A
LESSON *in*
PROPRIETY

Books by Jen Turano

MERRIWEATHER ACADEMY FOR YOUNG LADIES

— ONE —

A LESSON *in* PROPRIETY

JEN TURANO

BETHANYHOUSE

a division of Baker Publishing Group
Minneapolis, Minnesota

© 2025 by Jen Turano

Published by Bethany House Publishers
Minneapolis, Minnesota
BethanyHouse.com

Bethany House Publishers is a division of
Baker Publishing Group, Grand Rapids, Michigan

Printed in the United States of America

Library of Congress Cataloging-in-Publication Data
Names: Turano, Jen, author.
Title: A lesson in propriety / Jen Turano.
Description: Minneapolis, Minnesota : Bethany House, a division of Baker
    Publishing Group, 2025. | Series: Merriweather Academy for Young Ladies; 1
Identifiers: LCCN 2024039015 | ISBN 9780764243851 (paper) | ISBN 9780764245145
    (casebound) | ISBN 9781493450923 (ebook)
Subjects: LCGFT: Christian fiction. | Romance fiction. | Novels.
Classification: LCC PS3620.U7455 L47 2025 | DDC 813/.6—dc23/eng/20240906
LC record available at https://lccn.loc.gov/2024039015

Scripture quotations are from the King James Version of the Bible.

Cover design by Peter Gloege, LOOK Design Studio

Author is represented by Sarah Younger, Nancy Yost Literary Agency.

Baker Publishing Group publications use paper produced from sustainable forestry practices and postconsumer waste whenever possible.

25 26 27 28 29 30 31   7 6 5 4 3 2 1

In memory of Kristin Connors Turner,
my beautiful sister-in-law
who lit up any room she entered
and left us far too soon.

You will be missed every day.

Love you!
Jen

One

I'm sure you'll agree, my dear, if you take a moment to ponder the matter, that it might be for the best if we put all plans for our upcoming wedding on hold . . . perhaps indefinitely."

Miss Drusilla Merriweather sucked in a sharp breath, which immediately resulted in her choking on the sip of tea she'd just taken. Wheezing promptly commenced and continued for what seemed like forever, until she was finally able to settle eyes that were now watering on Mr. Elbert Herrington, her fiancé—or perhaps not, given the words that had just come out of his mouth—who was sitting across the table from her in the middle of Rutherford and Company's tearoom, watching her somewhat warily.

"Forgive me, Elbert," she managed to say in a breathy voice that now held a bit of a rasp. "It's quite unlike me to sputter about, but I fear all the sputtering was a direct result of me obviously mishearing you. It almost sounded as if you were suggesting we end our engagement."

Elbert leaned over a table draped in fine linen. "I'm afraid you didn't mishear me, Drusilla."

She stilled. "You're breaking our engagement?"

"I think it would be better if you'd do the breaking."

"Better for whom?"

Elbert settled back in his chair. "Surely you must realize that having you decide we won't suit, and then letting society know it was your choice to end matters, will allow you to maintain your dignity. It will also allow you to avoid having everyone assume there's something wrong with you, which you know is the conclusion everyone within the upper crust always arrives at if a gentleman ends an engagement."

Drusilla's mind went curiously numb, as if she simply couldn't comprehend the nuances of a conversation she'd certainly not been expecting to hold with a man she'd been engaged to for well over two years.

"What exactly is it that you think is wrong with me?" she finally managed to ask.

"I didn't say anything was wrong with you," Elbert countered. "I merely pointed out that if I were to dissolve our engagement, everyone traveling within our social set would assume I'd done so because you're deficient in some respect."

Drusilla pressed a finger against a temple that was beginning to throb. "I'm probably going to regret asking this, but what deficiencies, in your opinion, would everyone decide I possess?"

"I don't believe there's any need to delve into that," Elbert said, bestowing his most charming of smiles on her, but a smile she was not exactly finding all that charming at the moment.

"Why not?"

"Because disclosing any faults I believe you *might* possess, and faults society will undoubtedly pounce on if I end our alliance, will most assuredly leave you reaching for your smelling salts to stave off a fit of the vapors."

"I don't frequently suffer from fits of the vapors."

"You've fainted at numerous balls over the years."

"From lack of oxygen due to the tight lacing that's required to enhance a fashionable silhouette—but one that's not exactly conducive to gallivanting around a ballroom."

Elbert waved that aside. "There are many other ladies who present more fashionable silhouettes than you do who never faint dead away after they're done with a dance."

She was forced to set aside her cup when she realized she was gripping the delicate handle far too firmly. "Did you ever consider that those ladies are slenderer than I am and, as such, don't need to be laced as tightly to achieve that oh-so-fashionable profile?"

"An interesting theory, and one that now has me wondering if you should consider abstaining from sweets for the foreseeable future in order to avoid the threat of future fainting episodes."

Her jaw immediately took to clenching. "Are you suggesting I'm plump?"

Wariness once again flickered through Elbert's eyes. "I was merely voicing a solution to your fainting problem."

"I don't have a fainting problem, although I may soon have a temper problem if we continue discussing my figure, so . . . what other faults do you think I possess that society will bring to my attention if I don't agree to end matters with you?"

"I'm not sure disclosing that information is going to help with that temper problem you just mentioned."

Drusilla lifted her chin. "I'm sure my other faults will not be nearly as disconcerting as having you point out my less-than-svelte figure, so by all means, disclose away."

Elbert's gaze began darting around the tearoom, his smile returning when his attention settled on Miss Deerfield, a lady who'd been deemed a Diamond of the First Water, and who was currently enjoying tea with her aunt. After inclining his head when Miss Deerfield sent him a waggle of her fingers, Elbert turned back to Drusilla, his smile fading straightaway.

"I never realized you possessed the ability to turn difficult, my dear, but I'm going to suggest you discontinue with that unpleasant behavior posthaste, as it's not a trait any gentleman finds attractive in a woman."

Her teeth began to grind over that bit of ridiculousness. "As surprising as I'm certain you'll find this, Elbert, I'm not all that keen to adhere to any of your suggestions right now. What I am keen to do, though, is learn more about other deficiencies you believe I possess so I'll be better prepared to brace myself for any uncharitable comments sent my way after you toss me aside."

"As I've already mentioned, it would be better if you'd do the tossing."

"And as I just said, I'm not in the mood to entertain any of your suggestions right now. Therefore, please feel free to continue enlightening me about my evidently numerous and varied shortcomings."

Elbert opened his mouth, but instead of vocalizing a list of additional inadequacies, he was suddenly all smiles again, unquestionably because Miss Katherine Drayton and her sister, Julia, were now wandering past them on their way to a table, both ladies smiling broadly Elbert's way, although they barely inclined their heads to Drusilla as they passed.

Given that Elbert was considered one of the most handsome gentlemen within society, and that ladies were consistently determined to garner his attention, no matter that he was engaged to her, the warm smiles weren't exactly out of the ordinary.

"I hope the Drayton sisters didn't notice us arguing," Elbert murmured as he pulled his attention from where Katherine and Julia were now being assisted into chairs across the tearoom and settled a scowl she most certainly didn't deserve on her.

After glancing back to the sisters, who were now whispering furiously behind gloved hands as they continued looking Elbert's way, Drusilla returned Elbert's scowl. "I would say they definitely noticed there's something's amiss between us, but I have no idea why you'd be concerned about that. I would think people witnessing us engaged in a public argument would benefit your decision to end our engagement, not harm it."

"The last thing I want is for society to conclude the two of us parted on less-than-amicable terms, as that would hardly benefit my, or rather, ah, your reputation. That's why I'm now going to encourage you to discontinue glowering at me and smile at me instead."

"I have no intention of summoning up a smile to make it appear we're enjoying a lovely afternoon tea instead of engaged in a most disturbing affair. Truth be told, I'm finding it difficult to abstain from shrieking at you like a common fishmonger right now."

"You're far too prim and proper to resort to shrieking."

"You say that as if being prim and proper is yet another fault of mine."

Elbert gave a shrug of shoulders that were covered in fine wool. "I suppose it is a fault at that, as there have been numerous ladies who've broached your exceedingly proper attitude with me, and they weren't broaching it in a complimentary fashion."

"Ladies have told you they find me too prim and proper?"

"Indeed."

She narrowed her eyes. "Exactly what have they said about the matter?"

He returned the narrowing of the eyes. "I'm not appreciating this new demanding attitude of yours, but to answer your demand—know that I once sat between two young ladies at a dinner who regaled me with stories about your escapades when you attended the Sherwood Academy for Young Ladies together."

"I doubt they had many stories to regale you with as I never participated in any lively escapades while I was in school."

"That was evident fairly quickly since their stories revolved around all the time you spent in the library, reading your way through every etiquette and decorum book your finishing school offered."

Drusilla ignored the knot that began forming in her stomach at the mere mention of the hours she'd spent in the library—ones not spent because she'd been enthralled with learning everything she could about proper manners, but spent because her proficiency with her studies had earned her a small bit of praise from a father who'd been disappointed with her from the moment of her birth, as he'd been hoping for a son.

She'd even gone so far as to amass her own personal library dedicated to matters of etiquette, filling the space with tomes devoted to proper table settings, what wines were best paired with dinner selections, and how to achieve a pleasing effect when composing watercolors.

Her father, Morton Merriweather, had made a point of complimenting her dedication, which, given her desire to please a man who was mostly absent from her life, exactly explained her decision to become the most proper lady the Four Hundred had ever seen.

Not that her determination seemed to have paid off. In fact, it almost seemed to have had the opposite effect.

Needing a moment to get thoughts that were now skittering madly about in order, she selected a cucumber sandwich from a plate set in front of her, took a dainty nibble, and returned her attention to Elbert.

Annoyance was swift when she realized he was now watching Miss Thelma Whitting, who was sitting at a nearby table with her mother, although Thelma wasn't paying any notice to her mother but fluttering outrageously long lashes at Elbert instead.

Drusilla cleared her throat, then cleared it a second time, which finally had the desired effect of Elbert dragging his attention away from Thelma.

"Was there something else you wanted to add about your diligence to your decorum studies?" he asked, but only after he'd glanced back to Thelma, sent the lady a warm smile, then cocked a brow Drusilla's way.

She forced a hand that had taken to clenching to relax. "I wouldn't think I'd need to defend my attentiveness to my studies, as ladies are expected to excel with everything pertaining to proper manners." She took a second to smooth out a wrinkle she'd just spotted on the tablecloth. "As I'm sure you're aware, we women in the upper echelons of society are raised with the sole expectation of making an advantageous match and providing our husbands with a wife who's always above reproach."

"Of course I'm aware of that."

"Then why, pray tell, does it sound as if you agree with those other ladies and believe I over-excelled with my pursuit of achieving the pinnacle of proper decorum?"

"I didn't say I was in agreement, although I readily admit I was taken aback to learn from those ladies that most of the student population at Sherwood Academy found you somewhat insufferable."

"Insufferable?"

"Indeed."

Her hand took to clenching again. "Why would they think that?"

"I imagine it was a result of the teachers at Sherwood Academy encouraging the student body to strive to emulate your behavior. One lady at that dinner I mentioned even remarked to me that if you hadn't been born into a Knickerbocker family, you'd have been highly successful as a headmistress of a finishing school because your grasp of the rules rivaled that of Miss Sherwood, and your appearance . . ." Elbert abruptly stopped speaking, grabbed his teacup, and took a hefty swig.

Drusilla leaned forward. "Were you about to tell me that this lady thought my appearance suited that of a headmistress?"

Instead of immediately denying what any lady would have taken as a grave insult, Elbert winced instead. "She may have mentioned something to that effect."

Drusilla snatched up the remains of her cucumber sandwich, nibbled her way through half of it, returned it to the plate, then made a prolonged process of blotting her lips with her napkin as she strove to contain emotions that threatened to overwhelm her.

She'd truly had no idea that ladies within society spent their time making sport of her, and that they mocked what she considered her only credible achievement—that being possessed of impeccable manners—was hurtful to say the least.

She'd always known she wasn't a lady who'd ever take the Four Hundred by storm, or be deemed an Incomparable, not when she wasn't in possession of any great beauty, being merely "elegantly reserved," as her mother always put it.

Elegantly reserved simply meant she wasn't completely unattractive, but possessing a face that was less than riveting certainly didn't leave her standing out in a crowd, although people did compliment her on her blue eyes, which were evidently her greatest physical attribute. However, if possessing a less-than-beautiful face wasn't bad enough, she'd also been born with ordinary brown hair. And her shape, as Elbert had so kindly mentioned, wasn't slender, although she really didn't think she'd go so far as to call herself plump—more along the lines of unfashionably proportioned.

It was rather disheartening to learn that ladies she'd thought of as friends had been suggesting behind her back—and to her fiancé, no less—that not only would she be perfectly suited to running a ladies' academy, but that she also already looked the part of a headmistress, which in no way could be taken as a compliment.

"Not that I want to cut our luncheon short, Drusilla, but I have a pressing engagement soon," Elbert said, dragging her from her thoughts. "Shall we agree here and now that we're not well suited but intend to remain the closest of friends, and that you'll break the news to society in order to spare yourself any repercussions from the dissolution of our alliance?"

Drusilla's brow furrowed. "I don't know if we've ever been what I would consider friends, Elbert, and in all honesty, I'm still a little mystified as to exactly why you no longer care to marry me."

"Do I really need to spell it out for you?"

"You do, unless those deficiencies you just pointed out weren't brought to my attention because you fear others will pounce on them, but because those attributes of mine annoy you." She tilted her head. "If that's the case, it seems I'm being cast aside because I'm too plump, too prim, and too proper."

Elbert leaned forward, his gaze for once squarely focused on her. "My dear, my decision is not because you're too plump, prim, or proper—but because you're now all but penniless, or to put it bluntly . . . far too poor."

⇒ Two ⇐

I t was next to impossible to wrap her mind around the idea that Elbert had just called her *poor*, an obscene word within society if there ever was one, even if he wasn't exactly off the mark.

Drawing in a deep breath in the hopes of staving off the sense of panic that was threatening to overwhelm her, given that the repercussions of having her engagement nullified were beginning to sink in, Drusilla lifted her chin and met Elbert's gaze. "Am I wrong in concluding that your desire to end our engagement revolves around my dowry?"

"You no longer have a dowry."

"Through no fault of my own."

"I never said it was your fault," Elbert argued. "If anyone was to blame, it was your late father because he left the managing of the Merriweather fortune and assets to Mr. Sanford Duncan."

"Sanford was Father's trusted solicitor, as well as best friend," Drusilla countered.

"Sanford was anything but a friend to your father or family as he not only absconded with the Merriweather millions but also ran up outrageous debts he claimed were on behalf of your mother, telling a variety of vendors that the purchases were only made on credit because Merriweather finances were tied up in probate."

"I'm well aware of that, Elbert," Drusilla returned. "I'm also aware that the Pinkertons think Sanford ran up debts as some type of personal vendetta, given that he purchased an outrageously expensive yacht in Mother's name. With that said, though, I would have thought that you of all people would have had at least a few suspicions about what Sanford was doing before he disappeared, given that Father was intending to bring you on in some business capacity after we wed."

Elbert's brow furrowed. "To be more specific, your father was going to groom me to take over the company for him someday. However, since he didn't put that in writing, and as we weren't wed when he died, I had no legal standing to demand Sanford include me in any Merriweather ventures—something that would have only changed after we exchanged vows. It was hardly my fault that your mother decided a few months after your father died that we needed to delay our wedding until she was finished with her two-year mourning period."

"It wasn't exactly an unreasonable request since she had lost her husband of over twenty years and needed something to look forward to."

"Except that your mother's request gave Sanford the extra time he needed to put his diabolical plan into motion," Elbert pointed out. "And, before you ask, know that I did consider pressing the matter of becoming involved with Merriweather ventures at one point. However, my solicitor thought that would be a horrible idea."

She quirked a brow. "Because?"

He quirked a brow right back at her. "Come now, Drusilla. Given your father's unexpected death, you must realize that my solicitor and I discussed every possible scenario, including what would happen if you came to an untimely end before we were wed. Can you honestly say that were I already involved in

Merriweather matters and you suddenly passed away, that your mother wouldn't see that as an opportunity to get your sister, Annaliese, married off to the man who was already managing Merriweather business ventures?"

Drusilla frowned. "What would have been so horrible about marrying Annaliese? She's one of the most beautiful ladies in New York."

"Beautiful or not, everyone knows Annaliese is odd, which certainly wouldn't have helped my standing within the Four Hundred."

"Simply because Annaliese enjoys studying insects doesn't mean she's odd. Many ladies enjoy studying butterflies and the like."

"No, they enjoy painting pictures of them," Elbert countered. "Annaliese observes them in a scientific manner and also refuses to maintain her bug collection in a cabinet of curiosity, preferring to keep her bugs alive and stored in glass containers, which even the thought of would send any normal lady reaching for her smelling salts." He settled back in his chair. "Besides the bugs, though, she's submitted articles for all the newspapers stating her position against plume hunters and was also recently spotted in Central Park during a rally against the fur industry. She's turning into somewhat of a zealot with her questionable causes, and you mark my words, if she continues with her nonsense, she'll be thrown out of the Four Hundred once and for all."

"With you dissolving our engagement, I'm sure the Four Hundred will be turning their collective backs on my entire family since my mother will have no choice but to sell our last remaining asset—that being our house on Washington Square—to settle the remaining debts Sanford ran up in her name."

Elbert blinked. "Surely you weren't counting on me to settle those debts, were you?"

"How did you think we were going to settle the remaining debts?"

"I thought your mother would reach out to family members."

Drusilla pressed a finger against a temple that was definitely beginning to throb. "I have no idea how it came to be that we've been engaged for over two years and yet you don't seem aware of the fact that I only have one living relative—that being my aunt Ottilie. And before you claim that I never mentioned her to you, know that I distinctly remember telling you that she left for one of her frequent world adventures a few months before my father died, and that she wasn't at the funeral because we sent word to her solicitor, Mr. William Baumgartner, to have him contact her but never heard back from him."

"I don't remember you ever mentioning anything about an Ottilie before, but if she has the wherewithal to fund a world adventure, she certainly has the means to look after you and your family."

"Did you miss the part where I said we never heard back from her solicitor after we sent word to him about Father's death?"

"Your aunt's been on a world adventure for over two years?"

"She has, but that isn't unusual since Aunt Ottilie enjoys exploring places that are off the beaten track, although . . ." Drusilla wrinkled her nose. "Now that we're speaking of Aunt Ottilie, I suppose my family won't be truly homeless, as Aunt Ottilie gave Annaliese and me some property in Chicago before she left on her adventure when she stopped by for a quick visit at our house on Washington Square. If memory serves me correctly, there's some type of dwelling on that property as well."

"You certainly never told me you and Annaliese own any property."

"Because it's in Chicago and I never had any interest to travel there, not when my family used to own places in Paris, Rome, and England—all of which, of course, have now been sold."

Elbert leaned across the table. "Chicago's not exactly a fashionable destination, but I've heard that real estate is booming there of late." He edged forward another inch. "Do you happen to know if this property of yours is located anywhere near Prairie Avenue, where I know for a fact all the most prominent families live?"

"Aunt Ottilie never mentioned Prairie Avenue."

"How unfortunate, although . . ." He caught her eye. "Did she mention anything about it being near Lake Michigan?"

"There might have been a mention of views of some water."

"How encouraging, as that certainly puts a different light on matters since I imagine lakefront property is becoming desirable." Elbert settled back in his chair. "All we need to do now is have this property assessed."

"Because?"

"You could be sitting on a lot of money."

She crossed her arms over her chest. "And if I am?"

"There'd be no need for us to end our engagement."

"Except that even if this property is worth something, Annaliese and I promised our aunt we'd always keep it in the family."

"Why would you have done that?"

"Because Aunt Ottilie asked us to, and I certainly had no reason to argue the point as I had no way of knowing I'd ever be in a position where I needed funds. At that time, my family was one of the wealthiest in the country."

Elbert waved that aside. "I'm sure if your aunt was aware of your current circumstances, she'd be more than happy to rescind the promise she had you make."

"Perhaps she would, but since my aunt isn't around to discuss the matter, I need to honor the word I gave her."

"A woman giving her word isn't the same as a gentleman giving his."

Drusilla reached for another cucumber sandwich. "Honor isn't something that's incapable of transcending gender lines,

Elbert. It's a mark of a person's character, which means, no, I won't be setting aside my honor and selling off my aunt's property to avoid having you toss me over, even if I'm now going to have to figure out a way to make sure my family doesn't starve to death."

"You're not going to starve to death, as I did come up with another plan for you on the chance none of your relatives were available to take you in after we ended our engagement." He bestowed another one of his charming smiles on her. "You'll be pleased to learn that I've spoken with five wealthy gentlemen, all of whom would be more than happy to marry you."

"I beg your pardon?"

"You heard me." Elbert's smile turned more charming than ever. "You just say the word and five—that's right, *five*—gentlemen will present themselves on your doorstep, and all you have to do is choose one of them to marry."

"What's wrong with these gentlemen?"

"Nothing much," Elbert hurried to say. "They're simply members of the nouveau riche, which isn't nearly as troubling as it was, say, even two years ago, not since Alva Vanderbilt changed the dynamics of high society when she convinced Mrs. Astor to admit the Vanderbilt family into the highest social circles."

Drusilla began drumming her fingers against the table, earning a frown from Elbert in the process, which she ignored. "Out of blatant curiosity, tell me this. Why would any gentleman, even those from the nouveau riche set, want to marry me—a lady who is already twenty-two years old, almost twenty-three, and no longer possesses a fortune?"

"Because marriage to you will allow them unfettered access to the Four Hundred."

"And they'd be willing to overlook those deficiencies you kindly pointed out to acquire that unfettered access?"

"I assume so, because none of the men I spoke with were

21

even curious about the basics when it came to you. All they were concerned with was exactly how established your family was within society. Every one of them was suitably impressed to learn that you have Knickerbocker status, and . . ." His smile turned downright smug. "I know any of these men will marry you within the month, which will certainly allow you to avoid that whole starvation business."

It was almost impossible to ignore the urge she suddenly felt to lob her teacup across the table, an action that would undoubtedly wipe the smug smile directly off Elbert's face.

Three

You're starting to draw attention with that glare you're leveling on me," Elbert all but hissed.

Shoving aside the delightful image of Elbert having to duck to avoid a flying teacup, Drusilla glanced around the tearoom and found Katherine and Julia Drayton sitting forward in their seats, not even bothering to disguise the fact they were gawking at her and Elbert. After sending them a bit of a wink, which was completely unlike her and earned looks of confusion from the two ladies in return, Drusilla folded her hands demurely in her lap and returned her attention to Elbert.

"Do you honestly believe I care about giving the gossipmongers fodder to talk about, given that I've clearly been the object of their spitefulness for years?" Drusilla asked.

"Being the object of additional gossip could very well harm your chances with those prospective suitors I've found for you."

"I'd rather move to Chicago and find myself living in a tent than marry any man who only wants to marry me because of my position within society."

Elbert shoved a cucumber sandwich in his mouth, gave it a few rather intense chews, then washed it down with a hefty slug of tea. "You're being ridiculous, especially when I know you're simply refusing to accept one of the men I found for you out of spite. You should be grateful I've fixed what could have been a catastrophic financial situation for you."

"You're the one who created that catastrophic situation since I, along with my family, would have been financially fine if you would have upheld the deal you made with my father."

"There is no longer any deal to uphold since the Merriweather money is gone."

"But there's every chance the Pinkertons will eventually run Sanford to ground, and when that happens, I'll no longer be impoverished."

"Sanford is on the run with millions of dollars, and he's aboard a yacht that's capable of taking him anywhere in the world. Given that your family doesn't have the funds to continue paying the Pinkertons to search for him since bill collectors keep coming out of the woodwork, the likelihood that Sanford will ever be found is slim to none." Elbert caught her eye. "That means you have no choice but to meet these men from the nouveau riche set, choose one, then marry him."

"I think not" was all Drusilla had to say to that.

"You're being overly stubborn, another fault I never realized you possessed."

"Then it's a good thing you've decided to toss me over since I'm evidently riddled with unfortunate deficiencies."

"Perhaps you are at that," Elbert grumbled before he took another sip of his tea and set aside his cup. "Since it's evident the conversation is only going to go downhill from here, I suppose all that remains now is for you to allow society to know we've decided we no longer suit. However, since I'm truly not heartless, no matter that you obviously believe otherwise, know that I'm willing to allow you to keep the pearl bracelet I gave you as a betrothal gift. I will, however, need to have returned to me the Herrington diamonds, which includes the tiara, stomacher, bracelet, and necklace."

She stilled for the briefest of seconds before her lips took to curving as the true reason behind Elbert's insistence that she end their engagement suddenly became crystal clear.

"Are you smiling because you're pleased that I'm willing to let you keep the pearl bracelet?" Elbert asked, the wariness that was once again flickering through his eyes causing her smile to widen.

"I'm smiling because I've decided it's time for cake," she said before she waved a server over, ordered not one but two slices of cake, then returned her attention to Elbert, finding her soon-to-be-ex-fiancé frowning at her.

"I never said I wanted cake."

"I didn't order cake for you." She picked up her teacup and took a sip. "Since I'm already considered plump, and there's little likelihood I'll ever decide to marry, given the unpleasantness of our former alliance, I'm no longer going to worry about how slender I am."

"You seem oddly cheerful for a woman who's seemingly going to spend the rest of her life as a spinster, and who's also going to indulge in an overabundance of sweets, although . . ." Elbert tilted his head. "You might want to consider that if you don't marry, you won't have available funds for basic necessities, which means you won't have disposable income to indulge in sweets."

"Then I'll simply need to discover a way to secure a proper living for myself so I can purchase all the sweets I desire."

A chuckle was Elbert's first response to that. "In case you're unaware of this, you don't exactly possess any marketable skills."

"But according to you and a variety of society ladies, I over-excel with matters of proper decorum. Add in the notion that I also apparently look the part of a decorum instructor, and I'm sure I could find work in a finishing school."

Elbert opened his mouth, but Drusilla was spared the argument she knew was on the tip of his tongue when their server returned to the table, set a piece of cake in front of her, did the same with Elbert, and beat a hasty retreat, undoubtedly because she reached across the table and snagged the piece of cake in front of Elbert, earning a scowl from him in return. She immediately sunk her fork into it and stuffed a large bite into her mouth, a social faux pas if there ever was one.

"Delicious," she mumbled, taking a second bite and then a third before setting aside her fork when an intriguing idea flashed to mind. "Perhaps, instead of securing a position at a ladies' academy, I should consider opening a small etiquette school on my own, which would allow me to secure more funds since I could set the price of each lesson instead of drawing a salary."

"You have no idea how to go about opening a business, nor do you have the capital needed to get any type of finishing school open to begin with."

She grabbed her fork again, took three bites of cake, then realized she might be eating a little too quickly when she felt the most unladylike inclination to belch. She pushed the plate away from her.

"Contrary to what you seem to believe, Elbert," she began, "I'm not lacking in intelligence and fully understand that I'll need some form of capital to open up a small school." She felt a smile tug at her lips. "It just so happens that I have a way to secure that capital, and it's all thanks to you."

Elbert frowned. "What do you mean?"

"I'll sell your betrothal gift."

"The pearl bracelet won't bring you enough money to set up a small school."

"Of course it won't . . . but the entire Herrington diamond collection will."

Elbert settled an indulgent look on her. "You can't sell the Herrington collection because it doesn't belong to you."

"And that's where you're wrong. It would only *not* belong

to me if I was the one ending our engagement—something I'm convinced you're aware of, and something that exactly explains why you've been so determined to get me to agree to let society know that I'm the one who severed our alliance." She leaned across the table. "Tell me this—did you make a point to question those ladies who've been feeding you unpleasant little tidbits about me regarding the rules of retaining or regaining possession of any gifts a man bestows on his intended?"

Elbert scooted his chair backward a few inches, quite as if he wanted to maintain a certain distance between them. "I may have asked a question or two about broken engagements."

"And upon asking those questions, did you discover that if a lady ends an engagement, all betrothal gifts are to be returned, but if a gentleman ends matters, she's allowed to keep them, although most ladies in that position return the gifts because they don't care to have reminders of whatever scoundrel they almost married?"

It was clear she wasn't off the mark when Elbert's face began turning an interesting shade of red.

"I have no issue with you keeping the pearl bracelet, but you certainly can't keep the diamond collection," he practically growled, drawing the attention of Mrs. Winthrop, who was sitting at a table close to them and was now looking at Elbert with her mouth a little slack.

Drusilla refused a smile. "If you're still keen to have everyone in society believe we're parting on amicable terms, you might want to control that temper of yours and discontinue looking as if you'd like to throttle me."

Elbert was smiling a second later. "Keeping the Herrington diamonds is not an option because they're *Herrington* diamonds and you will not be a Herrington."

"To point out the obvious, they're not Herrington diamonds anymore because you gave them to me, which makes them Drusilla diamonds. And I, being in a bit of a financial pickle, know that those diamonds are going to be how I get my family moved and then settled in Chicago. Anything left over will be used to invest in some type of business."

His face began to mottle. "You cannot truly be considering selling them off to the highest bidder because that is quite beyond the pale, and you are not a lady who ever does anything beyond the pale."

"But it's *not* beyond the pale because, as I've already mentioned, proper rules of etiquette allow a lady to keep any trinkets she was given during her engagement period if she finds herself tossed aside. As an *overly* proper lady, something you suggested I am, I feel compelled to adhere to proper protocol in this matter. That means, since you're dissolving our engagement, I'm free to do whatever I want with the Herrington diamonds." She inclined her head. "However, since I'm not completely unreasonable, know that I'd be happy to sell them back to you."

"You say that as if selling me back the Herrington diamonds is doing me a favor."

"It is a favor, and before you ask, no, I won't give you a deal since I'm going to need every penny I can get to simply survive for the foreseeable future."

A vein began throbbing on Elbert's temple as he opened his mouth, but then snapped it shut when he shot a look to Mrs. Winthrop, who was now watching their exchange with eyes that were as wide as dinner platters. A blink of an eye later, he was on his feet, his color high and his gaze narrowed on Drusilla.

"I'll bring you an offer later this evening."

"Make sure it's a good offer, or I'm taking the diamonds to Sotheby's first thing tomorrow morning."

Elbert's eyes flashed before he turned and stalked out of the tearoom without another word, every gaze in the room following his departure.

Mrs. Winthrop was standing beside Drusilla a second later. "Good heavens, Miss Merriweather, what in the world just transpired between you and Mr. Herrington?"

28

"There's no need to fret, Mrs. Winthrop, as the matter was of little consequence."

"The two of you were almost shouting at each other at one point."

Drusilla nodded. "That is what happens when a man decides to end an engagement from out of the blue."

"Mr. Herrington just ended your engagement—and in the middle of Rutherford's tearoom?"

"Indeed."

Mrs. Winthrop patted Drusilla on the shoulder. "I would think you'd find that a situation of great consequence, not little, but would you care to have me fetch you some smelling salts, dear? I don't know if you realize this or not, but your tone is downright chipper, which given the circumstances, suggests you may be close to a state of hysterics."

Drusilla grinned, earning a blink from Mrs. Winthrop in return. "There's no need for smelling salts, Mrs. Winthrop. I assure you, I'm perfectly fine. In fact, I believe my life from this point forward is going to be far more pleasant than it ever would have been if I'd married a man I just discovered is a complete and utter bounder."

Rising to her feet after giving her lips one last dab on the chance she'd smeared chocolate icing on them while she'd been devouring bite after bite of cake, Drusilla sent Mrs. Winthrop a nod. She then turned and, with her head held high, sailed out of the room and toward an unknown future, but one that would no longer find her married to a most disagreeable gentleman.

⇒ Four ⇐

A shiver stole over Drusilla the moment she stepped from the hired hack and clapped eyes on a scene that seemed quite as if it had sprung directly out of a gothic novel—and one of the spookier gothic novels, at that.

Unlike the rustic lakeside cottage she and her sister had determined Aunt Ottilie had probably given them, rising up before her against a sky angry with billowing black clouds was an honest-to-goodness castle.

Unfortunately, it didn't seem to be one of those fairy-tale kinds of castles where princesses lived. Instead, it was more along the lines of a fortress that would house an evil sorcerer, that thought only reinforced when she noticed an entire flock of ravens—something her sister had once told her was called an *unkindness*—perched on top of two turrets, their caws swirling about in the wind as they peered down at her.

If ravens weren't bad enough, the castle also had an overabundance of gargoyles leering at her as well, the recent rain responsible for the water that was gushing out of their grotesque mouths.

"Think there's a possibility the driver took a wrong turn off Lake Shore Drive and this isn't our new home sweet home?"

Tearing her gaze from what appeared to be bats flittering in and out of what she believed was called a belfry, Drusilla turned and found her younger sister, Annaliese, climbing out of the hired hack, her eyes wide as she drew her traveling cloak tightly against her.

Her sister then smoothed a glove-covered hand over a ferret that was perched on her shoulder, one that went by the name of Pippin. Fortunately for Pippin, Annaliese had taken it upon herself to spirit the poor thing from a fur farm three months before, earning Pippin's undying devotion, the ferret so attached to what it obviously considered its new mother that it took to chirping in a most distressing fashion if it lost sight of Annaliese for any extended period of time.

Drusilla moved to her sister's side, ignored that Pippin immediately took to giving her the evil ferret eye, and took hold of Annaliese's hand. "I'm sorry to say that I think we're in the right place since that key Aunt Ottilie left with us opened that monstrosity of a wrought-iron gate we just drove through."

"I was afraid you were going to say that."

"Indeed." Drusilla squared her shoulders. "Nevertheless, since it's not as if we can turn around and traipse off to a less eerie house, we might as well head through the front door and hope the ghosts I'm relatively certain are floating about in there aren't the malicious types."

"You don't *actually* think it's haunted, do you?" Annaliese asked, glancing back to the castle and looking quite as if she expected ghosts to start wafting through the windows.

"I would love to say probably not, as I've never believed in ghosts, but given the way our luck has been of late, ghosts might very well turn out to be a problem. I hate to think what we're going to discover in the dungeon."

Annaliese shuddered. "We'll probably find the skeletons that belong to the ghosts haunting the place."

"An encouraging thought." Drusilla returned her attention to the ravens, who seemed to be returning her gaze. "I can't help but wonder what in the world Aunt Ottilie was thinking when she purchased a place that resembles that unnerving academy for wayward girls Father was determined to ship you off to after your unfortunate bird of paradise incident."

"Father threatened to send me to that wayward school after the roach incident, not the bird of paradise one," Annaliese corrected. "To refresh your memory, young ladies of the Four Hundred were up in arms against me, and not for the first time, after that unusual-looking roach darted across the floor during one of the family circle dance classes." Her lips curved. "How could I have possibly ignored the opportunity to scoop up the little darling and stash him in my reticule so I'd be able to study him once I was at my leisure?"

"I'm sure the ladies were expecting you to stomp on Xavier, not bring him home in your bag—or name him."

"Roaches are far too fascinating creatures to stomp on."

"Given that we're about to move into a moldy old castle, I have a feeling you're soon going to find yourself fascinated with a variety of unusual creatures."

"There might be some perks to moving into a haunted abode after all," Annaliese said before her attention drifted to the belfry, or more specifically to what now seemed to be an entire colony of bats whizzing about. It wasn't exactly surprising when excitement began flickering through Annaliese's eyes.

"Before you get any wild thoughts in that head of yours," Drusilla began, "I'm going to encourage you to resist the urge to capture a bat to study because I'm relatively certain they bite."

"I could always wear gloves."

"Or you could study them from afar and leave it at that since it's not as if we have expendable money to pay a physician to treat you for some dastardly disease you might pick up from a bat bite."

"An excellent point, although speaking of funds . . ." Annaliese gestured to the castle. "Not that I'm an expert on financial matters, since it wasn't as if we ever needed to count our coins before Sanford stole our fortune, but I'm relatively certain a castle is going to be expensive to maintain. Coal to heat the place will probably be astronomical, and I can't see Mother refraining from complaining incessantly once it begins getting colder if every room she steps foot in isn't at a comfortable temperature."

"Mother has proven herself to be rather adept at complaining over the past year," Drusilla said before she took a long moment to peruse her new home, stilling when an unexpected thought took that moment to fling to mind.

"You've got the most peculiar look on your face," Annaliese said, pulling Drusilla from her perusal.

"I'm sure I do because I might have just come up with an idea that could very well help us secure a more financially stable future." She took a few steps toward the castle, eyed it for another long moment, then turned. "Remember how that school for wayward girls had an ominous air to it?"

"It would be difficult to forget how spooky that school was considering it looked as if it had leapt off the pages of Jane Austen's *Northanger Abbey*. I haven't forgotten how relieved I was when, no matter how much Father offered to pay, I was denied entrance into that school because they had a two-year waitlist."

"And that a spooky old school didn't have any openings suggests that an ominous air isn't detrimental to the success of an academy for young girls or ladies."

Annaliese immediately took to shaking her head, freezing on the spot when Pippin began chirping up a storm.

After giving Pippin another soothing pat, Annaliese returned her attention to Drusilla. "If you're thinking what I think you're thinking, you've clearly taken leave of your senses. Not that I want to come across as a Doubting Delia, but we know nothing about running a school for wayward girls. Frankly, I've never even been acquainted with a wayward girl, and I know you haven't, so opening an academy for them is completely out of the question."

"There have been more than a few people who've thought you're a wayward girl over the years, which is why Father was determined to get you enrolled in that particular school."

"I would have never fit in at that school because holding an interest in studying bugs or wanting to ensure entire animal species don't go extinct due to the fur and plume trade doesn't make a girl wayward. It merely makes her curious, as well as compassionate, unlike truly wayward girls who enjoy creating chaos on purpose."

"A fair point," Drusilla conceded. "But I'm not saying I thought my idea was well formulated yet, although . . ." She cocked her head to the side. "There were men of the nouveau riche set in New York who were willing to marry me simply to enhance their social status. It might be worthy of consideration to explore the possibility of offering young ladies from the nouveau riche set an opportunity to secure a proper decorum education from ladies who are verified members of the New York Four Hundred."

"I'm not sure we're still verified, given our new unfashionable penniless status," Annaliese argued. "Besides that, what might truly stand in our way of opening any type of real academy is this—we're not businesswomen."

"And to that I must disagree. If you'll recall, I did take it upon myself to set up a meeting with the Pinkertons after they sent us notice they were abandoning our case due to the fact we could no longer pay their fee. I then negotiated a new contract with them, one that keeps them pursuing Sanford on a contingency basis, with their exorbitant fee only paid once they capture that repugnant man."

"That *was* a brilliant move on your part."

"Thank you, and finding success with the Pinkerton negotiations lends credence to the idea that you and I are capable of things we've never even dreamed about yet, and—"

A loud chorus of caws interrupted Drusilla, as well as caused the hair on the nape of her neck to rise when the ravens suddenly soared off the turrets and began swooping in their direction.

Pippin took one look at the advancing ravens and disappeared under the collar of Annaliese's cloak, causing Annaliese to squirm ever so slightly, undoubtedly because having a ferret under one's cloak probably wasn't all that comfortable.

After unbuttoning the top button of her cloak, Annaliese glanced back to the castle. "While I'll admit your academy idea may have merit, I'm afraid we're going to have a difficult time convincing anyone they're yearning to obtain lessons in propriety in a castle that might not only be haunted but truly may have more than a few skeletons lingering about."

"Oh, there's more than a few skeletons in that house, and everyone knows it's haunted."

Turning, Drusilla discovered the driver of one of the hacks they'd hired, who'd told her his name was Gus, setting down one of her large portmanteaus before he straightened.

"Why do you say it's haunted?" she asked.

"Because Norbert Tweed—that's Ottilie Merriweather's groundskeeper—and I often enjoy having an ale together down at the Mead and Vittles. He's told me all about the peculiar things that've been happening here. According to Norbert, this castle is one of the most haunted places in Chicago—and haunted by none other than Miss Ottilie Merriweather."

Drusilla blinked. "Are you telling me that Ottilie is dead?"

Gus blinked right back at her. "You didn't know that?"

"I haven't heard a word from Aunt Ottilie or even about her since she left on her adventure over two years ago."

Gus snatched his hat from his head. "I surely am sorry, then, for delivering what is some horrible news so bluntly. In my defense, though, when you hired me to take you to this address, I assumed you'd traveled here to finally get Miss Ottilie's affairs settled."

"We were unaware there was anything that needed to be

settled, but I'll look right into the matter after I have an opportunity to track down my aunt's solicitor."

"Then you're still plannin' on continuing with what I assume is some type of holiday, even after learning your aunt is haunting the place?" Gus asked.

"We're not here on holiday" was all Drusilla was able to get out of her mouth before the door to the hired hack suddenly flew open and her mother stepped out, the very sight of her causing Gus to take a few stumbling steps backward.

It wasn't exactly unexpected that Gus would take issue with her mother, Irma Merriweather, especially since she was dressed head to toe in widow's weeds and had also thrown on a floor-length weeping veil at some point while she'd been waiting in the carriage.

"Did I overhear correctly that the house we're supposed to live in is haunted?" were the first words out of Irma's mouth.

Drusilla refused a sigh. "I believe that's simply speculation from the locals at this point."

Irma peered through her netting at the castle. "Who's haunting it?"

"Miss Ottilie," Gus supplied before Drusilla could stop him, which had her mother raising a hand to her throat.

"Ottilie's dead?"

"That would fall under the whole speculation business as well," Drusilla muttered.

Irma ignored that as she shoved up her veil and settled her gaze on Gus. "Why do you think Ottilie's dead?"

Gus rubbed a hand over a chin that sported more than a day's worth of stubble. "I'm just repeating what Norbert told me. According to him, there weren't any signs of hauntings while Miss Ottilie was in residence, but that changed some months after she left Chicago."

"What type of hauntings began at that point?" Irma pressed.

"From what I've heard, the staff kept waking up to strange

noises," Gus said. "When they'd go to investigate, no one was ever found, but furniture was often rearranged, messages were scrawled onto the mirrors with soot from the fireplaces, and windows that had been locked the night before were wide open."

"Why did the staff conclude it was Ottilie haunting the place?"

Gus gave his chin another rub. "Norbert told me the messages scrawled on the mirrors seemed to be written in Miss Ottilie's hand, as she was known to make a very distinctive *S*. He also said the messages stated things like 'keep your feet off the sofa,' 'don't forget to water the roses,' and 'make sure to polish the silver every two weeks'—a telling message since Norbert mentioned that the butler, Bentley, neglected to regularly attend to that task after Miss Ottilie left."

Irma drew in a sharp breath. "Ottilie was always particular about keeping her silver polished."

"I don't know any lady who isn't particular about the silver," Drusilla couldn't help but point out.

"But only someone with the quirks Ottilie possessed would bother with silver after they've returned as a ghost," Irma argued. "That means there's no possible way I'm going to step foot in this castle because Ottilie never cared for me and will surely make a point of haunting me the most."

With that, Irma resettled the weeping veil over her face, turned on her heel, then marched back to the hired hack, climbed inside, and shut the door firmly behind her.

≈ Five ≈

O f any excuse I thought Mother would use to refuse to live here," Annaliese began, drawing Drusilla's attention, "using Aunt Ottilie's ghost wasn't anything I ever considered."

Drusilla felt the most curious urge to laugh. "I wouldn't have thought of that one either, but luckily for us, it's a flimsy excuse."

"I don't know how flimsy it is considering Aunt Ottilie and Mother truly never got along. Frankly, I wouldn't put it past Aunt Ottilie to single Mother out as the best person to haunt."

"Except that I highly doubt Aunt Ottilie is dead as we never received any notice regarding her passing from her solicitor, Mr. William Baumgartner."

Gus opened his mouth, probably to argue once again about Aunt Ottilie being dead, but before he could voice a single argument, the sound of carriage wheels rolling up the long drive interrupted him. A second later, two additional hired hacks, along with three wagons, came into view.

"I was beginning to worry the rest of our party took a wrong turn," Drusilla said as the hacks and wagons drew closer.

"They're just lagging behind because Thomas"—Gus nodded to the driver who was now bringing his hack to a stop a few feet away from them—"doesn't like to push his horses past a plod."

Annaliese was beaming a smile in Thomas's direction a second later, leaving poor Thomas looking somewhat dazed. "How delightful to learn there are hack drivers who concern themselves with the well-being of their horses."

Gus released a snort. "Thomas isn't concerned about the welfare of his animals. Our fares are based on how long it takes to get to a destination. If Thomas's horses are kept to a plod, he brings in a higher fare."

Annaliese's smile dimmed. "But my sister negotiated the same fare for all the hacks and wagons she hired today, so why would Thomas have kept his horses to a plod if there isn't a possibility for him to make more money?"

"Force of habit, I suppose, or . . ." Gus's voice trailed away as the door to the hack Thomas was driving began to open and then a foot clad in a high-buttoned shoe appeared, followed by the appearance of Miss Seraphina Livingston, who immediately pushed back the hood of her cloak as she took to perusing the castle with a frown on what could only be described as an exquisitely beautiful face.

Gus's jaw, along with Thomas's, instantaneously went slack at the mere sight of Seraphina, who didn't notice the gawking as her gaze was now settled on the ravens that had abandoned their tree and were once again circling the turrets.

In all honesty, it was a somewhat odd state of affairs that Seraphina had traveled with them to Chicago, considering that Drusilla hadn't set eyes on her old friend, nor heard a single word from her, since they'd both been twelve years old and enrolled in the Sherwood Academy together.

Seraphina had always been more outgoing than Drusilla, and could count dozens of girls at the academy as friends. But even though she'd been one of the most sought-after students there, she'd always made a point to include Drusilla in a variety of activities—until Seraphina's father had remarried and she'd been yanked out of the academy and sent off to a finishing school in Switzerland, never to be seen again until she'd arrived on Drusilla's doorstop a mere week ago. It had become clear almost immediately that Seraphina was experiencing a bit of a challenging situation.

What that situation was, exactly, Drusilla had yet to discover, as Seraphina seemed reluctant to discuss it. However, since it was very unusual for any lady to reside in a boarding school past the age of eighteen, and Seraphina had been attending her school in Switzerland four years past that, it was obvious that her old friend had experienced some manner of discontent with her family, which presumably started after Seraphina's father had married the widow Drayton, mother of Julia and Katherine, the two young ladies Elbert had been flirting with at Rutherford's tearoom the day he'd ended their engagement.

That discontent had evidently reached a tipping point after Seraphina had finally been summoned home, one that had then caused Seraphina to show up at the almost completely emptied-out Merriweather house on Washington Square, past midnight no less, dragging a portmanteau behind her and clutching a silk bag in her hand.

After apologizing for arriving at what was certainly an inappropriate hour, she'd proclaimed herself delighted that Drusilla still remembered her, then asked, because she'd overheard her stepsisters talking about how Drusilla was liquidating most of the Merriweather possessions, if Drusilla could recommend a jeweler who would be willing to relieve her of a few pieces of her late mother's jewelry.

Given the way Seraphina's gaze kept darting to the door as if she might need to bolt at any second, it had been obvious that something was gravely amiss. After asking Seraphina as delicately as possible if her father was aware she wanted to sell her late mother's jewelry, Seraphina admitted that her father had died over a year before. She'd then admitted she needed to lay low for a while, or more specifically, lay low for two years until she came into some money.

Recognizing a fellow lady in distress, and one who apparently had no one else to turn to, Drusilla had invited Seraphina to travel with them to Chicago.

It had been quite telling when Seraphina hadn't hesitated to accept that invitation, looking remarkably relieved as she made a point to promise to pay her own way just as soon as she could liquidate her jewelry.

"I feel the oddest sense of déjà vu because, if I didn't know better, I'd say I've just found myself back at the Swiss finishing school I attended for over ten years," Seraphina said as her gaze shifted from the ravens and swept over the castle.

"You truly were in finishing school for over ten years?" Annaliese asked.

Seraphina inclined her head. "Until I was summoned home after my father died. Quite frankly, if he hadn't passed away, I'd probably still be in Switzerland, diligently working my way through every social decorum instruction manual known to womankind. I'm sure I would have also been adding new languages to the five I already speak, and perhaps delving into a touch of Impressionism, an art form I've admired for a few years, but one I've yet to personally explore as my art instructor at the academy felt that Impressionism wasn't all that impressive."

"Ten years is a very long time to devote yourself to matters of propriety," Annaliese said.

"Quite." Seraphina grinned. "But before you take to feeling too sorry for me, know that I was also given the opportunity to dabble in some rather unusual pursuits that aren't common for ladies, taught to me by the likes of groundskeepers and retired military men who accepted guard positions at the school after they retired." Her eyes took to twinkling. "My favorite dance instructor, who turned out to be a master in fencing, even taught me fencing skills during school holidays since I never bothered traveling all the way from Switzerland to New York to enjoy Christmas or summer breaks."

Annaliese took a second to give a tug on the bodice of her gown, which had taken to moving, suggesting Pippin was trying to find a comfortable spot for a nap. "You didn't happen to ever stand in for any of your decorum instructors when they took unexpectedly ill, did you, or perhaps when they wanted to travel for the holidays early and knew you wouldn't be returning to New York?"

"Since I was enrolled in that school for far longer than any other student—so long, in fact, that I was actually older than some of the instructors—I often stepped in and lent a hand whenever there was a need."

Annaliese arched a brow Drusilla's way. "Are you thinking what I'm thinking?"

"That you're dying to learn what those other skills are that Annaliese procured during all the years she attended finishing school?"

Annaliese rolled her eyes. "Well, of course I'm curious about that, but I was actually thinking that your academy idea isn't such a bad one after all because it sounds as if Seraphina might very well surpass you in the whole being proficient with proper decorum business. She also has experience instructing students, something you and I lack."

"Academy?" Seraphina asked.

Before Drusilla could explain, Gus, who'd returned to unpacking their trunks, dropped another portmanteau to the ground, and none too gently at that, before he sent a nod Drusilla's way. "I only have a few trunks left, and it looks like the other drivers are almost done unpacking as well. That's why I'm going to suggest all of you gather any personal belongings you left in your respective hacks." He cast a glance at the sky. "If you haven't noticed, the sun will be going down before too long, and I, for one, don't intend on being around when the ghosts come out, even if I'm usually not opposed to charging an extra fee for lingering about."

Seraphina's lips twitched. "The castle has ghosts?"

"Allegedly," Drusilla returned. "But before Gus takes to telling us more ghost stories, which are hardly going to allow us to sleep well tonight, allow me to get Mother out of the hack so Gus can get on his way."

With that, and after asking Annaliese and Seraphina to see after the Merriweather staff members who'd gotten out of their respective hacks and were now standing in the middle of the drive, all of them gazing at the bats whizzing around the belfry, Drusilla squared her shoulders and marched over to the hack where her mother had taken to hiding out.

It was not an unexpected sight when she opened the door and found Irma sniffling into a handkerchief, something she'd been doing frequently ever since Sanford had made off with the Merriweather millions.

Tellingly enough, her mother had barely shed a tear for her husband after Morton Merriweather had died, probably because she'd never claimed to have been overly fond of her husband. Their marriage had been an arranged one, and Irma had barely tolerated Morton, just as he'd gone to extraordinary lengths to avoid her whenever possible.

Granted, Irma had certainly never wished him dead and had unquestionably been taken by surprise when Morton had suffered from what his doctor had deemed an unexpected failure of the heart while engaged in a business discussion with Sanford in his office. However, she'd seemed more distressed over being expected, per the rules of proper decorum, to mourn her husband for a full two years, her mourning period responsible for her having to forgo the many frivolities she'd always thrived on.

That right there was why Drusilla had not married Elbert the minute her one year of mourning was over, what with how her mother had retreated to her bed at the mere thought of missing her eldest daughter's wedding or, worse yet, not being able to host a wedding the Four Hundred would have deemed the wedding of the Season. Irma had only abandoned her bed after Drusilla assured her they'd postpone the nuptials—a delay that had allowed Sanford more than enough time to plan and execute the liquidation of the Merriweather fortune.

"You really are going to have to get out of the hack, Mother," Drusilla finally said, which earned her another sniffle before Irma narrowed red-rimmed eyes on her.

"I'm not getting out. This is a horrid place Ottilie gave you and Annaliese, and I won't step foot into a home that has bats circling around it or ghosts wandering the hallways, especially if one of those ghosts is Ottilie." Irma gathered her cloak tightly against her. "There are probably rats roaming around inside as well, along with a variety of other less-than-pleasant creatures."

"I once read that some bats are carnivorous, so perhaps these bats are of that variety and have taken care of any rats that may have tried to live in the castle."

Irma's mouth dropped open. "If those bats are carnivorous, what would stop them from trying to eat us, especially if they've found a way to access the interior of the castle?"

"That was probably not a well thought out answer on my part."

"Well thought out or not, you said it, which means I'm definitely not getting out of this hack now."

"What if I told you, now that I think about it, that I'm almost positive those carnivorous bats only live in tropical areas? Clearly Chicago is not a tropical paradise."

Irma pursed her lips. "I suppose that's somewhat reassuring, but if the bats aren't eating the rats, then there's undoubtedly an infestation of them in the castle. I imagine they'll be coming out in hordes at night with the sole intention of nibbling on our toes."

"Except that Annaliese's ferrets will take care of any bats or rats, which is what I should have said in the first place."

Irma frowned. "Annaliese has more than one ferret?"

"She has three—Pippin, Wiggles, and Fidget—but you probably thought there was only one because the ferrets look remarkably similar."

"Do all three of them ride around on her shoulder, taking it in turns?"

"Only Pippin does that. Wiggles and Fidget are more on the standoffish side."

Irma's gaze sharpened on Drusilla. "She doesn't have any other unusual animals that I don't know about, does she?"

"She used to have a colony of beavers, but since we had no idea what our housing situation was going to be like here, she decided not to bring them." Drusilla smiled. "They're currently living in the backyard of one of Annaliese's fellow animal activists, but I imagine Annaliese will send for them at some point."

"She'll never find herself a husband if she continues with her peculiar ways."

"Unless she happens upon a gentleman who loves animals as much as she does. But Annaliese's future husband prospects aside"—Drusilla caught her mother's eye—"the driver would like to get on his way, which means you're going to have to exit this hack, and before you argue with that, you need to remember that you have nowhere else to go."

Irma crossed her arms over her chest. "That's not true. We can always repair to the Palmer House. I've heard that it's quite delightful there."

"The Palmer House is a luxury hotel that we can no longer afford."

"Of course we can afford it because I know, given all the bellowing Elbert was doing regarding you holding the Herrington gems for ransom, that you managed to extract far more money from him than he wanted to give you."

"I wasn't holding the diamonds for ransom. I was simply making what I considered a sound business deal."

"It must have been some deal, given all that bellowing, although I do feel compelled to state yet again that it's very unbecoming for a lady to immerse herself in any type of business in the first place."

"Then you should start preparing yourself for additional unbecoming behavior from me since I've done a lot of contemplating about my life over the past few months, and I've decided that I will never again allow myself to depend on a man to take care of me, which means . . ."

"You've decided to remain a spinster?" Irma gasped before Drusilla could finish her thought.

"Indeed."

Irma raised a hand to her throat. "But marriage is the only way we members of the feminine set can enjoy financial stability."

"That way of thinking doesn't seem to have worked out well for either of us, Mother, which is why I say it's past time we Merriweather women figure out how to secure some financial stability on our own."

Two red splotches of color took up residence on Irma's pale cheeks. "Do not let anyone else hear you speak of such a thing, because with radical ideas like that, we'll never see ourselves returned to the fold of the New York Four Hundred."

"The Four Hundred turned their backs on us the moment they learned we were penniless. And not that I want to make you weep again, but you should probably prepare yourself for the fact that the upper echelons of New York society will undoubtedly continue giving us the cut direct if I follow through with an idea I was just discussing with Annaliese and Seraphina."

"Do not tell me this idea is a business idea, is it?"

"Securing financial stability for us is going to have to involve business, but it's not as if I'm about to suggest we open an ale house and start slugging mugs of ale around."

"I should hope not."

"Well, quite. But know that what I'm considering isn't improper in the least since the business I believe we could successfully run merely involves turning the castle into a finishing school, and one we could name something clever, such as the Merriweather Academy for Young Ladies."

Sheer horror immediately flickered through Irma's eyes right before she buried her face in her handkerchief and began weeping in earnest.

≈ Six ≈

E verything all right in there?" Annaliese called through
the door a few moments later, her question sending a
wave of relief through Drusilla, as she had no idea how
to proceed with a mother who'd now come down with a bad
case of the hiccups, brought about by all the weeping.

"Of course it's . . . *hick* . . . not all right," Irma called back
before Drusilla could answer. "Your sister . . . *hick* . . . has just
told me about her academy . . . *hick* . . . idea, a notion that . . .
hick . . . surely has your poor father . . . *hick* . . . turning over
in his grave."

"Perhaps Father would approve of Drusilla's idea, as it does
have the potential of being financially viable and he always was
intrigued with ways to make money," Annaliese stated, earning
a scandalized look from Irma, one she couldn't see since the
door was still shut.

"Your father would be appalled to learn . . . *hick* . . . that
Drusilla wants to . . . *hick* . . . use our good Merriweather name
for some ridiculous business . . . *hick* . . . venture she's come
up with that has something to do with turning the castle into
a . . . *hick* . . . academy."

It really came as no surprise when Annaliese, obviously having realized their mother was in an unreasonable frame of mind

yet again, called out that she'd fetch some water to help with the hiccups, leaving Drusilla alone again with a still-hiccupping and, need she add, difficult mother in the process.

A strained silence settled over them, broken only by intermittent hiccups until the door to the hack opened and Annaliese thrust a cup of water she'd undoubtedly fetched from one of the other hacks into Irma's hand. As Irma set about drinking it, frowning as she did so, which suggested the water was not to her liking, Annaliese turned to Drusilla.

"Thought you should know that Gus and the other hack drivers, along with the wagon drivers, have gotten everything unloaded. None of them are willing to take our belongings into the castle, though, because Gus just had to remind everyone that it's haunted. That means everyone is now anxious to get on their way, but they want to leave together, as they believe there's safety in numbers against ghosts."

Annaliese turned to Irma, who'd just finished her glass of water and was thankfully no longer hiccupping. "I truly understand, Mother, why you're reluctant to give up the safety of this hack, as we have no idea what we'll be facing once we go inside the castle. Nevertheless, as Drusilla has undoubtedly already told you, we don't have anywhere else to go. We also don't have funds to waste on paying hack drivers more than the fare they originally quoted us, but I'm afraid, if you don't get out of this hack soon, that's exactly what we're going to be forced to do."

Irma opened her mouth, closed it, opened it again, then after looking quite like a fish out of water for another few seconds, wrinkled her nose. "I don't think they'll charge us more if I simply stay here while the two of you do an initial inspection of the castle, making certain there aren't any bats, rats, or ghosts wandering about."

Knowing there was a very good chance they'd encounter at least one of those three obstacles, and also knowing there was absolutely no way they could rid the castle of any of those things before the sun went down, Drusilla settled for simply sending her mother a nod before she stepped out of the hack and shut the door.

After telling Gus that he'd hopefully be able to get on his way within the next ten minutes, Drusilla set her sights on the castle and headed up the drive, Annaliese and Seraphina joining her.

"I don't think there's any possibility we can inspect the entire castle for concerning creatures within ten minutes," Annaliese said as she settled Pippin more comfortably on her shoulder and Wiggles and Fidget, Pippin's siblings, began scurrying up the drive, chirping up a storm.

"I'm sure we can't, but Mother doesn't exactly seem to be in a reasonable frame of mind, something that has eluded her ever since Sanford disappeared with our money," Drusilla said. "I'm hoping we'll be pleasantly surprised and find that the castle has been very well maintained even though it doesn't seem as if any of the staff is still here, except maybe the groundskeeper, since no one has come out to greet us."

With that, Drusilla began climbing the limestone steps, stopping in front of a door that looked rather battered, as if it had taken quite the beating over the years.

She gave the door knocker a few raps on the off chance someone was inside, then withdrew the heavy set of keys Aunt Ottilie had given her from her reticle when she heard not a single footstep from the other side of the door. After eyeing the lock, she chose a skeleton key, inserted it into the lock, and smiled when a distinctive click sounded.

Her smile disappeared in a flash, though, when a spine-tingling creaking noise rang out the moment she began pushing the door open. The hair on the nape of her neck then stood at attention when she stepped into the entranceway and took note of the cobwebs hanging about, ones that drifted from the ceiling and down a long hallway, wafting over an honest-to-goodness cannon pointing her way.

Directly behind the cannon was what seemed to be an entire army of medieval suits of armor, each one standing perfectly erect and complete with helmet, breastplates, and full leg armor, and holding lances, clubs, and even a few threatening-looking maces.

"And this isn't creepy at all," Seraphina muttered. "And not that I want to embrace a pessimistic attitude, but being confronted with a cannon pointing at us, and one that has an entire cauldron of cannon balls stashed beside it, is not what I'd consider a welcoming touch."

"I'm sure the cannon is just for show," Drusilla said.

"Let's hope we don't personally discover otherwise," Seraphina said, earning a nod from Annaliese as she sidled closer to Drusilla.

"I don't think being confronted with a scene that would do justice to any haunted house is that pleasant surprise you were hoping for, Drusilla," Annaliese whispered.

"Too right it's not," Drusilla agreed before she squared her shoulders. "However, as long as the cannon doesn't suddenly start blasting cannonballs our way, and none of those suits of armor start moving around, or any ghosts drift through the cobwebs, I think we'll be fine, so . . . shall we continue on?"

"Since I don't think any of us want to sleep outside tonight amongst the ravens and bats, I don't believe we have a choice *except* to continue on," Seraphina pointed out.

"That's the spirit."

Seraphina batted aside a cobweb that had attached itself to the hood of her cloak. "Shall we walk toward our certain doom together instead of doing this single file?"

"Single file might allow at least one of us to escape if something tries to ambush us," Annaliese said as Wiggles and Fidget slunk up to join them, the ferrets taking one look at the suits of armor displayed in the hallway before they exchanged a few chirps, then turned and bolted toward the front door.

"Think that's a sign there's something terrifying waiting for us at the end of the hallway?" Seraphina asked.

"Since I've never seen them do that before, probably," Annaliese admitted.

"Perhaps we should arm ourselves with a few of the lances just to be on the safe side," Seraphina said, striding over to some armor and tugging a lance free, wobbling around a bit before she used both hands to hold out what seemed to be a very heavy object to Drusilla.

Drusilla frowned. "Do you honestly believe my sister and I have the slightest idea how to wield a lance, or worse yet, a mace?"

"An excellent question, and one that suggests it would be more dangerous to arm you and Annaliese, so I'll be responsible for our defense if we encounter any trouble."

"You know how to use a lance?" Annaliese asked.

Seraphina smiled. "I told you, I acquired some unusual skills in Switzerland." She took a second to look over the lance, tested the weight, seemed to settle for holding it exactly in the middle, then nodded down the hallway. "I'll lead the way."

Walking behind Seraphina, who was now pointing the lance in front of her and holding it in what appeared to be a practiced grip, Drusilla soon found herself moving out of the hallway and into a very large room, one that had a long, rough-hewn table in it that could have easily accommodated a hundred guests.

"Does anyone else hear that tinkling sound?" Annaliese whispered.

Seraphina stopped in her tracks and tilted her head. "It sounds like bells."

"Think the ghosts are doing that?" Annaliese asked right as the tinkling grew louder and was then joined by what sounded exactly like hooves rushing over the hard floor.

"It's not ghosts—it's goats!" Seraphina yelled, no longer bothering to keep her voice lowered as what appeared to be an entire herd of goats came clambering into the room, the bells hanging from their necks making a horrible racket, that racket joined by the sound of a honking noise that was being emitted from a goose that had just waddled into the room, moving as fast as its webbed feet would allow.

Before Drusilla had a chance to wonder why goats and a goose would be in the castle in the first place, the goat leading the group set its sights on her, changed direction, and charged her way.

≈ Seven ≈

M r. Rhenick Whittenbecker was a man who was accustomed to being surrounded by members of the feminine set.

Being the only son, as well as the eldest of the Whittenbecker family, which consisted of his parents, Franklin and Wilhelmine, and four younger sisters—Tilda, Eloise, Grace, and Coraline—he'd grown up immersed in a world filled with petticoats, ribbons, various shades of pink, and cute little bunnies his sisters simply couldn't live without.

He was also the only male cousin until recently to be born into any of the other Whittenbecker families, as well as the Akerman branches, his mother's side, which made him somewhat of a novelty in his female cousins' eyes and was exactly why those cousins had always clamored for his attention during every family gathering.

That clamoring usually resulted in the girls going to unusual lengths to garner his notice, which was exactly why he was more than proficient with rescuing girls from trees, tending to skinned knees and elbows, and then, once the girls began turning into young ladies, providing a sympathetic shoulder for them to cry on after they suffered what they believed were end-of-the-world problems, all of which normally involved young men who didn't return their affections or, worse yet, unfortunate hairstyles.

His familiarity with everything feminine was why, after he'd seen Ottilie's front gate open, he'd decided to drop by in the hopes that his dear friend had finally returned home because he was concerned that, as a lady living without the benefit of a gentleman's presence, her welfare might very well be in jeopardy, as there'd been some disturbing situations pertaining to her castle while she'd been away.

He'd not even made it to the castle entrance, though, before he'd spotted a young lady with red hair dashing down the drive, shouting something about mad goats. His first inclination had been to leap from Sweet Pea, a stallion his youngest sister had named because he'd made the mistake of bringing his new horse home on Coraline's birthday, which had made it impossible for him to refuse her request to name it, and race to the redhead's assistance.

That inclination had disappeared in a trice, though, when something furry materialized from the collar of the lady's cloak, something he'd first assumed was a fur wrap that had come loose due to all the dashing—until that bit of fur scrambled to the lady's shoulder, leapt to the ground, and then scurried off toward a grove of trees, leaving the young lady changing directions to charge after it.

Even with all his feminine experience, he'd never once witnessed a lady wearing what had appeared to be a ferret, but before he could contemplate the matter further or help her recapture a most unusual fashion accessory, a cloaked figure came rushing down the steps—gripping a lance, no less—one she evidently wasn't comfortable using against any of the numerous goats that were chasing her.

To his astonishment, that figure, clearly a woman, bolted for a stone wall that bordered the castle, tossed the lance over it, then made an impressive leap and disappeared over the wall, leaving the goats scrambling about as they tried to figure out how to continue chasing her.

Deciding the cloaked woman was probably safe for now, Rhenick nudged Sweet Pea in the direction the ferret-chasing lady had gone, reining his horse to a stop again when Norbert Tweed, Ottilie's longtime groundskeeper, came barreling into view, brandishing a rifle. A blink of an eye later, Norbert disappeared into the castle, and a second after that, additional goats came charging through the front door.

What a herd of goats was doing in the castle was a little puzzling, but considering they were heading directly for Sweet Pea and his horse was now tossing its head in an agitated state, which normally proceeded an attempt to unseat his rider, Rhenick abandoned the urge to puzzle out the goat situation or the ferret one, and swung from the saddle instead. His feet barely hit the gravel before Sweet Pea bolted away, leaving Rhenick behind as the goats immediately took to scrambling after his horse.

To say it was a most unusual state of affairs was an understatement, as was the fact that, instead of taking any type of decisive action, something he was known for always doing, he found himself in a bit of a quandary, unsure of which situation he should address first.

His indecision came to a rapid end when a shot rang out from inside the castle.

Breaking into a run, Rhenick took the steps two at a time, his progress impeded when he was forced to dodge a goat that was galloping through the door, one that gave him an uncalled-for ramming of its head before it charged past him, the ramming leaving him limping his way into the castle. He was then forced to edge his way along the wall in order to avoid another goat that was trundling down the hallway.

His edging stopped once he made it beyond the two dozen or so suits of armor that Ottilie had collected over the years, his gaze darting around the great hall before settling on a most unusual scene unfolding on the opposite side of the room.

Norbert was standing in front of a fireplace that gave new meaning to the word *gigantic*, the tail of his shirt only partially tucked into trousers that were being held in place by a single suspender, the other lying limply against Norbert's side, suggesting the man had been in a hurry to get to the castle and hadn't bothered to get properly dressed first.

The groundskeeper didn't seem concerned about being less-than-appropriately attired, though, as he was currently in the process of aiming his rifle at someone Rhenick couldn't see since Norbert was obstructing his view.

Stepping to the right, Rhenick returned his attention to the person being held at rifle-point, blinking—and then blinking again—when his gaze settled on not a man, as he'd been expecting, but a woman. That woman, unexpectedly enough, instead of cowering because there was a gun being pointed her way, or looking as if she were about to suffer a fit of the vapors over having recently been shot at—the proof of that being the large chunk that was missing from the fireplace behind her—was standing with perfect posture, staring Norbert down.

Rhenick's feet, seemingly on their own accord, began propelling him forward, the urge to protect the woman impossible to ignore, no matter if she'd done something that warranted being held in place by a rifle or not. His forward propulsion came to a rapid end, though, when he finally got an unimpeded view of the woman's face, the mere sight of it leaving him feeling as if the floor underneath his feet had dropped straight away.

To say she was the most exquisite woman he'd ever seen was an understatement, and given all the beautiful women he'd had the pleasure of spending time with over the years, that was saying something.

In all honesty, she wasn't what anyone would have considered a classic beauty, but there was simply something fascinating about her.

Her hair, being an intriguing shade of brown—which certainly wasn't considered all the rage these days, at least according to his sisters—was pulled back in a simple chignon, not a strand escaping the many pins he knew were required for that particular style, something that was quite impressive given her current circumstances.

He didn't know any lady who'd be capable of keeping every hair in place while dealing with a rifle-toting groundskeeper, but he was apparently now in the presence of a lady who gave new meaning to the word *composed*, as he had yet to notice her tremble even the slightest bit, nor did it appear as if her eyes were holding even a dollop of fear in them, and . . .

His train of thought disappeared when his attention settled more firmly on her eyes, ones that were the most compelling shade of blue he'd ever had the pleasure of seeing, and he felt he could drown in them if given half a chance, an unusual thought if there ever was one since he wasn't a gentleman whose thoughts normally traveled in a poetic direction.

Dragging his gaze from her eyes when he realized he was all but gawking at the lady, something he'd never done in his life, Rhenick gave himself a bit of a shake in the hopes of dissipating the stupor he'd descended into.

Thankfully, his sense of discombobulation lessened ever so slightly with the shaking, which allowed him to realize that while he'd been lost in some sort of curious trancelike state, the lady had begun speaking.

It was a more than peculiar happenstance when the mere sound of her voice left an honest-to-goodness shiver sliding down his spine.

"And there is absolutely no reason for you to continue pointing that gun at me," she said, her voice maintaining an even pitch, quite as if she wasn't in danger of being shot at any moment. "You're terrifying the poor goat that is even now trying to hide behind me, as well as a goose that has burrowed underneath my skirt. The burrowing is a circumstance I'd like to rectify as quickly as possible as I'm afraid the goose is soon going to realize she's trapped. I can't imagine I'll want her directly next to me when she tries to fight her way back to freedom."

"I'm sure you'd like me to set this down," Norbert scoffed, "but this is private property, and you have no business walking in here as if you own the place. Since you're a woman and all, I'll give you the courtesy of ten seconds to remove yourself, but if you're not out of my sight by then, don't think I won't shoot you."

Instead of immediately heading for the door, the lady narrowed blue eyes that were now flashing in a rather intimidating fashion on Norbert instead.

"I have no intention of removing myself from this castle as my aunt Ottilie transferred the ownership of it to me and my sister before she left the country. That means I have every right to walk into it as if I owned the place because, to put it bluntly, I do."

A sense of dread immediately began flowing through Rhenick's veins, undoubtedly brought about because if the lady was telling the truth, she was soon going to be facing far more danger than being held at gunpoint by Norbert. That danger, unfortunately, involved members of Chicago's underworld, who wouldn't hesitate to do whatever it took to obtain possession of land that was now considered one of the most coveted pieces of property outside of Chicago, and property that the most intriguing lady he'd ever clapped eyes on now claimed to own.

≈ Eight ≈

Deciding that the first order of business was to discern if the lady truly was the owner of the castle, although he had a feeling she was, as she didn't strike him as a lady prone to careless disregard for the truth, Rhenick cleared his throat, which resulted in him finding himself on the wrong end of Norbert's rifle.

He didn't hesitate to raise his hands in the air. "There's no need to shoot me, Norbert. I'm just here because I saw the gate open and thought Ottilie had returned. With that said, though, I don't get the impression this lady is here to harm anyone, so what say you set aside the rifle before someone gets hurt?"

"I'm not setting it aside until I see proof that she's Miss Ottilie's niece."

"Oh for heaven's sake," the lady said before she began fiddling with the cuff of her gown, stilling when Norbert directed the rifle her way again. "If you're considering shooting me because you're afraid I'm soon to whip a pistol out of my sleeve, know that it would be beyond ridiculous to stash a pistol in a sleeve that has a tailored cuff since it wouldn't be readily accessible. Besides, I don't even own a pistol, let alone know how to operate one."

"Then why are you acting all suspicious with your sleeve?" Norbert asked.

"You said you needed proof that I'm Ottilie's niece." She extracted a bracelet that had charms hanging from it. After flipping through the charms, she held one of them aloft. "There. It's a miniature of Aunt Ottilie, and since I doubt anyone who isn't related to her would attach her face to a bracelet, I'm sure you'll agree that this charm can be used as evidence that Ottilie is, indeed, my aunt. As further proof, my name is Drusilla Merriweather—Merriweather being a surname I share with Ottilie."

It was rather curious when a glimmer of satisfaction took that moment to sweep over Rhenick, undoubtedly because it seemed Drusilla wasn't married, as she'd not introduced herself as Mrs. Merriweather. Before he could contemplate the matter further, though, Norbert began peering at the charm Drusilla was dangling in front of him.

"Sure seems like it's a likeness of Miss Ottilie, but . . ." He nodded to Rhenick. "What do you think?"

Rhenick stepped closer and settled his gaze on the wrist Drusilla immediately thrust his way, getting a delicious whiff of lemon verbena in the process. Trying to ignore that the scent was tugging him straight back into discombobulated territory, Rhenick forced his attention on the miniature dangling in front of him. He lifted his head a second later and caught Drusilla's eye. "It would seem you are indeed Ottilie's niece."

"Of course I am," she said briskly, tucking her charm bracelet away before she glanced between him and Norbert. "With *my* identity now settled, who, pray tell, are both of you?"

After Norbert muttered his name and added that he was Ottilie's groundskeeper, Drusilla arched a brow Rhenick's way, which he responded to by presenting her with a bow.

"I'm Mr. Rhenick Whittenbecker," he began, anything else he might have wanted to add forgotten when his attention was captured by the unusual sight of a goose's backside trying to wiggle out from underneath Drusilla's hem.

He was in motion a heartbeat later, lunging forward with the intent of grabbing the goose. Regrettably, it quickly became evident that the whole lunging business was not going to work to his advantage after he tripped over his own feet in the process, causing him to slam into Drusilla and knocking her straight to the floor, with him tumbling directly after her.

If knocking a lady to the ground wasn't bad enough, instead of rolling to where he'd cushion her fall, he landed directly on top of her, the sharp intake of breath she immediately took suggesting he'd not exactly been successful with saving the lady as it seemed he'd injured her instead.

"In case this has escaped your notice," she said somewhat breathlessly, "I'm in very real danger of being squished—and by you, if that's in question."

The back of his neck took to heating because of course he was squishing her. He was at least twice her size, a good foot taller than she was, and . . .

"Still squishing me," she wheezed.

"Right," he muttered as he rolled to his left and landed on his back. Before he could extend her a well-deserved apology, though, his vision was obscured by a wet nose, one that turned out to belong to the goat that had been hovering next to Drusilla and was now snuffling its way across Rhenick's face.

A wet, abrasive tongue then began to scrape over Rhenick's cheek, leaving behind a great deal of slobber before Norbert finally had the presence of mind to grab the goat by its collar and tug it away.

"Sorry about that," Norbert said. "Billy's just a real friendly sort, but before he starts getting fresh with Miss Merriweather, I should take him and Mother Goose back to the barn." With that, Norbert began tugging Billy the Goat toward the hallway, Mother Goose letting out a squawk before waddling after them.

Swiping his sleeve over his slobber-covered face, Rhenick pushed himself to a sitting position and turned his attention to Drusilla, who was watching Norbert's departure, a frown marring her lovely face.

"Is it just me, or do you think it's odd that animals were wandering around the castle?" she asked.

"It does seem rather curious because I never noticed goats in here when Ottilie was in residence, although . . ." He nodded to a few bales of straw. "Given all that straw and the distinct scent of something unpleasant that's mixed in with the straw that's scattered on the floor, I'm thinking animals being inside has become a common occurrence these days."

She considered the straw-strewn floor before she turned her gaze to a chandelier that was dangling cobwebs directly over their heads. "Does it also seem odd that Aunt Ottilie's groundskeeper is still working here when her other employees probably left their positions after they decided my aunt had returned to the castle in the form of a ghost and was haunting the place?"

"You know the castle's rumored to be haunted?"

"I was recently made aware of that when my hack driver filled me in about the peculiar events happening here." She pulled her attention away from the chandelier and settled it on him. "You told Norbert that you're here because you thought Ottilie had returned, which suggests you don't believe the rumor that it's her ghost haunting this place."

"I've never put much store in rumors, and given that William Baumgartner, Ottilie's solicitor, never shared any official information with anyone in Chicago regarding Ottilie's death, I still have hope she's out there somewhere—unless you're here because William contacted you with unfortunate news regarding her demise."

"I've never heard anything from Mr. Baumgartner, even though we've sent him numerous telegrams over the past two

years, nor have I heard from my aunt after she transferred ownership of the castle to me and my sister and left the country."

"She really gave you the castle?" Rhenick forced himself to
ask.

Drusilla sat up and began dusting off the sleeve of her gown.
"I'd hardly show up here with the intention of moving in unless
she had, but why do I get the distinct impression you believe
there's a problem with my owning this place?"

He opened his mouth but got distracted by the sight of a
spider descending from the chandelier on a gossamer thread,
heading, of course, directly for Drusilla.

"What say we go out on the back courtyard to discuss this
further?" he asked as he pushed himself to his feet and grabbed
hold of her hand, pulling her to her feet and then hustling her
to the courtyard door.

"I'm almost tempted to ask if you spotted a ghost, which
could possibly explain why we're all but sprinting across the
room," she said as he shoved aside a bolt that was locking the
door, then shoved open a door that clearly hadn't been oiled
in months, given the squeaking it was doing.

"I didn't want to alarm you, but there was a spider," he said,
frowning when he got his first glance of what had once been
a charming courtyard when Ottilie had been in residence but
was now filled with overgrown vines and pots filled with dead
plants that had obviously been neglected for months.

"I'm not afraid of spiders because my sister enjoys collecting them, although I freely admit I don't admire them quite as
much as Annaliese does," she said before she wandered across the
courtyard, stopping once she reached a low stone wall that separated the courtyard from a cliff that led down to Lake Michigan.
She took a second to admire the view before she returned her
attention to him. "Now that we're well removed from that spider,
although I'm sure there are just as many spiders lurking out here,
tell me—why is it a problem that my aunt gave me this castle?"

"It's only a problem if you're truly determined to move in instead of selling the place."

"Because?"

He took a step closer to her. "This particular property is currently considered highly desirable, and it's coveted by men who will do whatever it takes to gain ownership of it. That means, unless you're willing to sell—and quickly at that, something I'm happy to admit I'm qualified to assist you with—your very life, along with the lives of everyone you've brought to Chicago with you, will unquestionably be in danger."

Nine

Considering she'd just been told she was in danger, it was rather unexpected that instead of feeling even a smidgen of apprehension about the matter, Drusilla was feeling downright annoyed instead.

That annoyance was a direct result of Mr. Rhenick Whittenbecker having slipped in that bit about him being qualified to help her, something that most assuredly meant he had some type of ulterior motive behind his offer of assistance—and a motive she wouldn't be surprised to discover had something to do with him wanting her property as well.

Needing a moment to get her annoyance in check, she presented Rhenick with her back and watched the small waves cresting on the lake, drawing in a few deep breaths when the sight and sound of the water did nothing to disperse her annoyance.

When she finally felt as if she'd be capable of speaking somewhat rationally to the man, she turned back to Rhenick. "Perhaps you could expand on how exactly you'd go about assisting me with the dangerous situation I'm evidently facing."

He immediately took to smiling, something that drew attention to what she hadn't neglected to notice was a far-too-attractive face, which was, given her past experience with a far-too-attractive ex-fiancé, not a mark in his favor.

"I can assist you because I'm acquainted with numerous developers in the area and can help you broker a lucrative deal with any of them."

She narrowed her eyes. "Which sounds lovely, to be sure, but what would you expect in return? A percentage of the sale, perhaps?"

His smile slipped just a touch. "I wouldn't expect anything."

It was difficult to resist a snort, and to avoid the temptation to do exactly that, which might be detrimental to her academy idea if Rhenick spread the word around that the headmistress of said academy made it a point to emit unladylike snorts at will, she spun around and faced the lake. After drawing in more than a few deeps breaths, she forced a smile and turned around. "Allow me to thank you, Mr. Whittenbecker, for your kind, and need I add unexpected, offer of support. However, know that I don't have any intention of selling."

"Why not?"

"I don't believe that's any of your concern."

"Given that I'm good friends with your aunt, and Ottilie would certainly want me to look after your safety, I disagree— unless you're about to tell me that your father, brother, or perhaps even your intended are traveling to join you soon."

She lifted her chin. "My father has been dead for over two years, I've never had a brother, and my intended tossed me over about five months ago. But know that I don't need any man to come racing to my rescue, as I'm perfectly capable of seeing after myself."

A trace of something that looked almost like disbelief flickered through Rhenick's eyes before he took a step closer to her. "I fear I must have misheard you, Miss Merriweather, because surely you didn't just say that your intended tossed you over, did you?"

She refused a sigh. "I'm afraid I did, although clearly the unusual events of this day are catching up with me as I had no intention of mentioning Elbert to anyone in Chicago, nor was

I intending on allowing anyone to know I'd once been engaged. However . . ." She caught his eye. "Since I *have* brought Elbert into our conversation, not that I'm going to speak further on the matter of my broken engagement, he made a point of telling me that the most prominent families in Chicago prefer living on Prairie Avenue. That suggests you may very well be mistaken about the desirability of this property."

"Your ex-fiancé isn't wrong in that Prairie Avenue is thought to be the most prestigious residence in Chicago," Rhenick said. "With that said, though, ever since Potter Palmer built a million-dollar mansion only a half mile from here, the wealthy are clamoring to emulate his lead." He frowned. "I'm curious, though, why this Elbert, who's clearly not an intelligent man, was discussing Prairie Avenue with you."

Drusilla returned the frown. "He was hoping I'd be coming into a windfall, but why would you assume Elbert lacks intelligence?"

"He tossed you over, didn't he?"

An unexpected ribbon of warmth began winding its way up Drusilla's neck to settle on her cheeks as the thought struck that no one, apart from her immediate family and Seraphina, had said anything negative about Elbert to her until now. And even though it hardly spoke well of her character to hear Rhenick question Elbert's intelligence, it . . .

"If you ask me, you're well shot of the man," Rhenick said, pulling Drusilla abruptly from her thoughts. "He hardly sounds like a charming sort, especially not if he was reconsidering tossing you over if you could hand him an unexpected windfall."

Before Drusilla had an opportunity to respond, Norbert came striding through the door that led to the courtyard and set his sights on her. "Thought you might have come outside to get some fresh air," he said once he stopped a few feet away from her. "My apologies for the way the castle smells right now. I wasn't expecting any of Miss Ottilie's relatives to come by, else I would've made a point to clean up the mess all the goats and Mother Goose made."

"Why were they left to make a mess in the first place?" Drusilla asked.

Norbert took a second to reattach his suspender before he lifted his head. "I've been using the goats as an alarm system ever since the staff left over a year ago."

"Because . . . ?" Drusilla pressed.

"There wasn't anyone left in the castle to alert me about peculiar happenstances."

"Peculiar happenstances that involve the ghost of my aunt Ottilie?"

Norbert's eyes widened. "Do not say you've already caught sight of her, because I've yet to get a true glimpse of her. Frankly, I've been feeling rather slighted because Miss Ottilie showed herself to numerous members of her staff before they bolted to take up positions elsewhere, but hasn't shown herself to me."

"No need to worry that Aunt Ottilie's slighted you again by already making an appearance for me because I haven't caught so much as a glimpse of her floating around," Drusilla returned. "In all honesty, I've never been a believer in ghosts. I also can't help but wonder why everyone assumed it was my aunt causing mischief in the castle since I never received a single telegram from my aunt's solicitor telling me there was even a chance my aunt might be dead, let alone an official notice of her death."

"I don't know why Mr. Baumgartner wouldn't have sent you word about all the trouble going on here, especially since he must have known Miss Ottilie transferred the castle over to you. Seems sketchy on his part, but you won't be able to ask him anything about that since he disappeared not long after the suit of armor incident."

"There was a suit of armor incident?" Drusilla forced herself to ask.

"Too right there was. A suit of armor was spotted strolling

around the great hall in the middle of the night, swinging a mace as it strolled and moaning up a storm." Norbert shook his head. "That was the final straw for the staff who lived here. They packed up their belongings and skedaddled off to new positions with a swell who lives in Hyde Park the very next morning."

"You weren't interested in skedaddling?" Rhenick asked.

"I don't live in the castle, and Miss Ottilie, or any other ghost for that matter, has yet to pay me a visit in my cottage."

"Let's hope none of them decide to pay me a visit either," Drusilla said. "But if we could return to the subject of William Baumgartner—you mentioned he left town, but surely he left a way to contact him, didn't he?"

"Not with me," Norbert admitted. "If you're interested in contacting him, though, you might want to visit the manager at Chicago Bank and Trust. That's where your aunt and Mr. Baumgartner have their accounts and where my wages get deposited as well." Norbert gave his nose a scratch. "But I wouldn't get your hopes up that the manager will give you that information since he wouldn't give it to me, even though I told him that I just needed to get word to Mr. Baumgartner because I needed a current address for Miss Fenna Larkin, who was once Miss Ottilie's personal assistant."

"Why did you need to find a current address for Miss Larkin?"

Norbert returned his attention to his suspenders, fiddled with one for a long second, then shrugged. "Can't hardly remember now, but it obviously wasn't all that important since I don't remember being all that bothered when the manager wouldn't give me Mr. Baumgartner's direction." He shook his head. "That manager told me the bank isn't permitted to give out personal information like that, and they'll only send a message to one of their customers if they deem it an emergency."

"I imagine the bank will agree to contact Mr. Baumgartner for me as he's my only connection to my aunt," Drusilla began, losing her train of thought when the sound of a goat bleating drew her attention. Turning to peer over the wall, she found three goats climbing up the cliff, all of them stopping once they reached the top, where they immediately began chomping on some tall grass.

She turned back to Norbert. "While I understand why you allowed the goats into the castle, needing an alarm system and all, I'm going to state here and now that since I, along with my family and staff, are now moving in, the goats are going to have to remain outside."

A hefty dose of what looked like horror flickered through Norbert's eyes. "You're moving in, not just here for a visit?"

"I am."

Norbert frowned. "I don't mean to be contradictory, Miss Merriweather, but I have a feeling you're going to want to reconsider, especially after the developers learn you're the new owner. To be blunt, your best option is to let it be known you're accepting bids on this place, then take the highest offer and get out of town as quickly as possible."

"Mr. Whittenbecker already told me about how determined a few men are to buy my property, but as I told him, I'm not selling, nor will I change my mind about that."

Norbert quirked a brow Rhenick's way. "Did you tell her who those determined men are?"

"I don't usually make it a point to disclose information to ladies that will undoubtedly terrify them."

"I think you might have to abandon that stance since Miss Merriweather doesn't seem to be grasping the extent of the danger she's in," Norbert said.

For a second, Drusilla didn't think Rhenick was going to comply, but then he drew in a breath before he inclined his head her way. "Know that it gives me no pleasure to have to tell you this, but if you refuse to sell, you're going to find yourself at odds with more than a few men involved in Chicago's underworld, and those men are not the type who will ever take no for an answer, even if it's being delivered by a most beautiful and charming lady."

⹁ Ten ⹁

I t was certainly uncommon to be the object of what seemed to be blatant flattery on Rhenick Whittenbecker's part, and in all honesty, Drusilla couldn't claim to not be a little charmed by it, until she realized that Rhenick and Norbert were both watching her warily, probably because she'd taken to smiling—an odd reaction to be sure after being told members of the criminal underworld might soon descend on the castle.

"Maybe she's in shock," Norbert muttered. "Think I should hie myself off to the wine cellar and fetch a bottle of Madeira? Miss Ottilie always swore it could cure you of any ailment, physical or mental."

"I'm not in shock, nor do I need a glass of Madeira right now, although I might need some to calm my mother down—if I can convince her to get out of the hired hack," Drusilla said, causing Rhenick, who was nodding in answer to Norbert's question, to stop nodding and frown.

"That sounds as if your mother isn't keen to live here, which I would think would be an excellent reason to sell this place as quickly as possible."

"Except that I gave my word to my aunt that I would keep the castle in the family. So no, I'm not able to sell it, no matter if that would delight my mother or not."

Rhenick cocked his head to the side. "That certainly puts a new twist on the matter, and also leaves me wondering why your aunt gave you the castle."

"Why would you wonder that?"

"Because Ottilie and I had a long discussion before she left Chicago about how she was being plagued by offers from developers," Rhenick said. "She was adamant about not entertaining any offers, as she had no intention of selling the place. That makes it more than curious that she gave the castle away."

"That is curious," Drusilla admitted. "However, it wasn't unusual for her to lavish extravagant and unexpected gifts on me and my sister."

"Which I can certainly see her doing, but what I can't see her doing is giving you an extravagant castle that threatens to put your life in danger."

"I can't see her doing that either, but . . ." Drusilla gave her temple a rub, stilling a second later. "There is the possibility that Aunt Ottilie wouldn't have expected Annaliese or myself to take time out of our busy schedules to travel here even for a visit, let alone move in, which might suggest . . ."

"Suggest what?" Rhenick prodded when Drusilla stopped talking as her thoughts began swirling madly about.

"I'm not quite sure just yet. I need a moment to think."

After glancing around the courtyard, Drusilla spotted a stone bench and made a beeline for it, brushing aside some old leaves before she sat down. She then took to rubbing a temple that was once again beginning to ache as she sorted through thoughts that weren't exactly cohesive yet.

It took a good few minutes before she felt she was capable of explaining where her train of thought was heading, time in which Rhenick and Norbert took to speaking in hushed tones to each other, their conversation coming to an abrupt end when Rhenick looked her way.

"Done thinking?" he asked.

74

"For the most part. And if you'll indulge me, I'd like to voice what I'm thinking and get both of your opinions on it."

Rhenick strode into motion with Norbert by his side, stopping directly in front of her.

"We're listening," Norbert said, holding a hand up to his ear, which either meant he was taking the fact that she wanted his opinion seriously, or that he was somewhat hard of hearing.

She fought an unexpected smile. "I suppose I'll start by asking this—what if my aunt gave me the castle as a way to keep it safe from the developers while she was gone? And also, what if her solicitor disappeared after rumors of Ottilie's ghost started swirling around because he knew certain members of the criminal persuasion were going to start pressuring him to settle her affairs?"

Norbert rubbed a hand over his face. "Begging your pardon, Miss Merriweather, but that's a lot of questionable what-ifs. Besides, I don't really understand why your aunt wouldn't have expected you to come and at least visit the castle since everyone knows Lake Michigan is beautiful in the summer."

"My aunt knows my family only summers in Newport, so she wouldn't have expected us to change our plans, not when the social Season in Newport is something we spend months preparing for—well, until we experienced a bit of a financial catastrophe. That catastrophe is the reason why we're now in Chicago, and why, since I can't sell the castle, I'm considering turning it into an academy for young ladies."

Rhenick's mouth went slack. "I would advise you against that."

"I wasn't asking for your opinion on that particular topic," she shot back before blinking at the distinct trace of snippiness that had been lacing her tone, something that would have most assuredly had her decorum teachers passing around a vial of smelling salts.

She blew out a breath. "Forgive me, Mr. Whittenbecker. I didn't mean to be terse with you. With that said, though, opening an academy is the only way I can think of to avert financial disaster, since I can't sell the place. And it'll also allow me to put to good use my only credible talent."

"I highly doubt you only possess one credible talent."

"Which is kind of you to say, but I'm not portraying false modesty just now. I honestly do possess a singular talent—that being that I'm overly proficient with all matters of social propriety. I had the honor of being top of my class at the academy for young ladies I attended and have recently been told that if I hadn't been born into one of the wealthiest families in the country, I would have excelled at being a headmistress of a finishing school, something I'm now going to prove wasn't the insult it was intended to be."

"You will not be able to prove anything if you're dead, a state you might very well soon experience if you don't at least consider selling."

Drusilla shook her head. "I gave Aunt Ottilie my word, and while I'm sure she wouldn't want me or my sister to be in danger, I'm not going to sell a castle my aunt might not have wanted to part with but merely gave to me as a way to keep it safe for her until she returns. Hopefully, if keeping the castle safe was her actual objective, she won't be too annoyed with me over turning it into an academy."

"Given Ottilie's philanthropic efforts to improve the lives of women in general, I'm sure she'll be anything but annoyed," Rhenick said. "However, even though it's admirable that you want to protect the castle for when your aunt returns—if she returns—can you not at least consider moving somewhere else until you hear from her, which will keep you safe from people who'll go to extreme measures to get their hands on this property?"

"If I wasn't experiencing that financial catastrophe I mentioned, of course I'd reconsider, but that's not an option." Drusilla's forehead furrowed. "Out of blatant curiosity, though, what exactly would those extreme measures be that you mentioned?"

"Given that you're adamant about not selling, I don't think that it would be comforting for you if I were to expand on that."

"I really must insist."

Rhenick raked a hand through his hair, leaving the black strands standing on end. "Well, if you insist—know that the most extreme measure would be finding yourself at the bottom of Lake Michigan without a way to get back to the surface."

"That *would* be extreme," Drusilla admitted as she gave the slightest bit of a shudder, something she suspected Rhenick had seen because his eyes narrowed for the briefest of seconds before he raked his hand through his hair again and started pacing around the courtyard.

He made four complete circles before he stopped to look out over the water for a long moment, then turned and strode back toward her, taking a seat beside her on the bench.

"You seem to believe you don't have any other option but to open an academy as a means to bring in some income. However, I have an alternative for you, one that will fix your financial situation, allow you to keep possession of the castle so you can return it to Ottilie when she returns, and lets you avoid the whole finding-yourself-on-the-bottom-of-Lake-Michigan problem."

Her sense of apprehension was immediate. "That sounds more like a miracle than a solution, but before you tell me what you have in mind, tell me this—why does it seem as if you've decided to take it upon yourself to assume responsibility for me?"

Something interesting flickered through Rhenick's eyes before he settled a smile on her. "I told you, I'm good friends with your aunt, and Ottilie would certainly expect me to step in, especially now that you have no other men available to protect you. The only way I can truly protect you, though, is this . . ." He leaned closer. "The way I see it, in order to keep you safe from members of Chicago's underworld, you're going to have to marry me, and the sooner the better as well."

Eleven

Trudging up the steps leading to his home on North Rush Street, an address that wasn't as fashionable as Prairie Avenue but still sported some impressive mansions all the same, Rhenick opened a door that was painted an unusual shade of red—vermillion, to be exact—chosen by his sister Eloise, who'd decided the previous year that vermillion was her favorite color and had asked if they could paint the front door that color in honor of her fifteenth birthday.

Birthdays in the Whittenbecker household were considered very important events indeed, which was why their door now stood out from all the other doors in the neighborhood, not that Rhenick was sure the neighbors appreciated that. However, given that Eloise seemed to be gravitating toward yellow these days, he had a feeling the neighbors wouldn't have to suffer the sight of a vermillion door for much longer.

After walking into the entranceway, Rhenick moved aside a few hats, ribbons, and even a pair of roller skates that were dangling by their laces from the hooks that were attached to the wall, finally making a space large enough to where he could hang up his hat.

He barely had a moment to glance in the mirror that hung beside the hooks before the sound of someone racing down the steps drew his attention, that distraction allowing him to ignore the fact that the glimpse he'd just gotten of his current expression suggested he was still lingering in what could only be described as a bewildered state.

He wasn't a man who experienced bewilderment often, if ever, but bewildered he most assuredly was, this unfamiliar state a direct result of the infuriated response he'd received from Drusilla after he'd broached the subject of marriage.

Infuriated wasn't exactly a response he'd ever thought he'd incur when it came to the subject of marriage.

"Rhenick, there you are," Coraline, his youngest sister, exclaimed as she skidded to a stop in front of him. "I've been waiting for you for ages, and now that you're finally home, I need you to come with me right this very minute and look over some outfits I'm considering wearing tonight. Then, after I've modeled each outfit, I need you to tell me which one shows me to advantage before I head off to Norma Jean McCormick's house."

"I take it Grace and Eloise aren't available?"

Coraline waved that away. "Oh, they're available, as is Tilda, who brought the twins for a visit, but I don't need a girl's opinion, and Edwin doesn't count as he's only five and knows nothing about fashion yet. That leaves you as my fashion adviser today."

A tingle of suspicion began tickling the back of his neck. "Why do you need me to advise you?"

"I require a male perspective."

He narrowed his eyes. "An unusual request, and one that has me wondering exactly what you're going to be doing at Norma Jean's this evening."

Coraline rolled her eyes. "There's no need for you to turn all suspicious. As I've mentioned often, Norma Jean's decided to become a playwright someday. She recently finished a new story and invited the girls over for a spur-of-the-moment gathering so we can read through her script later tonight."

Rhenick didn't need to ask who the "girls" were, as Coraline had been fast friends with a specific group of eight girls she'd met on the first day of Sunday school years before. Those girls could often be found lounging around the Whittenbecker music room, although thankfully they spent most of their time mooning over various local boys instead of pursuing musical endeavors. None of the girls were what anyone would call proficient with any musical instruments—or singing, for that matter.

"If you're merely spending the evening with the girls, why do you need my opinion about what you're going to wear?"

Coraline took to batting innocent lashes his way, but before she could get what he knew was going to be a less-than-completely-truthful response out of her mouth, additional footsteps coming down the stairs interrupted her.

"I imagine Coraline wants your opinion because she knows Norma Jean's brother, Seth, is currently spending some time at Norma Jean's house instead of his own after one of his latest inventions went horribly wrong." Rhenick's second-youngest sister, Grace, skipped over to his side, gave him a kiss on the cheek, and completely ignored that Coraline was now scowling at her. "From what I've heard, Seth blew a large hole out of his roof when something he was working on unexpectedly went airborne."

"Seth does seem to experience explosions more than your average inventor," Rhenick said right as a thought began forming in his mind, one that had his sense of suspicion intensifying. He returned his attention to Coraline. "You don't happen to want my opinion because you're hoping to make a favorable impression on Seth this evening, do you?"

"What young lady wouldn't want to impress a man who's already earning the reputation of being an inventor for the ages, as well as being delightfully mysterious?" Coraline countered.

"*Mysterious* is not a word I've ever heard used to describe Seth McCormick since he's got the air of an absentminded professor about him. However, non-mysterious ways aside, Seth and

I went to school together and he's exactly my age—twenty-eight. You're barely thirteen, which means Seth is far too old for you."

"Everyone knows that ladies mature far faster than gentlemen do," Coraline argued.

"Not that fast."

As Coraline immediately took to muttering about that, Rhenick turned to Grace, who was in the process of regarding him with a rather odd look on her face. "What?" he asked.

"Your hair is unusually untidy, which suggests something unexpected happened to you today."

Not certain he was up for an interrogation just yet, considering he was still in a rather bewildered state regarding what had transpired with Drusilla, Rhenick summoned up a smile. "I'm sure my hair *is* looking untidy. If you've neglected to notice, Chester, our less-than-efficient butler, is once again not manning his post. That not-unusual circumstance meant I had to hang up my own hat, and then any grooming I may have wanted to do, such as combing my hair after wearing a hat all day, came to a rapid end when Coraline intercepted me."

Grace returned his smile. "Mother sent Chester off to visit the doctor because he had a reaction to the silver polish he was using this morning."

Rhenick's smile dimmed. "Chester can barely manage to handle opening and closing the front door, let alone taking anyone's coat or hat. Why in the world would Mother have thought he'd be up for polishing the silver?"

"I think she believed that since Chester used to work in a steel mill until he came to work here not that long ago, he'd appreciate working with a form of ore again, especially when Mother recently read that proper butlers are always responsible for attending to the silver." Grace winced. "Unfortunately, as I said, Chester had a reaction to the polish, so I don't think polishing silver is going to be added to his list of butler duties once he gets that rash under control."

"I'm not sure I needed the imagine of Chester covered in a rash now imprinted on my mind," Rhenick admitted. "Nevertheless, his absence exactly explains why I'm currently looking untidy, as Chester wasn't available to point out the derelict state of my hair or, better yet, provide me with a comb the moment after I stepped foot into the house, something a competent butler would have done."

"I don't think there's any question about Chester's competency with his butler role, but Chester aside . . ." Grace considered him again. "While your explanation regarding your disheveled state is rather reasonable, for some reason, and one I can't quite put my finger on, I don't think our absentee butler is why you're looking out-of-sorts."

Hoping to avoid a full-out interrogation since he'd yet to fully comprehend how he'd made such a disaster with Drusilla Merriweather in the first place, Rhenick gave Grace's arm a squeeze. "Couldn't we simply leave it that I had a somewhat harrowing day, one I don't particularly care to discuss?"

Grace immediately took to exchanging a telling look with Coraline before she arched a brow his way. "I don't believe you've ever used the word *harrowing* before, which suggests something dastardly *did* happen to you, which means . . ."

Grace was striding to the foot of the stairs a mere heartbeat later, where she promptly stopped and opened her mouth.

A dulcet feminine tone was not what came out of that mouth, but an honest-to-goodness bellow, her bellowing resulting in the sound of numerous pairs of feet pounding down the stairs a blink of an eye later.

≈ Twelve ≈

A mere two minutes after his mother, Wilhelmine, and two other sisters, Eloise and Tilda, came barreling into the entranceway, Rhenick found himself being hauled into the sitting room, Coraline using somewhat of a sailor's grip to keep him moving at a fast clip. After shoving him onto a striped green-and-cream–colored chaise, she told him to stay put before she dashed out of the room again, clearly anxious to rejoin everyone else, who'd said they were repairing to the kitchen to request some coffee and treats.

In the Whittenbecker family, coffee and treats were considered a must in any unusual situation, and given that he'd never experienced a harrowing incident before, he wouldn't be surprised if an entire feast showed up at some point in response to what his family would certainly see as an unexpected disclosure.

"Did you get sent in here because you're in trouble too, Uncle Rhenick?" a voice asked from across the room.

Rhenick glanced around and discovered Edwin, Tilda's son and the only boy who'd been born into his family since his birth some twenty-eight years before, sitting in a small chair in the far corner of the room, his little five-year-old shoulders slumped and looking decidedly dejected.

"I'm here because your grandmother is probably even now

devising the best way to go about interrogating me and didn't want me to be privy to whatever strategy she's going to put into play," Rhenick said.

Edwin's nose wrinkled. "What's *interrogating* mean?"

"Asking questions."

"What is Grandmother gonna ask you questions about?"

"My harrowing day."

Edwin's nose continued wrinkling. "What's *harrowing* mean?"

"Disturbing."

His nephew nodded. "I've had a harrowing day then too."

"How so?"

An exaggerated sigh was Edwin's first response to that before he leaned forward. "Hattie punched me."

Rhenick blinked. "Your twin—as in sweet little Hattie—punched you?"

"She's not as sweet as everyone thinks," Edwin muttered. "You can ask Malcolm. He'll tell you I'm not wrong."

"Malcolm's a beagle. It might be difficult for him to tell me anything."

"All you have to do is take one look at him this evening to know what he's thinking because Hattie stuffed him into a doll dress and tied a bonnet on his head."

"Your mother used to put hats on my pony when we were children and also enjoyed tying ribbons in his mane."

"Bet she didn't do that *and* put flowers in all the rifle barrels of your toy soldiers."

Rhenick refused a grin. "That very well might have been crossing the line, but I'm not exactly sure why, if Hattie punched you, you're sitting in the naughty chair and not your sister."

"No one knows that Hattie punched me 'cause I'm no snitch," Edwin said. "I put myself in trouble because I wanted to punch her back, but . . ." His shoulders took to slumping again. "You told me that boys always have to treat girls, even their sisters, with the most udderly respect, so I'm gonna sit here until I don't feel like punching her."

"I think I used the phrase *utmost respect* instead of udderly," Rhenick began, "but I'm very proud of you for making the decision to take some time to gather your temper instead of giving in to the urge to punch Hattie."

"I'm still mad at her."

"Perfectly understandable, and know that I'll have a talk with Hattie because I have a feeling she knows you've been told you're not supposed to punch girls and she might be using that to her advantage, but . . ." Rhenick stopped talking and glanced to the door when the sound of feet marching in unison down the hallway reached him. "I think my interrogation squad is approaching."

"Think if I stay here with you, that squad will start askin' me questions 'bout what I'm doing in the naughty chair?"

"You know they will."

"I'm suddenly not feeling like punching Hattie anymore," Edwin proclaimed as he jumped from the naughty chair and scrambled for the door.

Unable to help but grin at his nephew's rapid retreat, Rhenick rose to his feet right as his mother breezed into the room and made a beeline for him. After helping her get settled on the chaise, he turned to his sisters, his grin widening as he watched them jostle one another around, looking quite as if they'd joined a game of musical chairs as they went about the business of trying to claim the most comfortable chairs for themselves.

In less than a minute, Tilda and Eloise were sitting on a fainting couch that wasn't hard as a board, while Grace was smiling smugly from her spot on a slipper settee that wasn't as soft as the fainting couch but wasn't completely uncomfortable.

Coraline, on the other hand, who'd suffered a tumble during the mad rush, was looking grumpy as she perched on the very edge of a wingback chair that had a tendency to creak if a person so much as shifted on it, even though it had been highly recommended by an interior decorator who'd set up shop in town, but one Rhenick wasn't convinced knew the slightest thing about furnishings.

"You'll be pleased to learn, dear," Wilhelmine began, settling a smile on him, "that coffee and tea have been ordered, along with some cheese. I know you're probably famished after the harrowing day you've experienced, but while we wait for everything to be delivered, perhaps you could take a moment to give us a few specifics about what happened to you."

"I hardly know where to begin as I fear my thoughts are still rather discombobulated," he admitted.

Wilhelmine's eyes widened. "You're experiencing discombobulation?"

"When you say it like that, it almost sounds as if I'm experiencing some type of grave malady that may soon see me on my deathbed."

"No one ever died from discombobulation, darling, but I do think I'm getting an inkling as to why you've experienced a harrowing day." Wilhelmine gave his hand a pat. "It involves a lady, doesn't it?"

"You've met a lady and didn't tell us about her?" Eloise demanded as his other sisters leaned forward and settled accusatory eyes on him, as if they believed he'd been holding back on them.

"There hasn't been anything to tell you as I only just met the lady who was mostly responsible for my very peculiar day," he said.

"And this lady is responsible for your discombobulated state?" Tilda pressed.

"I must admit that she is."

Wilhelmine settled back against the chaise. "You must tell us everything, and from the beginning, if you please, so that we'll be able to fully comprehend your peculiar situation."

Rhenick nodded and then took a moment to attempt to collect thoughts that were still scattered before he tilted his head. "In all honesty, it started off as a completely normal day, one where I got up before dawn, shaved, then fetched some coffee from the kitchen."

Tilda scooted forward on the fainting couch. "Why didn't your valet shave you and ring for your coffee since that's what you pay him to do?"

"Herman has difficulties getting out of bed before nine because he didn't used to get home from his previous job until after midnight."

"I forgot your valet used to work in an ale house," Tilda said as if that explained everything, which it actually did.

"I'm sure he'll eventually get accustomed to my schedule, but the staffing agency did warn me that Herman wasn't exactly qualified, given that he had no valet experience. I'm the one who decided to hire him anyway, though, since there was no telling when another unqualified candidate might show up at the agency looking for work." Rhenick smiled. "On the bright side, if I ever need an ale poured, Herman's an expert. He spent fifteen years behind the bar at the saloon he worked in before it burned down."

"While there's no question Chicago continues to suffer from less-than-qualified domestic workers," Wilhelmine began, "if we could return to your story, as the hour is growing late and I have a charity event to attend first thing tomorrow morning, that would be wonderful." Her eyes took to twinkling. "And not that I care to tell you how to go about telling a story, darling, but perhaps it would move matters along more rapidly if you began not from the moment you got out of bed, but from when events began to turn harrowing for you."

"You know if I hadn't started from when I got out of bed, someone would have interrupted me and asked me what I ate for breakfast."

"Everyone knows what you eat for breakfast. Two slices of toast, two eggs over easy, coffee, and occasionally you'll add a bowl of fruit, but usually only on Saturdays."

"I've always wondered why you only eat eggs over easy," Coraline said. "Is it that you enjoy the yolks being a little runny, which would explain why you don't ask for hard-boiled eggs, or even scrambled?"

"We are not going to launch into a discussion of the many ways Rhenick could eat eggs, not when he has yet to explain more about this lady who sent him into a discombobulated state," Tilda said firmly.

"You're the one who distracted him with the whole valet topic," Coraline didn't hesitate to point out.

A narrowed eye from Wilhelmine left his sisters abandoning their bickering, which left him free to launch into his story, garnering everyone's undivided attention when he got to the part of his day where he encountered a redhaired lady dashing out of the Merriweather castle with a ferret in tow.

Before he could get to the part about the cloaked woman, though, one of their housemaids, Charity, lumbered into the room, pushing a coffee cart that seemed to have a faulty wheel on it, the wheel obviously responsible for why the cart crashed into a table. Rhenick was on his feet a second later, scooping one of his mother's favorite vases out of the air before it had a chance to smash to the ground.

After setting the vase on a table that was far removed from the cart, Rhenick sent Charity, who was now looking more than frazzled, a smile before he asked her to return to the kitchen because she'd forgotten the teapot and Tilda had never been keen on coffee.

As Charity moseyed her way out of the room, clearly in no hurry to fetch the tea, Rhenick took it upon himself to serve his mother and sisters, save Tilda, a cup of coffee before he poured a cup for himself and retook his seat.

"Where were we?" he asked.

"The appearance of a redhaired lady and a ferret," Eloise supplied.

Rhenick took a sip of coffee that gave new meaning to the word *strong*, then set the cup on a saucer that was sporting a rather large chip in it. "Quite right, but before any of you decide that the redhaired lady is why I had a harrowing time of it today, she's not—well, not really, although her ferret does play a role in that, but I'm getting ahead of myself."

Eloise rose to her feet, her eyes gleaming in a rather unusual manner. "Since you were at the Merriweather castle, and everyone knows that Ottilie Merriweather is old money—as in old New York money—may I dare hope that this redhaired lady is a relative or friend of Miss Merriweather, come to visit from New York, and also hope that she was accompanied by a ferret because those creatures have become all the rage within the most fashionable set, or rather, the New York Four Hundred?"

Dead silence settled around the room for the briefest of seconds until Coraline crossed her arms over her chest and released a bit of a grunt. "If you're about to suggest that you get a ferret for your next birthday because you think that'll secure you invitations to the most prominent houses after you make your debut, you should just stick with asking that the whole house be painted to match the door instead." She smiled. "A red house will assuredly make you smile anytime you return home. Waltzing around the city with a ferret, on the other hand, would leave you in a perpetual grouchy state since ferret ownership isn't going to impress any of Chicago's most prominent society matrons."

Eloise's nose shot straight into the air. "My favorite color has recently changed to yellow, but know that if ferrets are all the rage within that oh-so-glamorous Four Hundred, me being one of the first to adopt one will certainly see me invited into the fold of Chicago's socially elite."

Tilda cleared her throat. "I hate to be the bearer of disappointing news, but I don't think acquiring a ferret, even if they are all the rage in New York City, will be enough to have the matriarchs of Chicago's high society issuing any Whittenbecker an invitation to their events."

"Why not?" Eloise demanded.

"We're too newly rich to hobnob with old Chicago money."

"Marshall Field started making his money right around the time Father did, after the fire of '71, and he and his family enjoy all the exclusive society events," Eloise argued.

"That's because Mr. Field owns a department store that all the ladies enjoy frequenting, whereas we own a construction company," Tilda said. "And before you say something about how construction companies are perfectly respectable, you have to remember that the majority of construction companies in Chicago possess dubious reputations—as in, they're run by members of Chicago's criminal underworld."

"But we're not members of the criminal underworld," Eloise countered.

"Of course we're not, darling," Wilhelmine said before she took a sip of her coffee and immediately set aside the cup, giving the distinct impression she wasn't satisfied with the coffee that had come out of the kitchen today. "Your father is an upstanding gentleman who would never dabble in criminal activities, but that hasn't stopped rumors from swirling around the upper crust of Chicago suggesting otherwise."

"What rumors?"

A sigh was Wilhelmine's first response before she rose to her feet and intercepted Charity, who was returning with a cup of tea for Tilda. She took the cup from the maid, probably in the hopes Charity wouldn't trip and spill hot tea everywhere, handed it to Tilda, and then squared her shoulders.

"I always hoped I wouldn't have to divulge what I'm about to divulge to all of you, but in the interest of avoiding a repeat occurrence of what happened when Tilda made her debut, know that I did try to get us included within the upper echelons of Chicago society, but failed miserably." Wilhelmine began wandering around the room, finally pausing beside the floor-to-ceiling windows. "It was very humbling to suffer a public dressing down in the middle of the Palmer House dining room, but that's exactly what happened to me."

Her eyes went distant. "There I was, dressed in what I thought was a most delightful outfit, dripping in diamonds and determined to introduce myself to an entire table filled with prominent society ladies." She pushed aside the curtain and peered out the window. "I was certain those ladies would welcome me into their midst after learning I was the wife of Franklin Whittenbecker, one of the most sought-after builders in Chicago, and then feel ever so honored once I extended them invitations to Tilda's debut dinner. Sadly, that's not what they did."

"What did they do?" Eloise asked.

"Nothing pleasant," Wilhelmine said before she turned from the window and began fiddling with one of the bracelets encircling her wrist. "I found myself being looked at as if I were something unpleasant one finds on the bottom of one's shoe the moment I stopped by their table. And then, I'll never forget this, Mrs. Getchell released a titter before she leveled ice-cold eyes on me and informed me that diamonds should never be worn in the afternoon. That was then followed up by Mrs. Peck stating that the Palmer House didn't enjoy serving women—and yes, I did note that she didn't call me a lady—whose husbands were involved in less-than-legitimate business endeavors. That right there is how I know without a shadow of a doubt that the majority of socially well-connected people in Chicago believe we're criminally connected."

"Didn't you explain to them that they were wrong?" Coraline asked.

"Since I was relatively certain they might have been right about the diamonds because no one at that table was wearing anything remotely sparkly, I wasn't going to argue with anything they said." Wilhelmine gave a bit of a shudder. "I gathered what little dignity I had remaining and bolted out the door, licking my wounded pride all the way home."

She squared her shoulders. "But enough of my sad tale of complete and utter humiliation. It's past time we return to a far more important matter, which is to delve further into Rhenick's harrowing day, or more specifically, exactly who the woman is who's responsible for all that harrowing business in the first place."

Thirteen

Before Rhenick could launch into the most troubling particulars of what could certainly be considered the oddest day of his life, Charity lumbered into the room again, precariously balancing a platter of fruit and cheese in her hands, one she unceremoniously dumped on the first table she encountered. A gesture to the platter was her way of suggesting everyone help themselves, and after bobbing what was supposed to be a curtsy, she lumbered out of the room again, calling over her shoulder something about fetching some plates and utensils.

"I say everyone should just grab a piece or two of cheese without the benefit of a plate because who knows if or when Charity will ever return," Wilhelmine said, earning grins all around before everyone moved to the table and began helping themselves to chunks of cheese.

Once everyone was resettled on their respective chairs or settees, with Coraline somehow managing to relieve Grace of her more comfortable spot, Rhenick finally returned to the events of his day, making a short account of everything leading up to his first sight of Miss Drusilla Merriweather.

Wilhelmine paused with a piece of cheese halfway to her mouth and frowned. "Good heavens, Rhenick, it's no wonder you've described your experience as harrowing. If I'm not mistaken, Miss Drusilla Merriweather undoubtedly suffered an attack of the vapors after she found herself almost shot, and I would guess it was quite a dramatic attack at that. After witnessing the poor lady in a most distraught state, you, being you, and because you have quite the experience with distraught members of the feminine persuasion, obviously felt compelled to step in and comfort Miss Merriweather. However, considering the shock she'd suffered, I'm going to say she was inconsolable, and probably needed an entire vial of smelling salts before her state of hysteria began to diminish."

Rhenick swallowed the piece of cheese he'd just popped into his mouth and shook his head. "Miss Merriweather wasn't hysterical at all. In fact, she was completely composed, an attitude I found quite extraordinary, given her circumstances."

"Did he just use the word *extraordinary?*" Grace asked, earning a nod from Eloise.

"He did—a telling remark if there ever was one—but what he hasn't told us about yet is anything to do with her appearance." Eloise caught Rhenick's eye. "May we assume Drusilla Merriweather possesses extraordinary looks that, of course, compliment her extraordinary level of composure?"

His lips curved. "She is a most beautiful lady with blue eyes that I would say are more aquamarine over an ordinary blue, and her hair is brown, although . . ." He gave his jaw a rub. "The word *brown* doesn't exactly do her hair justice, as it's more of a chocolate color, but not the darkest of chocolate, or perhaps it's not chocolate at all but more along the lines of the color of acorns, but only after a rain shower, the rain having left them all shiny looking, and . . ." His words trailed to nothing when he realized that his sisters were staring at him with their mouths agape.

"What?" he asked.

"You do realize that you've just taken to descending into

poetic prose, don't you?" Eloise finally asked as the rest of his sisters, along with his mother, simply continued to stare at him, quite as if they were at a loss for words—an unusual circumstance, to be sure.

"I don't know if I'd go so far as to claim I descended into poetic prose. I was simply describing Drusilla's appearance" was all he could think to say to that.

Eloise's brow furrowed. "You likened Drusilla Merriweather's hair to acorns after a rain shower. If that's not delving into poetic prose, I don't know what is."

Having nothing at his disposal to respond to that since Eloise had made a rather valid point, Rhenick rose to his feet and moved over to the cheese platter, needing a moment to collect thoughts that, clearly, hadn't returned to normal after becoming all muddled from the moment he'd clapped eyes on Drusilla.

It was an odd state to find himself in since he wasn't a man who dabbled in poetic turns of phrase, nor was he a man who'd ever blundered about with a lady like some sort of bumbling idiot, but that's exactly what he'd done with Drusilla, and . . .

"Ah, and here's Charity, with plates for us to use, no less," Wilhelmine exclaimed, pulling Rhenick from his thoughts right as Charity thrust some plates in his hand, bobbed another curtsy, then mumbled something about forgetting the utensils before heading out the door again.

"I suppose it's a sign that Charity's becoming more proficient with her position that she remembered the plates," Grace said before she took a plate from him and promptly began loading it up with cheese, still having to use her fingers.

It took a good few minutes before everyone got resettled, and after Rhenick got his plate of cheese balanced on his knees, he turned to his mother. "Where was I?"

"You'd just gotten to the part where Drusilla had been held at rifle-point by Norbert Tweed."

"Right, and directly after that, I was presented with the opportunity to become formally introduced to Drusilla, but I'm afraid that instead of pulling off an introduction with any sort of aplomb, I was made to look like a clumsy ninny, and all because of a goose and goat."

With that, Rhenick launched into the details regarding his various interactions with Drusilla, pretending not to notice when Eloise and Coraline disappeared behind their handkerchiefs when he talked about trying to rescue the goose, or when Tilda began frowning at him when he got to the part about telling Drusilla she was in danger, only to learn she wasn't able to sell due to a promise she'd given her aunt.

To give his sisters their due, though, they didn't interrupt him a single time, although his mother didn't hesitate to do exactly that when he got to the part about Elbert.

"She has an ex-fiancé?" Wilhelmine pressed.

"Indeed, and I think he's the reason why she informed me, after I broached the subject of marriage, that she was never going to entertain the idea of marriage again."

A telling silence settled over the room until his mother set aside her plate and sat forward. "The subject of marriage came up?"

"It took me by surprise as well," Rhenick admitted. "But after I told Drusilla she could end up in Lake Michigan, and not for a swim, she stated quite emphatically that she'd have to take her chances because she'd made the decision to open an academy for young ladies, which would provide her with much-needed funds to take care of her family." He gave his nose a rub. "Events then began taking a turn for the unfortunate because, being faced with a damsel in distress, or so I thought, I made the monumental mistake of coming up with what I believed was a brilliant solution that would solve all of her problems."

"Do not tell me that's when you brought up marriage, is it?" Wilhelmine asked.

Rhenick winced. "I'm very much afraid it was."

Tilda released a snort. "Please tell me that you didn't ask a lady you'd just met to marry you."

"I think it was more along the lines of me *telling* her she needed to marry me over any asking."

His mother immediately scooted closer to him on the settee and took hold of his hand. "It's no wonder you're experiencing discombobulation, my darling boy, because, if I'm not mistaken, after Miss Merriweather got over her initial shock regarding your unexpected solution to her problems, she realized it was a viable solution and agreed to marry you. That agreement has obviously left you with the realization that, as an honorable gentleman, you're going to have to exchange vows with a lady you don't know."

"You seem to be forgetting the part where Drusilla informed me she was wholeheartedly opposed to the institution of marriage in general."

Wilhelmine blinked. "She said no to your proposal?"

"I took the fact that she snatched up Norbert's rifle and aimed it at me as conclusive evidence she wasn't saying yes."

"She tried to shoot you?"

"Not at that particular moment because she got distracted when this figure dressed in widow's weeds materialized from out of nowhere, scaring me half to death." Rhenick smiled. "Since there'd been a lot of talk about ghosts haunting the castle, I thought I was being confronted with a spirit from another realm—until the figure shoved aside its weeping veil and I found myself being looked up and down by Irma Merriweather, Drusilla's mother."

"She didn't want to shoot you as well, did she?" Wilhelmine asked.

"Not at all, but she did want to learn some specific details about me, such as what I did for a living, where Drusilla would live if she married me, and if I was receptive to the idea of a mother-in-law moving in with a newly married couple."

Tilda arched a brow. "I take it Irma Merriweather had been doing some eavesdropping before she made herself known?"

"Indeed she had, and she seemed downright delighted to learn I'm a man of industry, but . . ." He blew out a breath. "Drusilla was not delighted in the least because as soon as she heard that our family owns a construction company, which obviously goes hand in hand with land development, she decided I was a cad of the worst sort and had only asked her to marry me because I was trying to get my hands on the Merriweather property."

"I can actually see her point on that one," Tilda said.

"Well, quite," Rhenick agreed. "Nevertheless, before I could assure Drusilla that her land was the last thing I wanted, she told me she was going to take a page out of Norbert's book and count to ten, and that if I wasn't gone by that time, she was going to shoot me."

"And that's when you made a hasty retreat?" Tilda asked.

"I didn't think that was necessary because she'd admitted earlier that she didn't know how to shoot a pistol, so I assumed she wouldn't know how to shoot a rifle either. Because of that, I didn't think I was in any real danger. I also thought I'd try one last time to convince her I wasn't after her land, but before I could do that, she started counting out loud, reached ten, and then, cool as you please, she took aim at me."

"And then she shot at you?" Eloise asked.

"Well, no, because she didn't seem to know that you needed to use the lever on a rifle before the hammer cocks. Unfortunately, though, that's when the cloaked woman returned—and no, I can't describe that woman because she had the hood of her cloak over her head—and she, without a word, simply took the rifle from Drusilla, armed it, then delivered explicit instructions as she handed the rifle back to her. Drusilla then sent me the most beautiful smile—right before she pulled the trigger."

"Maybe you should have been paying more attention to the rifle than to Drusilla's delightful smile," Wilhelmine muttered.

"Indeed. Although, clearly Drusilla wasn't shooting to kill, merely making a point since she didn't hit me, although I can't say that's completely true as, again, she doesn't know how to operate a weapon. Nevertheless, even though I didn't suffer a bullet, Drusilla did hit something—that being a chandelier, which plummeted to the ground in a shower of crystals, causing a bit of a ruckus in the process."

"Good heavens," Wilhelmine breathed.

"I know. It was another instance of extraordinariness because I don't actually know a woman who would follow through with shooting at a man, even if she wasn't actually capable of hitting one." Rhenick shook his head. "Thankfully, no one was injured, but before I could make any type of departure because it was obvious my presence wasn't welcome at the castle, the redhaired lady ran into the room with not one but three ferrets running beside her." He rubbed a hand over his face. "That's when things got really interesting because who knew that ferrets could turn vicious in the blink of an eye?"

"The redhaired lady ordered her ferrets to attack you?" Eloise asked.

"She mostly just snapped her fingers and pointed in my direction, and the next thing I knew, I was facing a full-on assault from cute little furry creatures that aren't very cute when their fangs are bared."

"I believe I'll rethink any interest I may have recently voiced in acquiring one of those," Eloise said.

"An excellent idea," Rhenick agreed. "Needless to say, my only option was to run out of the castle, ferrets nipping at my heels, but luckily, Sweet Pea had returned from his gallop away from the goats. He was standing right outside the door, so I jumped on his back and off we went, leaving behind a lady I know will never want to lay eyes on me again."

Wilhelmine rose to her feet, moved to stand in front of a bookshelf laden with the latest fiction novels of the day, and shook her head. "I have to admit, my dear, that I'm not certain the word *harrowing* does justice to what you experienced today, but not to fret. Even though you've clearly made a muddle of matters, I'm sure your sisters and I will be able to come up with a plan to salvage the misimpression Drusilla Merriweather undoubtedly has of you, a plan that will hopefully convince her you're not a disreputable sort, even though telling a woman she needs to marry you suggests exactly that."

⚞ Fourteen ⚟

I hate to be the bearer of bad news, but Mother is once again refusing to come out of her room," Annaliese said as she trudged up to join Drusilla, her appearance allowing Drusilla a brief respite from the drudgery of cleaning a medieval tapestry that had been hanging on the wall—until Drusilla had noticed numerous spiders gathered on the backside of it, something that Annaliese had informed her was called a *clutter*, as the spiders weren't actually touching one another but were spread out across the tapestry.

According to Annaliese, if the spiders *had* been touching, they would have been called a *cluster*, and given that the castle hadn't been properly cleaned since the household staff had abandoned their posts almost a year and a half before, Drusilla was relatively certain she'd happen upon a cluster of spiders at some point in time, something she was definitely not looking forward to.

She gave the tapestry one last thump with the raggedy old broom she'd found in the kitchen, giving a bit of a start when Annaliese edged up beside her and began plucking spiders from the apron Drusilla had also found in the kitchen, her sister setting each creepy-crawly gently on the ground instead of flinging them through the air, something Drusilla would have certainly done if she'd noticed the little darlings clinging to an apron she would have never imagined donning a mere month ago.

"These won't hurt you, at least not much," Annaliese said, scooping another spider into her gloved hand. "They're wolf spiders, from the family Lycosidae, and are a common spider found throughout the States."

"They seem to be quite common inside the castle. But what do you mean they won't hurt me *much*?"

"They'll only bite if they're feeling threatened."

"You don't think the spiders view being plucked off my apron as a little threatening?"

"An interesting point," Annaliese said before she set the spider on the ground and made a bit of a shooing motion when it simply stood there, undoubtedly wondering if it should hop back on Drusilla and see how tasty she was. Annaliese leaned over and gave it a prod, straightening a second later when the spider finally scrambled across the back courtyard.

"I think I got them all," Annaliese said after giving Drusilla a thorough perusal. "And since you're now spider-free, to return to the mother situation, know that besides refusing to leave her room, Mother has been overly enthusiastic with using the annunciator today, something that has left Mrs. O'Sullivan in a testy frame of mind."

"Why would Mother be ringing for Mrs. O'Sullivan when she just had breakfast delivered to her an hour ago?"

"I imagine she's decided she's in desperate need of a second pot of coffee."

"But she knows we have limited staff at the moment and she can't expect to be waited on hand and foot."

"I'm sure Mother's aware of that, but since she's still under the impression she'll run into another ghost if she steps out of her room, she's reluctant to do any fetching for herself."

Drusilla leaned her chin against the top of the broom handle, wondering how in the world it had happened that her life had turned so troubling of late.

In all honesty, during the three days that had passed since they'd landed in Chicago, she'd found herself thinking time and again that it would have been helpful if she hadn't enjoyed such a pampered life for most of her twenty-two years, given how difficult life seemed to be turning these days.

Pampered young ladies usually didn't find themselves responsible for putting an entire castle in order that hadn't seen a broom in forever, nor did they ever have to make do with a skeleton staff to accomplish that—how many rooms actually needed to be cleaned, she couldn't say as of yet, although she'd wandered through thirty-two at last count. She had the sneaking suspicion there were at least thirty-two more to go, if not more, given the size of the castle.

"Missed one," Annaliese said cheerfully as she plucked a spider from Drusilla's sleeve, yanking Drusilla straight out of her thoughts.

Annaliese set the spider down and straightened. "I'm sure that's all of them, but you might want to consider changing your clothes soon, and perhaps take a bath just to be on the safe side, although I wouldn't advise you asking Mrs. O'Sullivan to heat up the water since she is, as I mentioned, testy."

"Sound advice, but know that I'll talk to Mother and encourage her to avoid being a nuisance with the annunciator, which might have Mrs. O'Sullivan's testiness abating."

Annaliese leaned closer. "Mother might not be able to be a nuisance with it for much longer because when I left the kitchen a few minutes ago, Mrs. O'Sullivan and Mr. Grimsby were in the process of trying to disassemble the lever that's connected to Mother's room."

"I'm sure Mother will simply resort to ringing for Miss Tremblay, who'll then become testy as well, since Mother set her lady's maid the daunting task of unpacking and finding proper storage places for all of our clothes, the only thing of value we were able to salvage that the bank didn't demand we hand over to settle some debts."

"I'm sure that's exactly what Mother will do, but it's better if Miss Tremblay gets annoyed rather than Mrs. O'Sullivan because I shudder to think how we'd survive if we didn't have Mrs. O'Sullivan around to feed us."

"We do seem to be rather deficient in kitchen skills," Drusilla muttered.

"I believe *nonexistent* would be a better way to phrase that." Annaliese brightened. "But at least we can now claim to have the basic rudiments of cleaning down, something I never imagined either of us would ever obtain and . . ."

The rest of Annaliese's words got lost when the sound of *kraas* rang out, a term her sister had told her was the call ravens made. In the blink of an eye, the ravens came swooshing into view, where they promptly swooshed directly up to one of the turrets and got themselves settled on their roosting spot of choice.

Annaliese shaded her eyes with her hand and directed her attention the ravens' way. "Is it just me or have you been wondering if our dear aunt Ottilie might possess a bit of a macabre nature, given that she adored living in a creepy old castle that unquestionably possesses a rather sinister air about it?"

"It's not just you," Drusilla said right before the sound of a loud gong echoing through the air caused the ravens to take flight, and a second gong left her blowing out a breath. "Any guesses on who that'll turn out to be at the front gate? Another merchant, perhaps, or yet another developer who stopped in at the Mead and Vittles and had Gus or one of the other hack drivers apprise them of the fact we're now the owners of the castle?"

"My money's on a developer, although let's hope if that's the case, and Norbert turns them away, that they'll simply resort to pressing their face against the bars of the front gate and looking longingly at a property they covet instead of being like that man who worked for Mr. Loughlin MacSherry." Annaliese gave a shudder. "That man was lucky he didn't suffer a serious injury when he tried to scale the gate after Norbert told him we weren't receiving callers and ended up slipping and almost impaling himself on one of the iron spikes."

"I'm sure his boss wasn't happy to learn Norbert had to cut off the man's trousers to set him free, or happy to learn that man told Norbert that Loughlin MacSherry had sent him in the first place."

"At least we know now that Rhenick Whittenbecker wasn't lying when he told us that members of the criminal underworld are keen to acquire this property, since Norbert told us that Loughlin MacSherry is one of the most ruthless crime bosses in the area."

Drusilla lifted her chin. "Rhenick Whittenbecker might not have been lying about that, but that doesn't mean he wasn't lying about stopping by here on the pretense of merely wanting to see if Aunt Ottilie had returned home. Given that the man had the audacity to tell me that I needed to marry him—and for my own good, no less—he's fortunate I didn't try harder to shoot him."

"Was it that you weren't trying to aim at him, or that you're really far more inept with handling a weapon than I imagined?"

Drusilla's lips twitched. "I'll own up to ineptness, which is exactly why Seraphina promised, after she discovered that weapons room down by the dungeons, to train me up just as soon as we find some spare time."

Annaliese smiled. "She promised to do the same with me, as well as work with the ferrets to see if they're capable of learning how to attack on command. It was sheer luck they took my snapping of fingers as a sign to chase off Mr. Whittenbecker."

Drusilla returned the smile. "They did turn out to be amazingly competent at ridding us of that insufferable man's presence, just as they're turning out to be competent with ridding the castle of rodents, which has allowed us to concentrate our cleanup efforts elsewhere. But speaking of those efforts . . ."

She propped the handle of the broom against the now hopefully spider-free tapestry before fishing a list of chores she'd compiled that morning out of her apron pocket. After glancing over it, she lifted her head. "Next up for me is to investigate the giant fireplace in the great hall, since Norbert doesn't know if the coal furnace is still safe to use and the nights are still rather chilly."

"Does a fireplace need a specific investigation? I always thought you just piled logs into the grate and lit them on fire."

"That's what I thought as well, but Mr. Grimsby, who evidently knows a thing or two about chimneys because proper butlers are apparently supposed to be knowledgeable about such matters, believes something is blocking what he called the flue. The last thing we need is to burn the castle down, since that will truly leave us homeless and will also dash our hopes in opening up our academy."

"Too right it would, although I'm not sure the castle, since it's made of stone, would be easy to burn down, but there'd undoubtedly be smoke." Annaliese's eyes began to twinkle. "And not that this is something I'd normally recommend, but perhaps we shouldn't clean out that flue thing completely because if Mother smelled smoke, she'd leave her room in a heartbeat."

"Or she'd decide that Ottilie's ghost started a fire to force her out of her room, just like she's claiming that ghost drove her out of her first choice of rooms, those being what used to be Ottilie's personal suite."

"It still seems slightly suspicious that no one besides Mother has spotted so much as a whisper of an otherworldly being, which suggests that Mother either allowed the eerie nature of the castle to influence her imagination, or she feigned a ghost sighting as a way to convince you to take Mr. Whittenbecker up on his marriage proposal."

Drusilla allowed herself the luxury of an honest-to-goodness snort. "It was a ridiculous proposal, but since the mere mention of Mr. Whittenbecker sets my teeth on edge, I'm now going to hie myself off to the great hall to inspect a fireplace."

"Shall I come with you?"

"I don't think that's necessary, but you might want to check on Seraphina. She was heading back to organize some of those weapons she found, and that was a good hour or so ago. Might be best to make certain a ghost hasn't locked her in that dingy room where the weapons are stored."

"I don't believe even being locked in a dingy room by a ghost would bother Seraphina. She'd probably just find a weapon capable of blasting a hole in the wall, and blast herself out of there," Annaliese said before she turned and walked across the courtyard, disappearing a moment later.

Grabbing hold of the broom, since there was little question she'd need to use it in the near future, Drusilla strode for the castle as well, having to resort to shoving her shoulder against a heavy door that still needed oil, but one that led to a mudroom she'd made use of often of late.

After taking a second to wipe her feet, since she'd recently learned how time-consuming mopping a floor was, Drusilla moved into a hallway, passing a music room that had a piano still draped with a linen sheet. Resisting the urge to take a moment to uncover the piano and indulge in playing for an hour or ten, something that always relaxed her, she continued forward, barely glancing at the rooms she passed, having already investigated the library, receiving parlor, sitting room, and morning room.

Stepping into the great hall, she set her sights on Mrs. O'Sullivan and Mr. Grimsby, who were standing beside the enormous fireplace, a ladder propped up against the brick wall of the flue. She made it all of three feet toward them before she caught sight of Pippin scampering across the room, carrying what seemed to be a large rat in her mouth.

At any other time in her life, a rat-carrying ferret would have seemed rather peculiar, but given the way her life was unfolding of late, it didn't seem peculiar at all.

Before she could decide if she should address the ferret-carrying-a-rat situation, or pretend she hadn't seen it and hope she didn't stumble over a dead rat in the middle of the night, Annaliese came barreling into the room.

"Did you see . . . ?" was all Annaliese managed to get out of her mouth as she stopped and bent over, trying to catch her breath.

"Pippin's heading up the stairs."

"Probably to take that as a present to Mother, since my little darling seems to think Mother's shrieks are signs of affection," Annaliese muttered before she gulped a breath of air and took off, yelling for Pippin to stop at the top of her lungs as she took the steps two at a time.

"Mrs. Merriweather will never come out of that room if she realizes there truly are rats in here," Mrs. O'Sullivan said with a sad shake of her head, drawing Drusilla's attention.

"I'm sure she won't, but that'll be a problem for another day as it appears that you and Mr. Grimsby were inspecting that fireplace without me."

"We're not inspecting, simply pondering the situation," Mr. Grimsby said, who'd been the Merriweather butler for well over twenty years. "We got the damper fully opened, but it does seem as if something's blocking the flue because no light is getting through."

"What do you think it is?" Drusilla asked.

"Hard to say, but I'll know better once I get up the ladder."

"We've already been over this. I'm doing the inspection because you have a bad hip and Mrs. O'Sullivan is afraid of heights."

Ignoring that Mr. Grimsby had taken to muttering something about how it wasn't right that a proper lady was being forced to take on the role of chimney sweep because of his rather advanced age and bad hip, Drusilla set her sights on what turned out to be a very tall ladder and began climbing up the flue.

After reaching the top of the ladder, Drusilla stretched her arms above her head and poked what appeared to be a collection of twigs that had gotten lodged in the chimney.

"Did you find anything?" Mr. Grimsby called.

"I think it's some type of nest, but watch out below because I'm going to attempt to dislodge it," she called as she gave the twigs another poke, stilling when a rustle of wings captured her attention.

Less than a heartbeat later, a chorus of *kraas* began echoing eerily around the flue, right before something fluttered directly above her head and then landed on it, the unexpectedness of that leaving Drusilla losing her grip on the ladder and plummeting toward the ground.

Fifteen

A sense of self-preservation had Drusilla snagging hold of the ladder during her rapid downward descent, the velocity of which bounced her off one side of the flue and then the other. Thankfully, the bouncing didn't continue for long, but her shoulder felt ready to pull straight from its socket as she dangled for what seemed like forever until she finally got a foot on one of the rungs.

Before she could do more than appreciate that she'd managed to avoid a fall that could have seen her suffering a broken limb or worse, something began pecking at her head, eliciting a shriek from her, which spoke volumes regarding her current situation since she'd never resorted to shrieking before, not even when Anthony Sternman had put a frog down the back of her dress when she was all of ten years old.

Abandoning all thoughts of past frog misdeeds when the pecking began intensifying, Drusilla scrambled down the ladder, releasing her hold on it and dropping the remaining few feet to the fireplace floor when the pecking turned downright painful.

As far as descents went, *graceful* was not a word that sprang to mind, especially when she landed in a crumpled heap of what had been pristine ivory muslin at the beginning of the day, the pristineness disappearing the moment she hit the fireplace floor, her impact causing soot to billow up around her.

Any concern for her gown disappeared when she turned her head to the right and discovered a large raven peering back at her with eyes that seemed to be glittering with a great deal of malice. The malice observation was proven a second later when the bird darted forward, pecked her head, released a croak, then launched itself out of the fireplace with a flutter of black wings. Before she could breathe a sigh of relief over that fortunate situation, additional fluttering noises began reverberating down the chimney right before an entire unkindness of ravens whooshed down the flue and over her head.

It was quickly becoming clear why someone at some point in time had aptly named a group of ravens exactly that.

"Run!" she heard Mrs. O'Sullivan yell, but knowing it would hardly be a prudent move to stand when that would probably have numerous ravens flying into her, Drusilla crawled her way over the stones of the fireplace, then across the hearth, edging downward onto the cold, hard floor of the great hall as ravens continued to swirl over her.

"Keep down, Miss Drusilla," Mrs. O'Sullivan called. "I'll be right back with a broom and . . ."

Whatever else Mrs. O'Sullivan was saying got lost when the ravens began swooping directly over Drusilla, a few of them getting in pecks as they swooped, quite as if they'd figured out she was the one responsible for disturbing their nest and were keen to seek a bit of retribution.

Wincing when a raven landed on her back and sunk its beak into her neck, she rolled to her side in an attempt to dislodge it, stilling when a loud "Shoo" scared the bird away right before someone scooped her up from the floor.

A heartbeat later, she found herself flung unceremoniously over what was undoubtedly a male shoulder before said male bolted into motion, weaving and dodging his way across the hall before he broke into a full-out run once he reached the hallway.

A part of her couldn't help but be impressed that the man

hauling her around didn't seem winded in the least as he ran her out of the house, down the steps, and then lowered her onto a stone bench.

Any favorable impression she'd begun to hold for her rescuer disappeared in a flash, though, when she tilted her head back and found herself looking up at none other than Mr. Rhenick Whittenbecker—a man she'd hoped to never encounter again.

"Are you alright, Miss Merriweather?" Rhenick asked as he fished a handkerchief out of his pocket and took the liberty of pressing it against her forehead. "If you haven't realized, you're bleeding, and somewhat profusely at that."

"I'm perfectly capable of holding a handkerchief to my head without assistance" was all she could think to say, since reminding the man that she'd promised to shoot him if he ever darkened her doorstep again might very well be taken as a sign she wasn't appreciative of his remarkably timely assistance.

"I'm sure you are, but you have numerous wounds on your head. It'll be easier all around if I just stanch some of the blood for you." He gave the wound he was already attending to a dab before he moved the handkerchief an inch to the left and pressed it against another wound. "How in the world did it come about that you found yourself set upon by ravens? I've never heard that they're prone to attacking people."

"I'd never heard that either, but evidently if you dislodge a nest from a chimney where they're roosting, they turn vicious."

Rhenick frowned. "What were you doing in the chimney?"

"It needed cleaning."

He blinked. "And you decided to do that cleaning?"

"It seemed like a good idea at the time, what with how my sister is occupied with other matters, my mother is refusing to come out of her room, and most members of my staff are pushing seventy, except for Riley, our stable hand. Riley's afraid to step foot in the castle, though, because my mother claimed to have seen a ghost the other night."

Drusilla squared her shoulders. "But speaking of my staff, if you'll excuse me, I really do need to check on Mr. Grimsby, my butler, and Mrs. O'Sullivan, our cook, because the last I saw of them, they were in the process of fleeing from the great hall."

"You're in no fit state to get off that bench, so I'll find them," Rhenick said before he pressed a handkerchief that was now dotted with blood and soot into her hand. "Hold that in place while I'm gone. I'll be back momentarily, and then we can see about cleaning and dressing your wounds properly." With that, he got off the bench and strode toward the castle.

Drusilla watched him disappear through the door, but continued staring at the door even after he was out of sight because—it was difficult to hold a grudge against a gentleman who'd saved her from an unexpected bird assault.

It was also difficult to harbor ill-feelings toward a man who'd taken it upon himself to mop up her bloody forehead and then insist on reentering the scene of the crime, so to speak, to rescue members of her staff when doing so might result in him suffering some manner of personal injury as well.

Having a gentleman take control of a troubling situation was a novel experience to be sure, given that every gentleman in her life had left her to handle a world she willingly admitted she was ill-equipped to manage, unless he'd only rushed to her assistance because he was still determined to acquire the castle and land, and had viewed taking on a few ravens in order to accomplish that as a small price to pay.

Shoving aside thoughts that were leaving her with the distinct urge to throttle something—preferably Rhenick Whittenbecker, if what she'd been thinking turned out to be true—Drusilla took a moment to dab at blood dribbling down her face right as Annaliese came barreling around the castle. Her sister caught sight of her a second later and made a beeline her way, coming to a stop once she reached the bench, her eyes widening as she took to looking Drusilla up and down.

"What happened to you?"

"You didn't hear the ruckus coming out of the great hall?"

"There was a ruckus?"

"How could you not have heard it?" Drusilla asked. "Ravens were everywhere, and they weren't happy after I disturbed their nest in the chimney."

"You were attacked by ravens?"

"Indeed."

Annaliese blinked. "I'm sorry I missed that, as I don't believe it's usual raven behavior for them to go on the attack, but I missed all that excitement because I've been trying to find Mother."

"Should I ask why?"

"You do remember that my darling Pippin was running around with a rat in her mouth, don't you?"

Drusilla winced. "Do not say Mother saw that."

"Oh, she did more than see it because Mother heard me scolding Pippin right outside her room and evidently thought I was Mrs. O'Sullivan finally bringing her a tray." Annaliese shook her head. "The hysterics began the second Mother spotted Pippin, who promptly dropped her dead rat at Mother's feet, and then . . . the situation turned downright concerning when Fidget and Wiggles showed up."

"Should I ask why the appearance of your other two ferrets turned the situation concerning?"

Annaliese winced. "That would be on account that they wanted to bring Mother presents as well, but while the snake Wiggles dropped next to the dead rat was no longer alive, I'm afraid the rat Fidget had was very much so. Before I could do more than tell Fidget she was a *very* bad girl, the rat scurried into Mother's room, which caused Mother to dash down the hallway, screaming at the top of her lungs."

"Why do I get the distinct impression Mother will be changing rooms again?"

"I'm sure Fidget has already recaught the rat, but I did hear Mother yell something about never stepping foot in the castle again before she ran down the back stairs, screaming all the while." Annaliese glanced around the front yard. "I thought I'd find her heading down the drive, probably with the intention of running to Chicago, but I was wrong about that. She must have headed for the lake, where I'm hoping she didn't decide to attempt to swim her way to the city."

"You know Mother never steps a toe in any type of water unless it's an unusually warm day."

"Then let us hope she thinks it's too chilly for a swim and is merely brooding along the shoreline, contemplating the horrors she's faced of late." Annaliese leaned closer and peered into Drusilla's face. "Before I resume my search for Mother, though, are you certain you're alright?"

Drusilla waved that aside. "I'm fine, although I'm sure I must look a sight. I might have looked even worse, though, if Rhenick Whittenbecker hadn't shown up from out of the blue and rescued me from the ravens."

"Rhenick Whittenbecker rescued you?"

"He did."

Annaliese plopped down beside Drusilla, any thought of tracking down their mother seemingly forgotten. "Do you think intervening with the ravens might have been a calculated move on his part in order to get into your good graces, or . . . do you think it was a gallant reaction from a gentleman who saw a young lady in danger and did what gentlemen are expected to do—that being saving the damsel in distress?"

Even though Drusilla had just been thinking he'd had an ulterior motive for rescuing her, now that she thought further about the matter, it was highly unlikely Rhenick had had time to consider how his act of chivalry could be used to his advantage, as he certainly couldn't have known he'd arrive at the castle and find it being taken over by ravens.

That suggested that he'd acted instinctively, and also meant that he might very well have a chivalrous nature buried under what she'd assumed was a cold, calculating heart, which also meant that perhaps—just perhaps—he'd broached the whole marriage idea because of his concern regarding her safety.

"Looks like I won't need to track Mother down after all," Annaliese said, nodding across the front yard to where Irma was attempting to pull herself over a low stone wall, one that was only about three feet high, the stiff crepe of Irma's mourning gown evidently responsible for making it difficult for her mother to clear the wall.

Before Drusilla could do more than rise to her feet, Irma managed to pull herself to the top of the wall, stomach-side down. She then, instead of trying to sit up, simply remained on her stomach, quite as if she didn't know how to proceed from there.

"Do you think she knows she won't hurt herself if she just rolls to the ground?" Annaliese asked right as Rhenick walked through the castle door with Mrs. O'Sullivan on his arm, who looked as if she'd had a run-in with the ravens as well, since her hair was straggling from its pins. Mr. Grimsby followed a step behind, streaked with ash and looking rather like he'd run into a bolt of electricity, what with how his hair was standing on end.

After Rhenick got Mrs. O'Sullivan down the steps and then helped her take a seat on the very last one, Mr. Grimsby joining her, he turned Drusilla's way and frowned.

"You shouldn't be standing up," he called.

"My mother needs my assistance," she said with a wave at Irma, who'd just managed to sit up on the wall, dangling her legs over the side as she peered at the ground, clearly debating the risks to her person if she were to simply jump.

"I'll get her, but you need to sit down because I can see you wobbling from here," he called before he headed Irma's way.

Realizing she actually was wobbling, as well as realizing it was an odd circumstance that a gentleman had even taken notice of that, Drusilla retook her seat and watched as Rhenick strode closer to her mother.

"What do you think the odds are that Mother's going to do her best to convince Mr. Whittenbecker he needs to revisit the topic of marriage with you?" Annaliese asked.

"I'd say that's a given considering she's been badgering me relentlessly about that matter, insisting our family will only be able to return to a semblance of normalcy if I come to my senses and marry a man she believes has stellar recommendations.

"However," Drusilla continued, "even if Rhenick *has* returned to broach that particular matter with me, or if Mother succeeds in convincing him I might be more receptive to the idea now that I've had a few days living in a castle she believes is haunted, know that I haven't changed my mind in the least. Furthermore, if Rhenick tries to pursue the matter, I'm going to have to relieve Norbert of his rifle again, since I've already had a most trying day and have no intention of dealing with additional ridiculousness in the near or distant future."

Sixteen

It quickly became apparent that rescuing Mrs. Merriweather wasn't going to be your run-of-the-mill uneventful rescue attempt, especially not when Drusilla's mother all but launched herself at him when Rhenick got within a foot of her, almost taking him to the ground in the process.

Stumbling immediately commenced, unaided by the fact that Mrs. Merriweather now had her arms wrapped around his neck, which left her feet dangling in the air, until he finally found his balance, set her on her feet, and then found himself on the receiving end of an incredibly bright smile.

"My dear Mr. Whittenbecker," Mrs. Merriweather breathed as she took hold of his arm. "I cannot begin to tell you how relieved I am to see you again, and can only pray that you've returned because you want to give my darling, and need I add, occasionally stubborn daughter, another opportunity to reconsider your marriage proposition. Before we get into that, though, allow me to correct a grave error between us since we weren't properly introduced when Drusilla chased you off with a rifle the last time you were here, or perhaps it was the ferrets that had you on the run. Whatever the reason, though, I was unable to meet you formally, so know that I am Mrs. Morton

Merriweather, Drusilla's mother, but you may certainly call me Irma, as I feel we're soon to be the best of friends."

"And you must call me Rhenick" was all he could think to respond, since he knew full well that a friendship with the mother of a lady who might try to shoot him again was probably not going to happen anytime soon.

Irma's smile turned downright blinding in its intensity. "You are a charming man, my dear, as well as obviously brave since I'm sure you were somewhat apprehensive about approaching Drusilla again." Irma leaned closer. "What you should know right off the bat is that since we've learned the house is truly haunted, which I can personally attest to as I distinctly saw an apparition of my departed sister-in-law, as well as infested with rats and snakes, I'm convinced my daughter is now ready to admit she's in way over her head." Irma leaned closer still. "You mark my words, while Drusilla might have given you the impression she's reluctant to marry you, if you don't give up on her, she'll come around in the end."

"I don't believe chasing me off with a rifle suggested your daughter was only a bit reluctant to entertain the thought of marriage to me."

"But she didn't shoot you, did she, dear? I think you should take that as an encouraging sign."

"Given that your daughter didn't know how to operate that rifle, I'm not sure she wasn't actually trying to lodge a bullet in me."

Irma's smile dimmed ever so slightly before she squared her shoulders. "You may very well have a point, but again, since Drusilla's now had an opportunity to discover for herself that the castle really is haunted, I believe she'll be more receptive to a marriage proposition from you."

Realizing that Irma was not going to be easily dissuaded from her determination to see him married to her daughter, Rhenick decided a change of topic might be in order. "You must tell me how you came to conclude that the castle is well and truly haunted."

Her gaze darted around, quite as if she were ascertaining there were no ghosts nearby to hear what she was about to disclose. "I saw proof with my own eyes. If you can imagine—there I was, settling down to sleep in Ottilie's old suite of rooms, a suite my daughters insisted I move into as there are spectacular views of the lake from almost every vantage point. After spending a few moments saying good night to my lady's maid, Miss Tremblay, I then had her draw the drapes around the four-poster bed, waited for her to blow out the candles we'd used to sufficiently light the room, and closed my eyes, knowing sleep would soon be in my grasp as I was exhausted from the events of the day."

Irma shuddered ever so slightly. "I must have fallen asleep, for how long I'm not sure, but then I found myself wide awake and confronted with a ghostly figure that had opened up the drapes on the four-poster bed and was simply standing there, peering at me."

"How could you see the ghost if you blew out your candles before you went to sleep? And while I'm thinking about it, why use candles in the first place when I know Ottilie has gas lighting?"

"Norbert isn't certain the gas is still safe to turn on since it's not been used for months, so candles it is until we can have that inspected, but . . ." Irma glanced around again before lowering her voice. "I could see the figure because it was holding a candle, standing there calm as you please—until it pointed a finger at me and started talking. That's when I knew it was Ottilie."

"Because?"

"She told me that I, along with the girls, needed to return to New York because we were in danger. No other ghost who would be haunting this place knows I'm from New York."

Rhenick tilted his head. "And did this ghost sound like Ottilie?"

"I can't say for certain because, in all honesty, I was scared to death at the time. I do recall that Ottilie sounded like she had a cold, which is odd because I wouldn't think ghosts caught colds, seeing as how they're dead and all."

"What happened after she told you to return to New York?"

"She said I'd be sorry if I didn't listen to her because horrible things would happen to me. She then twitched the curtains shut, blew out the candle, and disappeared."

"Did you find it odd that a ghost could twitch something, or for that matter, light and hold a candle?"

A pursing of the lips was Irma's first response to that. "Now you sound exactly like Drusilla, who doesn't believe ghosts are capable of twitching anything either, let alone striking a match to light a candle. But while I have no idea how Ottilie managed those things, I know what I saw."

"Forgive me if I offended you," Rhenick said. "I simply have a lot of questions, as I've never spoken to anyone who encountered a ghost before, and my next question is this—what did you do after this ghost disappeared?"

"What anyone who finds themselves confronted with a ghost would do. I screamed and didn't stop until Drusilla, Annaliese, and Seraphina came rushing into my room."

"Did they detect any signs of this ghost?"

Irma's eyes took to flashing. "They did not, and to my annoyance, my daughters now believe that I've either taken complete leave of my senses, or that I claimed to have seen a ghost as a way to force Drusilla into considering other options to save the family instead of opening up a ladies' academy, but . . ." Irma's eyes stopped flashing as she took to smiling brightly at him again. "Speaking of options, here I am waxing on about my ghostly encounter when, clearly, you're here with a specific purpose in mind."

Rhenick opened his mouth, but before he could get a single word out, Irma held up a hand.

"No need to divulge the particulars of whatever tactic you've devised to further your quest to marry Drusilla, but know that I'm firmly on your side and will be cheering you on as you make your case to my daughter. And now, with that settled . . ."

In the span of a heartbeat, he found himself being herded toward the front of the castle until Irma abruptly stopped in her tracks. Her nose then took to wrinkling after she settled her attention on Drusilla, who was, thankfully, once again sitting on the bench with her sister, who, as luck would have it, didn't appear to have any of her attack ferrets with her.

"Is it my imagination or does it appear as if my daughter has been the victim of some sort of accident—and one that involved a great deal of dirt?" Irma asked.

"She apparently suffered a run-in with some ravens while she was cleaning out the chimney."

Irma raised a hand to her throat. "Do not tell me that besides rats and snakes we also have ravens living inside the castle."

"I believe the ravens were nesting in the chimney, which isn't technically living inside the castle."

"A comforting thought, but . . ." Irma was suddenly looking at him with horror in her eyes. "Surely I didn't hear you correctly, because it would be quite beyond the pale for Drusilla to turn herself into a chimney sweep." She sent him a rather weak smile. "Know that if she was cleaning the chimney, though, it must have been for a very good reason because Drusilla has never—as in ever—placed herself in a situation where dirt is actually involved, as that's not what proper ladies do."

"She seems to be taking all the dirt in stride," Rhenick reassured her. "Just as she barely blinked an eye over the fact she'd been set upon by rampaging ravens while she was in the chimney flue."

"Of course they'd be rampaging ravens" was all Irma said to that before she lifted her chin, tightened her grip on his arm, then hauled him into motion, not stopping until she was directly in front of Drusilla.

"Mr. Whittenbecker, or Rhenick as he has encouraged me to address him," Irma began, "has come to call on you, Drusilla. And since he just went to the bother of rescuing me from a situation where I could have very well lost my life, I expect you to afford him the courtesy of a few minutes of your time to hear what he's come to say—and without pulling a rifle on him, if you please."

Before Drusilla could do more than incline her head, which hopefully meant she was going to hear him out and not while holding him at rifle-point, a carriage rumbled into view—his mother's carriage, in fact.

"Who in the world is that?" Drusilla asked.

"It's not a developer, if that's your concern," Rhenick hurried to say. "It's my mother, Wilhelmine Whittenbecker, who was supposed to wait at the gate until I rode down there to fetch her if I thought you'd be receptive to hearing us out, but who must have been worried that my initial meeting with you wasn't going well since I've left her waiting for quite some time."

Before he could add any sort of explanation regarding why he and his mother wanted Drusilla to hear them out, the carriage came to a stop, the door swung open, and his mother stepped out, although Wilhelmine hesitated right beside the carriage door, obviously waiting for him to send her some sort of sign that it was safe for her to approach them.

Given the way Drusilla's eyes had taken to flashing, quite like her mother's had recently done, he wasn't completely convinced it *was* safe for his mother just yet, which was why he sent Wilhelmine a discreet shake of his head before he redirected his attention to Drusilla, who rose to her feet and took a step closer to him.

"While I was certainly willing, given how you intervened with the ravens on my behalf, to extend you a brief moment to hear what you came to say," she began, "I'm not certain that's still the case. You've obviously decided to try out some new tactic in order to get your hands on my land, but if you've brought your mother with you so that *she* can attempt to convince me to marry you, know that while I won't pull a rifle on anyone's mother, I won't hesitate to aim another one at you."

≈ Seventeen ≈

Knowing it would be best all around to make a point of dispelling any theories Drusilla had obviously come up with before someone got shot—not that he could actually blame her for developing theories in the first place since he was a grown man who'd shown up with his mother in tow, and after having botched a marriage proposition no less—Rhenick cleared his throat.

"I know the unexpected appearance of my mother probably looks somewhat suspicious, but it's not what you think."

She began tapping a toe against the gravel. "Do tell."

For the briefest of seconds, he found himself completely distracted from the conversation at hand because his gaze, on its own accord no less, had taken to lingering on Drusilla's face, the lingering allowing him to realize that there were so many little things he'd missed the first time he'd laid eyes on her— such as the hint of a dimple that was precisely in the middle of her chin, or the way her eyes seemed to be more along the lines of a greenish-blue shade today compared to . . .

"So your mother's *not* here to broach the subject of marriage?" Drusilla pressed, snapping him from his perusal of her face, although he couldn't help but notice that her eyes were flashing more intensely than ever, leaving him with the sneaking suspicion that he might already be making a muddle of things, but it was hardly his fault he found her face so compelling and . . .

"Your lack of response has left me believing that your mother *is* here to convince me to marry you, isn't she?"

Realizing he was definitely floundering, something he'd hoped to avoid this time around with Drusilla, Rhenick summoned up a smile, one that, unfortunately, wasn't returned. "Perhaps it would be best if I let my mother explain the particulars." He strode into motion, not stopping until he was directly beside Wilhelmine, who immediately settled a rather pitying look on him.

"Things not going well with Drusilla, dear?" she asked.

"Not going well is an understatement, which is why I'm now going to turn this delicate situation over to you, although be warned—any mention of marriage might put a rapid end to our visit and could very well see a rifle coming into play again, so I'd avoid that word at all costs."

It spoke volumes about his mother's no-nonsense attitude when she didn't bat an eye over what most people would find concerning news, instead sending him a nod before she took hold of his arm and pulled him into motion, reaching Drusilla a moment later.

Wilhelmine immediately dipped into a curtsy that left her knees creaking when she straightened, the creaking a direct result of the fact there weren't many people she bothered curtsying to and her knees were out of practice. To her credit, though, she ignored the creaking as he introduced her to Drusilla and Irma, Irma taking over the introductions when he reached Drusilla's sister and realized he had yet to be formally introduced to her.

After presenting Annaliese with a bow, it was a less than encouraging sign when she simply responded with a thinning of her lips, which suggested that she, unlike her mother, didn't

127

trust him in the least and probably wouldn't have any qualms about summoning her ferrets. Before he could think of anything that might soften her opinion of him, though, his mother ever so casually nudged him aside, then inserted herself between him and Drusilla's sister.

"Now that we've gotten introductions out of the way," Wilhelmine began, "it would probably be for the best if I got right down to why we're here since . . ." She abruptly stopped talking as her gaze settled on Drusilla. "Good heavens, Miss Merriweather, here we are, standing around chatting as if we're at some type of social event when you're bleeding from the head."

Before Drusilla could say more than "raven attack," Wilhelmine whipped a clean handkerchief from her sleeve and immediately took to dabbing Drusilla's forehead with it.

"I've never heard of an attack by raven before, but how unfortunate that you'd suffer such a thing upon your arrival in Chicago, which probably hasn't left you with a favorable impression of our city," Wilhelmine said, moving Drusilla's head to the right before she frowned. "However, you have more than a few wounds that need to be properly attended to, which is why I'm going to suggest we put all talk of what Rhenick and I are doing here on hold until after we get you inside and cleaned up."

Even though Drusilla was looking a tad bewildered, probably because a woman she'd just met was now trying to rub what appeared to be a particularly stubborn smear of blood mixed with soot from her cheek, she smiled. "While I appreciate your concern, I'm afraid it's not safe for us to move inside just yet since I'm relatively sure there are some ravens still running amok in there."

Whatever else she'd been about to say got lost when Wilhelmine turned her attention to a stubborn streak of soot that was marring her forehead, the effort with which his mother was now scrubbing at the streak leaving Drusilla wincing as she shot him a look that begged for an intervention.

He fought a smile and cleared his throat instead, which drew his mother's attention and earned Drusilla a reprieve from the scrubbing.

"Perhaps we should take our leave, Mother, and come back another day when Miss Merriweather hasn't experienced an unfortunate encounter with aggressive birds."

Wilhelmine waved that straight aside. "We can't leave this poor dear here with ravens on the loose and a head that's all pecked up. We need to sort those issues out for her, but before you go off to chase any lingering ravens out of the castle, be a dear and fetch my medical basket from the carriage."

The urge to argue was immediate, but since his mother was now sporting what his father always referred to as her stubborn look—an expression that usually meant anyone idiotic enough to argue with her was in for a rough time of it—Rhenick settled for sending her a nod before he headed for the carriage.

It came as no surprise when he had to burrow his way through abandoned slippers, hats, and numerous books littering the floor before he located the basket, but it was a surprise when he started walking back to rejoin the ladies and discovered Annaliese sprinting around the side of the castle, calling something about needing to catch Pippin before another rat got left as a present.

"Should I assume Pippin is one of Annaliese's ferrets?" he asked, handing his mother the basket and earning a rather dramatic sigh from Irma in return.

"She is," Irma said. "Unfortunately for me, though, Pippin enjoys bringing me all sorts of surprises."

"You know Annaliese will eventually figure out a way to train the ferrets to discontinue gifting you unsettling presents," Drusilla said as she eyed the canteen his mother had just pulled out of her basket somewhat curiously. "But to give the ferrets credit, they've been very diligent with hunting down rats, the proof in that being seen by the fact that all three ferrets are already plumper than they were when we arrived here just three days ago. They've put weight on so rapidly that Annaliese has been considering taking them out on daily walks to avoid having her little darlings turn overly plump."

Irma blanched. "You think there are still so many rats inhabiting the castle that the ferrets will be rodent hunting for the foreseeable future?"

"I should have probably stopped with 'the ferrets are very diligent with hunting down rats,'" Drusilla muttered.

"That might have been prudent," Wilhelmine agreed, taking a second to soak a piece of gauze with water from the canteen before she began blotting one of the peck marks on the side of Drusilla's neck.

"Speaking of being prudent," Drusilla began as Wilhelmine moved the gauze to another spot, "perhaps it would also be a prudent use of our time if, before your son goes off to address the raven situation, you explain why you're here."

"I'm certainly not here to convince you to marry Rhenick, if that's what you're thinking." Wilhelmine smiled. "Truth be told, I'm not even supposed to voice the word *marriage*, as Rhenick thinks it's a touchy subject with you. Nonetheless, because I'm sure he's right and it *is* touchy, I say instead of avoiding the elephant that's obviously in the room, we address the matter before we discuss anything else."

Wariness immediately clouded Drusilla's eyes. "I'm not certain there is any need to discuss what happened with your son the other day."

"Of course there is," Wilhelmine countered. "Being the mother to four daughters, I have an above average grasp of the way in which young ladies think, and I think you came to a completely erroneous conclusion regarding why Rhenick made that ridiculous suggestion of marriage to you."

"He made the suggestion because it would be the best way for him to gain possession of half the castle and surrounding lands since a woman's property becomes her husband's property the moment vows are exchanged."

"And I can certainly understand why you'd believe that because Rhenick explained to me how numerous developers have their eyes on your land. But that's not why he brought marriage into a conversation with you. Instead, he offered that rather unusual solution to keep you and your family out of harm's way simply because he completely took leave of his senses the moment he clapped eyes on you."

Eighteen

Words suddenly seemed difficult to come by, which was exactly why Drusilla found herself all but gaping at Wilhelmine, a direct result of the fact that Rhenick Whittenbecker, a gentleman who most assuredly attracted more than his fair share of feminine attention since he was a more than handsome man, had evidently told his mother he'd lost his senses because of her.

No gentleman had ever come close to losing their senses when they were in her presence. In all honesty, more than a few gentlemen hadn't even realized she was in their vicinity, a circumstance brought about because she was one of those women men didn't bother giving a second look to or even a second thought, for that matter.

It was a novel experience, being told a man had lost his head because of her, that condition evidently responsible for why Rhenick had decided they'd have to marry, and with all due haste.

There was a part of her that wanted to immediately dismiss what Wilhelmine had disclosed as pure fabrication. But another part of her, the part that couldn't ignore the current look on Rhenick's face—the one that suggested he was hoping a very large hole would open up at his feet so he could jump into it and escape a more than embarrassing situation—wanted to dwell on the idea that she might have, for the first time in her life, caused a man to lose all sense of reason.

The question of the hour now, of course, was . . . why?

The answer to that question certainly couldn't be because she'd been looking her best when Rhenick first saw her, not when she'd been traveling all day and had to have been looking haggard from the stress of the move, as well as the fact she'd been being held at gunpoint.

Her lips suddenly began curving when the pieces of *Why would Rhenick lose his senses around me?* took that moment to fall neatly into place.

"Should I take the fact that you're now smiling as a sign that you're willing to let bygones be bygones with Rhenick and put his ridiculous proposal aside once and for all?" Wilhelmine asked, drawing Drusilla from her thoughts.

She found herself nodding before she could stop herself.

"And you'll also forgive him his lapse in sanity because you're quite accustomed to gentlemen losing their heads around you?" Wilhelmine pressed.

Drusilla's nodding came to a rapid end. "Gentlemen don't make it a habit to lose their heads around me, but I'll forgive your son's lapse in sanity because I believe I've just figured out why he lost his head in the first place." She turned to Rhenick. "You obviously formed a misimpression of me, which then resulted with you coming to the erroneous conclusion that you were instantly smitten."

He gave his jaw a rub. "Why would you think I wasn't instantly smitten?"

"Because you were smitten by a fabrication—a lady you assumed was one who laughed in the face of danger because I wasn't descending into a fit of the vapors simply because Norbert was holding me at rifle-point." She smiled. "I assure you, I'm not that type of lady."

133

"But you weren't suffering from even a hint of the vapors as you faced Norbert down."

"A woman in my position doesn't have the luxury of suffering vapors, Mr. Whittenbecker. I have to embrace a pragmatic attitude these days, and that attitude was telling me at that particular time that I had no choice but to take control of the situation, as I had nowhere else to go with my family."

Rhenick tilted his head. "So if I'm understanding you correctly, you believe that the only reason I lost my head and then suggested we marry is because I mistook you for an extraordinary lady when you're telling me you're nothing of the sort?"

"Exactly."

His brows drew together. "I'm afraid I can't agree with that."

Her smile widened. "Well, of course you can't because I'm sure you think that admitting to me that I'm not extraordinary would hurt my tender feminine sensibilities."

"It would hurt anyone's sensibilities," he pointed out.

"I'm not that delicate. But since I now have a better grasp about why you suggested marriage in the first place, I'm going to suggest we put that unfortunate incident behind us and begin anew, but only if you agree to never broach the topic of marriage with me again."

Rhenick opened his mouth, but before he could get an agreement out of it, Norbert came huffing up the drive with Ernie, his mutt of undetermined parentage, loping along beside him. He stopped a few feet away from Drusilla, looked her up and down, and frowned.

"Everything all right with you, Miss Merriweather?" he asked.

"I've suffered a raven attack, so things have been better, but Mrs. Whittenbecker is setting me to rights, so I believe I'll live."

"Ravens got into the castle?"

"They came down through the chimney when I was trying to clean it."

"Don't know why you'd be cleaning the chimney when you have me around," Norbert said.

"If I'd have known how tricky it was going to turn, I might have at least asked you to hold the ladder for me, although perhaps not, as it's more important for you to guard the front gate."

"We can always send Riley down to man the gate if you need some tasks taken care of inside the castle since he's a stableboy and we only have my one horse and Miss Ottilie's contrary donkey, Moe, both of which I take care of," Norbert pointed out. "But speaking of the front gate, thought you should know that I've been turning away men left and right today—two of them being on the concerning side because one of them was here at the bequest of Giacomo Caggianni, a leader in Chicago's underworld, and the other was sent here by Umberto Zambarello." Norbert tilted his head. "To be fair to Umberto, rumor has it that he's turned legitimate on account that he wants to set a better example for his five daughters."

"So I shouldn't be as concerned about Umberto as that Giacomo Caggianni fellow?"

Norbert took a second to give Ernie a scratch behind the ears. "I wouldn't think Umberto's any less of a threat given that he's going to have to marry off those five daughters of his. Since they're known to be a handful, he's going to need a fortune to succeed with that, and everyone knows your property will turn into a gold mine for whoever acquires it. I suppose desperate fathers are just as dangerous as members of the underworld, especially ones who used to be a part of that world."

Wilhelmine took that moment to stop the dabbing she'd been doing and caught Drusilla's eye. "Norbert has just made a most excellent point, but know that I might be able to assist you with avoiding the antics of desperate men. However, before I explain further, I should probably explain how it came about that Rhenick and I were able to breach an impregnable gate since I certainly don't want you to think Norbert might have been shirking his duties."

Norbert shook his head. "No need to explain on my behalf, Mrs. Whittenbecker. Miss Merriweather surely already realizes that I'm a trusted employee who'd never shirk my duties, something her aunt was well aware of." He turned to Drusilla. "With that settled, know that I didn't hesitate to allow the Whittenbeckers through the gate, even though you'd been clear about your dislike of Rhenick, because he was in the company of his mother. Mrs. Whittenbecker and I attend the same church together, that being the Church of the Epiphany, and she's known for always lending a helping hand."

"And you let her through because you thought she wanted to lend me that hand?" Drusilla asked.

"Indeed, although I was in full agreement with Rhenick that she wait before following him up the drive, just in case you brought out one of those weapons Miss Seraphina unearthed after you caught sight of a man you recently chased away." He settled a warm smile on Wilhelmine. "Before I forget, though, allow me to say how thankful everyone was when you offered to play the organ last week during the service after the good reverend found himself once again without anyone available."

Wilhelmine winced. "I'm not certain how thankful everyone was as I readily admit I'm heavy-handed with the keys. Poor Reverend Michaelson was all but forced to bellow out the hymn I was attempting to play in the hopes he could drown out my abysmal rendition of that song."

Norbert shook his head. "You know Reverend Michaelson always belts out those hymns, and not just in an attempt to drown out whoever is sitting at the organ, but also to drown out the less-than-harmonious voices of the choir."

"It's a sad day when he's forced to rely on my dreadful musical talents for any given service, which, in a roundabout way"—she turned to Drusilla—"brings me to the reason why I'm paying you a visit."

"You wanted to inquire if my mother, my sister, or I can play a musical instrument?" Drusilla asked.

"Not exactly, although I'm sure all of you are proficient with a variety of musical instruments as it's my understanding that ladies from New York high society are taught from birth to be proficient in the feminine arts." Wilhelmine smiled. "I'm actually here to discuss that academy Rhenick mentioned you want to open and what your goal is with that academy."

"Our main goal will be to effectively teach lessons in propriety."

"And what would lessons in propriety actually entail?"

"I haven't created a syllabus just yet," Drusilla admitted. "But we'd definitely spend the first few months devoting ourselves to instructing students on the basics. Those would include proper decorum, composure, table etiquette, the art of conversation, and other social graces young ladies need to have a grasp of, such as watercolors, vocal lessons, and an introduction to a variety of musical instruments."

Wilhelmine was beaming a smile Drusilla's way a heartbeat later. "That was exactly what I was hoping you'd say, which means I can now finally get around to that business proposition Rhenick and I have come to offer you."

"A . . . business proposition?" Drusilla asked.

"Indeed, and one that I admit is rather self-serving, as I have three daughters who've yet to reach their majority, all of whom would benefit from more than a little instruction in the etiquette department."

"I thought you said you have four daughters."

"I do, but Tilda, the eldest, is already married. However, it's because of her that I came up with my business proposal for you." Wilhelmine took a second to reach out and dab at some lingering soot on the side of Drusilla's neck. "Tilda, I'll have you know, was fortunate to meet and marry a man she truly loves, and one who's rather affluent. Because of that affluence, my son-in-law was invited to dine with the Vanderbilts in New York. Poor Tilda, even though I provided her with an etiquette instructor before she made her debut, although not one who had much of an etiquette résumé since decorum teachers are few and far between in Chicago, found herself ill at ease during the dinner since she didn't know how to navigate her way through such an extravagant meal."

Drusilla leaned a little to the right, probably because his mother now seemed to be putting some elbow grease into the whole dabbing business. "May I assume you'd like to hire me to teach your daughters proper etiquette, as well as perhaps teach them how to play the piano or organ so your minister can stop belting out the hymns?"

Wilhelmine paused with her dabbing. "I have something a little grander in mind, and something that will also help all the families who are in similar situations prepare their daughters for futures that could see them comfortably settling into some of the most prestigious households in Chicago, if not the country."

"I must say you've captured my full attention now."

"I would hope so," Wilhelmine returned. "So allow me to get straight to the point. What Rhenick and I would like to propose is this: Whittenbecker and Company will provide everything you need, including materials and labor, to get your castle in tip-top shape."

Drusilla blinked. "That's very generous."

"Not when you take into account that I mentioned it's a rather self-serving proposition . . . and that I will need you to agree to a few teeny little conditions before we move forward."

"Such as?"

Wilhelmine gave a breezy wave of a hand. "They aren't anything drastic, simply things like how we need to coordinate our efforts so that you'll be able to open the academy within the month."

Another blink was Drusilla's first response to that. "I'm sorry, but did you say you want the academy opened within a month—as in thirty days?"

"Time is of the essence, dear, given that there are many a young lady, one of mine included, who'll be wanting to make a debut within the year. But don't fret that opening in a month is an impossible feat—not when I'll also be providing you with the full support of my domestic staff." She gave Drusilla's forehead another dab. "I do feel compelled to disclose that my staff will need a bit of direction at first since many of them are relatively new to their positions, but I'm sure your housekeeper will be more than up for the task of taking them in hand."

Irma took that moment to clear her throat. "I'm afraid we no longer have a housekeeper, as Mrs. Donaldson accepted a position with the Fish family two days after we learned our fortune was missing. With that said, though, our butler, Mr. Grimsby, will be perfectly capable of directing your staff, although he can be rather gruff at times, which might leave your staff unwilling to work with him."

Wilhelmine smiled. "My staff is made up of people who used to work in steel mills, shirtwaist factories, and even slaughterhouses. I assure you, they'll find taking direction from your butler to be a walk in the park."

Irma's forehead took to puckering. "But if you lend us the use of your staff, you're going to be shorthanded with running your own house."

"My house is always shorthanded even with a full staff, but you'll understand why once they turn up here—if your daughter agrees to my proposal."

With that, Wilhelmine directed an expectant gaze on Drusilla.

"It's a more than generous proposition you've presented me with," Drusilla began, "but even if we were able to whip the castle into shape within a month, I highly doubt we'd be able to get word out regarding the new academy, which means we might be capable of opening our doors, but there will be relatively few young ladies walking through them."

Wilhelmine's lips curved. "There's no need to concern yourself with getting any word out because I've already taken the liberty of reaching out to the mothers of my daughters' friends." Her eyes began to sparkle. "I'm sure you'll be delighted to learn that I've been able to comprise a list over the past two days of fifty-seven young ladies who are clamoring to be accepted into your new school. All you need to do to seal our business arrangement is to assure me that you, unlike the schools many of us here in Chicago have petitioned to get our daughters enrolled into, will accept every young lady I send to you, no matter if other schools deemed them unacceptable and refused to allow them entrance into their hallowed midst, normally for the ridiculous reason of an insufficient pedigree."

"I'm sure I wouldn't be opposed to any of the young ladies you'd send my way, but before we get into that . . ." Drusilla frowned. "Did you say fifty-seven young ladies already want to attend the academy?"

"I did." Wilhelmine's eyes took to sparkling more than ever. "Although I probably should have added *and counting.*"

≈ Nineteen ≈

A hundred questions swirled through Drusilla's mind over what was certainly an unexpected and potentially Merriweather-saving development, but before she could get a single word out of her mouth, such as discussing if they'd even be able to handle fifty-seven and counting potential students, Wilhelmine took hold of Drusilla's chin, turned her head to the left, then to the right, and frowned.

"My dear, you have a few wounds that are stubbornly refusing to cease bleeding, no matter how many times I dab them, which means further talk of my business proposal will need to wait until after we get you into your room and properly attend to those wounds once and for all."

Wilhelmine sent a nod Rhenick's way. "I believe now is the moment for you to address the raven situation, but do go about the matter carefully as it's obvious the ravens are an aggressive lot, but also try to hurry, dear. We don't want to keep Drusilla lingering out here."

Before Rhenick could respond to that, Norbert stepped forward. "Miss Drusilla won't need to linger outside until the castle is raven-free," he said. "She can just use one of the back servant stairs to reach her room."

"We have back servant stairs?" Drusilla asked.

"Two sets of them," Norbert said.

"Why two?"

"I suppose that would be on account of Captain Thurgood Harvey. He's the one who built the castle years ago and wanted a way for his men to be able to come and go without anyone detecting them."

"Why would Captain Harvey's men need to be able to do that?"

"I'm afraid I can't disclose that because Captain Harvey made me swear on the Bible when he hired me—he was a rather suspicious sort—that I would never tell a soul about anything I might see while in his employ."

"But you're no longer in his employ."

"Doesn't matter. I swore to *never* tell a soul—something I took to mean meant forever."

"Weren't you wary about accepting employment from a man who made such a peculiar demand?"

"Not when I was offered a job that paid me a handsome salary and allowed me to stay out of the mines and factories. It was worth it to keep my mouth shut when I saw some rather dubious things going on here—and no, I won't be disclosing those dubious things to you."

"Did he make everyone who worked for him swear to never divulge his secrets?"

"Sure did, although I always got the impression his men were loyal to a fault, most of them moving with the captain when he took off for Florida because he was tired of the cold winters here and wanted to seek out a warmer shore. The only one who stayed behind besides me was Sneaky Pete Smythe, who accepted employment with the new owner, that being Miss Ottilie, on account that he had a sister living in the area and didn't think she'd be keen to move down to Florida with a bunch of his old sea mates."

Drusilla's brow furrowed. "His name wasn't really Sneaky Pete, was it?"

"It was, but all the captain's men had names like that. There was One-Legged Tom, another was Stinking Stanley, and there was even a Dreadful Delbert." Norbert gave his nose a rub. "But talk of additional names should probably wait since I'm sure Rhenick's going to need help with those ravens. That means I need to show you where the servant staircase is sooner than later."

Before she could ask the burning question of what position a man named Sneaky Pete could have possibly taken on for her aunt, Drusilla found herself being helped to her feet by Wilhelmine, who made sure Drusilla was steady before turning to Rhenick.

"After you finish with the ravens," Wilhelmine began, "you'll need to have our footmen unload the baskets from my carriage. You might then want to start on lunch preparations since I'm sure everyone, after the morning they've experienced, would enjoy a hot meal." With that, Wilhelmine gestured Norbert toward the castle, then took a firm grip on Drusilla's arm, quite as if she believed Drusilla might still be a bit wobbly on her feet.

Irma immediately took hold of Drusilla's other arm, leaving Drusilla with the distinct impression that her mother had taken issue with Wilhelmine hovering over her daughter. Frankly, given that Irma was now considering Drusilla in what could only be described as a concerned manner, it almost seemed as if her mother wanted Wilhelmine to believe that it was an everyday occurrence for her to look after her daughter's welfare, something her mother had never done in Drusilla's life.

Drusilla leveled an arch of a brow on Irma, earning an innocent look from her mother in the process, then returned her attention to Wilhelmine. "Perhaps we can use the time it takes to get me up those mysterious servant stairs to speak further about this business deal of yours."

Wilhelmine waved that aside. "There'll be plenty of time to address that once we attend to your head, and after, or perhaps during, lunch. Considering you just suffered an assault by birds no less, I'm sure you must be famished, although . . ." Wilhelmine frowned. "I recently read in one of my etiquette books, which I've been trying to read more diligently ever since Tilda told me about her uncomfortable dinner at the Vanderbilts, that proper ladies shouldn't admit they're hungry, as it's considered by the upper crust to be a grave faux pas."

"Unfortunately, that is true, and most ladies would like everyone to believe they're capable of surviving on a tiny cucumber sandwich. However . . ." Drusilla smiled. "I'm not a lady who can exist on a meager diet, and willingly admit that I would be perfectly content to spend the rest of my life eating whatever I like—within reason, of course—something I'm fairly sure I'll be able to do since I've vowed to never marry and have absolutely no need to make certain my waist is capable of being squeezed into a gown with a twenty-something-inch waistline."

"I've always told people that you're capable of an eighteen-inch waist," Irma contradicted.

"My waist hasn't been capable of being squeezed to eighteen inches since I was sixteen," Drusilla countered. "In all honesty, having my former lady's maid get it to twenty-five inches was a feat in and of itself and forced my poor maid to have to resort to brute strength while tightening the laces of my corset so that she could then stuff me into my gowns."

"Twenty . . . five?" Irma all but sputtered.

Drusilla gave her mother's arm a pat. "My waistline, or lack thereof, is not the end of the world, Mother, and before you ask how it came to be that you were unaware of my less-than-waiflike figure, you've been in mourning for over two years, that state rendering you not nearly as observant as you used to be."

"I think you have a lovely figure," Wilhelmine said. "And I'm ever so pleased to learn you enjoy a good meal since Rhenick will soon be cooking up a storm." She leaned closer. "He's a genius in the kitchen."

Drusilla frowned. "I thought when you told him to start on lunch preparations that you meant he should unpack the supplies you brought with you and get everything ready for our cook to prepare the meal."

"It would hardly be a proper welcome to Chicago from the Whittenbecker family if we simply brought food and expected your cook to make everything," Wilhelmine countered. "And normally I wouldn't be so presumptuous as to include myself with eating any meal I brought a family, but given that we do still have matters to discuss, I hope you'll forgive what might come across as impertinence on my part."

"Sharing a meal with us that your son is going to prepare is hardly an impertinence," Drusilla said as they rounded the corner of one of the turrets, having to veer to the left to avoid Billy the Goat and a few of his friends who were chomping their way through high weeds, which was a benefit of having a herd of goats she'd not actually considered until just that moment.

After sending a nod to Norbert, who was standing a good ten feet in front of them and was evidently waiting to make certain they were still following, Drusilla glanced back to Wilhelmine. "Since it appears as if we might have a ways to go before we reach this mysterious staircase, tell me this, how long has Rhenick been cooking?"

"He learned his way around the kitchen when he was about twelve," Wilhelmine said. "That was back in the days when Franklin, my husband, was really starting to get his construction company up and running, and right around the time I gave birth to my third child, Eloise." She smiled. "Franklin and I didn't think we could have more children after we had Tilda, who's four years younger than Rhenick, but then Eloise came along, followed in quick succession by Grace and Coraline. Before I knew it, I was overwhelmed, because while our business was beginning to turn profitable, we didn't have much in the way of extra funds to hire on much staff. That's why Rhenick began taking over meal preparation as well as walking the floor with babies who didn't want to stop crying, or mending Eloise's many scrapes and bruises because, let me tell you, she was a handful from the moment she started walking."

"It sounds as if Rhenick might have a way with children."

Wilhelmine smiled. "That he does, my dear, and when you pair that with the idea that the food he prepares would give any chef a run for their money, it's little wonder the ladies of Chicago have had him in their sights for years."

"Your son does seem to be quite the catch," Irma proclaimed, leaving Drusilla with the distinct, and yet hardly proper, urge to roll her eyes.

Before she could give in to the urge to do exactly that, Norbert released a whistle, then sent them a wave right before he stepped behind a row of tall shrubs, sticking his head out of the shrubbery a second later.

"The door's behind here," he said before he disappeared again.

"Is it just me, or does it seem somewhat ominous that there's a doorway hidden behind shrubs?" Drusilla asked, earning nods from Wilhelmine and Irma before she slipped between the shrubs and the castle wall and edged to where Norbert was waiting, having to push aside bits of shrubbery to reach him.

"Lucky for all of you, someone left the candle and matches the captain's men always used right inside the door on the table," Norbert said. "After you get the candle lit, just go up the set of stairs that's about ten feet past this entranceway, but only go up to the first level. Once you reach that landing, turn right, then go all the way to the end of that hallway. There'll be a door there. I think it's green, but I'm not positive about that since it's been a few years since I've used this staircase. You should find yourself in a linen closet once you walk through that door, and then after you walk out of that closet, you'll find yourself on the second floor. After that, all you need to do is turn to the right, then turn left once you reach the main second-floor hallway. You should recognize your surroundings from there." After sending her a nod, he disappeared into the shrubbery again, right as Wilhelmine and Irma stumbled up to join her.

"From the sounds of things, it seems as if we might need a map to navigate this staircase," Irma muttered, brushing a few leaves from her hair.

"I'm sure Norbert made it sound more difficult than it really is," Drusilla said. "Although it might not be a bad idea to start making a few maps when we get some spare time because clearly this castle has more than a few secrets."

"I shudder to think what those might be," Irma said before she glanced through the doorway. "Seems rather menacing in there, what with how dark it is."

"Norbert said there's a candle." Drusilla shoved aside the trepidation that was causing the hair on the back of her neck to stand at attention and stepped into the gloom. Striking a match she located on a small table inside the door, she lit the candle that was next to it.

"Shall we?" she asked before she drew in a breath and began moving down a hallway that truly did seem as if it might have a few ghosts and ghouls wafting about.

⇒ Twenty ⇐

"I would like to state for the record," Irma said, causing Drusilla to jump ever so slightly when her mother stole up behind her and began following her down the narrow hallway that branched off in two directions once it reached the staircase, "that I don't believe this is a prudent decision on your part, but as your mother, I can't very well let you brave what will certainly turn into another disaster alone."

"That's a very motherly thing to say."

"And quite unlike me, which suggests I'm not feeling myself today, and . . ." Irma's words trailed to nothing before she suddenly released a strangled-sounding shriek that reverberated eerily around them.

Drusilla whipped around and found her mother swatting her hands madly about. "What's wrong?"

"I just walked straight into a spiderweb."

Drusilla peered through the gloom. "It looks to be more along the lines of a cobweb than spiderweb, and cobwebs won't hurt you."

Irma's brows slammed together. "Since you have as much experience as I do with spiderwebs and cobwebs, forgive me if I don't actually believe you have the ability to differentiate between the two."

"A valid point, but since I'm the one leading the way, you should take comfort in the fact that I'll be the one to run into most spiderwebs. Not that I know this for certain, as Annaliese is the expert on spiders, but I imagine that any spiders I run into will skedaddle by the time you pass through what remains of any webs I disrupt."

"Unless they decide, like the ravens did, to band together and attack us," Irma grumbled as Drusilla started moving up stairs that gave new meaning to the word *steep*, unsurprised when Irma's grumbles stopped when the stairs began creaking with every step they took, the creaks more unnerving than Irma's shriek had been.

The cobwebs—at least that's what Drusilla truly hoped they were—seemed to grow denser the higher they climbed, little wisps of webs sticking to her face as she fought her way through them. By the time she reached the first landing, she was covered in them. After taking a second to dash a web-covered sleeve across her face to rid it of little tangles of silken threads, she held the candle aloft and tried to get her bearings.

Directly to her left, the stairwell continued upward with a sharp turn, but once she stepped forward and into a narrow hallway, she realized that the hall seemed to run the entire length of the castle and that the staircase was positioned exactly in the middle.

She turned to the right, as Norbert had instructed, and walked forward, pausing when the feeble light from the candle glanced over the floor and what appeared to be footprints in a thick layer of dust captured her attention.

Curiosity had her kneeling to get a closer look, but before she could do more than realize the footprints were on the small side, Irma stumbled into her, sending Drusilla headfirst onto the floor, an *oomph* escaping her when her mother tumbled on top of her a second later.

The force of her mother's tumble had her dropping the

candle, causing the flame to immediately sputter out, leaving them in complete darkness.

"What do you think the odds are that Ottilie's ghost will show up next, making our current situation more unsettling than ever?" Irma whispered as she remained lying on top of Drusilla, seemingly content to remain there instead of on what was a remarkably dirty floor.

"Aunt Ottilie isn't haunting the castle."

"Of course she is, and I wouldn't put it past her to have been responsible for whatever it was that had you bending over like that, possibly in the hopes that I'd then fall over you and then we'd be stuck here in the darkness, unable to find our way to that door we're supposed to be looking for. It could be hours until someone finds us, and if I'm stuck here for hours, I will undeniably lose my senses and end up in a lunatic asylum, which was probably Ottilie's goal for me from the start and why she paid me a visit the other night."

"You're not going to end up in a lunatic asylum, nor was any ghost responsible for me kneeling down. I did so because I saw footprints on the floor, and before you tell me those were Ottilie's, know that I've never heard of any ghost leaving tracks behind."

"Oh" was all Irma said to that before she wiggled around a bit, quite as if she wanted to make herself more comfortable. "I suppose the creepy atmosphere is causing my imagination to race at full tilt, just as I suppose the footprints you spotted belong to Norbert since he told us he makes rounds throughout the castle at least twice a week."

"Norbert told me that he hasn't used this particular servant hallway and staircase for quite some time, and besides that, he wears big boots. The prints I saw were on the smaller side."

"Perhaps they were made by a member of Ottilie's staff before they bolted from the castle," Wilhelmine suggested from where she'd obviously had the good sense to stop a few feet behind them, sparing herself a tumble in the process. "Although, speaking of that exemplary staff, I feel compelled to admit that, if I'd been given advance notice that they were abandoning their positions because of a rogue suit of armor, something everyone in Chicago heard about, I wouldn't have hesitated to poach them."

"Given that it sounds as if you employ a rather inexperienced staff," Irma began, "I don't believe anyone, not even Ottilie, would have blamed you."

"How very kind of you to say, Irma, as I was worried my disclosure might have left you feeling at distinct odds with me as the poaching of Ottilie's staff is why the castle is in a rather derelict state."

"But you're not the ones who ended up poaching the staff," Irma pointed out.

"But I *would* have if I'd been given the chance," Wilhelmine reiterated right before she struck a match that she'd obviously had the foresight to pick up from the table, the weak flicker of the flame penetrating the darkness. "Let me find the candle, and then we'll look more closely at those prints." With that, Wilhelmine climbed over Irma, needing to strike a second match before she finally located the candle.

A blink of an eye later, and holding a candle that was once again lit, Wilhelmine pulled Irma to her feet, did the same with Drusilla, then held the candle aloft, nodding as the weak light traveled over a single set of footprints that marched down the hallway.

"Shall we follow them?" Wilhelmine asked.

"Don't you think it would be smarter to find that door Norbert told us about and get out of here as quickly as possible on the chance that whoever left those prints is still in here with us?" Irma whispered.

"I never thought about that," Wilhelmine whispered back,

the whispering somewhat questionable since it wasn't as if they'd been being overly quiet up until now.

"If they were left by a member of Ottilie's staff, that member is long gone by now, although . . ." Drusilla squatted down to look more closely at the tracks. "I think these are too fresh to have been made over a year and a half ago." She frowned and rose to her feet. "They're traveling away from the door we're supposed to be looking for, which means . . . we need to follow them to see if they lead to the stairs or travel down the other side of the hallway."

"Because?" Irma whispered.

"What if they were made by someone posing as that ghost that came to visit you in your room? And the reason we couldn't find that supposed ghost was because the person impersonating a ghost hustled themselves right into this hidden staircase, and hence, avoided detection."

"Or maybe no one could find the ghost because it was a ghost and it simply vanished into thin air like ghosts do."

"I think my explanation is more plausible, so we need to follow the prints."

"I don't believe we need to do any such thing," Irma protested. "I mean, honestly, Drusilla, it's not as if any of us are Pinkertons. We certainly won't know what to do if we run across whoever left those prints. I say we go back and fetch Rhenick and Norbert and let them investigate for us, or maybe this would be a wonderful task for Seraphina to take on, what with how you told me she spent years living in a spooky old boarding school. She probably has scads of experience with ghosts."

Drusilla took the candle from Wilhelmine and resisted the urge to roll her eyes yet again, an urge she'd certainly been resisting quite often. "You may go fetch Rhenick and Norbert if you want, but as I've vowed to learn how to deal with whatever life sends me without the assistance of gentlemen,

I'm going to follow the tracks. And no, I'm not going to ask Seraphina to do it for me. This is my castle, which means it's my responsibility."

"I'm not certain I care for this assertive attitude you've adopted of late," Irma complained, even though instead of heading for the door Norbert had told them would lead to a linen closet, she gave a wave of her hand toward the hallway. "I suppose you might as well get on with it, but know, if all of us come to a grisly end, I'm holding you responsible."

"Duly noted," Drusilla said before she edged past her mother and began heading toward the staircase, keeping the candle trained on tracks that turned toward the stairs and seemed to go up, although there was another set of tracks going down.

"This is a really bad idea," Irma said when Drusilla headed up the staircase, climbing her way to the next landing and then continuing upward when the tracks didn't head into the third-floor hallway but stayed on the steps.

"I might need to consider abandoning these widow's weeds once and for all as they're definitely far too heavy to accommodate any type of physical exertion, something I seem to be experiencing today," she heard Irma say to Wilhelmine as they continued to climb, cobwebs once again glancing over Drusilla's face. She slowed to a stop when she caught sight of a door looming in front of her, and a door where the stairs simply seemed to end.

Drawing in a deep breath, she forced feet that didn't want to move into motion again, then took hold of the doorknob, but before she had an opportunity to give it a twist, Irma was peering over her shoulder.

"Are you quite sure you want to open that instead of seeking out Rhenick to open it for us? He does seem to be a gentleman who'd probably know what to do if we found ourselves confronted with a real live ghost on the other side," Irma said.

"I don't think ghosts can be real live."

"You know what I meant, and who's to say that some of the ghosts that might be haunting this castle aren't of the malevolent type?" Irma countered. "If they're mean ghosts, they might attack us as soon as we open the door, and then we'll all be dead, and on the very day you learned that a gentleman had actually lost his senses because of you, which you know is a day we should be celebrating instead of courting death."

Drusilla grinned. She simply couldn't help herself.

"We are not courting death, merely contemplating walking through a door, and as has already been discussed, there was a reason Rhenick lost his senses around me, that being him having misconstrued who I am at heart."

"I don't believe he misconstrued who you were at all," Wilhelmine said as she crowded in behind them. "Especially not when you didn't hesitate to traipse on after these footprints, which suggests Rhenick's right and that you're a most exceptional young lady."

Having nothing of worth to say to that since it wasn't as if she was accustomed to anyone extending her any type of compliment, especially not one that had the word *exceptional* in it, Drusilla settled for sending Wilhelmine a small smile before she returned her attention to the doorknob.

"Any thoughts on what we might discover on the other side of this?" she asked.

"As long as it's not ghosts or more ravens, I think we'll be fine," Irma murmured.

"I think I'd rather take on a ghost than another raven," Drusilla murmured back before she gave the knob a twist and then stumbled through the door when it opened with barely any effort at all, quite as if it had been recently oiled.

Light blinded her as a stiff wind blew out the candle, and after shading her eyes with her hand, she realized she was now standing on one of the turrets, and . . .

A shriek rent the air, one that, of course, came from Irma, who stumbled into Drusilla a second later before she pointed a finger that was definitely shaking at something in the distance—something that was white, almost transparent, and wafting on the breeze.

⪦ Twenty-One ⪧

Rhenick strode from the kitchen and into the great hall, wanting to make certain it was still raven-free since the last thing he wanted was for Drusilla to find herself confronted with birds again when she returned from getting cleaned up.

Relief was immediate when he spotted not a single bird in sight, the few remaining ravens he'd encountered when he'd first entered the castle having decided to make use of the doors and windows he'd muscled open earlier.

After sending a nod to Mr. Grimsby, who was in the process of showing Rhenick's footmen how to lay a proper table, something his footmen had not been expecting to ever learn until Drusilla's butler had decided it would be beneficial for them to expand their domestic knowledge, Rhenick headed back to the kitchen.

He took a second to add a smidgen of salt to a simmering saucepot before he turned to Mrs. O'Sullivan, the Merriweather cook, who was in the process of chopping mushrooms.

"How are you coming with those?" he asked.

She gave the mushrooms a final chop and lifted her head. "That was the last one, so shall I move on to the lettuce next?"

"I think you should sit down and enjoy a nice cup of tea, something I suggested after we unpacked the provisions my mother and I brought." He smiled. "If you've forgotten, you've experienced quite the day already, and I'm perfectly capable of pulling a lunch together while you relax and keep me company."

Mrs. O'Sullivan waved that straight aside. "I'm not one to lounge about, Mr. Whittenbecker, and have always found the best way for me to relax is to work in my kitchen—one that I haven't neglected to notice you've taken over."

His smile dimmed. "I do beg your pardon, Mrs. O'Sullivan. I've just realized that I barged into your domain without a by-your-leave, a true impertinence if there ever was one."

Mrs. O'Sullivan released a bit of a tut. "I wouldn't say you were being impertinent, more along the lines of being determined to impress a certain young lady, that idea proven by the food you brought to cook for lunch today."

"Is it that obvious?"

"It's not subtle, that's for sure, since you're serving baked halibut in a mushroom cream sauce, paired with new potatoes, string beans, shrimp salad, and then strawberry ice cream to top off the meal."

He winced. "It's too much, isn't it?"

"Of course not, because Drusilla will definitely be impressed, which is what you're hoping to achieve." She smiled. "I should also mention that she won't simply be impressed because of the quality of the meal you're preparing, but because she's never had a gentleman make a fuss over her before, but . . ." Her smile slipped from her face. "If it turns out you're trying to impress her not because you actually find her extraordinary, but because you want to get your hands on this castle, know that I've spent years wielding a knife."

He inclined his head. "Point taken."

"Glad we understand each other," Mrs. O'Sullivan said.

"With that out of the way, I'll chop the lettuce for the salad while you finish pulling the tails from the shrimp."

A comfortable silence settled over them as they returned to work, Rhenick finishing the shrimp before he stirred the sliced mushrooms into the sauce simmering on the stove.

"Have you been the Merriweather cook for long?" he asked as he added more mushrooms to the pot.

"More than twenty years, a good fifteen of those years spent sharing the kitchen with the Merriweather French chef, Monsieur Boulanger. He left the Merriweather service to take up a position with the Rothchild family the second it became known that Mr. Sanford Duncan had absconded with the Merriweather fortune."

Rhenick abandoned the sauce. "Someone *stole* the Merriweather fortune?"

"You didn't already know that?"

"I knew something had happened because Drusilla mentioned a financial catastrophe, but she didn't elaborate, and she didn't whisper a thing about a Mr. Sanford Duncan."

"I shouldn't have said anything," Mrs. O'Sullivan muttered as she returned to the lettuce, worried her lip for a moment, then lifted her head. "Since I've already let the cat out of the bag, though, and you and your mother are apparently here to help, which is more than I can say about any of Mrs. Merriweather's fair-weather friends, who didn't offer her so much as a single coin when society learned what Sanford had done, I'll tell you exactly what happened."

As Rhenick stirred the sauce so it wouldn't scorch, Mrs. O'Sullivan took the next ten minutes to explain the basics of what had transpired with the Merriweather family, ten minutes in which he went from gently stirring the sauce to all but beating it, unquestionably because it was little wonder Drusilla had vowed to never marry, considering that the man who should have done everything in his power to protect her, one Mr. Elbert

Herrington to be exact, had abandoned her instead. Elbert had then had the audacity, from the sound of it, to arrange for Drusilla to marry one of several men he'd sought out, even though Drusilla had never met those men.

"And there you have it," Mrs. O'Sullivan finally said, wiping her hands on a towel. "The Merriweather ladies have certainly had a difficult time of it, Miss Drusilla more than her mother and Annaliese. To give that young lady credit, even though she's been given trials that would leave most women curled up in a ball and refusing to get out of bed, she's risen magnificently to the challenges she's been facing."

"And you believe it won't be too much of another challenge for her to open up an academy?"

"From what I've seen since her father died, Miss Drusilla is capable of handling anything that's thrown her way. Nevertheless, I can't say I wasn't relieved when I overheard your mother mention that bit about you and your family offering your assistance to get the academy doors open." Mrs. O'Sullivan caught Rhenick's eye. "Just between you and me, Miss Drusilla's been worried about the state of their finances because, even though she managed to get that no-good Elbert to pay her for the return of the Herrington diamonds, that money isn't going to last long. Having you help her open the academy sooner than later will surely take some of the weight off that poor dear's shoulders."

"*If* she agrees to let us help her, something she's yet to do."

Mrs. O'Sullivan smiled. "Oh, don't you worry about that. Drusilla is practical to a fault, and I can guarantee that she's already decided your offer is a godsent opportunity she can't ignore. But speaking of God . . ." She set aside the towel and moved closer to him. "I also overheard your mother and Norbert talking about the church you attend, and I would look upon it as a great favor if you could make a point to invite the Merriweather ladies to attend a service with you at some point. As I said, Mrs. Merriweather's friends, if you can even call them that, lifted not a single finger to help her, although all of them sent their agents around when the Merriweather possessions were put up at auction to pay off the exorbitant debts Sanford ran up in Mrs. Merriweather's name. Betrayals such as that are difficult to overcome, but I believe the ladies, along with Miss Seraphina Livingston, of course, would greatly benefit from making some new friends, and hopefully genuine friends at that."

"I'll be certain to ask if they'd care for me to escort them to a service soon, and you and Mr. Grimsby, as well as any other members of your staff, should know that you'll be welcome to attend as well."

Mrs. O'Sullivan stepped closer and gave his cheek a pat. "You're a good man, Mr. Whittenbecker, and—"

Whatever else she'd been about to say got interrupted when the sound of shrieking somewhere outside the kitchen captured their attention.

Rhenick was out of the kitchen in a heartbeat and running though the great hall, where he immediately caught sight of Irma, who was racing down the staircase as if something was chasing her. After jumping from the last step, she slid a good distance across the stone floor before she gained her balance, then took off for the front door, yelling over her shoulder that everyone needed to immediately abandon the castle as it was most assuredly haunted.

He didn't hesitate to run after her, although catching up with her turned out to be rather difficult because Irma Merriweather was unexpectedly fast on her feet.

"Mrs. Merriweather! Wait up!" he shouted when he got within a few feet of her, which had Irma stopping in her tracks, spinning on her heel, and then rushing directly for him, flinging arms that were decidedly shaking around him the second she reached him. She then buried her head against his chest and clung to him as if she was never going to let go.

Given that he was quite accustomed to members of his immediate and extended family throwing themselves on him whenever life seemed too difficult to bear, Rhenick gave her a few pats on the back, knowing there was little point in questioning her until she regained her composure.

"Step away from Mrs. Merriweather and then put your hands in the air where I can see them."

As Irma released her hold on him, Rhenick raised his hands and turned, finding the woman he'd first seen wearing a cloak standing in the middle of the drive, pointing a blunderbuss at him.

"I'm not here to harm anyone," he said, earning a grunt from the woman in return.

"Good to hear, but I imagine you *are* here in another attempt to relieve the Merriweathers of their property." She tilted her head and didn't bother to lower the blunderbuss. "I find myself wondering what unusual ploy you're intending to use this time since a marriage proposition didn't work out well for you last time."

Before he could state that he didn't have a ploy, Irma stepped forward. "For heaven's sake, Seraphina," she began, "put that gun away. Rhenick wasn't in the process of anything dastardly. He was simply consoling me."

Seraphina's brows drew together. "Consoling you because . . . ?"

"I've just suffered yet another hair-raising incident, but before I get into that . . ." She turned to Rhenick. "I must beg your forgiveness, dear. I normally don't make it a habit to accost young gentlemen, but clearly, as I just mentioned, I've suffered yet another fright and I fear I'm simply not myself right now."

"What type of fright?" Rhenick asked.

"It was of the ghostly variety."

"And you saw this after you and my mother got Drusilla to her room?"

"We never made it to her room."

A sense of dread was immediate. "Exactly where would Drusilla and my mother be right now then?"

"I'm sure they'll be along directly, but after we saw the ghost on the top of the turret, we became separated."

Seraphina frowned. "Why were you up in the turret?"

"That's where the footprints led us," Irma said, quite as if that made perfect sense. "However, when we opened the door after we reached the top of the servant stairs that led us outside, a ghost materialized directly in front of us. I was behind Wilhelmine and Drusilla, you see, and the second I caught sight of the ghost, I started screaming." She shook her head. "One would think that even in the afterlife a ghost would be affected by bloodcurdling screams, but it just continued floating about, which is why I'm sure you can't blame me for heading down the servant stairs as fast as I could. Unfortunately, I didn't have access to a candle, as Drusilla had been the one carrying it up the stairs, which meant I couldn't see a thing and had to feel my way along." She gave a bit of a shudder. "I thought for sure I'd be set upon by additional ghosts, but I finally managed to find a door and stumbled through it and then, I kid you not, I found myself in a room filled with mummies."

Seraphina's eyes widened. "Do not say you were set upon by mummies next."

"Not set upon, thank goodness, although I swear I thought I saw one of them move, but I wasn't going to linger around to make certain of that."

Seraphina was in motion a second later, striding for the house even as she said something about him looking after Irma while she went and tracked down Drusilla.

Knowing he couldn't very well leave Irma on her own so that he could help look for Drusilla and his mother as well, Rhenick offered Irma his arm and, after moving with her to the bench Drusilla had made use of earlier, helped her find her seat. He then sat down beside her, pleased to see her cheeks weren't nearly as pale as they'd been only moments before.

"I think it was the same ghost I saw in my bedchamber the other night," Irma said as she dusted what appeared to be cobwebs from her sleeve. "And now that your mother and Drusilla have seen it as well, there can be no doubt that the castle truly is haunted. That means we certainly can't live here, let alone open an academy, as I doubt any mother will allow her daughter to attend a finishing school in a place that has ghosts running amok and mummies cavorting about."

"I'm sure none of the mummies are doing any cavorting, but even if we determine there's something of a ghostly nature transpiring within the castle walls, I get the sneaking suspicion that isn't going to deter Drusilla from wanting to open her academy."

"That might not deter her, but I imagine, after what Wilhelmine just saw, she won't be keen to enroll your sisters in a haunted school. Since she's the one who found those fifty-something potential students, I doubt, once the other mothers learn your sisters won't be attending classes here, they'll enroll their daughters either."

"I don't think you understand how determined my mother is to assure my sisters receive their fair share of lessons pertaining to propriety," Rhenick countered. "A few ghosts, or even mummies, aren't going to scare her off."

Irma's shoulders slumped just the slightest bit. "That's unfortunate."

Knowing there was little he could say that would cheer Irma up, he spent the next few minutes simply sitting beside her in silence, that silence only broken when Irma would release somewhat dramatic sighs, until she sat forward.

"Looks like Drusilla and Wilhelmine escaped from the ghost," Irma said with a nod toward the castle.

Rhenick glanced to the castle and discovered Drusilla marching down the front steps, Wilhelmine on her right side, Seraphina on her left, and . . . he squinted when he realized Drusilla was carrying something.

Something that was white and looked to be as large as a woman.

Irma drew in a sharp breath. "Good heavens. Drusilla's captured the ghost, but . . . how could she have even done that? Or better yet—why is she heading our way with it?"

Before Rhenick could do more than open his mouth, Irma was on her feet and charging down the drive, her widow's weeds billowing behind her.

"Mother, stop!" Drusilla called. "It's not what you think."

It took Irma a good few yards before she finally stopped, turned around, then took a few hesitant steps toward Drusilla, who took that moment to toss whatever it was she was holding to the ground before she gestured Rhenick forward. "Look what we found on one of the turrets."

"What is that?"

"Someone's attempt at making everyone believe Aunt Ottilie is haunting the castle." She nodded to what seemed to be a rag doll, although a life-size one that was draped in a shimmery cloth. "That was hanging on the turret, and not only was it hanging, but someone devised a pulley system that attaches one turret to the other. It's obvious that the culprit went to all that bother as a way to convince people that this castle is, indeed, haunted."

"Are you saying I was scared half to death because of a prank?" Irma demanded as she marched up to join them, peering at the heap of white fabric. "That looks exactly like what the ghost that visited me was covered in."

"I'm sure it was cut out of the same bolt of fabric, but I don't believe any of this ghost business is a prank, Mother," Drusilla said. "It's more of a sign that someone is truly determined to run everyone off this property, but I have news for whoever that is—I'm not going anywhere, no matter how many ghosts they may throw my way."

≈ Twenty-Two ≈

During the week that had passed since Drusilla had found the facsimile of a ghost and decided on the spot to accept the Whittenbeckers' offer of assistance to get the academy up and running, she'd come to realize a few things.

For one—she was possessed of a bit of a temper, something she'd never considered before the whole fiasco she'd endured with Elbert, but a temper that was directly responsible for her now steadfast determination to maintain ownership of the castle.

Secondly—while Wilhelmine had implied that the reason she and Rhenick were offering up the services of Whittenbecker and Company Construction at no cost was to assure that the Whittenbecker sisters received a more-than-adequate education when it came to all matters of proprieties, that wasn't exactly true. Instead, and after inadvertently overhearing a conversation Rhenick had been having with his mother while he'd been finishing up what had turned out to be a delicious lunch the day of the ghost debacle, it seemed as if Rhenick believed that if the academy could be opened quickly and filled with the daughters of wealthy Chicago families, the danger from overzealous developers would diminish quite substantially.

He'd then gone on to tell Wilhelmine that Chicago developers made more than half their income from members of the newly rich set, which suggested they'd be remarkably hesitant to be responsible for Drusilla's academy failing, especially when the newly rich had been longing for just such an academy for years.

Given that Rhenick hadn't broached the matter of a marriage between them again, and Wilhelmine had made a point of telling her that the last thing Whittenbecker and Company needed was more business, as they had their hands full with the contracts they already had, Drusilla had come to the realization that she might have been wrong about Rhenick and that he wasn't a cad after all but simply a gentleman possessed of an unexpectedly kind nature.

He also seemed to be a considerate man, because he'd made a point to stop by Aunt Ottilie's bank to get the direction of William Baumgartner, and while the bank manager wouldn't turn over William's address to Rhenick, he had agreed to send William a message, asking him to contact Drusilla at his earliest convenience.

"Not that I want to alarm you, Drusilla, but if you're confronted with danger at some point in time, you're not going to have over a minute to consider exactly where you should aim that pistol in your hands because . . . you'll be dead by then."

All thoughts of how Rhenick was not turning out to be a cad disappeared in a trice as Drusilla turned her head and settled her attention on Seraphina, who was sitting on a tree stump in a meadow that was well-removed from the vicinity of the castle—a meadow Seraphina had decided would be sufficient to use as a training ground for all the weapons she'd uncovered so far.

"Forgive me, Seraphina. You're quite right, and of course I realize I can't dither before every shot," Drusilla admitted. "It's just that I've not hit the target once this morning, and I would like to return to my other tasks after being able to say I at least improved my shooting abilities somewhat today."

"You just need to get the target in your sights and pull the trigger. You're overthinking it." Seraphina considered the target in question before she nodded. "Let's try something new. I'll count to three, and once I reach three, you shoot. Ready? One . . . two . . . three."

Refusing to give in to the urge to study the target as she'd been doing during the three days she'd been practicing, Drusilla set her sights on the tree she'd been trying to hit and squeezed the trigger, a bit of a yelp escaping her as a boom immediately rang out and she stumbled a good foot backward from the recoil.

"Did I hit it?" she asked after she found her balance, glancing back to Seraphina, who was now peering through a pair of opera glasses she'd found in a room Aunt Ottilie had been storing gowns and accessories in, some of the fashions dating back at least forty years.

Seraphina lowered the glasses. "I'm afraid not. And here I thought your progress would improve after Rhenick left us to see if his niece and nephew had arrived yet. I was apparently wrong about that."

"Why would you think my progress would improve without Rhenick being here? He's the one who showed me how to properly hold my pistol because you were doing the same with Annaliese."

"He distracts you."

"He does not."

"He also makes you nervous," Seraphina added, not bothering to argue her first point. "That nervousness is why I thought, mistakenly so, that your aim would improve without him around."

Drusilla swallowed the argument she longed to make when she realized that Seraphina wasn't exactly wrong because . . . Rhenick did make her nervous, or perhaps it wasn't nervousness she felt when she was around him, but more along the lines of awareness.

She always knew exactly when he entered a room even if she wasn't facing the door, quite as if there was something in him that was attuned with something in her, whether she wanted it to be or not, a feeling that was, in all honesty, rather unsettling.

"Want to try a few more times before we call it a day and head back to the castle?"

Drusilla glanced at the watch encircling her wrist and shook her head. "I told Annaliese I'd meet her at ten to finish tidying up what used to be the mummy room. It's about quarter till, and I know she'll come looking for me if I'm late, bringing Rhenick's sisters with her since they seem to love Annaliese and stick beside her anytime they visit the castle."

"And you don't want to see the Whittenbecker girls today because . . . ?"

"It's not that I don't want to see them—it's that I don't want to see them out here, where I'm putting on a completely lackluster show with my pistol."

Seraphina frowned. "I have no idea why you'd be concerned about that as you've only just started learning how to operate a weapon, and it's not unusual to lack proficiency with weaponry at first."

"I'm soon to be the headmistress of the Merriweather Academy for Young Ladies. I can't very well let future students see me being anything less than proficient with everything because, as you should very well know, having spent eons of time in a boarding school, headmistresses are held to a certain standard. I'd lose all respect from the students if it got around that I can't figure out how to aim and shoot a pistol, especially when I'm relatively certain there are going to be a lot of our young ladies who've been shooting a variety of weapons since the time they could walk."

"Coraline told me that her friend Norma Jean knows how

to operate a cannon because her brother is some kind of mad inventor and seems to have a great interest in gadgets that blow things up."

"Perhaps we should store our cannon somewhere besides the entranceway to avoid tempting Norma Jean."

Seraphina grinned. "I've already had Norbert help me get it out of the castle, where it's waiting for him to cart to the barn just as soon as he can convince Moe, Aunt Ottilie's somewhat ornery donkey, to cooperate and allow him to attach a harness to him."

"I think Moe's contrariness is exactly why he must have appealed to Aunt Ottilie, but Moe's contradictory nature aside, I really do need to get back to the castle."

"I'll walk with you."

After taking a second to add three bullets to the chamber of her five-shot pistol since both Seraphina and Rhenick had suggested she make certain she was armed and ready at all times just in case a determined developer showed up with maleficence on his mind, Drusilla slipped the pistol into her pocket and entwined her arm with Seraphina's as they turned and headed across the meadow.

"Do you and Annaliese need some help with the mummy room?" Seraphina asked.

"I think we'll be fine because we have Rhenick's sisters available to help us today. Annaliese never hesitates to arm them with mops, brooms, and feather dusters." Drusilla smiled. "All of them seem to adore my sister, although that adoration may very well change once Annaliese gets down to the business of instructing them on how to paint the perfect watercolor, or worse yet, how to play a song on the piano without missing a note, something you and I both know will require hours and hours of practice on the girls' part."

"I always resented my music instructors ever so slightly because of all the practice time that's required to turn proficient, but at least Annaliese and I aren't going to be responsible for teaching the students proper posture, which always incurs resentment given the tedious nature of it."

Drusilla smiled. "That resentment is exactly why I volunteered to teach those lessons, as resentment goes hand in hand with being a headmistress. With that said, though, it's not as if either you or Annaliese are getting off easy, not when we already have almost sixty girls enrolled and we've had to divide them into thirds since it'll just be the three of us instructing at first. Once we make certain the academy is going to be financially solvent, we'll hire more teachers."

Seraphina steered them to the right when Billy the Goat suddenly appeared with Mother Goose, followed by the rest of the goats, none of whom had proven themselves to be overly friendly and made it a habit to chase anyone who got too close.

"Irma still not coming around to the idea of teaching a few classes for us?" Seraphina asked as they gave the goats a wide berth.

"Mother hasn't outright refused, but she hasn't said yes either, probably because I think there's a part of her that's still hoping I'll come to my senses, take Rhenick up on what wasn't exactly a marriage proposal, and then allow him to whisk all of us away to a house in the city after vows are exchanged, where she can put all memories of the time spent in a supposedly haunted castle behind her."

"It might be rather difficult to take Rhenick up on that offer of his since you told me earlier that he's not mentioned the word *marriage* again, obviously determined to honor your demand of him never broaching that particular topic again."

A whisper of what felt like disappointment slid over her, disappointment she wouldn't allow herself to consider too closely because it was absolutely ludicrous to feel any type of disappointment over the fact that Rhenick was abiding by a demand she'd made and avoiding the subject of marriage like the plague.

"Speaking of Rhenick, he's heading our way, and look, the twins are with him," Seraphina said, snapping Drusilla out of all thoughts of disappointment as she turned her attention to where Rhenick was rounding the castle.

Her heart took that moment to give a bit of a lurch, which she staunchly tried to ignore, albeit with little success, because Rhenick was carrying his niece, Hattie, who was looking remarkably grumpy, while Edwin walked at Rhenick's side, his hands gesturing wildly about as if he were presenting some type of argument, perhaps one that was behind why his twin was looking less than happy.

Seeing a gentleman so completely comfortable in the company of small children was an unusual sight to be sure, and that Rhenick seemed to be trying his hardest to stifle a grin, something that suggested he didn't want to offend the twins, well, it was little wonder her heart was acting a tad peculiar.

She drew in a breath in the hopes of alleviating the peculiarity and summoned up a smile when Rhenick drew to a stop once he reached her and Seraphina.

"Looks as if there might be some trouble in twin-ville" was all she could think to say, which wasn't exactly a riveting opening for a conversation, something Seraphina clearly picked up on because she took to looking at Drusilla quite as if she'd lost her mind.

Thankfully, Rhenick didn't seem to notice Seraphina's look as he opened his mouth to respond, but before he could get a single word out, Hattie brushed dark curls out of her eyes and leaned forward.

"Fidget's gone missing," Hattie said. "She slipped into a vent, and she might be lost forever."

"Fidget slips away all the time, but she always shows up again," Drusilla said.

Edwin turned a scowl on her. "That's what Miss Annaliese told us, but me and Hattie heard the aunts say that Fidget was

172

heading down a vent that leads to the dungeons." His eyes turned wide. "Aunt Coraline said there are mummies down there now, and poor Fidget won't stand a chance against mummies. But no one would let me and Hattie go down there to help find her, so now she's gonna be dead, just like the mummies." He shuddered. "She'll be turned into a mummy ferret, and then Mama won't let me and Hattie play with her ever again."

Drusilla knelt down in front of Edwin. "Fidget's not going to be turned into a mummy, nor are the mummies that are stored in the dungeons wandering about the castle."

Edwin's eyes grew wider than ever. "Do you think Fidget will turn into a ghost, then—like the ghost we heard our aunts say is haunting the castle and is the reason we're not allowed to explore the turrets?"

"Your aunts told you there's a ghost haunting the turrets?"

"We heard Aunt Coraline and Aunt Grace talking about how they heard tales from their friends about the ghost."

"And the turret?" Drusilla pressed.

"Mother told us we couldn't go up there because it was too dangerous," Hattie said. "She wouldn't say why it was dangerous, but me and Edwin know it's because of a ghost since she wouldn't let us go up there even when Aunt Coraline said she'd watch over us."

Drusilla resisted a sigh because, clearly, the twins were too intelligent for their own good.

In all honesty, it wasn't that the turrets were too dangerous. It was simply that after she'd found the ghostly rag doll the week before, she'd decided to return it to exactly where and how she'd found it, believing it could very well be used to trap whomever had been attempting to scare everyone away from the castle.

She'd not even told Norbert about what she'd found on the turret, knowing full well the groundskeeper was a little loose-lipped, especially when he went to the Mead and Vittles, where he evidently regaled all the patrons with the odd happenstances he observed on the castle grounds.

Her less-than-forthcoming attitude had most assuredly confused Norbert, especially when she questioned him about how a person would be able to enter the castle if they didn't have a key. But when she didn't expand on why she wanted to know that, she earned herself a rather long, very considering look from Norbert in the process.

It had been clear the man had known she was being deliberately sketchy, but after a full minute had passed with him considering her, he'd finally told her that entrance without a key could only be gained through a window, but that a window entry was highly unlikely as he made a point to keep all the windows locked, at least the ones on the floors with easy access from outside the castle walls.

Norbert had then been highly offended when Drusilla, with Rhenick in tow, had gone off to inspect the windows, his attitude coming to a rapid end when Rhenick found three unlocked windows on the ground floor, ones that had been conveniently located behind shrubs.

To say Norbert had been appalled over what he considered dereliction of his most important duty—protecting the castle— was an understatement, and he'd taken to checking the grounds every night instead of once or twice a week, as well as making certain no windows were ever left unlocked again.

Pulling herself from her thoughts when she realized little Hattie was undoubtedly waiting for her to commiserate over the fact the twins weren't allowed to visit the turrets or the dungeon, Drusilla was spared some type of flimsy explanation regarding the turret situation when Norbert came striding into view, his ever-present rifle resting against his shoulder.

"Got a situation down at the gate" were the first words out of his mouth.

"A situation?" Drusilla repeated.

"Umberto Zambarello is here again. It's his fourth dropping by this week, and this time he demanded that I tell you he's willing to double any offer Whittenbecker and Company has made you, and also tell you that he's not leaving until he gets an opportunity to speak to you in person." Norbert shook his head. "Seemed to me he's serious about that since he had one of his footmen pull out a chair, small table, and even a picnic basket."

Drusilla frowned. "Is Mr. Zambarello the scariest of crime bosses, or is he the one who's going legitimate?"

"Legitimate, but don't think that just because he's not dealing in gambling anymore means he's any less relentless. As you've been told, he has those five overly rambunctious and less than ladylike daughters on his hands. He also recently let it be known that he's increasing the dowry on his oldest girl, who's set to turn seventeen next year, to over a hundred thousand, which means he's going to have to build a lot of mansions and sell them to cover dowries like that in the coming years."

"I would think so, but unfortunately for Mr. Zambarello, he's not going to be able to plump up his bank account if he believes I'm going to be swayed with whatever it is he wants to offer me and turn over the castle and property to him." Drusilla squared her shoulders. "Nevertheless, since dear Mr. Zambarello seems to be a relentless sort, and since I have vowed to retain ownership of my property no matter what, I suppose I have no choice but to have a face-to-face chat with the man and set him straight once and for all."

= Twenty-Three =

I'm not certain Edwin believed, after he got a glimpse of the pistol in your pocket, that you're not going to use said pistol on Umberto Zambarello, no matter that you assured him you weren't a lady who usually resorted to violence," Rhenick said after Seraphina disappeared around the side of the castle with the twins, who'd been less than thrilled they hadn't been invited to watch the meeting with Umberto, what with how Edwin was convinced there was going to be some shooting involved.

Drusilla grinned. "I'm not sure he did either, but do you think it speaks well of my character that I was somewhat delighted by the mere idea he thought I was the type of adventurous lady who'd even consider shooting an opponent in the first place?"

"You took a shot at me not all that long ago," Rhenick pointed out before he stopped walking. "Besides the attempted shooting of me, though, what lady but an adventurous one wouldn't flee from a castle where shenanigans are obviously occurring, or flee when ravens that once attacked her are now making a habit of setting themselves up in a line on the turret, where they begin cawing ceaselessly the moment they spot her walking across the back courtyard?"

Drusilla shot a look to the sky to make certain there were

no ravens flying overhead before she leaned closer to Rhenick. "Annaliese told me that ravens are highly intelligent birds, and she believes the castle ravens might have memorized my appearance, which also leads her to believe they're going to stalk me from this point forward." The hair on the nape of her neck took to standing to attention when a chorus of *kraas* suddenly rang out, quite as if the ravens knew she was currently discussing them. "I may have to resort to drastic measures, such as taking some food up to the turret and leaving it there as a peace offering."

"Which might work, or it might simply attract more rats, something that will undoubtedly cause your mother to take to her room again, even though my mother has finally convinced her to get out and explore the castle more, which Irma seems to enjoy, but only as long as my mother is with her."

"Perhaps I should try to lure the ravens into the forest area and leave a peace offering there."

Rhenick smiled. "A sensible idea, but speaking of sensible, we should probably decide, before we reach the gate, how you want to proceed with Umberto. Would you like me standing directly beside you, or would you prefer me to linger in the background so that he knows you're the one who makes the decisions pertaining to Merriweather business and won't resort to directing questions my way when you don't agree to give him what he wants?"

For the briefest of seconds, she found herself devoid of an answer because, while Rhenick's question was a fairly simple one, the very idea that he was asking her what she wanted to do in this situation instead of taking charge because he was a man reinforced the idea she'd had often of late—that being the fact that she'd clearly misjudged Rhenick right from the start.

Rhenick, unlike other men, never ignored her opinion but actually sought it out often, a novel experience and one she couldn't deny she enjoyed.

Frankly, she'd come to enjoy quite a few things about Rhenick over the past weeks, as he was a man who was well-versed in a plethora of subjects and didn't expect to limit their conversations to the weather.

Many of the conversations they'd shared during the time they spent together revolved around the improvements that needed to be made in the castle, or discussing what classes should be considered of the utmost priority once the academy was up and running.

Rhenick, it turned out, possessed some incredibly helpful insights when it came to deciding what lessons would be the most beneficial to the young ladies of Chicago, that insight a direct result of him spending the majority of his time being surrounded by members of the feminine set. Those feminine members were not simply his sisters, but a variety of cousins, neighbors, and—not that he'd said this, but his mother certainly had—numerous young ladies who apparently longed to spend as much time in his company as possible.

Truth be told, she couldn't blame those ladies, not when she'd found herself—a woman who'd vowed to avoid the company of men—looking forward to the time she and Rhenick spent together, mostly because Rhenick never failed to make her feel as if she was the center of his attention, something she'd never experienced before.

He also never hesitated to answer any of the many questions she directed his way, and when she'd asked him about his love of architecture, he'd taken the time to explain how he developed his fascination for building when he was young and visited his father on different sites, then pursued his passion for creating structures when he went off to college and studied architectural design.

When they weren't talking about her plans for the academy or his love of design, they were immersed in castle renovations. Thankfully, those renovations hadn't been as extensive as Drusilla had feared, most of the work centering around maintenance issues such as getting the coal furnace up and running, fixing the water pressure to where it wasn't soaking a person anytime a faucet was turned on, and inspecting gas lines so that it would be safe to use the gas sconces that were installed on every wall.

"We could always put off this meeting with Umberto if you're having a difficult time deciding how to proceed," Rhenick said, recalling Drusilla to the fact she'd not said a word in reply to his question, which was not something any lady well-versed in proper decorum would usually do, not when turning mute in the middle of a conversation was certainly considered rude.

"Forgive me, Rhenick," she began. "I fear I was quite lost in thought, but know that I have a general idea of what I'm going to say to that man." She sent him a nod. "I'm going to keep it short and direct."

"And if he doesn't accept short and direct?"

"Then I may need you to intercede, as I would hate to lose my temper and begin shrieking at him in frustration since that would hardly be appropriate for a future headmistress to do." She smiled. "Shrieking, as I'm sure you know, would be very bad for business, especially if word got around that a lady who's supposed to be the picture of decorum displayed behavior that was anything but."

Rhenick drew her into motion again. "I don't think shrieking on your part would harm your academy in the least because what you don't seem to understand is this—the mothers of the Chicago daughters who are to be enrolled in your academy will not bat an eye if it's discovered that the headmistress of a soon-to-be-esteemed ladies' academy may have a bit of a temper. Not when her academy will go far in making sure that the embarrassment Tilda endured during a Vanderbilt dinner, or the embarrassment my own mother endured when she was snubbed at the Palmer House, won't happen to their daughters in the future."

Drusilla's pace slowed. "Wilhelmine never mentioned being snubbed at the Palmer House."

"I would have thought she'd have mentioned that at some point as a way to solidify why she wants you to open the academy. And while it's not my story to tell, I don't believe Mother would mind me explaining how she was given what amounts to a cut direct, and by ladies who not only snubbed her, but felt it was their job to point out what they thought were her glaring deficiencies."

A sliver of temper slid through her because, even though she knew it was simply the way society comported itself and had often witnessed ladies of the New York Four Hundred giving the cut direct to more members of the *nouveau riche* set than Drusilla could count, Wilhelmine had been more than kind to her, and because of that . . .

"Do you think your mother would be receptive to taking a few lessons in propriety?" she asked, earning a blink from Rhenick in return.

"I don't believe she'd be opposed to it, but you already have almost sixty students wanting to attend your school and only three instructors. Offering my mother personal classes might be too much for you to take on."

She waved that aside. "I wouldn't be giving those lessons. I'll ask my mother since she's already grown incredibly fond of Wilhelmine, especially after your mother somehow convinced mine to give up her widow's weeds, which has left my mother enjoying a far more comfortable existence of late. That comfortable condition has improved her frequently querulous nature by leaps and bounds. Because of that, I don't think she'd hesitate to extend a few lessons in propriety to Wilhelmine."

Rhenick settled a smile on her, but before he could do more than that, a whistle coming from the vicinity of the gate drew her attention, as well as caused her to realize that she'd almost reached the gate but had been completely unaware of that, what with how focused she'd been on Rhenick. It was a curious thing, losing track of her surroundings, something she'd never been prone to doing before, and . . .

"It's about time," a man yelled through the gate, snapping her out of her thoughts, her pace slowing when she got her first good look at a man she assumed was Umberto Zambarello.

To say he fit the image of a man who might still be a member of the criminal persuasion was an understatement, even if he'd supposedly gone legitimate, because he stood over six feet tall, had a scar bisecting one of his cheeks, and was as broad—if not broader—than Rhenick. Add in the fact that he was currently scowling at her with dark eyes that were narrowed in what could only be described as a menacing fashion, and it was little wonder that a shiver took that moment to travel up her spine.

She forced herself to meet his gaze directly. "I understand from my groundskeeper that you'd like a word with me. Mr. Zambarello, I presume?"

"Of course I'm Mr. Zambarello, and you're that Merriweather chit, but know that it would be easier to have that word if you'd open the gate and let me in," Umberto snapped. "I'm unused to being left lingering outside anyone's door."

"You wouldn't be left lingering if you'd simply accept that I'm not interested in selling, and calling me a chit is hardly going to convince me to have a lengthy talk with you, even with a gate separating us."

"Would addressing you as Miss Merriweather convince you to let me in?"

"I believe that moment has passed, not that I ever had any intention of inviting you inside as, again, I'm not selling the castle."

Umberto's eyes hardened. "Then why has Whittenbecker and Company had crews roaming around here?"

She lifted her chin. "How disconcerting to learn you've been spying on my castle, but to answer you're rude demand know that I, along with my sister, brought Whittenbecker and Company on because we needed a few maintenance issues addressed, nothing more."

"What kind of maintenance issues?"

"I don't see where that's any of your concern. But perhaps having you learn that I'm intending to open a finishing academy for young ladies in the near future will finally allow you, as well as all the other anxious developers, to realize that I am, again, not going to sell."

Umberto frowned. "I heard a rumor about this academy, but I didn't put much stock in it as the fees you would glean from tuition won't be able to compete with what I'm willing to give to buy you out."

"I'm not selling."

Umberto shot a look to Rhenick. "I find myself curious, Whittenbecker, how it came to be that you ended up being a man in Miss Merriweather's confidence. Could it be that you've been plying her with flattery, perhaps convincing her that you find her attractive when you and I both know she's nothing of the—"

Before Umberto could finish his thought, Rhenick surged into motion, pulling out the gate key Norbert had given him. A mere heartbeat later, he was shoving the gate open before he launched himself in Umberto's direction, taking the man to the ground before Drusilla could get so much as a squeak past her lips.

Her mind then went curiously numb as she watched Rhenick begin rolling with Umberto down the drive, but before she could do more than take a step in their direction—to do what, she had no idea—another carriage came racing toward the gate.

Before she knew it, the doors to that carriage were flying open and then a handful of very large men spilled out onto the drive, heading not in Rhenick and Umberto's direction, which suggested they weren't Umberto's men, but toward the now-open gate.

"My dear Miss Merriweather," one of the largest of the men called, "how delightful to find you outside for a change and with the gate open in obvious welcome. If you can now spare me but a minute or two of your time, I assure you, I'll make it worth your while."

A whisper of dread swept through her, but before she could contemplate her best response to what hadn't exactly seemed like a request, Norbert materialized at her side.

"Best get yourself back to the castle, Miss Merriweather," Norbert muttered. "Those are Loughlin 'Lackey' MacSherry's men, which means . . . we've got trouble."

With that, Norbert ever so casually aimed his rifle toward the men, who were in the process of steadily advancing toward them. To Drusilla's relief, the sight of Norbert's rifle left Loughlin MacSherry's men stopping in their tracks, her relief short-lived when another carriage came clattering toward and then *through* the gate, the man sitting beside the driver of this particular carriage sporting an enormous pistol, one he seemed to be directing Norbert's way.

Unwilling to allow her groundskeeper to suffer a bullet, Drusilla whipped her pistol out of her pocket and, remembering that Seraphina had told her to simply aim and shoot instead of pondering the matter too long, drew a breath and pulled the trigger.

Twenty-Four

For the briefest of seconds, silence settled over a scene that had been unquestionably chaotic right up to the point when Drusilla had fired off a shot—until a howl rent the air right before the carriage that had reined to a stop the moment she'd fired on it began trundling into motion again and, unfortunately, trundling directly toward her.

"You shot me!" the man sitting beside the carriage driver yelled as he clutched his right arm and swayed on the driver's seat as the carriage picked up speed.

Self-preservation had her spinning on her heel instead of begging the man's pardon, although given the circumstances, it probably wasn't a grave faux pas to not voice an apology, since it appeared as if the man she'd shot now wanted to run her over.

She made it all of ten feet before the sound of additional shots rang out, and then chaos once again surrounded her. She heard Norbert yell something about everyone laying their weapons down right as Seraphina raced into view, gripping the blunderbuss she'd unearthed from one of the dungeon rooms, which she immediately aimed and fired at the carriage that had been gaining ground on Drusilla.

Glancing over her shoulder, Drusilla found the carriage driver already steering the carriage off the drive to turn it around. The four men who'd jumped from the carriage while it had been chasing her froze in the middle of the drive, undoubtedly because Annaliese had now charged into view as well and was in the process of pointing the Frankenau purse revolver she'd found the day before in an old trunk of Ottilie's at them.

One of the men, the largest of the bunch, immediately stuck his hands in the air. "How about you just lower that pistol purse real nice and slow like," he began, not taking his eyes off Annaliese, who was now scowling at him, probably because the man was talking to her as if she were a child—and not too bright, to boot. "It sure would be a shame if it misfired and that beautiful face of yours got disfigured."

"It *would* be a shame, but I'm not lowering my weapon," Annaliese countered as she fumbled with the bottom of the purse, her fumbling coming to an abrupt stop when the pistol purse suddenly emitted a bang, which resulted in the four men spinning around in unison and heading down the drive, one of them yelling something about crazy ladies and questionable gun accessories in the process.

Before Drusilla could appreciate the fact that she was not going to be run over in the very near future, Pippin, Fidget, and Wiggles came scurrying into view, setting their sights on the four fleeing men after Annaliese gave a snap of her fingers and pointed in the men's direction.

To say the chaos increased exponentially was an understatement after Fidget caught up with one of the men and took to attacking his leg, Pippin and Wiggles doing the same to two other men a moment later. The fourth man then increased his speed, not bothering to help the others as he bolted down the drive.

Unfortunately for him, Billy the Goat, in the company of his entire herd, took that moment to charge through the trees, Mother Goose at his side, her long neck stretched out as she honked her way after the fleeing man, clearly intent on inflicting some damage, as well.

"Who would have ever thought that goats could be counted on to act as guardians of the castle?" Wilhelmine asked as she jogged up to join Drusilla, Irma panting beside her, both ladies equipped with brooms.

Irma rubbed at what was obviously a stitch in her side. "It was brilliant of Eloise to shoo the goats down the drive when we heard that first shot fired, but . . ." Her brow took to furrowing as she turned to Drusilla. "What in the world is going on?"

"I'm afraid some developers have turned desperate, but no time to explain since Rhenick still might be engaged in some fisticuffs with Umberto Zambarello."

"Good heavens," Wilhelmine breathed before she dashed into motion again, Irma dashing after her a second later, both ladies brandishing their brooms quite as if they were fully prepared to wield them.

After exchanging a look of alarm with Seraphina and An-naliese, Drusilla charged after them and reached the castle gate, coming to an abrupt stop and blinking rather owlishly at the sight that met her eyes.

Instead of finding Rhenick and Norbert holding off the men who'd taken the sight of an open gate as an invitation to abandon all sense of civility, there was no one in sight, save Umberto Zambarello. He, however, was sitting in the middle of the drive, nursing a bleeding nose, before turning his head to peer down the drive when a few distant yells rang out, yells that suggested that Billy the Goat had just gotten a few additional head rams in and the ferrets might still be enjoying sinking their teeth into additional legs.

Her lips began to curve—until she caught sight of Rhenick, who was limping his way toward her, his handsome face now battered and smeared with blood, his eyes already swelling shut, which explained the squinting he was doing.

He came to a stop directly in front of her and took a long moment to consider her. "Are you alright?"

Her lips began to curve again. "I'm obviously doing better than you are, but . . ." She winced. "I may have shot a man."

Rhenick blinked. "You don't say."

"I thought I was aiming over the carriage, but I seemingly wasn't aiming high enough and I hit a man instead. I don't believe it's a mortal wound, as he was perfectly capable of yelling at me, and he was still sitting upright when I think he encouraged his driver to run me over."

Rhenick stilled. "A man encouraged someone to run you over?"

"Indeed, but it was clearly an unsuccessful attempt as I'm still standing, and those particular men were run off due to the intervention of Seraphina and Annaliese, along with the ferrets, goats, one goose, and perhaps our mothers, although now that I think about it, our mothers showed up after the men were racing down the drive."

"I don't believe they would have been all that intimidated by our brooms," Wilhelmine called, drawing Drusilla's attention to where she and Irma were standing mere feet from Umberto, their brooms at the ready.

It was a curious state of affairs when a laugh began bubbling up Drusilla's throat.

"Not to point out the obvious," she called, "but I don't believe you need to be brandishing those brooms. Mr. Zambarello doesn't look to be much of a threat right now."

"We're not considering giving him a few wallops because he's a threat," Irma returned. "We're considering that because he had the audacity to get into a bout of fisticuffs with our dear Rhenick."

Umberto swiped a hand over a face that was just as, if not more, battered than Rhenick's. "He started the fight."

"Because?" Irma pressed.

"It was of little consequence as I merely stated what everyone is saying around town about Rhenick and Miss Merriweather—that being that he's resorted to flattery to gain her trust, something Miss Merriweather is obviously unfamiliar with given that . . ."

"Given that what?" Irma demanded when Umberto suddenly stopped talking, undoubtedly because Rhenick had taken to emitting a bit of a growl as well as balling his hand into a fist.

Umberto dashed a strand of hair out of his eyes before he lumbered to his feet and presented Irma with the slightest of bows. "I fear it won't benefit me in the least to continue with this conversation, Mrs. . . . ?"

"Merriweather," Irma supplied. "Drusilla's mother."

Umberto's eyes—or rather, the one that wasn't as swollen—narrowed on Irma. "May I dare hope, since I've learned there are no gentlemen in the picture with your family, that you're the head of your household and are actually the lady I should have been seeking out all along in order to discuss the more-than-fair offer I'm willing to make for the Merriweather castle and grounds?"

Irma narrowed her eyes right back at the man. "I should say not, as Ottilie gave the castle to Drusilla and Annaliese. However . . ." Irma tilted her head. "I find myself curious as to whether you're the Mr. Zambarello who has five unwed daughters?"

Wariness flickered through Umberto's eyes. "I do have five daughters, although there's no reason for you to say *unwed* in what sounded like an accusatory tone of voice."

"If my tone is accusatory, it's simply because I was told that your daughters are known to be somewhat rambunctious, and as such, may require you to settle overly large dowries on them, which I'm going to assume is why you've seemingly lost your mind since you thought it was a good idea to arrive here unannounced." Irma lifted her chin. "You then apparently proceeded to insult my daughter, prompting Rhenick to defend her, which then resulted in the two of you engaging in a brawl, which I believe speaks very highly of Rhenick's character, while leaving yours in tatters."

Umberto lifted his chin, quite like Irma had just done. "But again, I didn't throw the first punch."

"But you threw the first insult, which certainly isn't something you should be proud of. That type of behavior, if you're unaware, is considered vulgar in polite circles, and it certainly doesn't set a very good example for all those daughters of yours because they might very well conclude that the insults they may someday suffer are not out of line since their very own father doesn't hesitate to serve them up to uncooperative women."

Wilhelmine stepped directly beside Irma and shook her broom at Umberto. "I'm going to suggest you beg dear Drusilla's pardon now, as well as Rhenick's, and then take your leave, but only after I have your word that you won't be bothering the Merriweathers again about this property."

"Do you honestly believe I'm going to agree to that when I know without a shadow of a doubt that Loughlin MacSherry won't be abandoning his desire to secure this land anytime soon, nor will Giacomo Caggianni, not after Miss Merriweather lodged a bullet in his right-hand man."

Drusilla winced. "The whole lodging of a bullet was completely unintentional."

"Doesn't matter," Umberto argued. "Giacomo will take the shooting as a direct insult, and you mark my words, he'll be more determined now than ever to find a way to get this property."

"He can try all he wants," Irma snapped before Drusilla could respond, "but we Merriweathers are quite determined to open a much-needed academy for young ladies. And . . ." She drew herself up. "While all of you less-than-scrupulous developers seem to believe a household filled with ladies will be easily intimidated, know that Merriweather ladies are made of much sterner constitutions than I believe even we realized. As such, we're formidable enemies to make, especially when none of us will suffer the slightest qualm over putting to use any of our many unusual weapons—one of which is a rather terrifying cannon that will be waiting right inside the gate should you choose to not heed my advice and decide to show your face here again."

Twenty-Five

I'm not convinced that today was the best day to introduce me, Annaliese, my mother, and Seraphina to the members of your church, given that you still look like you've recently been in a brawl, even though it's been a week and a half since your tussle with Umberto," Drusilla said, causing Rhenick to turn her way. His eyes took to crinkling at the corners, something that drew attention to the fact that the skin surrounding those eyes was still tinged with various shades of yellow, green, and bruised-blue.

"Everyone in the congregation has already heard about my run-in with Umberto, and I wouldn't be surprised if everyone throughout Chicago has heard the particulars about that day, as well." Rhenick grinned. "Truth be told, I also wouldn't be a bit surprised if you find yourself inundated with offers to watch over you from the majority of the congregation, including quite a few of the ladies who are appalled that your welcome to Chicago has been anything but welcoming."

Drusilla smiled. "And while it's lovely to learn there are so many people willing to lend me their assistance, we haven't been paid a visit from a single developer after that dreadful day, so I'm hoping developers in general have decided to leave me alone from this point forward."

"A valid hope, and one that may come to fruition as Norbert told me that he heard down at the Mead and Vittles that word on the street is that the Merriweather castle is now filled with ladies who aren't afraid to defend their property, even if their abilities with weapons are somewhat questionable."

"Seraphina's an expert shot."

"True, but I don't think anyone took note of the shots she fired to purposefully chase men away. All anyone really noticed was Annaliese firing a less-than-accurate Frankenau purse at will, and you shooting Giacomo Caggianni's right-hand man when you realized he was heading your way."

"I was aiming for over his head."

"Which clearly suggests you might want to consider acquiring a pair of spectacles, but at least you didn't permanently maim that man. Norbert told me Caggianni's man only suffered a superficial flesh wound and barely needed any stitches to set him to rights."

Drusilla's eyes widened. "He needed stitches?"

Rhenick leaned closer to her. "If you're feeling guilty about that, allow me to remind you that the man was encouraging the driver to run you over."

"I suppose he was at that, so I'll desist with the guilt and concentrate instead on the unexpected positive outcomes of that particular day, one of which was, of course . . ." She sent a discreet nod to where Irma and Wilhelmine were sitting in the first pew, their heads bent closely together as they whispered back and forth, something they'd taken to doing ever since the attempted siege of the castle.

It was curious, the friendship that had sprung up between Irma and Wilhelmine, who'd taken to enjoying hours in each other's company, something that seemed to be a novel experience for Irma, who'd always surrounded herself with ladies of the Four Hundred but had never seemed to relish the time she spent with them.

It was also curious that Irma was now fully supportive of the academy idea and had even volunteered to teach a few classes, in addition to the lessons she'd agreed to give to Wilhelmine. She'd also taken to embracing a very unexpected motherly protective stance ever since the gate incident, as everyone was referring to it, a stance that seemingly required her to carry a pistol with her at all times, which was somewhat unnerving as she was experiencing as much success with her aim as Drusilla was.

"Why do you think our mothers keep turning around and smiling at us?" Rhenick asked, drawing Drusilla from her thoughts.

"Since you've been surrounded by the feminine set ever since you were born, I'm sure you know exactly why they're doing that." She lowered her voice. "They've got marriage on their minds—more specifically, a marriage between the two of us."

"I wasn't sure if you'd picked up on that."

She waved that aside. "Please. My mother has had marriage in mind between the two of us ever since you told me I needed to marry you. And, if I'm not mistaken, your mother has had marriage in mind ever since you told her you'd met an extraordinary woman."

He shifted on the bench. "If you believe that, you must also believe that my mother wasn't completely upfront with you regarding why she was offering you the assistance of Whittenbecker and Company."

"I don't think she was being dishonest," Drusilla countered. "Wilhelmine definitely wants me to open the academy, as that will benefit your sisters. Nevertheless, she's a mother with an eligible son, so the very idea that you met a woman you found interesting wasn't going to simply slip out of her mind. To give her credit, though, she's shown a lot of restraint for a marriage-minded mother, as she's not even broached the topic of marriage with me since the day we first met."

"I wouldn't let your guard down," Rhenick muttered.

"My guard is firmly in place because our mothers are obviously in cahoots. That idea was solidified earlier because after I offered to take Wilhelmine's place today on the organ, both she and my mother immediately took to objecting with the most nonsensical excuses, done so because they obviously want me to remain sitting by your side throughout the service."

She sent her mother, who was once again beaming a smile at her, a slight wrinkling of her nose before she squared her shoulders. "They'll eventually accustom themselves to the idea that we're simply meant to be good friends, especially when I've gotten the distinct impression, as you've not blundered about with me at all during the past month, that you realized I was right when I told you that you'd misinterpreted who I was during our very first encounter and that I'm not extraordinary in the least but merely ordinary."

His brows drew together. "Not that I want to argue with you, but I feel compelled to point out that you're certainly not ordinary. What ordinary lady wouldn't have suffered a fit of the vapors when under attack from some of the most dangerous men in Chicago?"

"I would have been run over for certain if I'd indulged in some vapors during that troubling event, which suggests my refusal to faint dead away was more an act of necessity than extraordinariness."

"Just because you reacted out of necessity doesn't mean you're an ordinary woman—far from it."

Heat immediately took to crawling up Drusilla's neck to settle on her face because she was not a lady accustomed to receiving compliments. Rhenick, however, seemed to find ways to compliment her on an almost hourly basis, and his compliments weren't of the practiced variety, like she'd heard Elbert extend to every woman except her, but the genuine kind that he simply threw into conversations as if they were of little consequence.

To her, they were of great consequence indeed.

He once told her that her hair reminded him of warm and rich chestnuts that were roasting over the fire. He'd then mentioned another time that he'd never seen eyes as lovely as hers, and then told her the very next day that while he knew it was rather untoward to ever mention a lady's figure, he liked how she'd abandoned the hourglass look most ladies were sporting, preferring her natural shape instead.

In all honesty, she'd come to believe that Rhenick Whittenbecker had the soul of a poet and . . . she'd come to realize that he wasn't using descriptive phrases or outlandish compliments because he wanted to get his hands on her property but simply because he seemed to genuinely like her and also seemed to genuinely get pleasure out of making her smile—or blush, as was frequently the case.

It was odd to discover she was even a lady prone to blushing, as she'd never made a point of blushing before, probably because she'd never been a lady who drew anyone's notice—until she'd met Rhenick.

He seemed to notice everything about her, and, if she were honest with herself, she'd begun noticing quite a lot about him as well—such as the fact that he was a sincerely caring man who was wonderful with his mother and who genuinely seemed to enjoy spending time with his many sisters, who clamored for his attention, something that never seemed to bother him, even if his sisters were interrupting his work.

"While I'm sure you're aware that I adore my youngest sister, Coraline," Rhenick suddenly said, leaning so close to her that his shoulder brushed against hers, "in the spirit of preparing you for the opening of your academy, I feel compelled to direct your attention to where Coraline and her somewhat motley band of friends are not exactly comporting themselves as young ladies should."

She turned her attention to where Rhenick was now oh-so-discreetly nodding and considered Coraline and her gaggle of friends, all the girls in the process of chatting like mad, seemingly unconcerned that they were in church and certainly weren't making a point to whisper.

Drusilla's eyes began narrowing when Norma Jean McCormick, one of Coraline's best friends, and a girl Drusilla had only just met before entering the church that morning, took the fan she was waving about and gave the girl sitting to her right, one Velma Chickering, a rap on the head with it.

Considering Drusilla had never once rapped anyone on the head with a fan, nor had she ever witnessed any of her contemporaries doing that, it was becoming more than obvious that she was going to have her work cut out for her once the girls started attending her academy.

It was also obvious that the academy might very well start off as a school for wayward girls after all, since there was a very good chance the majority of the girls were going to be exactly like Coraline and her friends.

She turned to Rhenick. "I never thought I'd say this, but I'm now thinking it's fortunate I've been told I already possess the look of a stern headmistress, which I'm now going to use to my advantage as much as possible as an intimidation tactic. Hopefully that tactic works reasonably well since I get the feeling I'm going to be facing quite a few challenges in the coming weeks."

"You hardly have the appearance of a stern headmistress, and I have no doubt you'll be up for all of those challenges," Rhenick countered. "In fact, I say it'll only take you a week to get everyone settled down and ready to learn how to become proper young ladies."

Drusilla glanced back to Coraline, who was directing her attention to a young gentleman who was sitting in the pew across from her.

That Coraline was in the process of fluttering her fan rapidly in front of her face suggested she was attempting to flirt with the man, the fluttering also suggesting that Coraline might benefit from a proper lesson in fan etiquette, as rapid fluttering of a fan in front of a lady's face was a discreet way for a lady to allow a gentleman to know she was engaged and sufficiently off the market, a message she doubted Coraline wanted to impart.

"While I appreciate your optimism," Drusilla began, ignoring the idea that heat had settled on her cheeks the moment he'd not hesitated to state she didn't resemble a headmistress, "I think it's going to take me at least the duration of the summer to get that particular group of young ladies to behave, and in all honesty, it may take me longer than that."

That notion was immediately reinforced when Norma Jean whipped open her fan again, smacking poor Velma Chickering straight in the nose. And even though it appeared as if the smacking was accidental, Velma had clearly had enough abuse as she didn't hesitate to give Norma what looked like a painful poking in the stomach with her fan in return.

"You might be right that my time frame was off regarding getting the girls in hand," Rhenick muttered before he gave her arm a soothing pat. "But misbehaving girls aside, Mother seems to be on the move, so you might want to prepare yourself for organ music like you've never heard played before."

Before Drusilla had a chance to brace herself, a blast of the organ pipes reverberated around the room, leaving her with the realization that truer words had never been spoken. And while it did appear as if Wilhelmine was simply running through a few scales to warm up her fingers, they were the most unusual scales Drusilla had ever heard.

"Maybe, for the sake of the congregation's ears, I should take over, no matter that our mothers want us to remain seated together," Drusilla said, pitching her voice a little louder than she normally would during a church service on account that was the only way Rhenick could hear her over the racket Wilhelmine was now making.

"Seraphina seems to have beaten you to that," Rhenick called

197

back as he nodded to where Seraphina was hurrying down the aisle, where she promptly slid onto the organ bench next to Wilhelmine.

Wilhelmine immediately stopped playing and gave Seraphina a pat on the cheek, sending the spectacles Seraphina had decided to pair with a cast-off gown of Aunt Ottilie's she'd found stuffed in one of her aunt's many wardrobes a little off-kilter.

"Mother appears to be fine with Seraphina taking over," Rhenick said. "But speaking of Seraphina, Eloise told me earlier, after Seraphina arrived here sporting a wig and looking quite unlike herself, that her change in appearance stems from some type of family situation, but I readily admit that wasn't much of an explanation."

"I'm afraid I can't say much more about the matter because Seraphina hasn't elaborated to me about her decision to disguise herself, except to say that she doesn't want to risk having anyone recognize her while she's out and about in Chicago. From what I gathered, if that information were to travel back to New York, it might cause some difficulties for her."

Rhenick frowned. "Isn't she worried that she'll be recognized once she begins teaching classes at the academy?"

"She intends to continue wearing a disguise while classes are in session," Drusilla said. "With that said, though, know that Seraphina isn't concerned that your family knows what she truly looks like, or that her name is Seraphina Livingston, because she trusts all of you to keep her secret. She simply doesn't want that to get out to the students and their families. That's why we've agreed that I'll simply introduce her as Miss Livingston and never mention her given name is Seraphina, which she thinks, paired with her less-than-noteworthy new appearance, will keep her safely away from her stepmother for a while."

Rhenick's brow furrowed. "Why is this the first I'm hearing about what sounds like Seraphina's evil stepmother?"

"Seraphina hasn't wanted to talk about her circumstances, and I haven't pressed her on the matter. All I know is that she needs to lay low for a while, although this development of her assuming a new look suggests she's involved in something far more troubling than a mere misunderstanding with her stepmother."

"The fact that she's added numerous moles to her face definitely suggests it's more than a misunderstanding as I don't know any young lady who'd want to do that unless absolutely necessary." He frowned. "Do you think she'd be receptive to having me look into whatever trouble she's avoiding in New York the next time I'm there?"

Before Drusilla had an opportunity to answer or appreciate the fact that Rhenick hadn't hesitated to offer his assistance, Seraphina began playing, Wilhelmine staying directly beside her on the organ bench to turn the pages of the hymnal, which effectively ended any and all conversation.

As the music flowed through the church—and music that rivaled that of anything played at the Academy of Music back in New York, given Seraphina's expertise—Drusilla settled back against the hard pew, allowing her thoughts to drift.

It wasn't surprising when her thoughts settled on how the castle was almost ready to open its door as a bona fide academy for young ladies, their targeted opening date being a mere week away—as long as nothing dastardly interrupted that target, such as ghosts making appearances again or unscrupulous men trying to force their way onto the property with their weapons at the ready.

Her thoughts came to an abrupt end when she realized Seraphina was finishing up on the organ and Reverend Michaelson, whom she'd met the previous week when he'd paid a visit to welcome her to Chicago, was walking to the pulpit. Once the reverend completed his opening prayer, Drusilla settled back against the hard pew and spent the next hour enjoying the service, something she'd missed over the past few months.

After the entire congregation finished the last hymn, Seraphina taking over on the organ again, Drusilla took Rhenick's arm and walked with him out of the church, her hold on his arm tightening when she realized everyone in the churchyard seemed to be looking her way.

"I'm quite unused to being the object of so much attention," she whispered once they reached the sidewalk, finding herself thankful when Rhenick gave her arm a reassuring squeeze and didn't relinquish his hold.

"And here I would have thought you were accustomed to attention since you spent so many years in the midst of this country's highest society."

"I spent most of my time as a member of the Four Hundred lingering on the sidelines, until Father died, and then I spent my time confined to our house on Washington Square, or occasionally going for a few rides in Central Park with my ex-fiancé, whose name I've decided will no longer pass through my lips."

Rhenick's eyes crinkled at the corners. "A fitting justice for that man if you ask me, but tell me this—how did you, as an engaged lady, and before you went into mourning, find yourself lingering at any society events? Where was this man who shall no longer be named during that time?"

Her lips curved. "If you must know, Mr. Nameless always danced the obligatory two dances with me, as well as sat beside me at dinner. However, he usually arranged it so there was a sparkling lady on the other side of him during any given meal, one who'd undoubtedly earned the title of Diamond of the First Water, and one Mr. Nameless would devote his complete attention to."

Rhenick shook his head. "It's little wonder you've vowed never to marry, but do know that not all men are like your former Mr. Nameless, who sounds like a complete scoundrel, and also sounds as if he's a gentleman who never deserved a lady like you in the first place."

For the briefest of seconds, it felt quite as if she and Rhenick were completely alone in the churchyard, until a group of ladies sauntered past them, murmuring hellos to Rhenick, their faces wreathed in smiles and their lashes fluttering madly about.

Reality returned in a trice when Rhenick inclined his head to the ladies in question, but then, when he immediately returned his attention to her and settled a charming smile on her—and not on the beautiful ladies who'd just attempted to draw his attention away from her—her world suddenly turned somewhat topsy-turvy and for good reason.

She'd never, not once in her entire life, captured a man's attention to such an extent where other ladies, and far more attractive ladies at that, couldn't distract him from paying attention to her, but that's exactly what seemed to have just happened.

"I'm so relieved I wasn't responsible for massacring the hymns today," Wilhelmine said as she, along with Irma, took that moment to stroll up and join them. "I'm also happy to report that Seraphina has agreed to play every Sunday until we find a permanent organ player."

Before Drusilla could add that she'd be happy to fill in as well, the crowd of churchgoers suddenly parted right in front of them, revealing a lady dressed in a tailored tweed jacket, the type that gentlemen normally wore, although she'd paired her jacket with a slim skirt instead of trousers.

Curiously enough, the lady was wearing a hat that resembled a helmet, one Drusilla thought might be called a pith something or other, but before she could consider the hat matter further, the woman began waving madly in their direction before she charged right for them, her charging causing a few members of the congregation to scurry out of her way.

"Yoo-hoo!" the lady called out before she set her sights on Irma, bustled up directly in front of her, and then did the unthinkable.

She reached out and pulled Irma into a hug, a departure from proper etiquette if there ever was one, that departure increasing when she suddenly gave Irma what appeared to be an honest-to-goodness squeeze.

Twenty-Six

Y ou don't know how long I've been waiting for the day when I'd finally get to meet you in person, Mrs. Merriweather," the woman said, completely ignoring that Irma had gone stiff as a board once all the embracing started. "Truth be told, I was planning on visiting the castle tomorrow because I only learned yesterday, when I arrived in Chicago after a lengthy absence, that the New York Merriweather family had come to town. Why, you could have knocked me over with a feather when someone told me who you were when I spotted you across the church. But how wonderful to find you attending the same church service I just happened to be attending as well. I'm ever so happy you're here, as I get to greet you a day earlier than expected, although I am sorry it's under these circumstances."

The woman gave Irma another squeeze, eliciting an honest-to-goodness grunt from Irma in return, which the woman blatantly ignored as she continued hugging her. "With that said, and before I get down to paying my condolences, let's agree here and now to abandon all formality right from the start, which means I insist that you call me Fenna."

"Informality might be rather premature," Irma said, her voice muffled because Fenna was continuing to hug her. "I have no idea who you are, and am now going to suggest you abandon this unexpected hugging business before *I* do something unexpected, such as scream."

The lady, Fenna Somebody-or-Other, froze for the briefest of seconds before she released her hold on Irma, took a step backward, then whipped off her hat, and, oddly enough, presented Irma with a bow. "I do beg your pardon, Mrs. Merriweather, as I'm sure I must have startled you with my enthusiastic greeting, which must be exactly why you haven't realized who I am—I'm Fenna, Fenna Larkin—your sister-in-law's very best friend as well as assistant."

When Irma began looking as if she were at a complete loss, a clear sign she had no recollection of Ottilie ever mentioning this woman, Drusilla stepped forward and cleared her throat, then cleared it again, and louder this time because Fenna hadn't bothered to turn toward her. Instead, she was keeping her attention firmly centered on Irma, smiling brightly, as if the smiling was going to result in Irma recalling who she was and then exclaiming how delighted she was to finally meet Fenna as well.

"Might you be the assistant who Norbert has mentioned to me, and who traveled to Egypt with my aunt?" Drusilla asked, stepping closer to Fenna in the hopes the lady might realize she was speaking to her.

Fenna, thankfully, turned to Drusilla and then raised a hand to her throat. "On my word but you're Drusilla, of course." She took a step closer. "Ottilie told me all about you and your sister, and she showed me miniatures of you two. Why, you're just as darling as your miniature suggested."

Since Drusilla knew exactly what miniature Aunt Ottilie would have shown Fenna, as well as knew it was not a likeness that was overly complimentary, she was a little surprised to be deemed a darling, but before she could summon up a thank-you to a rather dubious compliment, Fenna was looking over Drusilla's shoulder, her ever-present smile dimming ever so slightly.

"I don't see Annaliese anywhere, although I thought I saw her red hair from where I was sitting in the back of the church. Do not tell me that she's already left to return to the castle, as I was anxious to ask her if she's had any additional encounters with those pesky plume hunters your aunt mentioned she seems to enjoy tangling with."

It was becoming evident that Fenna had not been exaggerating about Aunt Ottilie mentioning her nieces, and often from the sound of things.

"I'm sure Annaliese will be along directly, as we rode here together, although I'm not certain it would be wise to mention plume hunters to her while we're still at church because there's many a lady sporting feathers today, which I'm sure Annaliese has also noted. She's most likely already in a questionable state about that, and that state could turn somewhat contentious if you remind her of the plume hunters who were responsible for collecting the feathers on all the hats here today."

A smack to her forehead was Fenna's first response to that. "I do beg your pardon, Drusilla, as you're perfectly right and I should hold my tongue, at least until a more private moment. And how silly of me to think Annaliese had already departed since of course you rode here together, what with how Merriweather Castle, as our dear Ottilie always called it, isn't exactly a hop, skip, and a jump away. But speaking of dear Ottilie, allow me to say how very sorry I am to learn, although I've had my suspicions for a while now, that she's no longer with us."

Drusilla frowned. "Why would you think she's no longer with us?"

Fenna returned the frown. "Because you and your family are here, and gossip has it that you and your sister are the new owners of Merriweather Castle."

"I'm afraid that gossip, which began permeating through

town after I shared a few snippets regarding our arrival in Chicago with a hack driver who rushed right out to tell everyone, might have gotten a little mangled in the telling, as it isn't completely accurate."

"Are you saying that you and Annaliese aren't the new owners of Merriweather Castle?" Fenna asked.

"We're the owners, but we're not the owners because we received word of Aunt Ottilie's passing. She gave us the castle when she was in New York before she left on her last adventure."

A furrow appeared on Fenna's forehead. "She gave it to you?"

"Indeed."

"Ottilie never mentioned a thing to me about giving away her castle," Fenna muttered as she began tapping a finger against her chin, stilling mid-tap. "I find myself curious, though, as to whether—if rumor actually has it correctly and you're considering turning the castle into an academy for ladies—if this was Ottilie's idea. She was, after all, a supporter of advancing women's rights through education."

Drusilla inclined her head. "Opening an academy isn't a rumor, although it wasn't an idea Aunt Ottilie and I discussed. Aunt Ottilie told me that she wanted to keep the castle in the Merriweather family, and after Annaliese and I swore we would never sell it, my aunt handed us the keys and here we are." She caught Fenna's eye. "I'm quite relieved to hear that you thought the academy was Aunt Ottilie's idea, though, as that reinforces my feeling that she would approve of what Annaliese and I are doing, something I've pondered quite a bit of late. I'll now set aside any qualms regarding turning the castle into an academy I had, and simply concentrate on all the tasks I need to complete before we open the doors in a week, perhaps two, to almost sixty young ladies for an abbreviated summer session."

Fenna blinked—several times, in fact. "You're opening *next* week?"

"Hopefully, but that depends on if we stay on schedule, although classes will only be held three days a week since it is summer."

Fenna shoved her hat back on her head. "That still seems quite industrious of you because, forgive me if I'm wrong, but didn't you land in Chicago a mere month ago? I would think it would take much longer to turn the castle into a school, what with all the artifacts Ottilie has lying about in different rooms."

"That's exactly what I thought as well, until . . ." Drusilla turned and nodded to Rhenick. "My sister and I secured the services of Whittenbecker and Company, and I'm pleased to report that they've been very thorough, as well as fast, with getting the castle in order. The Whittenbecker family has also kindly lent me the services of their entire staff, and that staff has been working diligently to relocate Aunt Ottilie's artifacts to the lower levels of the castle, freeing up space for classrooms."

Fenna settled her attention on Rhenick, her eyes widening a second later. "Mr. Whittenbecker. My goodness but I didn't realize you were standing there. It's been a long time, although I doubt you remember me, as we only met briefly when you paid a visit to Ottilie well over two years ago. I was on the staircase, carrying a heavy urn filled with sand we'd collected in Egypt, which is why I only nodded to you after Ottilie told you who I was and then continued on my way to the mummy room."

Rhenick considered her for a moment, then, quite as if one of Thomas Edison's lightbulbs suddenly went on in his head, he smiled. "Miss Fenna, of course I remember meeting you now, although forgive me for faltering for a second, a direct result of the fact that the one time we met, you were wearing a turban."

"Good heavens, but you're right." Fenna thrust out her hand to him, which he immediately took, but before he could kiss it, she gave his hand a rather vigorous shake.

"As you can see," she continued as she kept what seemed to

be a firm grasp of his hand, "I've abandoned my love for turbans and have taken to wearing a pith helmet instead because people in Chicago were making a point to frequently remark on my turbans, and not in a positive fashion."

Rhenick's eyes twinkled. "I find it difficult to believe that a pith helmet doesn't garner some remarks as well."

Fenna's eyes twinkled back at him as she finally released his hand. "Oh, it does, but a pith helmet suggests I'm a lady of adventure, so I don't mind the remarks this particular hat attracts."

"A delightful way of choosing to view the gossip about you in town, but tell me this. After we were introduced, I remember Ottilie telling me that she had you hard at work cataloging the artifacts she'd brought home over the years, a task I have to imagine was rather daunting."

"Oh, it was daunting, and was exactly why I didn't accompany Ottilie on her last adventure." She leaned closer to him. "Not that this is well-known, but Ottilie had decided to write a book about her collection, as well as her life, and that right there is why she wanted me to devote the months she was originally intending to be gone to finishing up the cataloging and completing the notes pertaining to where she'd found the pieces in her collection."

She shook her head. "If I finished all that before she returned, she then wanted me to begin organizing notes that were more personal in nature so that she could include colorful tidbits about the unusual events she encountered while uncovering some of her artifacts."

"How were you expected to do that when Aunt Ottilie wasn't around to tell you her stories about those tidbits?" Drusilla asked.

Fenna glanced around, then edged closer to Drusilla. "Your aunt kept personal journals, and she gave me a few of them to read right before she left, claiming I'd find them riveting reads."

Rhenick smiled. "I imagine Miss Ottilie's journals were riveting reads indeed."

"And one would have thought that would've been the case except the three journals she lent me before she left were more along the lines of tepid, but only because she gave me the first three journals she'd ever written—when she was ten." Fenna returned Rhenick's smile. "And while Ottilie did seem to enjoy an unconventional year when she was ten, the antics she got up to were rather mild."

She switched her attention back to Drusilla. "I have, though, been itching to learn how Ottilie's life played out over the years because she neglected to give me additional journals before she left town."

"Why didn't you simply help yourself to additional journals, as it was at Aunt Ottilie's bequest that you gather this information so she could publish a book after she returned?"

Fenna shrugged. "Helping myself to additional journals wouldn't have been untoward, as you're quite right and it was at Ottilie's request. However, I decided I needed to get the more mundane and dry research surrounding the artifacts out of the way first, which is why I repaired to the small cottage I keep outside the city since I knew that being away from Ottilie's staff would keep me from becoming distracted from the work at hand."

"You didn't live in the castle?" Drusilla asked.

"I did not because Ottilie was a lady who enjoyed her space, and I didn't want to put a strain on our friendship, although I did sleep over at the castle if Ottilie wanted to work late." Fenna took to fiddling with the brim of her hat again. "But to return to why I didn't help myself to Ottilie's journals—it took me almost seven months to assemble the notes on the artifacts. During those months, I had no reason to stop by the castle, which is why I had no idea that strange occurrences had begun to happen there, nor did I know that the staff, save Norbert, had up and left due to those strange occurrences."

Her lips thinned ever so slightly. "Imagine my surprise to hear all of that, and not hear it from inside the castle, where one would expect to hold an important conversation, but through the wrought-iron spindles of the front gate. That was where I then learned I would not be able to retrieve any of Ottilie's journals that day as I was being denied access to the castle and grounds, and that access wasn't up for debate."

Twenty-Seven

rusilla allowed that disclosure to settle for a moment before she frowned. "Who took it upon themselves to deny you access to the castle?"

A bit of a sniff was Fenna's first response to that. "I would think that's obvious as I mentioned everyone was gone, save Norbert."

"*Norbert* wouldn't let you through the gate?" Drusilla pressed.

"He would not."

"Did he give you an explanation as to why you were being denied entrance?"

"He was somewhat sketchy about everything, merely saying that William Baumgartner instructed him, after Ottilie's staff up and left, to deny anyone access to the castle from that point forward. From what little Norbert disclosed, Mr. Baumgartner thought it would be too easy, with no one around but Norbert, for someone to make off with Ottilie's treasures." She caught Drusilla's eye. "Norbert then told me that I could only come in if I were to get express permission from Mr. Baumgartner. The problem with that, though, was when I went to seek out Mr. Baumgartner, I discovered, oddly enough, that he'd left town."

"And you found that odd because . . ."

Fenna's nose wrinkled. "I would think you'd find it odd as well if you consider that the majority of Ottilie's staff had been scared from the property *except* Norbert. He's the one who told me I couldn't get into the castle unless Mr. Baumgartner gave his permission, and then Mr. Baumgartner just happened to no longer be around."

The hair on the nape of Drusilla's neck stood to attention. "Exactly what are you implying?"

"I'm not implying anything. I'm saying that it's curious how Norbert was the only staff member left standing in the castle."

Drusilla rubbed a temple that was beginning to ache. "I find myself wondering why you've decided to tell me this now, instead of making an appointment to speak with me directly after you learned I was in Chicago. Surely you would have assumed I'd want to hear your suspicions about a man who's still roaming around Merriweather Castle, wouldn't you?"

Fenna waved that aside. "I told you. I just returned to the city a few days ago so I didn't know you were here. And while I know I mentioned that I was intending on traveling to the castle to extend my condolences, in all honesty, I wasn't sure how I was going to be able to do that, as Norbert could have very well turned me away at the gate again."

She edged closer to Drusilla. "I certainly didn't know you would be attending church services here today. But if you ask me, this was a fortuitous meeting if there ever was one because, now that I've become aware that you intend to open an academy in the very near future, I feel it's my moral obligation to disclose some of my more worrisome suspicions about Norbert."

"Like what?"

Fenna lowered her voice to practically a whisper. "I think Norbert had something to do with why Ottilie never returned, and I also think he might be behind why Mr. Baumgartner left town."

"What?"

"Try to keep up with me," Fenna muttered. "To be as clear as I possibly can, know that there's a very real possibility that Norbert wanted the castle to himself, and knew if the staff remained, or if I would pop in now and again to work, he'd be unsuccessful finding the treasure he'd obviously learned Ottilie had hidden there."

Drusilla blinked. "Treasure?"

"Indeed. Or rather, a map that Ottilie believed could lead to one of the largest forgotten pirate lairs ever found."

"Aunt Ottilie had a treasure map?"

Fenna frowned. "You haven't run across a large trunk filled with maps, ones that Ottilie spent hours of her time perusing before she left town?"

"I've run across a lot of trunks, but none of them had maps in them."

"How curious, and it leaves me wondering if Norbert may have spirited that particular trunk away to his cottage, as Ottilie's great passion in life was pursuing treasure."

"She pursued treasure?"

"Why do you think Ottilie and I went to Egypt?"

"I would think you went there to view the pyramids."

"Well, of course we viewed the pyramids," Fenna scoffed. "But our main objective was to locate the final burial spot of a pharaoh that was indicated on a map she purchased from a questionable sort in Boston."

Drusilla shot a look to Rhenick, who looked as confused as she felt, before returning her attention to Fenna. "Am I to understand that you and Ottilie found the remains of a pharaoh?"

"Of course not," Fenna didn't hesitate to say. "Ottilie's never found success with any of the maps she's acquired over the years. But to continue with my suspicions, I think Norbert might have decided that Ottilie was on to something real this time and wanted the castle to himself in order to find a copy of the map Ottilie was using on her last adventure."

"Did *you* get the impression Ottilie might have been pursuing clues to a real treasure?"

"I'm always skeptical when it comes to treasure maps, but I will say, if any treasure maps were to have merit, the ones in the trunk we found waiting for us once we returned from Egypt—ones that Captain Harvey, the original owner of the castle, sent to her—were undoubtedly the closest Ottilie had ever seen to the real thing."

She caught Drusilla's eye. "If Ottilie never told you, Captain Harvey was a smuggler back in the day, although I've always thought he might have been a pirate as well. From what little Ottilie told me about the maps in the trunk, Captain Harvey purchased them from a former 'friend,' although I'd bet good money that friend was an old pirate. He then decided to send them to Ottilie because he and your aunt used to discuss maps all the time and your aunt had the spare time, along with the patience, to inspect every map in that trunk."

"Why wouldn't the captain sort through them on his own? I thought he'd retired, which suggests he would have had time to study them as well."

"I asked Ottilie that very same question, and she told me that the captain didn't trust his staff. He did, however, trust Ottilie, hence the reason we returned to the castle and found a trunk stuffed with maps waiting for us."

"Did you ever get an opportunity to study these maps?"

Fenna released a sigh. "Best friend or not, Ottilie was somewhat territorial when it came to treasure maps, so I'm afraid, other than catching a peek at some roughly drawn areas with Xs marked in red, I didn't see anything that might help determine exactly where she went, or what map she might have been perusing, although . . . I think wherever she went, Captain Harvey went with her." She gave a bob of her head. "I know for a fact that Ottilie asked Norbert to send a telegram to Captain Harvey, which means Norbert knew what that telegram said since he placed it for your aunt. And then, after Ottilie received a return telegram from the captain, she began to pack for a new adventure, but she was rather close-lipped, telling me it was a spur-of-the-moment adventure but that she wouldn't be gone more than seven months, eight at the most."

"And you believe that she left on this spur-of-the-moment trip because she thought she'd found a genuine treasure map?"

"Indeed."

"And you also think Norbert knew this and wanted the castle to himself in order to find a copy of this map?"

"Indeed again, and before you ask, know that Ottilie always made copies of her maps, and would leave at least one copy behind in case something went wrong."

"Where would my aunt have left this copy?"

"I would guess she left it in that trunk I already mentioned," Fenna said. "I was hoping she'd given the trunk to William Baumgartner, and so I was going to ask him about it, or at least ask him if he knew where Ottilie had sailed off to, when I went to seek his permission for access to the castle. As I said, though, he'd already left town."

"If I'm understanding correctly, you believe that Norbert's responsible for Aunt Ottilie's disappearance, as well as the disappearance of her solicitor, whom I'm not exactly certain is missing as Rhenick asked the manager of Ottilie's bank to get word to him regarding my arrival in Chicago. That man, if I'm not mistaken, never gave Rhenick the impression he would be unsuccessful getting that word to Mr. Baumgartner."

Fenna arched a brow Rhenick's way. "I suppose the question of the hour now is whether that manager heard back from Mr. Baumgartner."

Rhenick shook his head. "I've not received any word from the manager, but it's not as if much time has elapsed."

Fenna grabbed hold of Drusilla's hand and gave it a squeeze. "I would think the bank would have sent Mr. Baumgartner a telegram, which takes no time at all to be delivered. That he never responded to that telegram suggests that he may very well be missing since I'm sure he would have arrived back in town lickety-split if he knew you were here, or at the very least, sent you a telegram acknowledging that he's aware you're in Chicago."

"A valid point."

Fenna gave Drusilla's hand another squeeze. "Indeed, and that means you can't very well open your academy until you get to the bottom of this nasty business because—what if Norbert hasn't found that trunk yet? That would mean he's still searching the castle for it, and is undoubtedly more than annoyed that you've shown up because he doesn't have unlimited access inside the castle to roam around, searching at his leisure."

She sent Drusilla a knowing look. "Surely you'll agree that it would be highly inappropriate to host young ladies in the Merriweather Castle knowing that you may very well have a possible murderer on the loose, and a murderer who may be responsible for the disappearance of numerous people to date."

Twenty-Eight

Rhenick settled his attention on Drusilla, who'd closed her eyes the moment they began trundling away from the church in the open landau he'd chosen to bring out today, done so because Drusilla had spent most of the past month enclosed in the castle.

There was little doubt that she was just as concerned as he was regarding their recent exchange with Fenna, that idea reinforced when she took that moment to release a sigh.

Drusilla wasn't a lady prone to sighing, but that she was doing so now suggested she was currently revisiting everything Fenna had disclosed, as well as revisiting the fact that Fenna, when Drusilla had suggested she travel with them to the castle in order to get to the bottom of the matter with Norbert, had adamantly refused.

Not only had she refused, she'd told Drusilla that she would only step foot in the castle if Norbert was no longer there, or better yet, if he were safely jailed behind bars, where he'd be incapable of doing away with her exactly like Fenna believed he'd done away with Ottilie.

If all that hadn't been concerning enough, Rhenick, directly after Fenna had accused Norbert of doing away with Ottilie, had spotted the groundskeeper standing on the far side of the churchyard, his eyes narrowed on Fenna. Given that Norbert had last been seen manning the front gate, and had told Rhenick not to worry about the castle as he had the safeguarding of it well in hand, it was clear that something was amiss.

It hadn't taken long before Norbert realized Rhenick had spotted him, but instead of joining them with an explanation regarding why he was at church instead of watching over the castle, Norbert simply turned and melted into the crowd without a word.

"I'm afraid Fenna Larkin is right," Drusilla suddenly said, drawing Rhenick from his thoughts.

"About what?"

"That it would be irresponsible for me to open the academy right now, what with the serious allegations she tossed Norbert's way." She blew out another sigh. "Even if she's way off the mark about Norbert having anything to do with Aunt Ottilie's disappearance, or William Baumgartner's for that matter, the fact remains that both of them are missing. Add in the notion that someone wants everyone to believe the castle is haunted and I can no longer avoid the fact that this is not an opportune time to invite students into a castle that's plagued with issues that could very well turn dangerous."

She caught Rhenick's eye. "You're the one who warned me that there are men out there who'll go to extreme lengths to get what they want, and men who are probably behind the ghost infestation. And while I'm still determined to retain possession of the castle, I can't open the academy in the hopes that it will simply cause all these developers to give up and leave me alone. What if they're just biding their time until my defenses are down? If that's the case, logic suggests they'll turn more threatening, which means that until we sort out all these mysteries, which seem to be stacking up around us, the Merriweather Academy for Young Ladies will need to be put on hold."

Seraphina, who was sitting beside Drusilla, took off her spectacles and tucked them into her reticule. "I hate to have to say this, given how much work everyone has done to get the castle in order, but until we get to the bottom of everything, I don't believe we should open our doors next week either."

Drusilla turned her attention to Annaliese, who was sitting beside Rhenick. "What do you think?"

Annaliese tucked a strand of hair behind her ear and frowned. "I think a delay is necessary as well. We certainly can't expect to run an academy effectively, something we've never done before in the first place, with so many obstacles plaguing us, the most troubling one being if we were to discover that Norbert truly is a madman and does something mad while classes are in session."

Drusilla arched a brow Rhenick's way. "And you?"

Rhenick raked a hand through his hair. "A delayed opening is probably unavoidable until we get to the bottom of all the mysteries surrounding the castle. I would suggest we start getting to that bottom with Norbert first, since he could be the key to everything."

"I doubt Norbert will confess to being a murderer."

"I doubt that as well, but he's at least a place to start." Rhenick sat forward. "However, before we get down to figuring out our interrogation technique, I need to ask you a rather delicate question."

"You want to know how I'm going to deal with Coraline and her friends' serious breach of etiquette today during the service?"

"That hadn't even crossed my mind. But now that you've broached the topic, how *are* you going to handle my sister?"

Drusilla shrugged. "I'm not going to do anything about it because Coraline is perfectly capable of behaving herself. Today was the first time I've ever witnessed her being overly exuberant."

"That's just because my mother has made a point of keeping an eagle eye on Coraline whenever she's at the castle, but my sister obviously saw an unexpected opportunity today because Mother was preoccupied with Irma, I was sitting next to you, and my father didn't attend service today since he's suffering from a bad cold."

"What did you sitting next to me have to do with Coraline misbehaving?"

Rhenick took a moment to consider the question since he certainly wasn't going to spit out the entire truth of it to her, not when the truth revolved around the idea that his sisters all knew he was still completely enamored with Drusilla, even though she seemed content to merely maintain a friendship with him.

That enamored state, which his sisters brought up every evening when he returned home from the castle, didn't seem to be diminishing in the slightest, although . . . it did seem to be changing, transforming into something deeper, something Eloise, who fancied herself an expert on romance because she made a point of reading Jane Austen, was convinced was love.

Frankly, he was relatively convinced it was love as well, since he found himself looking forward to seeing Drusilla first thing in the morning, enjoyed every minute he spent with her during the day as they worked side by side on different projects, and then found himself thinking about her whenever he left the castle to attend to other projects that demanded his attention. He'd then taken to returning to the castle after he was finished with his other obligations for the day, making it a habit to take over preparing the evening meal from Mrs. O'Sullivan a few nights a week because Drusilla made a point of cleaning her plate every time he made her a meal, something she told him was rather unladylike, but something she couldn't help as his cooking was simply far too delicious for her to resist.

The problem with the whole being-in-love business, though, was this—he had absolutely no idea how to address the matter since Drusilla had asked him to never bring up the topic of marriage again, and he had the sneaking suspicion that she probably meant he was supposed to avoid all areas surrounding matrimony, including any talk of romance.

Granted, he hadn't actually agreed to her request, but he certainly didn't want to give her a reason to end what had turned out to be a delightful friendship, even if he wanted to turn that friendship into so much more.

Seraphina suddenly cleared her throat in a more-than-telling fashion, which snapped him directly out of what were certainly interesting thoughts. Before he could recall what Drusilla had asked him, Seraphina took it upon herself to answer the question for him.

"I'm sure what Rhenick would tell you about Coraline misbehaving while he was sitting beside you is this—she knows, as everyone else does, that the two of you spend the majority of your time discussing new ways to improve the castle, and when you're doing that, you're usually oblivious to everything else around you."

Drusilla wrinkled her nose. "We don't spend all our time discussing the castle. A lot of times we talk about his family, or I tell him about my time in finishing school and exactly how it came to be that I earned the title of Far Too Prim and Proper."

"You were hardly prim and proper when you were dealing with those developers last week, as most exceedingly proper ladies don't shoot at other people," Annaliese pointed out.

"That was an extenuating circumstance."

Annaliese rolled her eyes. "You shot at Rhenick a month ago."

"Another extenuating circumstance," Drusilla said before she turned to him. "Weren't you saying something about having a delicate question you wanted to ask me?"

He grinned. "Not enjoying your sister pointing out specific circumstances where you're not prim and proper?"

"Not in the least," she said, although her eyes were twinkling ever so slightly. "So, to avoid additional examples where I've set aside my usual adherence to proper decorum, what was your question?"

His grin faded. "I wanted to know if you'll be left facing another dire financial situation if you're forced to delay the opening of the academy, as I know you've been counting on tuition money to set your finances to rights."

She worried her lip for a second. "That is a concern, but I believe I'll have enough money to make do until we can safely open the academy."

He caught her gaze. "If you find that you can't make do, I'll be more than happy to extend you a loan."

She sent him a rather wobbly smile. "And while that's very kind of you, know that I won't be taking you up on your offer, as I have the sneaking suspicion you'd refuse to accept repayment from me since you've been a little vague about agreeing to allow me to reimburse you for the cost of all the supplies and labor you've incurred fixing up the castle. To remind you, I'm quite determined to learn how to become self-sufficient. But I do thank you for the offer."

Since there was no doubt he *would* refuse repayment, and little doubt she wouldn't react well if he blundered about yet again and blurted out what he really wanted to say—that her financial troubles would be over if she'd simply marry him— Rhenick settled for sending her an inclination of his head as Seraphina sat forward.

"You wouldn't have to set aside your goal of becoming self-sufficient if someone would simply point me in the direction of a reputable jeweler, and I could finally get around to selling some of my mother's jewelry," Seraphina said. "I'm perfectly happy to invest in a venture I know will eventually be a great financial success."

"You're not selling your late mother's jewelry because we're not going to delay the opening of our academy indefinitely." Drusilla lifted her chin. "I fully intend to swing those doors wide open come September, which means we need to concentrate our efforts on solving every mystery connected with the castle once and for all, and we need to solve those by the end of August."

Before Rhenick could ask how Drusilla thought any of them would be capable of solving a single mystery, let alone several, the landau began to slow as it approached the castle gate. Riley Murphy, the Merriweathers' one and only stable boy, waved to them from the other side as he rattled a set of keys in his hand and went about unlocking the gate.

"It seems as if Norbert didn't leave the church in such a hurry because he was anxious to return to his post," Drusilla said as Riley swung the gate open. As he stepped aside to make room for the landau, Drusilla told Rhenick's coachman to pull the landau over once it cleared the gate. She then hopped to the ground after it came to a stop, not bothering to wait for either of the two groomsmen to assist her—not that they'd made so much as a single move to abandon their positions, probably because both of them had only recently worked in one of the shipyards and weren't exactly familiar with groomsmen duties in general.

After sending his groomsmen, Jimmy Stillwater and Mannie Bracken, a look, which must not have been a very telling look since neither of them made a move to assist Seraphina or Annaliese from the landau either, Rhenick stepped to the ground, offering his hand to the other ladies. He quirked a brow Jimmy and Mannie's way, earning some winces in return as his groomsmen evidently finally realized what they'd been expected to do.

Deciding he'd have to make arrangements for Jimmy and Mannie to spend some time with Mr. Grimsby, who'd been downright militant with teaching other members of Rhenick's staff how to adequately perform their duties, Rhenick strode over to join Drusilla, his attention settling on Riley, who was in the process of shaking his head.

"I wouldn't say, Miss Drusilla, that Norbert originally intended on leaving the castle today, or intended on asking me to mind the gate. That was just a result of what happened after he spotted a carriage parked a ways down Lake Shore Drive. As soon as he saw it, he called over to me—I was helping him prune some roses by the gate—and told me he needed to go investigate a suspicious-looking carriage. Then he fetched his horse and off he went."

"Did he say why he thought it was suspicious?"

"He mentioned something about it might belong to one of those developers, but he never told me what he discovered after he returned here about forty-five minutes ago."

"Norbert's here?" Rhenick asked.

"He was, but only to fetch Ernie as well as a large rucksack, which left me thinking he might not be coming back for quite some time."

⩗ Twenty-Nine ⩘

Leaving with his dog and a rucksack certainly doesn't make Norbert look guilty at all, does it?" Seraphina muttered as they walked up the drive and headed for the castle, everyone having opted to not use the landau as the day was beautiful and there was a lovely breeze blowing in off the lake.

"I hate to jump to conclusions when Norbert has been growing on me, something that took me by surprise after our first disastrous meeting, but . . . innocent people usually don't bolt without an explanation," Drusilla said. "I suppose we can at least be thankful, since Norbert figured out that Fenna Larkin might have told us something unfavorable about him, that we don't have to worry about having a possible murderer roaming around the castle, unless he sneaks back onto the grounds because he's still determined to find that trunk of maps."

"Perhaps the goats should return to the castle, and I think I should put some bells on the ferrets as another way to at least get a heads-up if Norbert does return in a sneaky fashion," Annaliese said right as Irma and Wilhelmine trundled past them in Wilhelmine's phaeton, Rhenick's mother calling over her shoulder that the girls had decided to have lunch with their father and weren't going to join them.

225

"That was very sweet of your sisters to forgo an afternoon by the water in order to spend time with your father," Drusilla said as Wilhelmine and Irma continued barreling up the drive.

"My sisters can turn somewhat hovering anytime one of our parents isn't feeling up to snuff, even though Father assured me this morning that it was just a summer cold," Rhenick said.

Drusilla smiled. "Summer cold or not, it speaks highly of your sisters that they'd want to spend their Sunday with their ailing father instead of seeking out a more amusing afternoon. That suggests your sisters aren't going to give me nearly as much trouble as everyone seems to think they will once the academy opens."

He returned the smile. "I never said they're not exceptional young ladies, but that doesn't mean they're not a little too exuberant at times, and they definitely have a penchant for mischief."

Before Drusilla could respond to that, Irma and Wilhelmine came strolling down the drive to join them, Irma waving a piece of paper in Drusilla's direction.

"Riley forgot to give you this telegram and told me to tell you that it was delivered about an hour ago and that the telegram boy was practically beside himself because it's a telegram from a Pinkerton agent."

"It must be an update from Agent Pearson," Drusilla said, taking the telegram from her mother. "He told me he'd make an effort to check in every month or so, even if there wasn't much to report."

Rhenick moved closer to her. "Is this Agent Pearson looking into Ottilie's whereabouts for you?"

"He's actually searching for the man who absconded with the Merriweather fortune. I haven't even spoken to Agent Pearson yet about Aunt Ottilie, as I was unaware she'd actually gone missing during my last meeting with the Pinkertons before I left New York. Truth be told, I wasn't all that concerned that we hadn't heard from my aunt until we got here since she was never one to adhere to a strict schedule. With that said, though, given all the odd happenstances we've encountered, I think continuing to believe Aunt Ottilie simply got delayed is wishful thinking. That means I'll ask Agent Pearson in my return telegram if he'd be willing to look into Aunt Ottilie's disappearance as well."

Irma's forehead puckered. "I'm not sure why you think a Pinkerton agent would want to take on more work for us, as I didn't think they were even still investigating Sanford and his whereabouts since we don't have the means to pay the exorbitant fees they charge for private cases."

"Do you not recall that I told you, before we left New York, that I'd struck a deal with the Pinkertons and that they agreed to stay on our case on a contingency basis?" Drusilla asked.

"I don't recall that, although I readily admit I was in a rather depressed state for a year or two, but . . ." Irma frowned. "You struck a deal with the Pinkertons?"

"I wasn't very well going to simply walk away and forget what Sanford had done to our family merely because we weren't capable of paying the going Pinkerton rate," Drusilla said. "And before you ask, I offered to pay double the Pinkertons' normal fee, but only if Agent Pearson found Sanford, or more importantly, our money. Since the Pinkertons are well aware that Sanford made off with millions, they didn't hesitate to agree to my terms."

Drusilla smiled. "I imagine Agent Pearson will be agreeable to another contingency case, especially when Aunt Ottilie's also worth millions, having inherited half of the Merriweather fortune from her parents with Father inheriting the other half. It might be difficult, though, to uncover answers, as it appears that Norbert, who I've been told might have had something to do with Aunt Ottilie's disappearance, could have intentionally disappeared, as well."

"Norbert's disappeared?" Irma asked.

"It appears so, but before we delve into the particulars of yet another peculiar afternoon, what say all of us get a little more comfortable?" Drusilla suggested before she urged everyone into the house, then rang for Mrs. O'Sullivan and asked for a coffee and tea cart after she reached the sitting room.

A sliver of warmth crept through her when Rhenick sat down beside her after she'd taken a seat on a settee, but before she could contemplate exactly why she was suddenly feeling a bit flustered, Irma sat down on the other side of her and shifted around in an obvious attempt to get more comfortable, her shifting leaving Drusilla with no choice but to scoot closer to Rhenick, which did nothing for her flustered state as she was now practically pressed up against the man.

"Now that everyone is all nice and cozy," Wilhelmine began as she sent Irma a hint of a wink before she nodded to the telegram Drusilla was still holding, "perhaps you should open that and see what it says."

Taking a second to do exactly that, Drusilla scanned the contents of the telegram, then scanned them again to make certain she'd read it correctly the first time.

"What does it say?" Irma asked.

Drusilla lifted her head. "Sanford was spotted by one of Father's old business associates a few weeks ago in Florida, on the Gulf side, and he also spotted Sanford's yacht docked in a harbor down there."

"I would have thought Sanford would have hied himself off to some obscure Scottish estate since he always talked about living in Scotland someday," Irma said. "What else does it say?"

Drusilla glanced at the telegram again. "Just that Sanford apparently named his yacht . . . the *Revenge*."

Irma's eyes took to flashing before she began drumming her fingers against the arm of the settee, something that was quite unlike her.

"Are you alright?" Drusilla asked.

"It's difficult to say because this is quite a lot for a lady to have to take in." Irma lifted her chin. "Nevertheless, I suppose there's no delaying telling you what I probably should have mentioned months ago, especially not when Sanford has returned to the States, and undoubtedly done so because he's apparently not done with me yet, given what he named his yacht—and with my money, no less."

"You think you're the object of his revenge?"

Irma's lips thinned. "Unfortunately, I don't *think*, I *know* I am, although I had truly hoped his thirst for revenge would have been appeased after he left me destitute, but clearly that's not the case."

Drusilla stilled. "I'm not sure I understand what that means."

"It means that Sanford must have somehow learned I wasn't tossed out into the streets." Irma blew out a breath. "I wouldn't be surprised if he's already on a train, heading this way, or if he's sailing his yacht up some river that'll dump him into Lake Michigan, where he'll then be able to sail practically right outside our front door."

"But showing up here would place Sanford at great risk, although . . . do you think his thirst for revenge might be why he'd be willing to incur such a risk, and if so, why would he want revenge against you in the first place?" Drusilla asked.

Instead of answering her, Irma rose to her feet, moved to the window, pushed aside a heavy velvet curtain, and peered through the glass. When she finally turned, she then stalked her way to a dainty chair done up in a peach floral motif and actually flung herself into it, an unusual action that sent alarm slithering up Drusilla's spine.

"I suppose before I explain anything, I should admit right from the start that I've been less than upfront regarding how it came to be that our fortune went missing," Irma finally said. "Know that I'm not proud of withholding the truth from my own daughters, but know that I did so because . . ." She released a dramatic sigh before she, surprisingly enough, slouched back against the chair. "I believe I'm indirectly responsible for your father's death, and directly responsible for us being left destitute."

Silence was swift until Annaliese walked across the room, snagged hold of a chair, and muscled it over to where Irma was still slouching, plopping down on it a second later. "Father died because he had a weak heart."

"True," Irma didn't hesitate to say. "But what precipitated his heart going out was the apoplectic fit he suffered, apparently brought on after Sanford told your father that he was tired of hiding the fact he was in love with me, had been in love with me since we were children, and knew for a fact that I was in love with him."

Annaliese blinked. "You were in love with Sanford Duncan?"

"I've never been in love with any man, and certainly not with Sanford," Irma countered. "Yes, Sanford and I were good friends growing up, and yes, I knew he was somewhat infatuated with me. However, my father had been in talks with Morton's father from the time I was thirteen, using those talks to hammer out a marriage contract that was acceptable to both families. It was agreed upon that Morton would receive a substantial dowry from my father, as well as the benefit of combining two Knickerbocker families, which I would benefit from, as our social position would be firmly cemented from that day forward, as would be the social position of any children we might have."

"I was almost tossed out of the Four Hundred after rescuing one tiny little roach, which I had the audacity to name, no matter that I'm from a Knickerbocker family," Annaliese pointed out. "That suggests our societal position wasn't firmly cemented in the least."

"Of course it wasn't," Irma agreed. "Not that any of us realized that at the time, but since I was given the cut direct the moment our fortune went missing, something that has certainly been a difficult spoonful of medicine to swallow, I've now realized that it was beyond ridiculous for me to believe that my society position was unshakeable."

She lifted her chin. "To return to my story, though, I should have been more aware that something was odd with Sanford because after your father died and during my first year of mourning, he was overly attentive to me, going to great lengths to distract me from the monotonous manner my days had turned while observing my mourning period."

"Weren't you worried," Drusilla began, "since you said you were aware that Sanford was infatuated with you when you were younger, that his infatuation might return once Father was no longer in the picture, and he was spending so much time with you?"

"I thought Sanford had put his infatuation aside directly after he learned your grandfather had solidified a marriage contract with Morton," Irma said. "Sanford certainly understood how marriages worked between the socially elite, and knew that Morton had more to offer me than he ever would, given that Sanford was not a Knickerbocker, nor was he in line to inherit more than a modest fortune."

Irma gave her temple a rub. "Looking back, I was a complete idiot because, not long after my wedding, Sanford began running across Morton at all his clubs. Before I knew it, Sanford had turned into Morton's most trusted solicitor as well as good friend."

"But where did you fit into this friendship between Father and Sanford?"

"Sanford and I remained friends, and he was the gentleman who frequently escorted me to society events your father didn't care to attend, something that evidently led Sanford to believe I was secretly in love with him."

"It certainly wasn't your fault," Mrs. O'Sullivan began as

she wheeled a coffee and tea cart into the room, followed by Mr. Grimsby, "that Sanford assumed you enjoyed having him escort you around town because you were in love with him. One would have thought he'd have realized that, like most society matrons whose husbands were never around, you were simply looking at his attentiveness as one would look at Mr. Ward McAllister's attentiveness to Mrs. Astor, the only difference being that Ward was married while Sanford was not."

"Perhaps I should have questioned why Sanford never married," Irma muttered. "Although, in my defense, I simply thought he appreciated his bachelor state far too much to consider tying himself down." Her lips thinned. "That belief came to a rapid end, though, when Sanford learned Drusilla and Elbert were delaying their wedding until I was out of mourning. He then took me completely by surprise when he suggested, and over what I thought was simply one of our casual dinner engagements, that we should start planning for a double wedding, with one couple being Drusilla and Elbert and the other being me and Sanford."

"Good heavens," Drusilla breathed.

"Indeed, and to make matters even more concerning, as I was trying to wrap my mind around what had almost sounded like a peculiar proposal, Sanford rose to his feet, moved directly next to me, bent down on one knee, and then declared his never-ending love for me."

Drusilla blinked. "That must have been a bit of a shock for you."

"Well, quite."

"What did you say after Sanford declared his never-ending love for you?" Annaliese asked, sitting forward.

"I'm afraid, given the shock I'd just been delivered, I told him that he needed to discontinue being ridiculous or he was going to ruin the friendship—and only friendship—that was between us." Irma winced. "That was definitely a mistake because Sanford descended into a rant, spouting all sorts of crazy things, starting with how he'd been biding his time to be with me for years, had deliberately befriended Morton as a way to remain close to me, and then admitted what he'd said to Morton the day Morton died, which left me realizing that I was in the presence of a man who seemed to be suffering from some type of delusional state." She caught Drusilla's eye. "That's when I told Sanford that his emotions were obviously getting the better of him, which he didn't appreciate, and had him storming out of our dinner."

"He didn't storm for very long because he continued managing Merriweather affairs to his very great advantage for almost another year," Drusilla pointed out.

"Oh, he was back the next day," Irma said. "Bearing flowers and begging my pardon, telling me that he'd had too much wine the previous night, and that while he would always love me, it truly was a friendship type of love. He then said that he hoped he hadn't ruined our friendship by his behavior the night before."

"And because of that, you let him stay on in his position and never thought to tell either me or Annaliese what had happened?"

Irma's lip quivered. "I know that was a mistake, Drusilla, but in all honesty, I was a little frightened of Sanford at that point. I truly thought it might be for the best if I just didn't say anything about his less-than-acceptable behavior to anyone because I was afraid he'd begin being a little loose with his tongue and twist our relationship around to all the gentlemen in Sanford's many clubs. That would have certainly cast aspersions on a reputation I've always taken great pains to maintain. I also figured it was best not to make any waves since Elbert would be taking over for Sanford in a year, and then I'd be able to distance myself from him. I never in a million years thought that I'd infuriated Sanford to such an extent that he'd decide to completely ruin me to extract his revenge for my not returning his love."

Drusilla reached out and took hold of Irma's hand. "Do you actually believe, though, that he could even now be traveling here with the express purpose of extracting additional revenge against you?"

"Unfortunately, given the months that have elapsed since Sanford sailed away on his yacht, I think he's had time to think the matter through. And, if I'm not mistaken, he's either decided that I'll be more agreeable to marrying him now since I've been shown how difficult life can be without money, or he's decided he needs to assuage his desire for further revenge, which, in his mind, might mean he's decided he needs to get rid of me once and for all."

Thirty

To say that it had been one of the most unusual days Drusilla had ever experienced was saying quite a lot, given the unusualness of her life in general these days. "You're certain you'll be alright for an hour or so while I follow Mother home in her phaeton, then gather up a change or two of clothing before I return?" Rhenick asked, drawing Drusilla's attention as she stood in the hallway, getting ready to do a last sweep of the castle to make certain the doors and windows were locked.

She smiled. "I'll be fine, although I must admit I'm relieved you offered to stay at the castle for the foreseeable future, as it appears we've got quite a few threats being leveled against us right now."

Rhenick returned her smile. "And I must admit that I was surprised you accepted my offer since I know you're determined to embrace your independence these days."

"I was rather surprised myself, until it struck me that I'd be a complete ninny if I declined your kind offer because embracing a sense of independence certainly shouldn't mean I need to refuse assistance or advice from a gentleman simply on principle. Especially not when you've been nothing but helpful to me . . . well, after you decided you might have made a blunder by telling me we needed to get married."

"You'll notice that I haven't broached that topic again, per your demand, although I have been wanting to clarify something with you."

"Clarify?"

"Indeed, and clarify that no matter that I did blunder rather badly the first day we met, I'm well aware of the fact that the manner in which I approached the subject of marriage with you was completely beyond the pale."

"I, ah, see."

Rhenick's eyes took to crinkling at the corners. "I don't think you truly do, so to explain a little more sufficiently, know that, in my mind, marriage proposals should be dealt with properly and not in some willy-nilly fashion. Properly, if you're curious, involves a gentleman presenting himself to his intended on bended knee, where he'll then declare an earnest proclamation of his love for said intended, and then ask her to do him the very great honor of becoming his wife."

For a split second, Drusilla found herself waiting with bated breath to see if Rhenick was about to drop to one knee, and then, when he did no such thing, a smidgen of what felt exactly like disappointment stole through her.

Before she had an opportunity to contemplate the disappointment, though, Rhenick told her he was off to escort his mother home before he turned and strode through a door Mr. Grimsby and Chester, the Whittenbecker butler, were already holding open for him.

"I believe you're now expected to return with Mrs. Whittenbecker back to Rush Street," Mr. Grimsby said to Chester, which had the man giving a bit of a start, as if he'd just recalled he truly was supposed to return with Wilhelmine to the house he actually worked in since his butler lessons were done for the day.

As Chester hurried through the door and down the steps after Rhenick, Drusilla turned to Mr. Grimsby, who gave his face a bit of a rub before he shook his head.

"I'm not certain Chester is ever going to be able to grasp the intricacies of what it takes to become a proper butler, but he fixed the fireplace screen in five minutes flat because he spent years working with iron."

Drusilla grinned. "It does seem as if Chicago might be suffering from a lack of appropriately trained domestic workers. Wilhelmine was saying something to Mother about how Coraline's lady's maid singed off a bit of Coraline's hair the other evening while trying to style it in an upsweep."

"Isn't Coraline the youngest Whittenbecker sister, and as such, too young to be wearing her hair in a chignon just yet?" Mr. Grimsby asked.

"Indeed, but she's rather proficient with persuasion and convinced her lady's maid that the rules of putting your hair up had changed."

"You're certainly going to have some challenges with Mr. Whittenbecker's sisters, but speaking of Mr. Whittenbecker . . ." Mr. Grimsby took one last glance out the door, nodded to where Rhenick was already on Sweet Pea and trailing behind Wilhelmine's departing phaeton, then closed the door and settled a stern gaze on her.

She fought the inclination to fidget when Mr. Grimsby simply continued considering her as his stern expression didn't waver in the least.

"You wanted to say something about Rhenick?" she finally asked.

Mr. Grimsby gave a bob of his head. "Indeed, although I'm not quite certain how I should phrase what I need to say, so perhaps it might be best for me to simply spit out what I, along with Mrs. O'Sullivan, have been thinking."

"Why do I get the distinct impression I'm soon to be in for a lecture?"

"It's not a lecture, my dear, but as you have absolutely no one to advise you, or rather, no one to advise you who possesses years of worldly wisdom as Mrs. O'Sullivan and I do, I feel duty bound to lend you some advice. That advice revolves around this—your determination to keep every gentleman at arm's length will not see you happy, especially not when a man like Rhenick Whittenbecker would be only too happy to get closer to you."

"Rhenick *is* closer to me than any gentleman has ever been because we've become friends."

"After being privy to the conversation you and Mr. Whittenbeck just shared—and no, I won't be apologizing for eavesdropping as I was manning the door and couldn't avoid it—it seems to me as if Mr. Whittenbecker was hedging around a little, waiting to see what your response would be to him explaining that a lady like you deserved a proper proposal, but you made no response at all."

"Because I had no idea *how* to respond."

"You could have said that you've come to the realization that you may have been a little hasty demanding that he never speak about marriage with you again."

Drusilla blinked. "That would have been completely untoward, as well as forward of me, and besides that, I don't recall ever mentioning anything to you or Mrs. O'Sullivan about me changing my mind regarding the whole marriage business."

Mr. Grimsby moved to where he'd left some polishing rags beside a suit of armor. "The only reason you haven't admitted that you might have changed your mind is because you're stubborn and don't want to admit that you were wrong when you decided to lump all gentlemen into a they're-all-cads category. Clearly Mr. Whittenbecker is nothing of the sort, just as, clearly, you like him and enjoy spending time in his company."

"As I already mentioned, we've become friends. Of course I like him."

Mr. Grimsby picked up a cloth, squinted at the suit of armor, then took to polishing what looked to be a fingerprint off it. "In my humble opinion, starting off a relationship as friends is the best way to begin. And how could you not be friends with Rhenick since he's a very impressive man with ambitions that I know will see him eventually become one of the most sought-after architects in Chicago? More importantly than that, though, and what has impressed me and Mrs. O'Sullivan the most about him is that he's incredibly caring and protective of his mother and sisters. He's also a gentleman who respects women in general, and that right there speaks to who he truly is at heart."

Before Drusilla could respond to that, although she wasn't certain how to respond as it certainly hadn't escaped her notice how dedicated Rhenick was to his family, or how he truly did seem to respect her opinions, Seraphina and Annaliese came striding up the hallway, the sound of the bells Annaliese had attached to her ferrets' collars jingling merrily away.

"I think they're going to be alright with the bells," Annaliese said, stopping beside Drusilla and sending a fond look to her ferrets, who were now scampering in and around the suits of armor, looking quite as if they were in the midst of a ferret game of hide-and-seek. "I'm not sure they'll continue to be alright, though, if we bring the goats back into the house, as Fidget doesn't seem to care for goats, nor does she care for Mother Goose because I caught her chasing the goose around the backyard the other day, obviously with the intent of chasing her right off the castle grounds."

Drusilla winced. "Since the last thing we need right now is a goat, ferret, and goose war, we'll keep the goats and goose outside for now, but I am going to have Riley leave the barn door open at night from this point forward since the goats could alert us if anyone takes to snooping around the grounds."

"You think Norbert might come back?" Seraphina asked.

"I'm not sure what to think about Norbert, especially after I found his keys on my office desk."

Seraphina frowned. "That's rather odd."

"Everything about our lives seems odd these days," Annaliese muttered. "But oddness aside, I think I'll go check in with Mother, who curiously enough, seems as if she's in good spirits, even knowing Sanford may be on his way to Chicago to do her in. After that, I'm going to head off to bed, as I could certainly use some sleep."

"I could use some sleep, as well," Seraphina said. "But given that we seem to be incurring more threats against us on an hourly basis, I'm fairly sure, even with Rhenick returning later to take turns with Riley on patrols around the grounds tonight, I'll be sleeping with one eye open."

"One would think," Drusilla began as she headed for the stairs, Seraphina falling into step on her right with Annaliese doing the same on her left, "given how much we've dealt with today, that the odds of us experiencing additional drama would be slim to none, which means we should be able to enjoy a very peaceful night of sleep indeed."

Thirty-One

The sound of her door creaking open had Drusilla waking with a start, but before she could do more than swing her legs over the side of the four-poster bed and jump to the ground, Annaliese was stealing into her room, candle in hand and a finger to her lips.

"What is it?" Drusilla whispered.

"There's a suit of armor strolling around the great hall."

"What?"

"Shhh . . . you heard me. A suit of armor is moseying around the castle."

"How do you know that?"

"I just saw it after hearing the ferrets' bells tinkling. I thought my little darlings were back to chasing one another around the armor, so I went to shush them so they wouldn't wake anyone else up and . . . that's when I saw it, right in the great hall, swinging a mace as it walked about."

"Please tell me you only saw one suit of armor down there."

"That's all I saw, but I wasn't going to investigate the matter by myself, so I might be mistaken about that."

"Let's hope you're not," Drusilla said as she slipped a robe over her nightgown, stuffed her feet into slippers, and headed for the door. "We should probably arm ourselves."

"Already have that covered," Seraphina whispered as she edged into the room, handing Drusilla a pistol, Annaliese a sword, and keeping the blunderbuss for herself. She nodded toward the door. "Shall we?"

It didn't take long to make it down the hallway and tiptoe down the stairs, the sound of the ferrets' hisses and squeals reaching Drusilla's ears the moment she stepped off the last stair.

"They're not happy," Annaliese murmured right before another squeal rang out, followed by a thud, which seemed to suggest the suit of armor might have given one of the ferrets a kick and sent it flying into . . .

Before Drusilla could finish the thought, Annaliese was in motion, racing down the hallway and roaring quite like one would expect a mama bear to roar when protecting its cubs.

Drusilla was running after her sister a second later, with Seraphina by her side, skidding to a stop once she reached the great hall and discovered Annaliese already faced off with the suit of armor, and one that was currently swinging the mace it was carrying and advancing on her sister.

Knowing she couldn't very well shoot at whoever was underneath the armor—and there was no question it was human, given the heavy breathing that was coming out of the helmet—because there was a good chance she'd end up hitting Annaliese, Drusilla glanced around, spotted a mace that was, thankfully, on the smaller side, and dashed over to it.

After thrusting her pistol into the pocket of her robe, she snatched up the mace and sprinted toward her sister, having to use both hands to lift the weapon, as it was still far heavier than she'd anticipated, before she swung it at the suit of armor, a resounding thud reverberating around the room when it made contact with the breastplate.

For the briefest of seconds, nothing happened, but then the suit of armor began listing forward, quite like a falling tree, hitting the hard floor a heartbeat later, where it bounced ever so slightly, and then there was silence—until Wiggles and Pippin came charging out from underneath the table.

A bit of chattering erupted between the ferrets, quite as if they were coordinating an attack before Wiggles pounced on the breastplate and squeezed herself through the crack that separated the helmet from the rest of the suit while Pippin slipped underneath the chainmail.

It wasn't exactly unexpected when the person underneath the suit began yelling a second later.

"Get 'em off me," a distinctly male voice boomed out of the helmet.

"Ferrets aren't like dogs," Annaliese said, moving up to the man and doing not a thing to retrieve her ferrets. "They don't respond well to commands, although they do seem to have quite the mean streak, especially when someone harms one of their own, which I believe you did to their sister. Unfortunately for you, Fidget, the ferret you kicked, appears to be coming out of her stupor, and I'm sorry to have to tell you that you made a grave error by kicking her, as she's the most vicious of my little darlings."

A bit of wiggling was the man's first response to that, probably because he was wearing a suit of armor that didn't allow him much mobility and that also seemed to have rendered him rather helpless on the floor. Deciding she might as well take advantage of his less-than-threatening state, Drusilla leaned over and yanked up the visor on the helmet, revealing a man she'd never seen before.

"And who do we have here?" she asked right as Wiggles poked her head out from the armor on the man's sleeve while Pippin slithered out from the bottom of the breastplate.

"I ain't sayin' nothin'."

"Which is too bad, as it seems as if Fidget now has you in her sights, and it's only a matter of time until she attacks."

It was rather telling when the man immediately changed his mind and muttered that he'd tell her who he was, but only after she got rid of the ferrets.

Less than five minutes later, and after Irma, Mr. Grimsby, and Mrs. O'Sullivan rushed into the great hall to help, Drusilla stepped back from the man who'd now been relieved of his armor and was sitting on the floor with his hands tied behind his back, taking a moment to consider him.

There was no question that he was a man who was accustomed to living it rough, what with how his reddish-brown hair was shaggy and looked as if it hadn't been washed in weeks. His face was weathered and lined, and his build was on the wiry side, while the clothing he'd been wearing underneath the armor was well-worn and patched in places.

"Now that we've gotten you out of all that armor, and my sister has taken the ferrets a safe distance away from you," Drusilla began, "what say we start with the basics, such as your name."

"Name's Blackeye Bailey."

"And why are you in the castle, Blackeye Bailey?"

"I used to live here when I, ah, was a boatswain for Captain Thurgood Harvey, until he sold the place to Miss Ottilie and moved himself down to Florida."

Given the way the man's eyes had taken to darting around the room, looking at everything but Drusilla, it wasn't much of a stretch to conclude he wasn't exactly being truthful.

"That doesn't tell me what you're doing here."

"Maybe I was just missin' the place and wanted to come back and mosey around the great hall."

"And you also wanted to don a suit of armor because, what? You made a habit of doing that when you worked for the captain?"

Blackeye Bailey nodded. "All of Captain Harvey's staff liked wearing the armor. We found it amusing."

Drusilla wrinkled her nose. "I don't buy that, so how about you try again, and the truth this time, if you please."

"That was the truth."

She took a second to pull her pistol out of her pocket, which had the immediate result of his gaze locking onto it. "While I might believe men would take to dressing in armor once their workday was through, perhaps to engage in mock battles, you and I both know that's not why you donned armor tonight, nor did you do it because you were feeling nostalgic."

A bead of sweat began trailing from his forehead and down the side of his face. "There ain't no reason for you to keep that pistol out because I have no desire to suffer a bullet. How about I just tell you that I work for someone who has their eye on this property. I was asked by that someone to do what I could to encourage you to go on back to where you came from."

"May I assume this isn't your first time wandering around this castle impersonating a knight? And no, I'm not talking about when you were still working for Captain Harvey."

"Could be I've put on a suit of armor once after I left Captain Harvey's employ."

"When you were asked to scare my aunt's staff away a year and a half ago?"

"That would be the time," he muttered.

Drusilla shifted the pistol to her other hand as she tried to get her thoughts in order before she frowned. "Have you been working with Norbert to continue making it appear that the castle is haunted?"

He blinked, blinked again, then gave a shrug, although it wasn't much of a shrug since his hands were tied behind his back. "I ain't no snitch."

"I'll take that as a yes, but who are you and Norbert working for?"

"I ain't gonna snitch about that either."

Realizing she was getting nowhere, she decided a change of

tactics was in order. "Why didn't you and Norbert continue on in Captain Harvey's employ when he headed for warmer shores?"

"I have family in this area." He smiled, revealing a few missing teeth. "Besides that, me and Norbert decided, since Captain Harvey was going off to Florida, we'd miss the snow."

"Because pirates have such a fondness for snow."

"I never said nothin' about me being a pirate."

"With a name like Blackeye Bailey, you didn't need to, but speaking of names, I doubt that's really yours."

"'Course it is."

"No, it's not, and I know this because Norbert told me that everyone who was a longtime employee of Captain Harvey left Chicago with him, save one man—Sneaky Pete Smythe, to be exact."

It wasn't much of a stretch to realize she was on the right track about him being Sneaky Pete when he took a marked interest in the new chandelier Rhenick's crew had recently hung in the great hall.

"May I suggest," she began, "since we've established your true identity, that we turn once again to the person who hired you?"

Sneaky Pete's lips thinned. "I don't see how telling you that would benefit me at all, and again, I ain't no snitch."

"But it *would* benefit you because, if you were to cooperate, I might feel compelled to make certain my sister keeps a tight hold on Fidget instead of encouraging her to set the ferret down and aim her in your direction."

Thirty-Two

Sneaky Pete's forehead immediately took to perspiring more than ever. "I wouldn't think a lady keen on opening a school to teach proper manners would stoop to threatening a man with what sounds like torture techniques since that's hardly fitting behavior for a lady who's supposed to be all prim and proper."

Drusilla gave a wave of her hand. "I'm sure you'd love if I'd invite you to enjoy a cup of tea instead of setting ferrets on you, but having been woken from a sound sleep to discover a suit of armor strolling about has left me with little desire to cling to the proprieties right now. With that said, if you don't want to suffer a round of torture, I suggest you start talking, and start by telling me who sent you."

Sneaky Pete glared at her for a long moment before he swung his attention to Annaliese, who gave Fidget a bit of a tickle before sending Sneaky Pete a wink.

Obviously taking that as a sign Annaliese wasn't opposed to setting aside proprieties as well and setting her ferret on him, Sneaky Pete stared at the ceiling for a long moment before he returned his attention to Drusilla.

"Fine, since all of you seem prone to violence—and violence by ferret, at that—I suppose I have no choice but to tell you that

I first donned the armor a year and a half ago after Umberto Zambarello offered me a large fee if I was able to convince Ottilie's staff they wanted to work for him."

Of anything Drusilla had been expecting him to say, that hadn't been remotely close. "You scared off the staff because Umberto wanted them to work for him?"

"His missus was tired of having to hire domestic servants that weren't what anyone would consider good at their jobs. Everyone knew Ottilie Merriweather had the best staff west of the Mississippi since she'd brought most of her staff back with her after living in London for a few years. That's what prompted Umberto, who adores his wife and calls her his angel, to tell me he'd make it worth my while if I could arrange matters to his satisfaction."

"Did he offer to make it worth your while again if you scared me straight on back to New York?"

For a moment, Sneaky Pete didn't answer, until Annaliese took to smoothing a finger over Fidget's head, which immediately drew the man's attention. He blanched. "I'd think you'd be able to figure that out on your own, what with how all those developers haven't been shy with lettin' you know they want to buy you out. Word around the city has it that you're gonna open that academy soon. That's got some developers real nervous-like because it's one thing to threaten you when you're here all alone and quite another to come after you when the castle is filled with young ladies from some of the wealthiest families in Chicago. That would be bad for business."

Seraphina cleared her throat. "Perhaps we should consider *not* delaying the opening, as that might put an end to our developer problem once and for all."

"And while I have to agree with you there, we're still facing the Sanford problem, the Norbert problem, and lest we forget, the Aunt Ottilie problem," Drusilla muttered before she returned her attention to Sneaky Pete. "I find myself curious as to how you accessed the castle tonight. I know for a fact all the windows and doors were locked."

Sneaky Pete had the audacity to smile. "I sure would like to oblige you and your curiosity, Miss Merriweather, but Captain Harvey made me swear on a Bible that I would never divulge the castle's secrets."

"You no longer work for Captain Harvey."

"Doesn't matter. A swear's a swear, ain't it?"

Before Drusilla could argue with that, someone started pounding on the front door, and after telling Seraphina and Annaliese to guard Pete, Drusilla strode through the great hall and into the hallway, Mr. Grimsby by her side, who snatched an umbrella out of the umbrella stand before he moved closer to the door.

"Who is it?" he yelled through the door.

"It's Rhenick, Mr. Grimsby."

"Thank goodness," Mr. Grimsby breathed before he un-locked the door and swung it open. "I'm quite relieved to see you, Mr. Whittenbecker, as we've got a bit of a situation here."

"I know. I spotted the ghost fluttering from the turret on the ride up the drive."

Drusilla blinked. "The ghost is back?"

Rhenick blinked right back at her. "That's not the situation Mr. Grimsby was referring to?"

"He's referring to the strolling suit of armor that we took the liberty of capturing, although it turned out that underneath the armor was a man who goes by the name of Sneaky Pete."

After raking a hand through his hair, Rhenick stepped closer to her. "Do I want to know how you managed to capture this Sneaky Pete?"

"I clubbed him with a mace and then the ferrets went after him."

His lips curved straight into a grin. "An unexpected method to subdue a marauding suit of armor, but since you managed the very impressive feat of capturing him, we should make certain he's acting alone and that he set the ghost in play over the turret before he donned his armor."

"He hasn't given me any indication that he has a partner, but I haven't questioned him about that since I didn't know someone had brought the ghost out." She smiled. "I'm relatively sure he'll tell us the truth about that since he seems rather leery of Fidget, who's champing at the bit to get a piece of Pete since that man kicked her earlier."

Rhenick's eyes began to twinkle. "Ah, you're continuing to keep the guard ferrets on active duty?"

"Indeed, and we've already used the threat of Fidget to get some answers—the most important ones thus far being that Sneaky Pete has been working with Norbert and was also hired by none other than Umberto Zambarello. Umberto evidently hired him last year to frighten everyone from the castle, save Norbert. Turns out Umberto wanted to present his wife with a household staff that held the reputation of being competent."

Rhenick frowned. "And here I was expecting you to tell me that Sneaky Pete was hired by the Caggianni family, as I'm sure they're still rather annoyed with you for shooting one of their men."

"They have no reason to be annoyed with me because that was an accident on my part, and besides, they're the ones who had the audacity to try to force a meeting with me when they saw the gate was open," Drusilla returned. "With that said, I'm actually relieved it was Umberto who sent Sneaky Pete instead of some of the more frightening developers because after I get Sneaky Pete safely secured in the dungeon, I intend to head to Umberto's residence to have a bit of a chat with that man."

"Given the current time, I doubt Umberto's going to be receiving callers, as he's probably retired for the night."

"Agreed, but since this isn't a social call, I have no problem rousing him from his bed. Besides that, it'll be to our advantage

JEN TURANO

to take him by surprise, as he'll be more unguarded with the answers I'm going to demand from him."

"Or we could have the authorities take him by surprise since we're going to have to contact them anyway."

"Except that I suspect someone on the police force is working for one of those developers, as no authority figure has ever come to the castle to take a statement regarding what happened the day I shot that man from the Caggianni family. Where I'm from, when someone is shot, there are always statements taken."

"The Caggianni family wouldn't have notified the authorities about your accidental shooting, not given their less-than-lawful business endeavors."

"Perhaps not, but I sent Norbert off to the police station to file a report regarding the incident. Norbert told me that no one was available to take the report, and the authorities have yet to send anyone to speak with me about what transpired. That means someone is on the take, and also means that it'll be up to us to get answers out of Umberto."

"Or it could be that Norbert never went to the police station," Rhenick pointed out.

Drusilla's shoulders slumped the slightest bit. "I didn't even consider that. Nevertheless, I'm determined to get answers, and have no intention of allowing an authority figure who could be corrupt to stand in my way. Given that Umberto is the only lead I have who can explain the nonsense that went on tonight, Umberto is who I intend to speak with. I also intend to speak to him sooner than later, which means we'll need to leave the castle for the city within the next five minutes, or perhaps ten, as it would hardly be proper for me to arrive at that man's house wearing my nightgown and slippers."

Thirty-Three

Twenty minutes later, Rhenick found himself back in his carriage, with Drusilla by his side, as Seraphina drove them toward the city after stating in that no-nonsense way of hers that she was probably more lethal with a weapon than anyone present, including Rhenick. Because of that, she'd proclaimed that it was in everyone's best interest for her to travel to Umberto's house as well, and then added that it wasn't up for debate.

Because Seraphina had already been carrying her blunder-buss, had a rapier attached to her side, and seemed to have what appeared to be two sticks of dynamite shoved into a bag—even though he'd pointed out that dynamite was rather unstable, which had simply earned him a roll of the eyes from Seraphina, as if she knew exactly how volatile dynamite was but was ca-pable of handling it properly—he and Drusilla had agreed that of course Seraphina would be more than welcome to join them.

It really hadn't come as much of a surprise when Seraphina had then insisted on driving them to Umberto's house on South Michigan Avenue, saying in an offhand manner that she was beyond proficient with handling the reins, as well as being quite capable of employing evasive maneuvers, although where she'd learned those was anyone's guess.

Considering that Seraphina had truly not appeared to be in the mood to debate the matter, and he was perfectly familiar with members of the feminine set who weren't in favorable moods, she was now sitting on the coachman's seat, while his somewhat puzzled coachman and groomsmen had been sent off to patrol the castle grounds. That had left Annaliese and her ferrets free to keep an eye on Sneaky Pete, who was now secured in one of the dungeons.

"I appreciate you deciding to accompany us, especially after Seraphina turned all bossy, which most men wouldn't have appreciated in the least," Drusilla said as she clutched the strap attached to the coach's ceiling, the strap getting more use than it ever had before as it wasn't a usual occurrence for one of the Whittenbecker family carriages to be traveling along at what amounted to breakneck speed.

"There's nothing to appreciate, as I certainly wasn't going to stay behind while you and Seraphina went off to chat with Umberto, nor was I bothered by Seraphina's bossiness, as I'm quite accustomed to bossy ladies, given the family I grew up in." Rhenick smiled. "I mean, granted, Seraphina seems quite capable of protecting you, especially as she's armed with dynamite, which will definitely put an interesting twist on the evening if she brings that out at any point. But even though I know she'll keep you safe, Umberto and I work in the same industry. We've always maintained a rather cordial attitude with each other, a cordiality that may help us get a few answers tonight."

"That cordiality might be a thing of the past considering you and Umberto were engaged in a rousing bout of fisticuffs recently."

"An excellent point, although I'm sure Umberto has realized by now that he acted completely beyond the pale when he cast aspersions on your appearance. I'm sure he's also realized that I was completely justified in my response of slugging him, as he'd bestowed a grave insult on a lady I hold very dear to my heart, something I'm sure Umberto, as well as the other developers, have realized by now."

Drusilla's eyes, oddly enough, began to twinkle in the lantern light. "Given what Umberto was implying last week, I don't believe any of the developers think you're in my company as often as you are because I'm very dear to your heart. Instead, they, as I was guilty of at first, believe this is a plot to get your hands on the castle. With that said, though, know that my tender feminine sensibilities were not injured when Umberto remarked on my plain appearance, as I'm rather accustomed to people mentioning my less-than-beautiful features. I'm happy to report that I've grown immune to those types of slights over the years."

Something heavy settled in the pit of his stomach. "Anyone who has ever had the audacity to call you plain clearly has something wrong with their eyesight, as you are a remarkably beautiful woman and, in fact, are the most beautiful woman I've ever had the pleasure of meeting."

For the span of a few heartbeats, Drusilla considered him, but then her lips curved into a smile that left his mind going curiously numb.

"I find myself unable to conjure up anything clever to say in response to what was a truly lovely thing to say to me," she said, her voice no louder than a whisper. "With that said, I'll simply say thank you and leave it at that, although . . . this might be one of those moments in a friendship where those hugs I've seen you often bestowing on your sisters might be in order."

The sound of the carriage wheels rumbling against the cobblestones faded straightaway as he found himself captured by Drusilla's eyes, eyes that were still twinkling in a compelling fashion, although they were now holding a hint of warmth in them as well.

What that warmth meant, he couldn't say for certain, but what he could say was this—ever since he'd first set eyes on

Drusilla, he'd felt the most compelling urge to take her in his arms and hold her tight. Quite honestly, though, he'd also wanted to be given an opportunity to kiss her, to be able to take her face between his hands and then lower his lips to hers.

That she was asking him to give her a hug, something he got the distinct impression she was not overly familiar with receiving, was promising to the say the least, and . . .

The carriage took that moment to make a sharp turn to the left, sending him careening off the seat and to the floor, but before he could so much as pull himself back onto his seat, or lament the loss of hugging Drusilla since it seemed as if the moment had come and gone, the carriage pulled to a smart stop. The rapidity of the stop had him sprawling to the floor again, which was why his first sight when the door swung open was of the blunderbuss Seraphina had jammed in a holster slung low on her hip, followed by her face looming in front of his when she stuck her head into the carriage.

Given that one of Seraphina's imitation moles looked to be coming undone from the adhesive she'd used to attach it to her face, it was clear that she might need to watch how fast she drove a carriage in the future, as adhesives might not be up for the task of keeping moles in place when she was racing against the wind at excessive speeds.

"What happened to you?" were the first words out of Seraphina's mouth.

"Your driving," he muttered, earning a grin from Seraphina before she lent him a hand from the carriage, Drusilla stepping out behind him a second later. She settled her gaze on a very large house that had numerous fountains tinkling away on the front lawn, along with statues of cherubs and angels lining the front walk.

"It's, ah, difficult to describe," Drusilla finally said.

"Rhenick told me to look for a fussy house once I reached South Michigan and Thirty-Third Street," Seraphina said, her gaze settling on one of the pillars flanking the front porch that looked to have some sort of vine motif carved into the marble. "I have to say this one stood out right away, as the rest of the houses on this street are more on the tasteful side, although . . ." She tilted her head. "That seems to be a lovely stained-glass panel in the front door. I would hate to have to blow it up if no one answers that door." With that, Seraphina strode into motion, leaving Drusilla and Rhenick behind.

"She's rather terrifying," Rhenick said, earning a quirk of the lips from Drusilla before she took hold of his arm and pulled him after Seraphina, who was already standing in front of the door, eyeing a door knocker that was shaped in the form of a cherub.

"Everyone ready?" Seraphina asked.

"Quite," Drusilla said, which left Seraphina sending her a nod before she gave the knocker a few raps, then returned her attention to Drusilla. "We probably should have discussed a strategy before I knocked on the door, but I'm thinking you should be the lead interrogator because you didn't have an issue with speaking your mind to Umberto before." Seraphina nodded to Rhenick. "You'll be the muscle in the background."

"I thought you were the muscle," he argued.

Seraphina's lips curved. "I'll be the surprise muscle, but we'll only use me if Umberto doesn't cooperate." She reached up to give the knocker another rap, pausing mid-reach when the door swung open and a man wearing a dark formal jacket thrown over his nightclothes took to looking down his very long nose at them.

"It's the middle of the night," he said in a clipped voice that held a distinct British accent.

Drusilla stepped forward. "And we apologize for the inappropriateness of the hour, but we have a matter of some urgency to discuss with Mr. Umberto Zambarello. You may tell him that Miss Drusilla Merriweather has come to call."

The butler blinked. "Good heavens, you're Miss Ottilie's niece, aren't you?" He presented her with a bow. "I'm Bentley, miss, your aunt's former butler, but . . . what are you doing in Chicago? Or better yet, what are you doing here and at this late hour?"

"I'll be more than happy to have that conversation with you later, but for now, Bentley, if you could fetch Mr. Zambarello, I'd be much obliged, as I need to speak to him about another one of his employees."

Before Bentley could do more than frown, the sound of slipper-clad feet came flip-flopping down the hall, Umberto coming into view a second later. He faltered ever so slightly as he caught sight of them, but then he was flip-flopping their way a second later, stopping directly in front of Drusilla.

"While I realize we parted on less-than-amicable terms the last time we spoke, Miss Merriweather, arriving on my doorstep in the middle of the night is an impertinence that's inexcusable, especially when I'm sure whatever it is you want to speak with me about could have waited until tomorrow."

"Of course it's an impertinence, but one I was willing to make given the impertinence you directed my way when you sent your man to my castle tonight with the express purpose of trying to scare me back to New York."

Umberto scowled. "What in the world are you talking about?"

"I really don't have the patience to deal with you pleading ignorance, Mr. Zambarello. You know full well I'm speaking about Sneaky Pete."

"Who?"

Drusilla crossed her arms over her chest, but before she could get another word out of her mouth, the sound of rapidly approaching footsteps drew everyone's attention, and then a lady wearing a mobcap and a robe embellished with feathers came bursting into view. She stopped dead in her tracks, glanced to

Drusilla, then to Rhenick, and finally to Seraphina, her gaze lingering on the blunderbuss in Seraphina's hand before she marched over to stand directly beside Umberto.

"Do not tell me that you've been running numbers again and these miscreants have arrived in the middle of the night because they just finished a job for you, or are here to tell you that the job went horribly wrong," the woman said through teeth that had taken to clenching.

"Now, angel," Umberto began, "you know I've left gambling behind. I'm a completely legitimate man of business these days."

Drusilla, to Rhenick's surprise, released a bit of a snort. "Completely legitimate unless you take into account that you sent Sneaky Pete to my home tonight with the express purpose of breaking into it and then masquerading as a ghostly knight. Since you clearly did that to frighten me into leaving town, if you ask me, you're not exactly finding complete success as a legitimate man of business. In fact, you might want to consider telling people instead that you're an occasionally legitimate businessman. You might also want to extend the lady you just called *angel* an apology, as I'm relatively certain you've been telling her some rather large fibs of late about your business dealings in general."

Thirty-Four

It was quite telling when the lady Drusilla believed was Umberto's wife began swelling on the spot before she rounded on her husband, her dark eyes flashing, which resulted in Umberto edging ever so slowly away from her.

"You promised me, Umberto, that you weren't going to hire any questionable characters anymore, but if this lady has the right of it and you've been dealing with a man named Sneaky Pete—well, how much more questionable can you get when a person has the word *sneaky* attached to their name?"

"I have never met a man who went by the name of Sneaky Pete," Umberto argued.

It was difficult to refuse the inclination to snort again, but since she'd only just snorted a mere moment before, a second snort would be pushing the boundaries of proper decorum a little too far, even if she was facing some rather extenuating circumstances.

"While I understand your need for self-preservation, as this lady I'm assuming is your wife looks quite ready to inflict some bodily harm on you," Drusilla began, "I have no qualms explaining the truth of the matter to her so . . ."

She nodded to the lady in question and took a moment to explain what she knew about Sneaky Pete, ending with, "And then your husband arranged for Sneaky Pete to infiltrate my aunt's castle because he wanted to present you with your heart's desire, which was being in possession of a competent staff."

The lady shot a glance to Umberto, pursed her lips, then returned her attention to Drusilla before she promptly dropped into a curtsy. "I beg your pardon for not introducing myself straight from the start but as you deduced, I am Umberto's wife, Elena Zambarello. You are, of course, Miss Drusilla Merriweather, who I have heard my husband muttering about of late, his mutters revolving around the notion he believes you're an unreasonable woman who won't accept a more-than-generous offer for your castle." Elena drew herself up. "It's now more than obvious that your unreasonableness was completely warranted, given that I'm getting the distinct impression something underhanded has been transpiring in regard to you—and something my husband has been a part of."

She turned to Umberto. "You will now tell me exactly what you've been up to, starting with how it came to be that we, out of everyone in Chicago, ended up with Ottilie Merriweather's staff."

"There was nothing underhanded about how the Merriweather staff came to work for us," Umberto protested. "I simply had a conversation with a man who was watching the Merriweather Castle's front gate one day when Norbert, the usual gatekeeper wasn't around. Although . . ." Umberto tilted his head. "Come to think of it, that man's name might have actually been Peter, but he never mentioned the word *sneaky* in our conversation."

Elena's eyes narrowed. "Why would you have gone to the castle in the first place if Ottilie Merriweather was out of town?"

"I kept checking in to see if she'd returned because I have more clients who want to build houses on North Lake Shore Avenue than available land, and I wanted to make her an offer that would be worth her while." He held up his hand, forestalling whatever it was Elena seemed about to say. "Before you take to chiding me about that, don't think I was the only one stopping by the castle. There were a good dozen other developers who wanted her land, although the majority of them have given up their pursuit these days."

"Ottilie Merriweather is rumored to be one of the wealthiest women in the country because she evidently inherited millions from her parents and grandparents," Elena shot back. "Unless she'd allowed it to be known she wanted to sell, why would you, or any other developer, think she'd be persuaded by a financial offer to give up her castle simply because her land is highly desirable?"

Umberto waved that aside. "Ottilie Merriweather is rarely in town, and she's an unmarried woman without children. Seems to me it's somewhat selfish of her to own so much land when there are at least a hundred families who would gain a better quality of life if she sold to a developer. Just think how those children would benefit from getting out of the city smog and breathing in lakeside air instead."

"That's a ridiculous reason to justify what seems to be a concerning case of stalking on your part, as well as stalking from other developers," Elena snapped. "But to return to what we were actually speaking about, explain to me, if you please, exactly how it came to be that we were the family who ended up with her staff."

Umberto gave his nose a bit of a scratch. "Would you believe we were unbelievably lucky because I just happened to mention to that Peter fellow that we were looking to bring on additional domestic workers right around the time Ottilie's entire staff was looking for a new employer?"

Elena folded her arms over her chest. "I probably should have asked this directly after you hired Ottilie's staff, but why did they want to leave her employ in the first place?"

"Ah . . ." Umberto glanced to Bentley. "Didn't you tell me

when I interviewed you that everyone was convinced the castle was haunted?"

"Indeed," Bentley said before he frowned. "Although I'm unable to help but wonder, after learning Sneaky Pete was behind the suit of armor incident, as well as being the man who told me you were hiring, if all the hauntings we experienced were at the hands of Sneaky Pete."

"I don't think anyone can blame you for wondering that, as I'm wondering the same exact thing," Drusilla said, earning a scowl from Umberto in return.

"Except that I didn't specifically ask Peter to scare anyone out of the castle," he argued. "The employment conversation simply happened after he told me that Ottilie had not returned and no one had heard from her. He then added that talk was beginning to swirl around that something dreadful might have befallen her."

"That makes it sound as if, after Sneaky Pete implied to you that my aunt might be dead, you saw that as a prime opportunity to make off with Ottilie's staff."

"If Ottilie was dead, her staff was going to have to find new positions anyway, so it's not as if I did anything except not pass up an opportunity that had unexpectedly landed in my lap."

Drusilla's brow furrowed. "But no one knew for sure what had happened to my aunt—and still don't know—so I'm curious as to whether you might have helped this opportunity along somehow. Perhaps offered some type of incentive to Sneaky Pete to encourage him to send members of the Merriweather staff your way?"

Umberto shot a glance to Elena, who responded with an arched brow before he winced. "I might have told him I'd give him a fee for anyone he sent to my household who ended up accepting a position."

"To a man named Sneaky Pete, the promise of a fat payout was probably enough motivation for him to stuff himself into an old suit of armor, squeeze his head into a steel helmet, and wander about the great hall, moaning every few feet as he swung a mace around." Drusilla cocked her head to the side. "Should I assume that tonight's fiasco was an opportunity you couldn't pass up either because you knew, if you didn't make one last-ditch effort to scare me from the castle before I open my academy for young ladies, that you probably wouldn't get another chance?"

"I did *not* hire Sneaky Pete to roam around your castle tonight, nor have I ever done that. To reiterate, I simply told him that *one* time we spoke well over a year ago that I'd appreciate it if he'd let everyone know I was hiring."

Elena began tapping a toe against the marble floor. "You should have realized the man would resort to unusual tactics, as I have to imagine Ottilie Merriweather's staff was perfectly content in their positions since a woman who was rarely in residence wouldn't have exactly been difficult to work for."

"She was absolutely delightful," Bentley interjected, blanching a second later as if he'd just realized he'd said that out loud, and in a tone that suggested it wasn't all that delightful to work for the Zambarello family.

"A telling statement if there ever was one," Elena said before she considered Umberto for an uncomfortably long moment, then turned to Drusilla. "I know you're hardly likely to believe me, but I've been married to Umberto for what feels like forever at the moment, and I can normally tell when he's being untruthful. I don't get the feeling he's lying about the Sneaky Pete incident tonight. However, before we discuss that further, I would like to revisit something you said—that being an academy. Surely you weren't suggesting you're going to open an academy in the castle, were you?"

"You haven't heard?" Drusilla asked.

"The only thing I've heard about an academy of late is that Mrs. McCormick finally got her daughter, Norma Jean, who would give any of my girls a run for their money in the questionable-behavior department, enrolled in a ladies' academy after spending the past few years being turned down by every finishing school east of the Mississippi."

"Mrs. McCormick has enrolled Norma Jean in my academy, the Merriweather Academy for Young Ladies."

Elena's gaze sharpened on Drusilla. "Are there any specific qualifications girls need to possess in order to gain admittance into your academy?"

"We're not going to be as stringent with enrollment requirements as many academies are, if that's what you're asking, but I won't be admitting any young ladies for a while, as I've recently decided, given the unfortunate circumstances I'm currently facing, that I'll need to delay the opening of the academy."

Elena took a step toward Drusilla. "May I assume those unfortunate circumstances revolve around the developers who are determined to acquire your castle?"

"That would be one of the unfortunate circumstances I'm facing."

"May I also assume, then, that if that particular threat were alleviated, your academy opening might not be as delayed?"

"That would be a fair assumption."

Elena smiled. "Then allow me to offer you my assistance in the pesky developer matter." She turned to Umberto. "To begin, you, my dear, will cease any and all attempts to convince Miss Merriweather to sell out to you, just as you're now going to come completely clean and admit to me, and the truth if you please, whether or not you hired Sneaky Pete to scare Miss Merriweather from the castle tonight."

"I haven't had any contact with Sneaky Pete since he stopped by my office over a year ago to collect those fees I mentioned."

Drusilla frowned. "I now find myself wondering why Pete didn't accept a position with you as well when you brought on the rest of my aunt's staff."

"He told me another developer had offered him a job, one that got him back on a boat again, which is why he decided to take that position instead of accepting a job with me as a gardener."

Drusilla turned to Bentley. "Did Pete mention anything to you regarding where he was going to work?"

Bentley shook his head. "I'm afraid not, although it seems rather curious that a developer would just happen to have a boating position available. I wouldn't think builders in general have much need to have many boats around."

"Unless you're Loughlin MacSherry," Elena said slowly.

Drusilla blinked. "The criminal underboss?"

"Ah, so you've heard of him."

"He's another developer who'd like to secure my property."

"Interesting," Elena murmured.

"How so?"

"Because even though MacSherry promotes himself as a developer and builder, he uses that as a front to conceal how he really makes his money—that being smuggling."

"Smuggling?" Drusilla repeated.

Elena nodded. "He has an entire fleet of ships that he claims to use to bring in building supplies, but everyone knows that the majority of items MacSherry brings into Chicago aren't building supplies at all but stolen goods or opium."

Umberto's brows drew together. "I was unaware that you knew about MacSherry's true business endeavors."

"Just because we've decided to leave Chicago's underworld behind doesn't mean I've abandoned all of the friends I have who still remain in that world," Elena said. "Frankly, if I'd done that, I wouldn't have any lady friends at all since it's not as if Mrs. Palmer is beating down my door, asking me to join her for tea at the Palmer House."

"I don't recall you ever having tea with Mrs. MacSherry or any of the MacSherry family," Umberto pointed out.

"No one has tea with the MacSherrys as that could put your very life in danger, which brings me around to Sneaky Pete again." Elena worried her lip for a moment. "I'm sure, as there's a chance he's been working for MacSherry for over a year, that Pete is well-aware of how ruthless the man is. That means it's doubtful that Sneaky Pete, when he was caught in the act tonight, would have fessed up to working for MacSherry." She nodded to Umberto. "Instead, he blamed you, my darling, a ready stooge if there ever was once since you were responsible for Sneaky Pete seemingly coming up with the haunted castle scenario as a way to collect those fees you offered him."

Drusilla gave her forehead a rub as she tried to keep up with the conversation. "I can certainly understand why Sneaky Pete wouldn't want to tell us he was working for MacSherry, but why would MacSherry want to acquire my land if his most profitable business doesn't revolve around building contracts?"

"I'm sure that's somehow connected to your castle once be-longing to another smuggler—Captain Harvey," Elena said. "Since MacSherry's a smuggler as well, I'm sure he realized that the captain chose the castle's location for a specific reason, that being that you can sail a boat close to shore, load and unload questionable cargo, and then store that cargo in a remote castle that's surrounded by undeveloped land."

Drusilla's lips began to curve. "But that's absolutely bril-liant, and now has me questioning what other secrets the castle has yet to reveal."

"I would hazard a guess and say that Sneaky Pete is probably familiar with a lot of those secrets," Elena said. "But before you head out to question that man again, know that I was being perfectly sincere when I offered to handle your developer problem for you. I can guarantee that Umberto will no longer be plaguing you with offers, and I would guess it'll take me no longer than a week to get all the other developers interested in the castle to lose that interest."

"Even Loughlin MacSherry?"

"I can take care of MacSherry."

Drusilla tilted her head. "What would you expect in return for your assistance?"

"While I would love to claim I'm only offering my assistance as a way to make amends for Umberto stealing your aunt's staff," Elena began, "I'm afraid I'm not that altruistic. I, again, have five daughters who have yet to reach their majority, and I've been told they're somewhat unmanageable."

"Ah. You'd like my assurances that I'll agree to admit your daughters into my academy in exchange for your assistance."

"I believe that would be a fair exchange."

"Should I ask exactly how you intend to intervene on my behalf with MacSherry?" Drusilla couldn't resist asking.

Elena smiled. "It would be best if you aren't privy to any details, especially when that will allow you to claim complete ignorance if anything unexpected were to happen and the authorities feel compelled to pay you a visit."

Thirty-Five

"While I understand that it's after midnight," Drusilla began as the carriage careened wildly down the road, which wasn't exactly a surprise with Seraphina driving again, "one would have thought, when we stopped at the police station, that they would have at least sent a single officer to accompany us back to the castle, as we do have a criminal stashed in the dungeon."

"Agreed," Rhenick said. "However, I suppose they figured, since it *is* after midnight, and since you happen to have said criminal tucked safely away in an honest-to-goodness dungeon, that there was no reason to send anyone tonight, as Sneaky Pete will still be in that dungeon come morning."

Drusilla opened her mouth, but not a word came out, because the carriage took that moment to make a sharp turn to the right, which left Drusilla sliding across the carriage seat and bouncing off the carriage wall. She pushed herself upright, but then went sliding to the left a second later when the carriage made another abrupt turn.

"Perhaps we should share a seat as that might allow both of us to avoid finding ourselves on the floor," Rhenick suggested.

"That's an excellent idea considering Seraphina seems to be putting her evasive driving skills into play, as she's worried

Loughlin MacSherry's men might be following us." Drusilla patted the seat beside her.

An immediate response was impossible to get out of his mouth after Rhenick had to all but launch himself in the direction of the opposite seat, barely managing to sit down before the carriage took another fast turn. "Sweet Pea is undoubtedly delighted to have Seraphina at the reins because he's a horse that loves galloping whenever possible. With that said, though, I didn't notice anyone tailing us earlier, or notice any suspicious carriages parked outside Umberto's house, so our current speed might be a little excessive, especially when I swear that last turn Seraphina made left us tooling along on two wheels."

Drusilla grinned and then released what sounded like a snort when the carriage careened over a pothole that left her bouncing right up against him. She shoved herself away, leaving him rather disappointed, before she pushed hair that had had the audacity to slip from her chignon out of her face.

"Considering that Elena seems terrifying in her own right, even if the Zambarello family has gone completely legitimate, I doubt there are many people, even Loughlin MacSherry, who'd risk incurring the wrath of that lady by skulking around her residence, even if someone had been following us after we left the castle."

"She's definitely not a woman to cross, which makes me wonder how you're going to handle her interest in getting her daughters enrolled in your academy."

"Since I told Elena, if she's able to get the developers to abandon their interest in the castle, that I would see her daughters promptly enrolled, that's exactly what I intend to do."

Rhenick frowned. "Surely you must know that you'll face indignation from other parents if you admit the Zambarello sisters, given that their father was, until recently, involved in the criminal underworld."

"Of course I know that, but it would hardly speak well of me if I start discriminating against future students simply because of their backgrounds." She looked out the window, although there was nothing to see as it was completely black outside. "If you think about it, Reverend Michaelson's choice of Scripture from the book of Romans that we heard only yesterday, although it seems as if that service was at least a month ago, could have been hand-selected for me as it dealt with how we're expected to live peaceably with one another. It would hardly be living peaceably with anyone if I exclude young ladies from the academy simply because of who their parents are."

She returned her attention to him. "Truth be told, I've been thinking that there's a reason for why my life went off the rails, a reason He Who Shall Not Be Named tossed me over, and a reason I was forced to come to Chicago. What that reason is exactly, I'm still not sure, but one thing I am certain about is this—I've been given an opportunity to not only claim a sense of independence I never would have known if I'd entered into what amounted to nothing more than an arranged marriage, but I have also been given an opportunity to help other young ladies gain an advantage in life, even if it's an advantage simply gained by learning how to properly comport themselves. That could very well allow some of these ladies to lead a life they never would have imagined, but that won't happen if I set superficial boundaries in place regarding who may attend my school and who may not."

He smiled. "Forgive me for questioning your decision because that was a very compelling argument. So compelling, in fact, that I'm sure if you simply explain your stance on inclusion to any indignant parents exactly as you just explained to me, no one will give you any trouble."

Drusilla returned his smile, but before she could do more than that, the carriage bounced over yet another rut, sending her careening into him, where she promptly grabbed hold of his jacket lapels and hung on for dear life as the carriage veered to the right.

Curiously enough, even though they were in very real danger of being tossed from the carriage altogether if they continued the way they were, Rhenick found all trepidations of their mad midnight ride disappearing when Drusilla looked up, her face mere inches from his.

Instead of pulling back, which was exactly what he expected her to do, her gaze locked with his for what seemed like an eternity, until that gaze shifted to his mouth. Any notion that he might have had about not giving in to the distinct urge he felt to kiss her faded straightaway.

He leaned closer, settled his hand at the nape of her neck, tilted her chin up with his other hand, leaned closer still, and then his lips met hers, the emotions that immediately swept over him surpassing anything he thought kissing Drusilla would be like, and . . .

The carriage took that moment to stop in its tracks, the sudden lack of motion sending him lurching off the seat and taking Drusilla with him.

A second later, she was sprawled on top of him, an honest-to-goodness grunt escaping her.

"That was quite unexpected," she muttered as she pushed herself up from where she'd been lying against his chest.

"Unexpected because we've now found ourselves on the floor?"

Her lips curved. "Unexpected as it brought a rather abrupt end to our kiss."

His lips began to curve as well. "And I will now say that I wasn't expecting you to say that."

"And to that I'll say that I wasn't expecting you to kiss me in the first place, but now that we have, I don't believe there's any need for us to pretend it didn't happen, as it was most enjoyable, and—"

"Got a bit of a situation out here," Seraphina said as she pulled open the carriage door, stuck her head in, and blinked. "What are you doing down there?"

"Suffering effects of your driving, of course," Drusilla returned without batting an eye, although she did send him a hint of a wink, the wink suggesting that even though she was, indeed, one of the most proper ladies he'd ever met, underneath that prim and properness might very well be a lady possessed of a mischievous spirit.

He could only hope he'd have an opportunity to explore more of her mischievous side in the very near future.

"It doesn't actually appear as if either of you suffered overly much from my evasive maneuvers," Seraphina said, a distinct trace of amusement in her voice.

Drusilla grinned, took the hand Seraphina held out to her, and climbed off of him a second later, sending him an apologetic wince when her elbow dug into his side before she practically fell out of the carriage.

After pushing himself upright, Rhenick climbed out of the carriage and moved to stand beside Drusilla and Seraphina, who were already directing their attention to the castle gate, one that was standing wide open and had no one manning it.

"What do you think the odds are that finding the gate open is not going to be a precursor of yet more trouble?" Drusilla asked.

"Slim to none," Seraphina didn't hesitate to say. "And because of that, I think we should leave the carriage behind and approach the castle as cautiously as possible, and with our weapons at the ready."

It wasn't exactly unexpected when Drusilla whipped her pistol from her pocket while Seraphina drew out a rapier, holding it in one hand while grasping the blunderbuss in the other.

"You should go first," Drusilla said, sending him a nod. "That way, if we encounter any trouble, whoever is behind that trouble will be expecting you, as the man, to protect us, but then when you're engaged in battle, Seraphina and I will swoop in to assist you, taking the miscreants by surprise."

The sound of jingling reached his ears before he could respond, the jingling explained when Billy the Goat came charging around the side of the castle, Mother Goose squawking by his side, the rest of the goat herd galloping behind them.

"That's definitely not a good sign," Drusilla said.

"Nor is it that we've yet to get a glimpse of Rhenick's coachman or his two groomsmen, which suggests that something has, indeed, happened," Seraphina added.

Waiting until the goats and Mother Goose hurried past them, Rhenick stayed to the shadows as he made his way to the front steps, then crept up them with his back to the wall, apprehension sliding over him when he realized the castle door was wide open, something Mr. Grimsby would have never allowed to occur.

He stepped into the entranceway, where he was promptly met with the sight of Fidget scrambling down the hallway, emitting sounds that Annaliese had told him were called *donks*, something she'd also told him ferrets used to communicate with one another.

Unfortunately, Wiggles and Pippin were nowhere to be found, but that didn't stop Fidget from continuing to chatter about as she scurried up to Drusilla, stood on her hind legs, and gave Drusilla a bat with a front paw. She then dropped to all fours and began gamboling down the hallway, releasing little yips as she went.

"I think she wants us to follow her," Drusilla said, lifting up the hem of her gown before charging after the ferret.

Striding after her, Rhenick soon found himself winding his way down curving stone steps that led to the dungeons, Drusilla coming to a stop once she stepped off the last stair, her eyes narrowed as she glanced around the room. "There's no one here."

"In here" came a voice from behind the door where they'd stashed Sneaky Pete a few hours before.

"Annaliese?" Drusilla called.

"Yes. It's me. We're locked in here," Annaliese called back.

"Hold on. Let me find a key."

Five minutes later, and after Drusilla had dashed up to her room to retrieve her key ring, she was swinging the dungeon door open, Annaliese stumbling out a second later. She was followed by Mr. Grimsby, who was sporting a cut on his forehead; Mrs. O'Sullivan, who was nursing a bloody lip; Miss Tremblay, the lady's maid, who was sniffling into a handkerchief; and Riley, who looked as if he wanted to punch somebody.

"Where's my coachman and groomsmen?" Rhenick asked after sticking his head into the dungeon and discovering it empty.

"I think they're tied up in the carriage house," Riley said. "I'll go check now."

As Riley hurried away, Drusilla peered into the dungeon, then backed out and arched a brow Annaliese's way. "Where's Mother?"

Annaliese released a shaky breath. "I'm not sure where she is, but I know who she's with . . . Sanford."

"What?"

"He showed up about an hour ago after he took the coachman and groomsmen by surprise. He then relieved them of the set of keys they'd been given so they could open the gate, which Sanford had bypassed because he was able to breach the grounds by coming here by way of the lake. Then, if I'm piecing events together properly, after securing Rhenick's men, he walked through the front door as bold as you please and kept right on going until he found me and Mother in the parlor."

Drusilla frowned. "What did he say when he walked into the parlor?"

"He wished us a good evening, told Mother that she was looking as beautiful as ever, then told her that he was certain she'd had enough time to come to her senses and should be all too willing to marry him now. He then went on to say that after they were wed, he'd be happy to return all the Merriweather money he stole, plus hand over the yacht to her."

"What did Mother say to all that?"

Annaliese's eyes crinkled at the corners. "She told him that she would rather face life as a complete pauper than ever consider marrying a scoundrel like him. Clearly, that didn't go over well with Sanford, who then told Mother that they were going to go off on a little trip together to give her time to consider the matter more thoroughly. I had a feeling he was going to turn nasty when Mother told him she wasn't going anywhere, so I whistled for my darlings, but before Pippin and Wiggles could do more than run into the room, fangs bared, events took a turn for the curious."

"More curious than Sanford showing up?"

"Indeed, because right as Pippin set her sights on Sanford, the ghostly figure that Mother saw when we first moved here came waltzing into the room, sporting a pistol in one hand and a rifle in the other." Annaliese shook her head. "Before I knew it, the ghost was threatening to shoot Pippin and Wiggles, which meant I had no choice but to scoop them up. While I was doing that, the ghost began brokering a deal with Sanford."

Drusilla blinked. "Brokering a deal?"

"Indeed, and in a feminine voice that sounded, as Mother had mentioned after she'd seen the ghost the first time, as if she had a cold, or was trying to disguise who she really was."

"But what kind of deal did the ghost want to broker?"

Annaliese gave her nose a rub. "The ghost told Sanford that if he would help her rescue her partner from the dungeon and get all of the staff locked in that dungeon instead, she would show him how to get back to his yacht without him having to go down the cliffs he had to climb to access the castle in the first place."

"That's right around the time Mr. Grimsby and I tried to take Sanford and the ghost by surprise by rushing into the parlor, armed with a rolling pin, spatula, and a few knives," Mrs. O'Sullivan said. "Sanford took me out with one slap to the face, and poor Mr. Grimsby didn't fare any better with the ghost, who conked him over the head with the rifle."

"By that time," Miss Tremblay added, "Riley and I had heard the commotion, so we went to investigate, but we probably shouldn't have rushed into the room without a plan because we found ourselves threatened with being shot, and a few minutes later, found ourselves exchanging places with Sneaky Pete."

"Which suggests we were wrong about Sneaky Pete working alone tonight," Rhenick said.

"He was clearly not alone," Annaliese said. "I'm sure he and his ghost partner were supposed to divide and conquer, the ghost probably being responsible for setting the stuffed ghost floating over the turret while Sneaky Pete started wandering around the great hall. I think Sneaky Pete's partner must have taken to hiding after we caught him but then saw an opportunity to escape, as well as rescue Sneaky Pete, when Sanford showed up."

"Any idea where Sanford might be heading with Irma?" Rhenick asked.

"I heard him ask Sneaky Pete if he knew what the best way was to get back to the Atlantic undetected. Sneaky Pete suggested Sanford wind his way through the Great Lakes, which means, if my grasp of the Great Lakes is accurate, he's heading north. Sanford didn't hesitate to agree to take Sneaky Pete and his partner with him after Sneaky Pete told him he was familiar with the waterways around the lakes."

"What we haven't been able to figure out, though," Mr. Grimsby began, "is why Sneaky Pete and his accomplice seemed downright desperate to get away from Chicago."

Rhenick ran a hand through his hair. "I would hazard a guess and say they're desperate because we uncovered tonight that Umberto was not responsible for Pete being here. Loughlin MacSherry was instead."

"The underworld boss you said was ruthless?" Annaliese asked.

"That's the one, and MacSherry isn't going to be pleased that Sneaky Pete wasn't successful in running Drusilla out of town." He blew out a breath. "It's going to complicate tracking Sanford down, though, since Pete's with them. He'll be familiar with the lakes, given that he's been working on the water for MacSherry and spent years on the water when he worked for Captain Harvey."

Drusilla worried her lip for a second. "It sounds like the only way we'll have a chance to find them is if we can find someone who has access to a boat and knows how to navigate through the lakes."

In the blink of an eye, the perfect solution sprang to mind, and one that went by the name of Seth McCormick, Norma Jean's brother and the man his sister Coraline was somewhat infatuated with.

"I might know someone who'll help us out," Rhenick said. "He's an inventor, as well as a friend of mine, and he's been tinkering around with what he calls a motorboat, a boat he's somehow managed to get running off kerosene. He's spent hours on the lakes as he's done that tinkering, so if anyone can locate Sanford, it's Seth." He sent Drusilla a nod. "I'll go speak to him now, and while I'm gone, I'm going to suggest that all of you try to get a little rest."

"I doubt any of us will be able to do that," Drusilla said.

"You can at least close your eyes because, if Sanford realizes that Irma isn't going to change her mind about sailing off into the sunset with him, the situation is bound to turn concerning. We'll be much more capable of handling anything concerning if we're not stumbling about half dead on our feet when we finally catch up to them."

Thirty-Six

D rusilla shifted on the makeshift bench she was sitting on in Seth McCormick's motorboat, surprised to discover she was wide awake even though she'd not been able to get any of that rest Rhenick had suggested a few hours before.

"I can't thank you enough for providing us with a boat as well as agreeing to captain for us today," she said, earning a smile from Seth as he shoved a strand of black hair that was definitely longer than most men were sporting these days out of his face.

"There's no need to thank me, Miss Merriweather. I've been itching to test the improvements I made to the motor but haven't found the time, as I've been tinkering around with a prototype for a water tank that might be able to deliver reliable hot water through pipes and by using only one faucet. This adventure of yours has gotten me out of my laboratory and breathing some fresh air for a change."

"I'm not certain the air we're breathing can be considered fresh, considering all the smoke your engine is coughing up," Annaliese said, her voice rather muffled since she'd wrapped a scarf over her face to avoid breathing in all the smoky air.

"That's due to the kerosene," Seth explained. "I might need

to refine the filter, but you'll get a break soon because we need to make it to shore so I can fill up the tank from the cans of kerosene I brought with us."

"Are you sure traveling with kerosene is a good idea? I've always heard that it's incredibly combustible," Annaliese asked.

Seth's brow furrowed for the briefest of seconds before he brightened. "I've only caught on fire three, or, eh, maybe it was five times." He nodded to a stack of floatation devices. "I came prepared, though, so if you do spot fire, just grab one of those and jump overboard."

Before Annaliese could do more than gape at a man who'd just delivered a less-than-reassuring statement, Rhenick lowered the binoculars he'd been using to scan the water and nodded. "There's a yacht anchored in that cove up ahead, but we're still too far away for me to make out the name on the side of it."

"Perhaps we should put into shore right past the opening of the cove, then go on foot to get a better look since we can't very well sneak closer since Mr. McCormick's motorboat isn't what I would call the stealthiest of machines," Annaliese said.

"I might have to see if I can weld a muffler onto the motor," Seth practically shouted as his motorboat began making more noise than ever. "But mufflers aside, I bet someone on that yacht stopped in that particular cove because they know Miss Sally runs a beachside green grocery and lunch counter that caters to the local fishermen."

"I can see Mother demanding a snack in an attempt to find a way to escape," Annaliese said. "I can also see Sanford trying to appease her since I heard him mutter something to Mother before he shut me in the dungeon about how much he'd missed her."

"Then let's hope that is Sanford's yacht and that everyone is on shore instead of still onboard since that might make it easier to rescue Mother," Drusilla said as Seth began steering the motorboat toward a patch of sandy beach that was past the entrance to the cove.

Unfortunately, before they made it to shore, smoke began billowing from the engine, right before flames shot out of it and began licking their way over the side of the boat.

"Everyone out!" Seth yelled, waiting until Drusilla, Annaliese, and Seraphina had flung themselves into the water before he tossed them floatation devices.

Thankfully, the floatation devices weren't needed since they'd already made it to shallow water. And after turning to check on Rhenick and finding him and Seth in shallow water as well, using two buckets Seth had wisely included on the boat to douse the flames, Drusilla waded to shore. After stumbling her way onto the beach, she took a second to wring water from her skirt as Annaliese and Seraphina did the same beside her.

She gave her skirt a last wring and lifted her head, finding Seraphina smiling brightly back at her.

"What could you possibly be finding amusing at this particular moment?" she asked.

"I'm not smiling because I'm amused. I'm smiling because we finally have a moment to ourselves, and a moment I'm now going to encourage you to use wisely, and by wisely, I mean use it to explain to me exactly what it was that I interrupted between you and Rhenick." Seraphina plopped down on the sand and patted the spot beside her. "You will also divulge, and in great detail if you please, if I interrupted something romantic in nature, which I'm convinced I did. Then, I'm hoping you'll tell us that you've changed your stance about never wanting a gentleman to court you."

Before Drusilla could muster up a response to any of that, Annaliese's mouth went slightly agape as she dropped down beside Seraphina. "You believe my sister was engaged in something of a romantic nature?"

Seraphina nodded. "I do, but I didn't personally see the

romance, which is why I'm now waiting with bated breath for Drusilla to tell us everything."

"It's hardly proper for a lady to kiss and tell," Drusilla heard pop out of her mouth before she could stop the words, words that left Annaliese gaping again and Seraphina looking rather smug.

"I knew it," Seraphina exclaimed. "But how unfortunate that my evasive driving techniques interrupted you, especially if that came before the two of you declared your affections for each other."

"There were no declarations of any affections" was all Drusilla could think to say to that.

Seraphina seemed to deflate on the spot. "And isn't that simply a shame since the two of you make such an adorable couple."

Drusilla took a seat on the sand beside Seraphina. "I don't know why you'd think Rhenick and I make an adorable couple."

"Please," Seraphina returned with a wave of a sandy hand. "The man absolutely dotes on you, looks at you as if you're the most beautiful woman in the world, and would give you the moon if you ask for it." She smiled. "That is completely adorable behavior, and you cannot tell me that you're immune to Rhenick's charm, as you seem to always be smiling when you're in his company, which is also adorable."

"She does seem to be smiling a lot of late," Annaliese agreed.

"She'd be smiling even more if she'd simply set aside her stubbornness and admit that her vow to never consider marriage was made in haste."

"I'm sure you'd swear off any romantic encounters as well if you'd endured what I did at the hands of He Who Shall Not Be Named," Drusilla muttered.

"Undoubtedly, but since you've now learned that all men are not like that dastardly scoundrel, and that there are men like

Rhenick out there, who, again, adores you, don't you think it might be time to reevaluate your stance on romance in general?"

Drusilla blew out a breath. "I suppose I'm not completely opposed to doing some reevaluating."

"Excellent," Seraphina exclaimed. "Just as it's excellent that I get the distinct feeling that you, my dear Drusilla, might have enjoyed that kiss you admitted you shared with Rhenick. And, to point out the obvious, when a lady enjoys kissing a gentleman, that's a sign there's a budding romantic relationship on the horizon—and the near horizon, at that."

Drusilla found she didn't have an argument readily available to that because . . . she *had* enjoyed Rhenick's kiss.

Truth be told, she enjoyed quite a bit about Rhenick these days, and that *was* presenting her with quite the conundrum because she *had* vowed she would never become involved with a gentleman again as she was determined to embrace a sense of independence.

The problem with her vow, though, and why she might need to reevaluate her decision, was this—Rhenick wasn't like any gentleman she'd ever known.

Yes, he'd made a muck of their first encounter, but then, after they'd begun working together, he'd started to become her friend, and a friend who respected her opinion and didn't expect, simply because he was a man, that his opinions were more valuable than hers.

Besides respecting her opinion, though, Rhenick was an enjoyable gentleman to spend company with. Conversations were never forced between them, and he had an easy manner that left people disclosing their problems to him, something she'd seen his sisters do on numerous occasions.

"You might not want to let Mother, when we retrieve her, or Wilhelmine either for that matter, learn about the kiss," Annaliese said, pulling Drusilla from her thoughts. "They'll be planning a wedding before you can stop them, and I don't think you'd stand a chance of protesting a wedding if Mother, Wilhelmine, *and* Rhenick's delightful sisters decide that the two of you share a mutual affection for each other, and not simply of the friendly sort." She smiled. "And while I'm no expert when it comes to the matter of kissing, I'm relatively sure that most friends don't kiss each other in a romantic fashion."

Thankfully, before Drusilla had to come up with something to say to what hadn't exactly been a mistaken opinion on her sister's part, Rhenick and Seth came striding up to join them, their faces blackened from the smoke the fire had caused and their clothes soaking wet.

"We're going to have to find another ride back because the motorboat isn't going to stay seaworthy for long," Seth said before he dropped the two large rucksacks he was carrying on the sand. "I managed to save the bag of weapons you brought, as well as my own."

Annaliese tilted her head. "What type of weapons did you bring?"

"Just some prototypes I've been working on." Seth rubbed a hand over his face, smearing soot in the process. "I included my latest invention, something I'm currently calling a flame-thrower, which I think might come in handy because I'm sure it'll stop everyone in their tracks once I fire it up, which will make rescuing your mother easier."

Annaliese blinked. "And while a flamethrower sounds down-right enticing, you might want to show some caution when wielding it, especially if we make it onto the yacht my mother's money paid for. I'm sure Mother would love to be able to enjoy a few abduction-free rides on it after we rescue her before it goes up in flames."

"Duly noted," Seth said before his eyes went a little distant, then he blinked and focused on Annaliese again. "Rhenick told me how Sanford made off with your fortune, but if we're successful capturing him, do you think your money will be returned to you?"

"Not a question I was expecting, but I suppose, since Sanford told Mother that he'd return the money if she married him, if we do capture him, there is a chance our bank accounts will be sufficiently plumped up in the near future."

"That's what I'm thinking as well, which leads me to another question."

Instead of asking that question, though, Seth leaned toward Annaliese and began perusing her face, his brow furrowing in the process.

Annaliese shot a glance to Drusilla when Seth didn't bother saying a word, simply continued staring at her for what was beginning to turn into a very long moment.

Having no idea why Seth was considering Annaliese so closely, although he might simply be doing so because Annaliese was unusually beautiful, even when in a bedraggled state, Drusilla settled for sending her sister a shrug.

"Hardly helpful," Annaliese muttered before she returned her attention to Seth, then gave a snap of her fingers, something that left Seth blinking a time or two back at her.

"You said you had another question?" Annaliese prompted.

"Has anyone ever told you that your face is oddly symmetrical?" was Seth's unexpected response to that.

"They have not, but is that a good thing?" Annaliese asked.

"It's unusual."

"I'm not certain that's a good thing, but . . . your question?"

He gave himself a shake. "Right. My question." Instead of directing that question to Annaliese, though, Seth turned to Drusilla instead. "I find myself curious, if your fortune is returned to you, if you'll return to New York, which I know will disappoint Norma Jean, as she and her friends have been talking about nothing else but attending your academy."

It was a question that, curiously enough, didn't take much

consideration because, given what had happened to her in New York, she had no desire to return to the city of her birth. Especially not when the good people of Chicago had been more welcoming toward her and her family than the New York Four Hundred had ever been.

"Drusilla has far too much she already enjoys in Chicago to want to return to New York," Seraphina answered for her as she sent the barest of winks in Rhenick's direction before she rose to her feet and nodded toward the water. "However, I don't think now is the time to linger about and discuss that further because, if none of you have noticed, Seth's motorboat is once again smoking, something that's certain to draw attention at some point. Heaven forbid if Sanford is the one to notice that smoke because he'll surely pick up anchor and sail away."

"Seraphina's right," Drusilla said. "We should get moving."

After sending her a nod, Seraphina grabbed hold of one of the rucksacks as Seth did the same with the other, and with Annaliese trailing behind them, they set off for the cove.

Rhenick held out his hand and pulled Drusilla to her feet, frowning when she took a second to wring more water from her skirt. "I'm sure the weight of your gown is going to make for an uncomfortable stroll," he began, "but know that I'm more than capable of carrying you if you find yourself growing weary."

The very thought of being held in Rhenick's arms sent a blaze of heat settling on her cheeks, which she staunchly tried to ignore while hoping Rhenick wouldn't notice. "I'm sure I'll be fine, but thank you for the offer."

"It'll still stand if you find yourself tiring," he returned, presenting her with his arm, which she didn't hesitate to take before they began walking toward the cove.

"You never answered Seth's question about whether you would be returning to New York if your fortune is restored to you," he said.

286

"That's because Seraphina went ahead and answered for me."

Rhenick drew them to a stop. "You want to stay in Chicago?"

She smiled. "There's nothing for me anymore in New York. And even though I haven't been in Chicago long, it already feels like home, much more than I think New York ever did."

Rhenick returned her smile before his gaze drifted to her lips, his smile fading ever so slightly as he stepped closer.

Anticipation was swift, but before Rhenick had an opportunity to kiss her again, something she knew without a doubt he was about to do, a loud clearing of a throat pulled her directly out of a moment she knew full well would have been most extraordinary—if they hadn't been interrupted yet again.

Thirty-Seven

After giving herself a bit of a shake, Drusilla stepped away from Rhenick and turned, discovering Annaliese standing a few feet away from her, a brow already arched in Drusilla's direction.

"Not that I want to point out the obvious," Annaliese began, "but this might not be the right moment for romantic shenanigans, since we do need to keep our wits about us as we're about to undertake a rescue. I may be wrong, but I'm relatively sure none of us have ever undertaken such an attempt before, although . . ." She tilted her head. "I can't say for certain Seraphina hasn't."

"I completely forgot your sister was in our near vicinity," Rhenick muttered.

"I doubt you'll be forgetting that again," Drusilla muttered back as she fought a grin, losing the *I will not grin* battle when Annaliese marched up beside her, grabbed hold of her hand, and pulled her forward, quite as if she didn't trust her older sister to behave herself.

Ten minutes later, and after having to fight her way through the tall grass that bordered the beach, along with a slew of mud that a recent storm had left behind, they finally made it to the cove. After taking a moment to glance around, Drusilla moved to crouch down in the tall grass next to Seraphina, who already had binoculars out and was scanning the area in front of them.

"There's a man over by that shack, but as I don't know what Sanford looks like, you'll need to decide if that's him," Seraphina said, passing the binoculars to Drusilla.

In the span of time it took to direct the binoculars to a small shack where a woman, presumably Miss Sally, was serving up food to a man who was unquestionably Sanford Duncan, Drusilla's sense of apprehension over the upcoming rescue attempt turned to downright temper.

That a man she'd once called *Uncle* had stolen Irma and was attempting to whisk her away, obviously with the intent of forcing her to marry him, was beyond unacceptable, and she vowed there and then that he would be stopped, no matter if Seth's flamethrower needed to come out in order to achieve putting an end to Sanford's malicious intentions once and for all.

"That's Sanford all right," she said as Rhenick crawled his way over to join her, pulling out his binoculars and scanning the area before he turned to Drusilla.

"If you didn't notice, your mother's sitting on a blanket with Sneaky Pete and another woman, although I can't tell who that is because she's facing away from me. Since Sanford appears to be ordering food, it seems your mother might very well have convinced them to drop anchor because she was in need of a snack."

"May I take another look?" Seraphina asked, taking the binoculars from Drusilla and lifting them to her eyes. "I have to admit that Sanford doesn't look anything like I expected. He certainly doesn't appear mad, but more along the lines of a wealthy man of business."

"I'm not certain Sanford is completely mad," Drusilla admitted. "He had enough of his senses remaining to pull off an embezzlement scheme without a hitch, and one where he ended up with millions. I doubt a true madman would have been capable of that. With that said, though, he's definitely suffering from some type of delusional malady, probably brought about after he realized his love for my mother was unrequited."

"Delusional or not," Annaliese said, "the very idea that Sanford set out years ago to gain Father's friendship in order to remain close to Mother suggests he'd probably benefit from an extended stay in an asylum because that's not what I'd consider rational behavior."

"It sounds to me as if Sanford, at the very least, is destined for a long prison term since kidnapping is a felony," Seth added. "But may I suggest we continue this conversation at a later date, as we have no idea how long everyone is going to be lingering on the beach?"

"I think *we're* lingering because none of us are exactly accustomed to retrieving kidnapped mothers," Annaliese admitted.

Seth returned his attention to the beach. "I readily admit that I have no experience with situations like this, as I spend a good majority of my time well removed from people in general." He squinted at where Sanford was now rejoining Irma and nodded. "However, it seems to me as if our most likely chance of success, which I'm thinking is at twenty-five percent right now, would be to stage an ambush. We outnumber them, even though none of us are exactly trained up in ambushing techniques, unless . . ." He arched a brow Seraphina's way.

"I have never ambushed anyone," Seraphina said. "Although there was the time when my boarding school was set upon by a band of drunken men come to serenade us and I was given the responsibility of getting them to leave."

"I doubt Sanford or Sneaky Pete have been indulging in spirits, so I'm not certain how helpful your experience will be, but . . ." Annaliese's brows drew together as she turned to Seth. "Did I hear you correctly that you think we only have a twenty-five percent chance of success, which means we have a seventy-five percent chance of failure?"

Seth's brows drew together, as well. "I see your point. Those aren't very good odds, but I'm relatively sure those odds will increase if I bring out the flamethrower, and before you protest, know that no one is actually on your mother's yacht, so I won't be able to burn it down." He gave his nose a rub. "I should probably disclose, though, that I've had a few issues with controlling the flames, but I'm fairly certain I've fixed that problem."

"What'll happen if you haven't fixed it?" Drusilla forced herself to ask.

"Let's just hope that it's fixed, but if something should go amiss, we still have the element of surprise, so we'll simply need to use that to our advantage."

After disclosing that less-than-reassuring statement, Seth began crawling through the tall grass that separated them from the beach with Seraphina and Annaliese beside him, while Drusilla and Rhenick trailed behind.

Barely a minute passed before they reached sandy ground, Seth opening up his rucksack and immediately pulling out an odd-looking contraption that was comprised of a large canister and some type of metal tubing. He nodded to Rhenick. "I'm assuming you have a pistol."

"Already in hand," Rhenick said.

Seth nodded to the lake. "I don't know if you saw this, but there's another ship pulling into the cove, which means we're running out of time." He switched his attention to Drusilla. "What are the odds of you, Annaliese, and Seraphina agreeing to stay behind?"

"Less than the odds of us finding success with the use of your flamethrower," she returned.

His lips quirked. "I'll say one thing for sure—all of you are going to make some interesting proper decorum instructors because, from what I know about ladies, which isn't all that much, the proper ones don't tend to involve themselves with matters that might turn dangerous."

Drusilla's lips quirked in return. "We're definitely not the type of ladies who are going to hide our heads in the sand while you and Rhenick go off to rescue my mother."

Seth shot a look to Rhenick, who shrugged. "Don't think I'm idiotic enough to try to change their decision, as I know full well how contrary determined ladies can be. However . . ." Rhenick turned to Drusilla. "Can we at least agree that it would be best if Seth and I went first, with the three of you following, as we are larger than you and will provide some cover if Sanford or Sneaky Pete decide to shoot at us?"

"I suppose that wouldn't be too much to ask," Drusilla said, which earned her a lovely smile from Rhenick before he checked the chamber of his pistol as Seraphina opened up the other rucksack, handed Annaliese a pistol, gave one to Drusilla, and kept her favorite, the blunderbuss, for herself.

A mere moment later, Drusilla found herself running across the sand in Rhenick's wake, stumbling over a piece of driftwood right as shouts rang out and then the sound of a pistol being fired split the air.

That was all it took for Seth to stop in his tracks and aim the flamethrower in the direction of Sneaky Pete, who took one look at Seth's invention and tossed his gun aside before he sprinted off toward the water right as a huge plume of fire burst out of the flamethrower.

It quickly became evident that Seth had *not* fixed the problem with his recent invention, as the flame sputtering out of the tube suddenly erupted into something far more than sputters, which resulted in Seth tossing the flamethrower aside as he yelled for everyone to take cover since there was no question that an explosion was imminent.

Thirty-Eight

To say that Irma's rescue attempt was not going smoothly wasn't an exaggeration since a mere moment after Seth's flamethrower literally blew up, Sanford snatched hold of Irma, flung her over his shoulder, and sprinted after Sneaky Pete, who was racing full tilt toward a dinghy that was pulled ashore right on the edge of the water.

Rhenick's gaze darted around the beach and landed on Drusilla, who was struggling with Sneaky Pete's accomplice, an accomplice who looked remarkably like Fenna Larkin. Before he could take a single step toward her, though, Seraphina came charging to her aid, pulling the woman off Drusilla a second later.

Glancing to his right, he found Annaliese running into the water after Irma, Seth splashing behind her, his face completely black and his hair standing on end—at least the parts that hadn't been singed right off his head after the flamethrower exploded.

Deciding Drusilla and Seraphina had matters with the woman well in hand, Rhenick ran for the lake, diving under the water before he surfaced and struck out to intercept Sanford and Sneaky Pete, who had managed to get Irma thrown into the dinghy and were trying to drag it into deeper water.

He made it to within feet of them before a shot rent the air, followed by another, and then another, and then a loud voice that sounded as if it were coming out of a large horn wafted over the water.

"Raise your hands in the air, drop your weapons, and wait for one of our Pinkerton agents to escort you back to shore."

"Agent Pearson!" Drusilla suddenly called out. "What are you doing here?"

"Miss Merriweather! Thank goodness you're alright, and I'm here trying to do my job, but it appears as if you've gotten the jump on me."

As Drusilla took to grinning, Rhenick put his hands in the air and turned, noticing that the ship Seth had pointed out earlier had pulled alongside the *Revenge* and that there were already numerous dinghies in the water, all of them filled with what Rhenick assumed were Pinkerton agents.

Before he knew it, he was being escorted by one of those Pinkertons back to the beach, where Miss Sally, the owner of the cove shack, was waiting for everyone, that woman having had the good sense to throw water on Seth's questionable flame-thrower. As soon as everyone began wading out of the water, Sally bellowed that she was off to the refreshment counter, letting everyone know she was open for business, quite as if her little cove hadn't just witnessed a troubling attack but simply the arrival of potential customers.

After Drusilla called to the Pinkerton agent who'd taken hold of Rhenick's arm that he was with her, the agent released him and went off to help other Pinkertons go about the business of securing Sanford, Sneaky Pete, and a woman who did turn out to be Fenna Larkin.

Slogging out of the water, Rhenick moved to join Drusilla, who immediately introduced him, as well as Seth and Seraphina, to Agent Pearson.

"I cannot tell you how relieved I am to see you, Agent

Pearson," Drusilla exclaimed after introductions had been completed. "It's been quite the wild morning to say the least, and given that we lost the use of our boat after it caught on fire, and then seemed to be losing the fight to prevent Sanford from making off with my mother again, your appearance certainly saved the day. With that said, I find I'm now brimming with curiosity to hear how you managed to find us, or what you're doing here in the first place?"

Agent Pearson, a man who looked to be in his early fifties and had a face that was lined with enough wrinkles to suggest he'd seen more than his fair share of life, smiled. "We're here because of that lead we received about Sanford being spotted in the Gulf of Mexico. Unfortunately, by the time I got to the port where he'd been spotted, he was no longer there. I had no idea where he might have gone until another agent had the good sense to pull out a map and we realized he could sail his yacht up the Mississippi and eventually land in Lake Michigan. Knowing that's where your family had gone, I decided that Sanford had learned that as well, so here I am, although a bit late to the party."

He gave a rueful shake of his head. "We arrived at the castle after you'd already left this morning, but Mrs. O'Sullivan got us up to speed on what had happened, and then Mr. Grimsby told us you were heading north on the lake, so that's the direction we headed."

Agent Pearson nodded to where Sanford, Sneaky Pete, and Fenna were now sitting, their hands tied behind their backs and looking quite as if they'd rather be anywhere else. "Do you know who those two are with Sanford?"

"Sneaky Pete Smythe and Fenna Larkin," Drusilla said. "They weren't directly involved with Sanford until last night— well, not that I know of, but I'm sure we'll uncover a few of their secrets now that they're in custody. Those secrets will need to wait to be revealed, though, as I believe I want to start with questioning Sanford first, as he is the man who upended my entire world. In all honesty, though, I've begun wondering if that upending might have been a blessing in disguise."

Five minutes later, and sipping iced tea that Sally had brought him from her snack shack, charging him a hefty fee for it in the process, Rhenick watched as Drusilla, after she'd given Irma a long hug, settled herself on a piece of driftwood that put her within feet of Sanford, unable to help but wonder what she'd meant when she'd said that the upending of her world might have been a blessing in disguise.

There was the possibility that she'd said it because the loss of the Merriweather fortune had allowed her to escape a future being married to a man who sounded like a complete cad. However, she could have also been referring to the opening of her academy as a blessing, since it was clear she thrived on challenges and probably hadn't been faced with many when she'd been an heiress.

Either of those two possibilities would perfectly explain her statement, except for the fact that Drusilla had glanced his way directly after uttering the word *blessing*, which left him thinking, or rather hoping, that she looked at becoming acquainted with him as a blessing, which might suggest she was becoming somewhat fond of him, that idea reinforced given that they'd shared a more-than-delightful kiss only the night before.

Considering everything that had happened since, he'd not had much time to ponder the matter of their kiss in general, but the one thing he did know was this—Drusilla had seemed to enjoy it. That right there suggested she *was* somewhat fond of him, or maybe, since she might find him a blessing in her life, could be more than somewhat fond of him, although how much more remained to be seen.

"I don't think there's any reason for me to be anything but direct," Drusilla said, pulling Rhenick from his thoughts as she settled her gaze on Sanford. "With that said, I'd like for you, a man I once called Uncle Sanford, to explain to me how you could have, even if you'd been annoyed with my mother, stolen everything from us, going so far as to leave us without a roof over our heads. Well, except for the one Aunt Ottilie thankfully gave me and Annaliese, although I'm not certain you even knew about the castle."

Sanford's brow furrowed. "Of course I didn't know about the castle. Your father, contrary to what everyone believes, didn't tell me everything. Regardless, you should know that I never meant to leave you without a roof over your head because I assumed Elbert Herrington would step in and save the house on Washington Square. I had no inkling that dreadful man would break off your engagement, but know that after I learned he'd done exactly that, I immediately made plans to leave Scotland, where I'd been letting a house."

Drusilla frowned. "You would have me believe that you raced across the ocean to save us from a situation you were responsible for?"

"Too right I did, as you're my family." He sent a nod Agent Pearson's way. "I knew the Pinkertons would have been put on the case, as I did make off with a great deal of money, which is why I couldn't risk docking on the east coast and taking a train to Chicago. Luckily, the Mississippi turned into a viable option, so here I am."

"But you didn't exactly swoop in and save us," Drusilla pointed out. "You swooped in and made off with my mother."

"I thought it would benefit your mother and me as a future couple if we were able to talk out our differences in private."

Drusilla began rubbing her temple. "I have no idea what I can even say to that."

"Then allow me to take over the conversation from here,"

Irma said, moving to join Drusilla on her piece of driftwood, where she promptly settled eyes that were flashing on Sanford. "We, if you haven't figured this out, are never going to be a future couple, and not simply because you're soon going to find yourself behind bars, although . . ." She tilted her head. "Given what is clearly a delusional frame of mind on your part, you may find that the courts will sentence you to a very long stay in an insane asylum."

Sanford frowned. "I assure you, the last place I deserve to be is in an asylum."

Irma returned the frown. "And to that I say it's debatable. You've taken at least a slight leave of your senses since you seem to believe we're some star-crossed lovers who are finally being given an opportunity to be together."

"We've been waiting to be together since we were eight years old and vowed we'd marry someday."

"Children often claim to their best friends they'll marry someday, but no one ever actually expects those children to honor those types of vows once they get older."

"Ah, so you do admit we were best friends," Sanford said.

"We were the only children of a like age to live on the same street."

"But we remained friends even as we matured, and to remind you, I made a point of attending your debut even though I had to cut short my grand tour."

Irma sat forward. "I never asked you to do that, Sanford, and, if you'll recall, I even wrote to you that Father had his eye on Morton Merriweather as a potential suitor for me."

"And I wrote you back and told you to tell your father that you didn't need any potential suitors, as you were going to marry me."

Irma crossed her arms over her chest. "If you'll recall, you and I often spoke about the fact that my father placed great emphasis on his Knickerbocker status and had married my mother simply because she was a Knickerbocker as well. It then stands to reason that my father would only want me to marry a Knickerbocker, and while your family was very well-connected, you weren't Knickerbockers. Morton was, though, which is why I thought you were jesting about the two of us marrying because you knew all of that."

"I suppose I can understand why you'd think I was jesting, but I certainly can't see why, after Morton died, you wouldn't agree to marry me, as your father was long dead and could no longer exert any influence on any decisions you might want to make."

Irma released a sigh. "Did you ever consider that me telling you I couldn't marry you when you suggested we begin planning a double wedding was actually me making my own decision?"

"But decisions can be changed," Sanford argued, quite as if he wasn't going to even contemplate that her decision had been to not marry him. "Why, look at me, even though I decided to render you penniless, I've now decided I'm perfectly happy to return every penny to you. Well, as long as you agree to marry me, that is."

Drusilla leaned closer to Irma. "I'm afraid there's no point trying to reason with him further, Mother. His delusions when it comes to you are obviously deeply rooted, no matter that you're certainly due this opportunity to speak your mind to him."

"I fear you may be right, my dear, which means we shall now simply turn him over to the Pinkertons, where I'm sure they'll see him delivered to the nearest jail, or perhaps they'll take him to be seen by a doctor to explore the extent of his delusions. Hopefully, at some point, someone will manage to get Sanford to divulge where he's stashed our money, but until that day happens, we'll simply concentrate on opening the academy and pray that venture will see us firmly on the road to financial stability once again."

Agent Pearson stepped forward. "You won't need to wait to learn where Sanford stashed your money because the man who reached out to us after he spotted Sanford in the Gulf of Mexico also spotted him an hour later leaving a bank. We Pinkertons, being rather motivated by that lovely fee Drusilla promised us, tracked that bank down and then recovered an account that was under the name of M. Weather, a take on Merriweather, if I'm not mistaken."

He settled a smile on Irma. "I'm pleased to inform you that you'll soon be reunited with a good chunk of your fortune, although know that we won't close the case until we've discerned exactly where Sanford stashed the rest of your funds. Given that there's quite the hefty sum in the bank account we recovered, know that there is absolutely no reason for you to ever have to concern yourself with financial problems again."

Thirty-Nine

I t had not escaped Drusilla's notice that there seemed to be something bothering Rhenick, since he'd taken to raking his hand through his hair, something he was prone to doing whenever he was troubled.

Before she could question him about the matter, though, Agent Pearson nodded to some fellow Pinkertons, who set about getting Sanford to his feet, who didn't struggle the slightest bit until he realized, as the agents led him to a dinghy, that Irma wasn't going with him.

"I shall be counting the seconds until we find ourselves together again, my love," he called in Irma's direction after the agents had to resort to muscling him into the dinghy, where two of them immediately sat on either side of him to prevent him from jumping overboard.

Irma turned her gaze away from a man who'd caused her no end of difficulties. "Perhaps a stay in an asylum truly is needed because we may very well be mistaken in that he's not merely slightly delusional but borderline insane." She gave Sanford one last glance before she squared her shoulders and turned her attention to Sneaky Pete and Fenna. "But Sanford's questionable mental state is something we can revisit later, as we still need to decide what's to be done with those two."

Before Drusilla could do more than consider people who'd obviously been responsible for the haunting of Merriweather Castle, Fenna Larkin took to settling a bright smile on Irma.

"I don't think there's anything to be done with us except let us go. As has already been noted, I'm great friends with Ottilie, a friendship that, unfortunately, Loughlin MacSherry became aware of. That friendship is exactly why he began demanding I take on a project for him, and as I'm sure you've been made aware, MacSherry isn't a man one can refuse, not if one wants to continue breathing."

"And while I'm sure you would love nothing more than for us to turn you free," Drusilla said before her mother could do more than take to looking rather confused over Fenna's unlikely explanation, "I'm afraid I'm unwilling to do that since I'm relatively certain you're not being truthful with us. In all honesty, I'm not convinced you were ever good friends with my aunt. And since my aunt actually seems to be missing, and you just admitted you've been doing some work for Loughlin Mac-Sherry, I now find myself wondering if you, along with Sneaky Pete, had something to do with my aunt's disappearance."

Fenna's eyes widened. "I would never do anything to dear Ottilie."

"You were never friends with Miss Ottilie, something she was very much aware of, and is exactly why she turned ownership of the castle over to her nieces before she left on her trip."

Fenna sucked in a sharp breath right as Norbert, surprisingly enough, in the company of an older gentleman, stepped around Agent Pearson and marched through the sand to join them.

The groundskeeper's gaze traveled to Fenna, then to Sneaky Pete, before it settled on Drusilla. "Miss Drusilla," he began with an inclination of his head. "It's ever so wonderful to see that you've managed to survive the machinations of these two criminals relatively unscathed, and know that I'm truly sorry I was forced to disappear without a word."

He shot another glance to Fenna before he returned his attention to Drusilla. "I didn't believe I had a choice in the matter, though, since I was certain Fenna was going to tell you some fairly large lies about me." He directed a nod to the man standing beside him. "As luck would have it, I'd already made plans to meet Mr. William Baumgartner at an inn directly outside of Chicago. He sent me a telegram asking to speak with me about the situation in the castle, that being you and your family having moved into it, something he found out about after Rhenick had the bank send him a message."

The man beside Norbert stepped forward and presented Drusilla with a bow. "I must beg your pardon for not responding to the telegram I received from the bank, but know that it was only because I needed to consider the matter carefully and weigh how much danger I'd put you in if I arrived back in the city." He straightened. "I'm Mr. William Baumgartner, Miss Ottilie's solicitor, and Norbert told me that you're Miss Drusilla Merriweather."

Drusilla dipped into a curtsy. "It's a pleasure to meet you, Mr. Baumgartner, but before we exchange polite pleasantries, I have a few questions for both you and Norbert."

"I'd be surprised if you didn't," Mr. Baumgartner said.

Drusilla inclined her head to the solicitor before she turned to Norbert. "I'm curious why you didn't simply explain to me your concerns about Fenna instead of stealing off to meet with Mr. Baumgartner."

"I surely did consider that," Norbert began, "until I realized there was every chance you wouldn't believe me since Fenna is very good with telling tall tales." He shook his head. "I knew the only person who was going to be able to clear my name was Mr. Baumgartner, because he was aware of what Miss Ottilie's suspicions were about Fenna. That's why it was fortunate we had that meeting already set up outside of town, especially after I saw Fenna watching the castle before everyone left for church. Once everyone got on their way, Fenna immediately pulled her buggy from where she'd been lurking in the shadows and began following you—suspicious behavior if there ever was some."

Norbert gave his nose a scratch. "I never trusted the woman after she turned difficult about gaining access to the castle. That's why I decided to follow her, and I started getting worried when she stopped her buggy at the church and scooted right on inside, my concern growing when, after the service, she made a beeline for you and started talking your ear off."

"She was telling me about her suspicions about you," Drusilla said.

"I figured as much because I was pretty sure she'd spotted me following her at one point. That's why I hurried back to the castle and packed a bag, just to be on the safe side in case things went sideways. After that, I fetched Ernie and off I went to meet Mr. Baumgartner. I was hoping he'd be able to answer some of the questions I had about the strange occurrences that have been going on now for months."

Drusilla glanced to Mr. Baumgartner. "And were you able to provide Norbert with the answers he desired?"

"I believe so, and know that Norbert convinced me to travel to the castle to explain everything to you so you'd understand the danger you were in, which is how it came to be that Norbert and I are currently here, speaking with you now."

"But how did you manage to get here at this particular moment?" Drusilla asked.

"That's a story in and of itself," Norbert said. "But the short of it is this—Mr. Baumgartner and I caught a ride with the Pinkertons after we ran smack into them as they were leaving the castle this morning." He winced. "In all truthfulness, we didn't have a choice but to go with them because Mrs. O'Sullivan told them I was involved with some shady dealings surrounding the castle and the Pinkertons decided it would be a better use of their time if they just took us with them since they didn't want to delay going after Sanford and your mother."

"How did you convince the Pinkertons you weren't up to anything suspicious?"

Norbert nodded to Mr. Baumgartner. "One of the local Pinkerton agents recognized Mr. Baumgartner and knew, given Mr. Baumgartner's stellar reputation, that he definitely wasn't involved in any shenanigans. By that time, though, we were already aboard their ship and sailing up Lake Michigan. When the *Revenge* was spotted, we were told to stay behind because the situation might become dangerous. That local Pinkerton who recognized Mr. Baumgartner returned to the ship just a few moments ago with some man who's muttering something about losing his true love, and that agent thought we might be able to help clear up the situation with the two suspects who were still on the beach."

"There's no reason for you to involve yourself in this, Norbert," Fenna snapped.

"Of course there is because you told Miss Drusilla you were close with her aunt, which is an out-and-out lie. You were her assistant, nothing more."

"I traveled the world with her."

"You went on one trip to Egypt with her as her assistant," Norbert countered. "That she didn't ask you to go on her last adventure suggests she was beginning to realize you might have been up to something shady."

Fenna lifted her chin. "The only thing I did that might have been considered shady was when, after I was approached by Loughlin MacSherry and agreed to deliver an offer from him for the castle to Ottilie, I might have neglected to disclose to her that MacSherry was paying me a fee."

Norbert let out a grunt. "I'm sure that's not the only shady thing you've done, just as I'm sure Miss Ottilie figured out your connection to Loughlin MacSherry right from the start, as well as figured that MacSherry was going to continue to use you to exert pressure on her to sell. That's probably why she began to make plans to take a spur-of-the-moment adventure and why she had Mr. Baumgartner transfer ownership of the castle to her two nieces, which he just recently told me she had him do as a way to protect ownership of her property while she was gone."

Mr. Baumgartner cleared his throat and glanced to Drusilla. "Before another word is said, allow me to beg your pardon for never explaining the true reason why your aunt gave you and your sister the castle."

"You might also want to beg my mother's pardon for never responding to the telegrams she sent you after my father, Ottilie's brother, died."

Mr. Baumgartner glanced around, presenting Irma with a bow a moment later. "You would be Mrs. Merriweather, of course, and indeed I do need to beg your pardon for neglecting to respond to your telegrams. I assure you there were numerous reasons why I didn't, and if you'll indulge me for a few minutes, I'll explain why."

He took a second to rock on his heels in the sand before he nodded. "Ottilie had me transfer ownership of the castle because she knew MacSherry wanted it. She also knew he was a ruthless man and thus wanted to put some distance between her and him, which is exactly why, when Captain Harvey sent her a trunk filled with maps, she claimed she'd found one with potential. She then sent Captain Harvey a telegram, and a mere week or so later, they were off on a treasure hunt together."

"Ottilie didn't happen to mention where she was going to be doing that treasure hunting, did she?" Drusilla asked.

"I'm afraid not, although she left that trunk of maps in my care." Mr. Baumgartner gave a shake of his head. "Sadly, I've looked at every map in that trunk numerous times and haven't been able to decide with any certainty if she and Captain Harvey had been pursuing one specific map. I have noticed that a few of the maps look like copies, which may be a clue, although I'm not sure about that or what they may be a clue about."

Drusilla turned to Agent Pearson. "It seems as if we'll be needing your services to look into my aunt's disappearance, so I'll have Mr. Baumgartner send the trunk of maps to the castle, and we can look them over together." She returned her attention to Mr. Baumgartner. "May I assume that you left town for a specific reason, and that there was also a specific reason why you never answered the telegrams my mother sent you regarding the death of my father?"

"I was very sorry to hear about your father's passing, but I didn't dare respond, not when Ottilie had warned me about MacSherry and that she feared there were members of her staff who couldn't be trusted—most specifically Fenna. I was afraid Fenna might have bribed someone in the telegram office to contact her or MacSherry about any telegrams I might send, or more specifically, tell her who I was sending them to. I promised your aunt I wouldn't say a word about you or your sister, nor let anyone get near the will she also left in my possession, one that names you and Annaliese as her sole heirs if anything happens to her, although she did bequeath a token amount to your mother."

Irma blinked. "Ottilie left me something in her will?"

"She didn't want you to feel slighted, but know that your daughters are due to inherit far more of Ottilie's fortune than you are."

Irma's lips twitched. "That sounds more like Ottilie, but . . ." She took to frowning. "Since you did disappear from Chicago, may I assume that someone started questioning you about who Ottilie's heirs were?"

Mr. Baumgartner nodded to Fenna. "She started stopping by my office not long after Ottilie left town, then began increasing her visits about seven months after Ottilie left, demanding to know where Ottilie had gone, when she was expected back, and if I thought something might have happened to her, and if so, did that mean I, as Ottilie's solicitor, was responsible for having my client declared dead. Since I got the distinct impression Fenna was only going to become more persistent, I decided, in order to protect Drusilla and Annaliese, I needed to leave town."

"And I thank you for that," Drusilla began, "although my sister and I certainly ruined your plan when we showed up in Chicago and let it be known almost immediately that we were now the owners of Merriweather Castle."

Mr. Baumgartner smiled. "That definitely wasn't part of the plan. Your aunt never thought either of you would even come to visit the property she gave you, let alone move into the castle, which, as I've already intimated, she was only intending on transferring to you on a temporary basis. Know, though, that your aunt would have more than compensated you for taking her gift back." He leaned closer to Drusilla. "She was thinking about buying both of you cottages in Newport, ones that would rival Mrs. Astor's cottage, to make up for any disappointment you might have felt over being asked to turn the castle back over to her."

"She wouldn't have needed to do that, as Annaliese and I would have understood the reason behind the transferring of ownership," Drusilla said. "I'm simply sorry that we ruined the plans you and Ottilie put into place to safeguard the property, which we wouldn't have ruined if someone hadn't stolen our fortune, making the castle the only property we had available to live in."

"Norbert told me about the trouble you've experienced, which makes me feel even sorrier that I never returned your telegrams, as there was no need for any of you to suffer from lack of funds. I have the authority to relinquish the trust funds your aunt set up for you and Annaliese."

Drusilla blinked. "We have trust funds?"

"Five million apiece, and funds that your aunt made sure could never be able to be accessed by any husbands if or when you married, as your aunt wanted both of you to have a way to be financially independent."

"Ottilie left her nieces five million apiece?" Fenna repeated.

"And that's just the money she set aside in trusts," Mr. Baumgartner said. "They'll inherit far more than that, but only, of course, if we get conclusive evidence that Ottilie is indeed deceased."

Fenna exchanged a glance with Sneaky Pete before she returned her attention to Drusilla. "Pete and I may have some information that might help you find out exactly what happened to Ottilie, but information like that always comes with a price."

≕ Forty ≕

It was difficult to resist the inclination to give Fenna a bit of a shake, but after realizing it would hardly be appropriate to shake a woman who had her hands tied behind her back, Drusilla settled for quirking a brow Fenna's way instead.

"You want me to pay you for information that might lead to Ottilie's whereabouts—a woman you've told me numerous times was one of your dearest friends, even though Norbert seems to think otherwise?"

"Ottilie *was* a dear friend of mine. If she wasn't, why would she have shown me that miniature of you, or told me about Annaliese and plume hunters, or also told me that her sister-in-law's name is Irma?"

"I would imagine she told you information about my family while the two of you traveled to Egypt together, as well as showed you a miniature of us during that time, but . . ." Drusilla narrowed her eyes. "I have a feeling it's far more likely that after you and Sneaky Pete got rid of the staff at the castle, and then you continued haunting the place, probably at the direction of Loughlin MacSherry, you made a point of looking through Aunt Ottilie's personal effects. If I'm right, you would have undoubtedly run across some of the letters I, along with

JEN TURANO

Annaliese, sent to our aunt over the years, as she was notorious for saving our every scribble."

Norbert made a bit of a process out of clearing his throat, drawing everyone's attention. "Fenna wouldn't have had to look hard for your miniatures as Miss Ottilie never took her charm bracelets with her. They were what she considered special treasures, so she kept them in a jewelry box that's probably still on her dresser." He settled a scowl on Fenna. "And while it doesn't surprise me to learn that you've been riffling through Miss Ottilie's belongings for months, and don't think I haven't figured out that it was you leaving all those messages on the mirrors because you had access to Miss Ottilie's handwriting and could have easily copied her distinctive S, what I haven't figured out is how you've been able to access the castle."

"There's no secret to how we got into the castle," Sneaky Pete said. "We just used the tunnel."

Fenna immediately leveled a glare on Pete. "There is absolutely no reason for you to admit anything we might have done, especially when doing that is the same as handing the Pinkertons a confession of guilt on our part."

Sneaky Pete glared right back at Fenna. "I'm not admitting anything that's considered a crime except that we had access to the castle because of the tunnel, which Norbert undoubtedly knows about. Besides that, it might benefit us to cooperate because you know the Pinkertons are going to find out about the tunnel anyway since we showed Sanford how to access it so he could get to his boat without scaling down the cliffside. He'll most likely tell them all about how we got away from the castle once the Pinkertons start questioning him."

"Except that Sanford's clearly taken leave of most of his senses so the Pinkertons probably wouldn't have put much stock in anything he'd tell them," Fenna snapped.

As Sneaky Pete took to looking like he might not have considered that, Norbert took a step closer to him. "While it's true

311

I know about the tunnel, I'm not sure how you could have used it when Captain Harvey had the entrance sealed off right after he decided to retire."

"Just because the entrance was sealed off doesn't mean the person who was sent to do that sealing did a credible job," Sneaky Pete muttered.

"You were the one responsible for carrying out Captain Harvey's order?" Norbert demanded.

"Sure was, and I decided to make sure it wasn't sealed off properly because I thought the new owner might appreciate my foresight in keeping the tunnel accessible, and would, of course, reward me for that foresight." He shook his head. "That almost worked to my advantage after Loughlin MacSherry approached me, telling me to let him know when the captain was going to sell because he knew all about Captain Harvey being a smuggler. MacSherry also knew the castle was perfect for clandestine activities and wanted to be the first in line to buy it."

"If that's true, why isn't he the owner of the castle now?" Drusilla asked.

"He was out of town when the captain decided to sell." Sneaky Pete shook his head. "That was a bone of contention with MacSherry for certain, and believe you me, he was really upset that I hadn't been aware of what the captain was planning in advance.

"MacSherry eventually stopped holding me responsible and decided he'd just bide his time and wait for another opportunity to gain ownership of the castle. He thought that time had come after Ottilie didn't return on schedule, which is when he reached out to me again, telling me he'd pay me a handsome fee if I could provide him with a list of Ottilie's heirs before that became public knowledge."

Pete inclined his head in Fenna's direction. "Since Fenna had been Ottilie's assistant, I got MacSherry's permission to bring her into the job as well. But it didn't turn into the easy money

---

we thought it would because Mr. Baumgartner wouldn't tell her who Ottilie's heirs were. He then left town, and Norbert wouldn't let her back into the castle. That's when we decided our only hope was to continue making it appear as if the castle was haunted, something that would allow me and Fenna to snoop around at our leisure." He shrugged. "It wasn't difficult to unseal the entrance to the tunnel, and Fenna and I have been using it ever since."

Fenna released a hiss. "Be quiet, you fool. There's no need to keep telling them things they haven't asked to be told."

Sneaky Pete hissed right back at her. "It's called leverage. I'm sure the Pinkertons would rather take a man like Loughlin MacSherry into custody over the two of us, as we're only guilty of breaking into a castle, scaring a few people, and looking through some papers, as well as trying to find a copy of a treasure map. None of which are exactly crimes we'd spend much time for in jail."

"Why were you interested in finding a copy of that map?" Drusilla asked.

Fenna shot a look of clear warning to Pete before smiling Drusilla's way a second later. "We weren't actually looking for the map. I'm sure Pete simply meant to say we were trying to find more of Ottilie's journals."

"Sure enough that's what I meant to say," Pete said with a bob of his head. "And just so everyone knows, it wasn't a crime for my sister to help herself to Ottilie's journals since Ottilie had already given her a few of them to use for research."

Fenna settled another glare on Pete. "We weren't going to let anyone know we're brother and sister."

"It's not a crime for us to be related," Pete shot back. "Nor was it much of a crime for us to continue to haunt the castle in the hopes that, when Ottilie was declared dead, whoever her heirs were would hear about the hauntings and not hesitate to take Loughlin MacSherry's money and head directly out of town. Questionable behavior like that is known as criminal mischief, and given all the concerning crimes that happen in Chicago these days, criminal mischief doesn't get a person more than a slap on the wrist."

"Unless that criminal mischief might lead to a felony offense if something you and your sister did led to the death of my aunt," Drusilla said as she narrowed her eyes on Fenna. "I'm now wondering why you and your brother seemed so certain Ottilie was dead, which might have been exactly why you started asking Mr. Baumgartner questions and perhaps also had you searching for a copy of that treasure map. If I'm guessing correctly, you might have wanted to start looking for that treasure on your own—especially if you had reason to believe Ottilie was no longer capable of looking for it herself."

"That's ridiculous," Fenna snapped. "Ottilie was always running off chasing treasure, but she never found anything."

"But I doubt she'd ever been sent treasure maps that had been the property of a pirate before, something you mentioned while you and I were speaking at the church."

Drusilla turned her attention to Agent Pearson. "Do you think there might be enough circumstantial evidence to take Fenna and Sneaky Pete in to question them further about their part in my aunt's disappearance?"

Agent Pearson inclined his head. "Given that they've admitted they were working for this Loughlin MacSherry, it's not a stretch to think he would have asked them to make arrangements to have your aunt disappear once she left on her trip. The question of the hour would be exactly how they made that happen."

"That almost sounds as if you're accusing Pete and me of Ottilie's . . . murder," Fenna all but sputtered.

"Since you and your brother obviously had some malicious intent in mind toward Ottilie Merriweather, and she has, unfortunately, disappeared, I can guarantee a judge will agree to have you held for attempted murder until we can get to the bottom of exactly what happened to Ottilie," Agent Pearson said.

"There is absolutely no reason to hold me or my brother as I have no qualms telling you that, if you want answers, all you need to do is track down Captain Harvey's men," Fenna rushed to say, obviously not as reluctant to provide some answers now that she might be facing a murder charge. "If anyone knows what happened to Ottilie, they do because MacSherry paid them a very handsome fee to take care of his Ottilie problem, although . . ." She shot a glance to Pete, paired with the barest hint of a nod. "Know that Pete and I don't know any of the details, nor did we have anything to do with her disappearance."

Agent Pearson blinked before he cleared his throat. "You can be certain we'll be tracking Captain Harvey's crew down, but know this, if Ottilie Merriweather *is* dead, you and your brother will be considered accomplices in her death and will, of course, be charged accordingly."

⇒ Forty-One ⇐

Rhenick knew it was certainly safe to say that the two days that had passed since Sanford, Fenna, and Sneaky Pete had been taken into custody, had been on the exceptionally busy side.

After everyone had returned to Chicago, and then taken well-deserved naps as sleep had been in short supply ever since Sneaky Pete had been discovered strolling about in his suit of armor, there'd been absolutely no opportunity to speak with Drusilla in private.

In all honesty, Rhenick wasn't exactly certain how to broach what he wanted to speak with her about as she had been rather adamant regarding her aversion to the topic of matrimony. However, given that they'd shared a kiss, and she hadn't seemed opposed to his kiss, it seemed as if some sort of private talk needed to be held between them.

The question of the hour was how he was going to approach the talk because his sisters all had differing opinions on the subject.

Tilda believed he should just be direct and ask Drusilla if her opinion of matrimony had changed since they'd kissed, while Grace and Coraline thought he should completely start from scratch and take to properly courting Drusilla before even uttering the word *marriage* in her presence.

Eloise, on the other hand, believed he should simply drop to one knee at his earliest convenience, proclaim himself madly in love with Drusilla, and hope for the best, which, frankly, he thought was the suggestion that might have the most potential.

Blinking out of his thoughts when he realized Sweet Pea had stopped moving, undoubtedly because they'd reached their destination, Rhenick stepped from the two-person buggy he'd chosen to bring out today and handed the reins to a groom waiting outside the Palmer House.

After the groom assured him that Sweet Pea would be more than adequately attended to, Rhenick walked into the hotel, taking a second to appreciate the grand lobby that sported numerous crystal chandeliers and fresco paintings on the ceiling before he headed across the marble floor and toward the dining room.

A smile curved his lips as he walked into that room and his gaze immediately settled on Drusilla, who was sitting at a table with not only Irma, Annaliese, and Seraphina, but his mother and four sisters, as well.

He strode across the room, nodding to Mrs. Marshall Field and Mrs. Potter Palmer, before he set his sights on his mother, who was dressed almost exactly like Mrs. Palmer, which left him wondering if Irma had been helping his mother with her wardrobe selections of late.

After reaching his mother's side, he bent over and kissed her cheek, sent his sisters a smile, nodded to Seraphina, Annaliese, and Irma, then moved to stand beside where Drusilla was sitting, his smile widening when she held out her hand to him, which he dutifully took hold of and kissed.

It was rather encouraging when her cheeks turned a little pink.

"We were thinking you might have decided not to join us," she said as he sat down in the chair beside her, unable to help but wonder if Drusilla had been responsible for where he was sitting, and if so, if that might mean he really should consider Eloise's option of simply declaring his intentions and seeing what happened. If she wasn't opposed to sitting beside him, perhaps she wouldn't be completely opposed to the idea of marriage to him, or at the very least, opposed to a formal courtship where they could really get down to becoming well-acquainted with each other.

"May I assume something troubling has happened again since your brow is furrowing in a rather telling fashion?" she asked.

He shoved all thoughts of matrimony and courtship aside and summoned up a smile. "Nothing troubling has happened. I was merely delayed because one of the water closets my men recently installed in the castle was malfunctioning, and no, you don't want to know the details of that. I was then delayed again because Norbert tracked me down to tell me about a hidden staircase he'd never seen before and only found because Fidget ran past him with a mouse and disappeared behind a bookcase. Turns out that particular bookcase hides the entrance to another staircase, which suggests your castle still has numerous secrets to reveal."

"How delightful," Drusilla exclaimed right as numerous servers approached the table, setting bowls of soup on the charger plates already set in front of everyone. They then turned and headed back for the kitchen, Drusilla clearing her throat and nodding to Grace, Coraline, and Eloise after the servers disappeared.

"Not to make any of you nervous, but as I mentioned earlier, one of the points of this luncheon is to allow me an opportunity to study your proficiency with cutlery and general ease with maneuvering your way through lunch. You certainly won't be graded, as this isn't an official academy lesson, but it will help me know what to expect when we open our doors next week, as many of the students are direct friends of yours. I imagine most of you share similar familiarity with the rules of propriety."

"Norma Jean McCormick," Coraline began, "believes that complete adherence to proper etiquette might be somewhat overrated, and she's hoping you won't be a complete stickler for insisting everyone adheres to proper decorum all the time as that might dim her exuberance for life."

"I'm afraid Norma Jean's exuberance for life might dim ever so slightly, because yes, I will expect all students to behave themselves, and there will certainly not be any beating of anyone over the head with a fan, which I saw Norma Jean doing during church.

"With that said, though, I'm not an absolute stickler for every lesson in propriety that I've studied over the years. My decision to open an academy, even though high society frowns on ladies engaged in any type of business endeavors, wasn't a decision most proper ladies would have made."

"Norma Jean might bring up that deviation from the proprieties if she happens to feel another urge to use her fan as a weapon," Coraline pointed out.

"I'm more than capable of dealing with Norma Jean, but I thank you for the advanced warning. And, with that settled, shall we enjoy our soup?"

"Should we assume no slurping is allowed?" Eloise asked.

Drusilla's lips twitched. "I don't think that's a question that even needs to be asked."

As his sisters began taking a marked interest in the many different spoons that were laid out on the right side of the charger plate, Grace finally picking up the largest one after shooting a glance to Seraphina, who might have ever so casually pointed to her large spoon. Rhenick picked up his soup spoon as well, unable to help but smile as he stuck it into the bowl.

"Do not say you're smiling because you saw Seraphina being less than subtle as she tries to help your sisters out. Smiling will only encourage her to continue giving them assistance once they need a fork," Drusilla whispered before she took a perfect spoonful of soup.

Rhenick watched her take another before he tried to emulate her, grimacing when a bit of soup dribbled from the spoon and marred the white linen of the tablecloth. "I'm not smiling because of Seraphina, although I would bet good money she's going to become a favorite instructor. I'm smiling because we've not had an opportunity to discuss anything much of late since you've been busy getting your affairs in order, but you've evidently decided to stay in Chicago to run your academy instead of returning to New York."

"Why would you have thought I'd return to New York? I already told you, right before we rescued my mother, that I was planning on staying in Chicago."

"I thought you might have had a change of heart after you discovered you have a trust fund, and then learned that a good portion of the Merriweather fortune was going to be returned to your family. With money like that, it would be perfectly reasonable to expect you to change your mind about the academy since that's going to be quite the challenge to get up and running, and besides that, you lived your entire life up until this point in New York."

Drusilla set aside her spoon. "But I'm sure I also told you that I never felt as if I belonged in New York, undoubtedly because the few friends I thought I had there were evidently making a point to mock me behind my back."

She nodded to Seraphina, who was in the process of taking a spoonful of soup, but she was doing it in almost slow motion as his sisters watched her every move. "Seraphina would never mock me behind my back."

Rhenick fought a grin when Coraline suddenly reached out and pressed one of Seraphina's moles back into place, one that seemed to be in the process of falling off Seraphina's face. "Seraphina is definitely a lady you can count as a good friend, but I thought you might want to return to New York because of all the society events there."

"I'm sure there are social events to be enjoyed in Chicago, and I freely admit I'm looking forward to exploring the city now that I've decided this is where I'm meant to make my home."

"And it's meant to be your home because . . . ?" he pressed.

Drusilla tilted her head. "There are numerous reasons. One of those, of course, would be proving to myself that I have what it takes to make a success of the academy, which will definitely be easier to accomplish now that Loughlin MacSherry is no longer in the picture."

"What?"

She took another spoonful of soup and frowned. "Forgive me, Rhenick. I should have told you that straightaway, but I only just learned about an hour ago, when Elena Zambarello tracked me down in the lobby when I first arrived here, that MacSherry left town. He's also apparently made the decision to stay out of Chicago for the foreseeable future in order to 'lay low,' as Elena put it."

"Because?"

Drusilla leaned closer to him. "He learned that, after Fenna and Sneaky Pete realized they were facing some serious felony charges, they began singing like canaries, and their song of choice was exactly how MacSherry was responsible for almost every mystery tied to the castle."

"He fled to avoid arrest?"

"That, and the fact that Elena threatened to tell MacSherry's wife about the many mistresses her husband has stashed around the city." Her eyes twinkled. "Turns out that Elena made it a habit over the years to collect information on their competition when Umberto was still involved with the underworld, information she didn't hesitate to use against MacSherry since she's determined to get her daughters enrolled in the academy. From what I understand, MacSherry skedaddled out of town not long after his meeting with Elena because MacSherry's wife is rumored to be more terrifying than he is—or even Elena, for that matter."

"No wonder MacSherry left town," Rhenick said before he took another spoonful of soup, then sat back when the servers returned to whisk away everyone's soup bowls. His lips began curving when Coraline promptly earned a discreet shake of her head from Drusilla when his sister tried to stop the server from removing her soup, obviously done so because there'd been a bit left at the bottom of her bowl and she evidently meant to finish it.

Once the server all but pried the bowl from Coraline's hand, the other servers began setting down cheese plates that also contained bread and a fig spread.

His lips curved straight into a grin when all of his sisters took to considering the cheese as if they were afraid it might bite them, until Annaliese picked up a small pronged fork, used it to spear a slice of cheese, and promptly slid it into her mouth.

"Annaliese will be a favorite instructor, as well," Drusilla murmured before she returned her attention to him. "However, I fear with trying to watch your sisters, I've lost track of our conversation. Did I tell you yet that Sneaky Pete has been more forthcoming with details since he's been behind bars?"

"You did say he was singing like a canary."

"Indeed he is, and he expanded on what part MacSherry played in Ottilie's disappearance by telling Agent Pearson that

MacSherry asked him to contact his old mates who still work for Captain Harvey and get them to agree—for a very large fee, of course—to get rid of Aunt Ottilie, along with the captain, since there couldn't be any witnesses."

Rhenick blinked. "MacSherry actually had Ottilie murdered?"

"Well, here's the interesting part," Drusilla said after she'd taken a dainty bite of cheese. "Sneaky Pete doesn't think his old mates went through with it, even though MacSherry received a telegram from Captain Harvey's first mate about seven months or so after Aunt Ottilie left on her trip, telling him the deed was done and Ottilie was now swimming with some Caribbean fishes."

"She was in the Caribbean?"

"Perhaps, but Pete didn't know for sure, and he doesn't have any proof that Ottilie is still alive, but he told Agent Pearson he has a feeling. He also had a feeling about that treasure map Ottilie was using, which was why he and Fenna were determined to find a copy of the map because they believed—again, because of some feeling Sneaky Pete was getting—that Captain Harvey and Aunt Ottilie were on the trail of something big, although whether they're still on that trail is up for debate."

"So Sneaky Pete and Fenna really were on a double mission— one for MacSherry and one for themselves."

"It does appear as if that's the case, but that's all the information I have about the matter so far, although know that Agent Pearson has already agreed to investigate Aunt Ottilie's disappearance. He's also sending some agents with William Baumgartner to retrieve the trunk of maps he stored for my aunt in a bank vault outside of Chicago."

Rhenick smiled. "I suppose learning all of that did leave you feeling as if it would be safe to open your academy, but . . . you said there were numerous reasons why you feel as if Chicago is meant to be your home."

She returned his smile. "The academy isn't the main reason Chicago feels like home, Rhenick. It's the people I've met here that make it feel that way, especially your family. And, if I'm being perfectly honest, *you* make it feel as if this is truly where I belong."

Forty-Two

As Rhenick blinked somewhat owlishly back at her, quite as if he thought he'd misheard the words that had just come out of her mouth, Mrs. Potter Palmer suddenly appeared at their table, smiling broadly at Irma and interrupting what Drusilla had hoped might have turned into a bit of a life-changing moment for her.

"Forgive me for interrupting," Mrs. Palmer said as she dipped into a curtsy. "But I've just learned that you're Mrs. Morton Merriweather of New York City, no less, and wanted to be one of the first ladies to welcome you to Chicago. I'm Mrs. Potter Palmer."

Irma smiled and inclined her head. "How delightful to meet you, Mrs. Palmer, and allow me to say that I adore this lovely hotel of yours, and am quite impressed with the meal I've been served thus far." She nodded to Wilhelmine. "Have you ever been introduced to my dear friend Mrs. Franklin Whittenbecker?"

Mrs. Palmer considered Wilhelmine for a moment before she shook her head. "I'm afraid not, which means we need to remedy that situation straightaway."

It took a good five minutes for Irma to introduce everyone sitting around the table to Mrs. Palmer, but after everyone had been properly greeted, and Rhenick had finally been able to return to his seat after Mrs. Palmer bid them a lovely good day and glided out of the restaurant, Wilhelmine took to grinning.

"That was quite unexpected, and you could have knocked me over with a feather when Mrs. Palmer asked me—after she'd asked Irma, of course—if I would extend her the pleasure of my company during the book salon she's hosting next week."

Eloise's eyes began to gleam. "I think there's real promise for my debut after all, and that's with me not even having been trained up in the manners department by Miss Drusilla, Miss Annaliese, and Miss Livingston."

As the servers took that moment to arrive at their table once again, this time bearing a lovely chicken in cream sauce, everyone took to chatting about Mrs. Palmer and her unexpected appearance. Everyone except Rhenick, who wasn't saying much at all, but was simply watching Drusilla instead with something interesting in his eyes.

"What are you thinking?" she finally asked.

"I'm thinking I would really like to be done with lunch so that you and I could continue the conversation we were having before Mrs. Palmer showed up."

Her stomach took to fluttering, quite as if a collection of butterflies had taken up residency there. "I wouldn't mind continuing with that conversation either."

A mere second after those words left her mouth, Rhenick rose to his feet, set his napkin aside, inclined his head to his mother and Irma, who were now watching them with wide eyes, and then helped Drusilla to her feet. He took hold of her arm, drew her around numerous tables and out the door, straight across the lobby, and then down the steps of the Palmer House, nodding to one of the waiting grooms, who dashed off like a shot, leading Sweet Pea and a buggy over to them a moment later.

After helping Drusilla onto the seat, Rhenick took his place beside her and, after setting Sweet Pea in motion, turned and sent her a grin.

"I bet that just broke at least a hundred rules of etiquette," he said cheerfully.

"I don't believe I've ever gotten up mid-meal and abandoned the people I was dining with, although I am curious as to why Eloise called out for you to choose her idea—or better yet, I suppose I'm more than curious to discover exactly what idea she was speaking about."

He considered her for a long moment, then returned his attention to the road as he steered Sweet Pea around a delivery wagon. "I don't think Eloise's idea is the way to go."

"Why not?"

"It might be too abrupt."

"Because . . . ?"

"It's difficult to explain."

"Would it be helpful if you took some time to think about how to explain as we drive to . . . where are we driving anyway?"

He smiled. "I really haven't given that much thought, but I suppose if we return to the castle, we'll have some privacy, as we left everyone else behind at the Palmer House."

"The castle it is."

A comfortable silence settled over them as Rhenick drove through the streets of Chicago, one that left Drusilla realizing that somewhere during the time she'd spent in Chicago, she'd become completely at ease in Rhenick's company, something that was quite telling as she'd never been at ease during the two and a half years she'd been engaged to He Who Shall Not Be Named.

That man, in all honesty, had always made her nervous, what with how he consistently seemed to find fault with her. He also only listened to her with half an ear, if at all, preferring to settle his attention on any lady but her, which had left her with the distinct feeling that she was always found lacking when compared to the more sparkling ladies of society.

Rhenick, on the other hand, listened to everything she said, and he seemed to enjoy her opinion on a variety of different subjects, whether it was on what style of water closet she thought young ladies would best enjoy at the academy, or what she wanted to do about the ravens that, no matter how much she hollered at them, wouldn't abandon their preferred perch on the turrets.

He also, without a shadow of a doubt, respected women. But besides respecting them, he enjoyed women, and not simply because they were pretty or charming, but because he saw women as people—or better yet, not as inferior beings who needed to be spoken to as if they were lacking in intelligence.

"It's a good thing you decided you were going to continue on with your plans to open the academy or this would be a rather awkward moment," Rhenick said, drawing her from her thoughts as he pulled Sweet Pea to a stop a few feet from the castle gate. He set the brake, swung himself down from the buggy, and was holding his hand out to her a second later.

"What would have been awkward?" she asked as she put her hand in his and stepped from the buggy.

He nodded toward the gate. "Take a look for yourself."

She leaned forward and squinted at the gate. "Is that new?"

"It is."

"Was there something wrong with the old gate?"

"It was missing something" was all he said before he pulled her into motion, her pace slowing when she finally understood why he'd said the moment would have been awkward if she'd not decided to continue with opening the academy.

Her eyes immediately took to swimming with tears, an unusual circumstance to be sure, but tears were certainly justified because where the gate had merely been wrought-iron bars when she'd passed through them that morning, they now sported an intricate bit of scrolling on top. More importantly, though, forged across both sections in a beautiful script was this—*The Merriweather Academy for Young Ladies*.

"Did you have this made for me?" she whispered.

He smiled. "I asked Chester to make it, and, clearly, he's far more proficient with iron than he is with his butler duties."

"Mr. Grimsby thinks Chester may have potential, but . . ." Drusilla allowed her gaze to linger on the gate. "It's beautiful."

"It's also a gift, which means you will not pester me to figure out how much it cost so that you can add it to the ledger of expenses you've been keeping."

"I wasn't planning on pestering you. I was simply planning on saying thank you for the sweetest, most thoughtful gift I've ever received."

He rubbed a hand over his jaw. "It's a gate, Drusilla, not exactly on the lines of jewelry, which I know full well, having all those sisters as well as an entire army of female cousins, ladies find the sweetest gift of all."

"I was given the Herrington diamonds, and I didn't find them sweet in the least."

"That's because the man who gave them to you was an idiot."

She grinned. "He was, wasn't he?"

"Indeed, but it is now duly noted that you're not impressed with diamonds. Although, is there any specific gem you may be impressed with?"

She stilled. "Why do you want to know?"

He took to considering her for a long moment before he stepped closer. "I think I might as well take Eloise's advice. But before I do that, there's something I feel I need to say first." He took hold of her hand. "I was wrong when I broached the topic of marriage with you the day we first met because you are a lady who deserves—before you're extended a proper proposal, one that's complete with a bended knee, moonlight, and perhaps a violin playing softly in the background—to be properly courted."

The butterflies immediately returned.

"Properly . . . courted?" she asked in a breathy tone that certainly didn't sound like her normal voice.

"Indeed, and that proper courtship should last as long as you want it to last, and should be a time where you get to learn everything there is to know about your intended. It is also a time where you should be spoiled outrageously, although know that even after you're married, you should expect to be spoiled outrageously as well."

"I don't believe I've ever been spoiled, let alone outrageously, although . . ." She glanced to her new gate. "That is definitely along the lines of spoiling me."

"Again, that's just a gate. Spoiling, at least in my humble opinion, would entail showering you with flowers and chocolate simply because you enjoy those things, or taking you to a country fair because you saw a flyer posted in town and decided you longed to go to enjoy the festivities offered there. It would also entail a great deal of dancing, if that's something you enjoy. But if it's not, it could simply be grabbing a few books and heading to the lake, where a picnic meal would be waiting for you, comprised of your favorite foods."

"It does seem as if you know what you're about when it comes to spoiling a lady" was all she could think to say.

He raised her hand to his lips and kissed it. "Per Eloise's suggestion, although this is going to be a modified version of her advice, I would like to get your permission to properly court you, Miss Drusilla Merriweather. I would then love to spoil you outrageously, but you see, I can't do that quite yet as I don't know nearly enough about you. I don't know what type of flowers you prefer, although I do know that you enjoy perfume that's lemon scented, so perhaps instead of flowers, you'd prefer if I presented you with a lemon tree.

"I also want to discover, if our courtship leaves you with the impression you might like to turn it from a proper courtship into a proper so-much-more, how you would like to mark a betrothal. I will tell you right now, though, that I don't have any Whittenbecker family jewels at my disposal, but I'd be more than happy to start a collection of jewelry to give you, but not until I know exactly what jewels you prefer."

"I like sapphires."

"Which I think is a most fitting gem as sapphires match your eyes, and know that sapphires you shall have if you decide you'd be agreeable to allowing me to properly court you."

Drusilla glanced to the gate again, then back to Rhenick, who was now watching her closely. "May I ask you something?"

"Of course."

"What was Eloise's original suggestion?"

He smiled. "She thought I should simply drop to one knee, proclaim my love for you, and ask you to be my wife."

Drusilla blinked. "But you decided not to take that suggestion because you believe I need a proper courtship?"

"Exactly."

"I . . . see."

Rhenick was lifting her chin a second later, his gaze locked with hers. "What's going on in that head of yours?"

She smiled ever so slightly. "You just mentioned love—or rather, said that Eloise suggested you proclaim your love for me."

"She did suggest that."

"Does that mean you actually believe yourself to be in love with me?"

"I *know* I'm in love with you, which is why I want to properly court you so that you can discover whether or not you might be able to fall in love with me as well."

Warmth immediately began flowing through her as she realized in that moment that she didn't need to discover if she *might* be able to fall in love with the man because—she was *already* in love with him.

Her lips curved straight into a full smile. "You don't need to properly court me."

Rhenick blinked. "Why not?"

"That probably came out wrong, because you can certainly take to courting me, but you don't need to do that for the express purpose of allowing me time to discern if I could come to love you because . . . I already do."

Rhenick's mouth went a little slack. "You do?"

She grinned. "I know, it's taken me a bit by surprise as well, but you see, Mr. Rhenick Whittenbecker, you are the only person in my life—except perhaps for Annaliese, of course—who has ever seen me for who I truly am."

"You're extraordinary."

Her grin widened. "In your eyes, I do believe I am, and that right there is certainly how it came to be—well, besides the fact that you're incredibly charming, and authentically charming at that—that I have fallen in love with you."

He returned her grin. "This is not how I expected any of this to go, but, before we're joined by everyone, and I would say that's going to happen soon because they probably only lasted five minutes at the Palmer House after we bolted, I have a proposal for you."

"A proper proposal?"

"Indeed, and it's this—Miss Drusilla Merriweather, it would be a great honor if you'd accept my hand in marriage, but I don't want to marry you straightaway, even though I'm completely in love with you. I'd like an opportunity, as I already mentioned, to properly court you first."

She wrinkled her nose. "How long would a proper courtship last?"

"A few months?"

"That seems awfully long, especially if you think a proper courtship precedes a betrothal and then we'd be betrothed for a few months and then get married."

He tilted his head. "What did you have in mind?"

"I would go with a few weeks of courtship, followed by a month or so for a betrothal period, and then plan a wedding that would coincide with the fall break we can most certainly add into the academy calendar. Unless I just leave Annaliese, Seraphina, and my mother in charge of running things for a few weeks while we go off on a wedding holiday."

"I have a feeling, given Seraphina's background, that she'd be able to run the academy with one hand tied behind her back."

"Does that mean you think a fall wedding might work for us?"

"Since I've already told you that I intend to spoil you outrageously, we can have a wedding whenever you want. I will also court you for however long you want and be betrothed to you for however long you want." He smiled. "Have I missed anything else you may want?"

She leaned an inch closer to him. "I believe you're being most accommodating, although there *is* something else I want. Something I've been wanting for a few days now."

"And that would be?"

"A kiss—and a proper kiss, at that. One where we can take our time and not be interrupted by Seraphina, Annaliese, or anyone else."

A blink of an eye later, Rhenick was pulling her close, his eyes warm as his gaze lingered on her mouth. "I believe we should add that, during your proper courtship, followed by a most proper betrothal, and then a proper wedding, which I know my sisters and mother are going to adore helping you plan, we need to make certain that I give you more-than-a-few proper kisses. Perhaps we should set aside time every day to adhere to a proper kissing schedule."

A laugh slipped through her lips, but before she could laugh again, Rhenick's lips were pressing against hers, and it didn't take long to realize that, as far as kisses went, Rhenick Whittenbecker knew how to deliver a proper kiss indeed. That meant she was certain to spend the rest of her life being properly kissed, and by a man she knew without a doubt was going to make the most proper and perfect of husbands.

Read on
for a sneak peek at
the next book in the

Merriweather Academy for Young Ladies

series.

Available April 2026.

One

In hindsight, taking a small group of students from the Merriweather Academy for Young Ladies to a country fair to assess their progress regarding the rudimentary rules of civility wasn't quite the brilliant opportunity Miss Annaliese Merriweather had expected it to be. Not when two of the five young ladies had slipped away from the group—undoubtedly intent on delving into mischief.

Resisting the inclination to heave a perfectly justifiable sigh, Annaliese summoned up what she hoped would be taken as a stern look.

Truth be told, she wasn't a lady who was predisposed to stern looks, but if she'd learned anything during the scant four months she'd taken up the unexpected role of decorum instructor, it was this: Young ladies who'd spent their lives with little instruction pertaining to the rules of propriety were far more likely to respond to a stern look over any expression that hinted at even a smidgen of geniality.

After tucking a strand of flyaway red hair behind her ear, Annaliese settled her attention on the student most likely to fold

337

under pressure: Miss Coraline Whittenbecker, who'd recently become related to Annaliese through the marriage of Drusilla Merriweather, Annaliese's sister, to Rhenick Whittenbecker, Coraline's brother.

"Any thoughts as to where Norma Jean and Velma might have wandered off to?" she asked, which earned her a rather deer-in-the-lantern-lights look before Coraline began taking a marked interest in the dirt she was scuffing her sturdy button-up boot through.

"Um, well, not that I know this for certain," Coraline began as she continued with her scuffing, "but Norma Jean might have gone off to speak to her brother, Seth."

"And she didn't ask permission from me to do that because . . . ?"

"I'm sure she didn't want to interrupt your scolding of that man you felt was mistreating his performing bear."

"I didn't feel he was mistreating the bear. He was mistreating it, as I'm sure the poor bear didn't appreciate being poked in the stomach with a stick when it couldn't maintain its balance on a tricycle."

"And I'm sure everyone in the vicinity of the bear is now aware of its mistreatment since you were really loud when you were taking that man to task over the poking incident."

"My distraction with the bear was hardly a credible excuse for Norma Jean to meander off without a word to me."

"Maybe not, but after Pippin jumped off your shoulder and looked like she wanted to tussle with the bear man, your distraction level increased." Coraline stopped her scuffing and looked up. "Everyone knows your ferrets can turn vicious when provoked. I'm sure Norma Jean decided that you would have your hands full managing Pippin for the foreseeable future and left the group without bothering you, thinking she'd be back before you had your ferret under control again."

Annaliese took a second to give Pippin, the neediest of the

three ferrets she'd rescued months before, who was lounging around her neck and taking a well-deserved rest after her almost-attack on a horrid bear owner, a scratch. After earning a chirp from Pippin in return, she resettled her attention on Coraline and frowned. "While I understand why Norma Jean might not have wanted to interrupt me while I was engaged in an altercation, what I don't understand is why you didn't accompany Norma Jean and Velma. You've been quite vocal about how dreamy you find Seth McCormick to be, and I would think you'd have been champing at the bit to speak to him when presented with such a prime opportunity."

"Coraline's no longer smitten with Seth McCormick," Miss Phoebe Studebaker blurted.

Coraline turned to Phoebe and leveled a scowl on her.

Phoebe missed the scowl because she'd returned to ripping off a piece of the turkey leg she was clutching in her now grease-stained gloved hand, a piece she shoveled into her mouth. A few rapid chews commenced before she swallowed, patted her chest, which elicited a very unladylike belch, then opened her mouth. "Coraline, like a lot of other girls, finds Riley, your stable hand, to be far dreamier these days than Seth."

Before Annaliese could do more than realize the apparent dreaminess of her stable hand was behind why so many young ladies at the academy had broached the subject of adding riding lessons into their weekly schedules, let alone address the belching situation, Coraline crossed her arms over her chest.

"I don't recall asking you, Phoebe, for your input regarding my interest in Seth McCormick or Riley," Coraline grouched.

Fighting a smile, Annaliese settled her attention on Coraline again. "You're certain Norma Jean went off to have a word with her brother?"

It was rather concerning when Coraline adopted the deer-in-the-lantern-light look again. "Nothing is ever completely certain when it concerns Norma Jean, but she did point Seth out to me when we were strolling past the steam engine display. She also said something about needing to have a word with him regarding her need of some extra pin money." Coraline sent her a bright smile. "There's no need for you to be worried about Norma Jean meandering off, though. It's not as if she's out there all alone since she took Velma Chickering with her. Velma has a wicked right hook, taught to her by her uncle, Ewart Chickering, who decided he wanted nothing to do with the family pig-raising business and became a pugilist instead."

"Which is impressive, to be sure, but I doubt Velma's pugilistic abilities, if you're mistaken and your friends decided to pursue a little adventure instead, perhaps wanting a glimpse of the mermaid lady, will be very effective if they find themselves wandering into an area that's unfit for young ladies. If you neglected to notice, I've made certain to keep us clear of any areas that seem even remotely questionable today."

Coraline's smile dimmed. "I wouldn't think there are any questionable areas here, as the advertisements we saw plastered around Chicago stated this fair was to be a family event."

"And I'm sure whoever designed those advertisements did so with the belief that parents would steer any children around dubious attractions, such as the tent I saw selling large tankards of ale next to the mermaid attraction, which is why I said we couldn't view the mermaid lady today."

Coraline glanced at Phoebe and Mabel, and a look was exchanged, one that probably had some kind of code attached to it that Annaliese was clearly unfamiliar with. Coraline nodded. "While I'm still certain there's no need for you to worry, maybe it would be best if we track down Norma Jean and Velma sooner rather than later to be on the safe side. As luck would have it, I think I remember where to find Seth."

With that, Coraline turned on her heel and began barreling through the crowd, moving at a pace that was just shy of a full-out run, which caused the apprehension Annaliese was already experiencing to increase significantly.

Not wanting to lose track of any additional students in her charge, she grabbed hold of Phoebe and Mabel's hands and bolted after Coraline.

"I don't think there's any need for this amount of exertion," Phoebe muttered before she tried to take another bite of her turkey leg as they dodged through the fairgoers, leaving a trail of grease smeared on her cheek when she missed her mouth. "Norma Jean makes a habit of meandering through the streets of Chicago, and she's never run into more than a smidgen of trouble when she's been doing her meandering."

"It was more than a smidgen of trouble when she almost got abducted a few months back," Mabel argued around the large mouthful of turkey she'd just taken.

"I forgot about the almost-abduction," Phoebe admitted.

"Norma Jean almost got abducted?" Annaliese asked, even though what she really wanted to ask was if Mabel had perhaps been sleeping her way through the table-etiquette lessons of late, because speaking with your mouth full had certainly been addressed, and numerous times at that.

Mabel swallowed and gave a wave of her greasy turkey leg, which sent grease flying. "Indeed she did, and it all started when Norma Jean spotted a bright yellow phaeton." Mabel bit off another piece of turkey, gave a few vigorous chews, and nodded. "She decided to stop it and interview the man driving it because she'd been thinking about adding a phaeton into a play she was writing—you know she longs to become a playwright someday— which turned out to be a grave error in judgment on her part."

"In Norma Jean's defense, she could have hardly known that the man tooling around in that phaeton had recently nicked it from Mr. Ogden's front drive," Phoebe argued before she chucked her partially finished turkey leg toward a rubbish bin. After the turkey made it into the bin—an impressive shot, since they were moving at a rapid pace—Phoebe gave her mouth a swipe with her now grease-drenched glove. "It was her fault, though, that after she stopped the phaeton by standing in front of it in the middle of the road, and after the driver told her to get out of his way, she made the monumental mistake of not taking that as a firm no and leapt up alongside the driver instead."

Annaliese slowed their pace and, after checking to make certain that Coraline was still in sight, settled a frown on Phoebe. "Surely you're mistaken. Norma Jean didn't truly jump into a stranger's phaeton, did she?"

"Not mistaken. That's exactly what she did," Phoebe said. "And then, after she settled herself next to the driver, a squadron of policemen came barreling onto the scene, having been alerted about the phaeton theft by Mr. Ogden. From what I've been told, they were making an awful racket by blowing their whistles, and they gave chase when the thief sped off down the road. That's when Norma Jean realized that she'd gotten herself into a pickle. She then made the mistake of telling the thief she was from a wealthy family, and if he'd simply let her get out of the phaeton, she'd make sure he was well-compensated."

"And he, being a thief, decided to hold her for ransom instead?" Annaliese asked.

"Too right he did, and who knows what would have happened to Norma Jean if Seth hadn't arrived on the scene. He stepped out of his barbershop and saw the phaeton careening down the road and immediately jumped on his horse and took off after it because he'd been itching to get a closer look at Mr. Ogden's phaeton as well as gauge how fast it was capable of traveling."

"Norma Jean, thankfully, spotted her brother," Mabel added before she tossed her practically eaten-to-the-bone turkey leg toward a bin, missed, frowned, but was all smiles a blink of an eye later when a strapping young lad picked it up for her, placed it in the bin, and then began sauntering their way.

He stopped in his tracks, though, when Annaliese sent him her stern look, then began sauntering in the opposite direction.

"What did Norma Jean do after she spotted Seth?" Annaliese asked.

"She began yelling at the top of her lungs, Seth heard her and went about the tricky business of rescuing her."

"He used some new contraption he'd been working on," Phoebe explained. "He'd evidently visited a ranch and decided ranch hands might find their job easier if they had a better way to lasso errant livestock, so he invented a lasso that shoots out the barrel of a pistol."

Annaliese's brow furrowed. "That would have to be some pistol, as the rope needed to make a lasso would take up quite a bit of space."

"It looks like a portable cannon," Mabel said. "Seth just happened to have it attached to his saddlebag that day because he was heading back to the ranch for some target practice."

"From what was said, his invention—'the cowboy assistant,' I think he calls it," Phoebe added, "didn't work as he intended."

Annaliese's eyes widened. "Did it burst into flames like the flamethrower he used a few months back?"

"There were no flames involved," Phoebe said. "But I guess, when he pulled the trigger, the lasso part of the rope never opened, but the speed at which it shot out of the gun was practically as fast as a bullet. When the rope hit the thief, it knocked him straight off his seat and out of the phaeton."

"Unfortunately," Mabel continued, "that left the phaeton without anyone holding the reins. Norma Jean told us she saw her life flash before her eyes and was sure she wouldn't live to see another adventure, but then Seth jumped from his horse into the phaeton and saved the day." Mabel released a rather dramatic sigh. "There's just something about a man who knows how to rescue damsels in distress that makes a girl's heart go pitter-patter." She heaved another sigh, this one more dramatic than the last. "Nevertheless, even though Seth is a swoon-worthy gentleman if there ever was one, we girls have come to realize that he might be a tad too old for us right now, which we've decided is why he never pays any of us much mind when we coerce Norma Jean into taking us over to his house to watch him work on his inventions."

Phoebe released a snort. "I'm not sure watching is an apt way to describe what most of us do. *Ogling* would be a better way to phrase it."

Mabel's nose shot into the air. "I'm sure Miss Merriweather perfectly understands our ogling, as she does have eyes in her head, and anyone with eyes can see that Seth McCormick is a more than scrumptious-looking gentleman. I'm also sure that Miss Merriweather is accustomed to frequent ogling as well, since she's one of the most beautiful ladies you and I have ever seen and has undoubtedly experienced more than a few oglers in her day."

Mabel came to a complete stop, jerking Annaliese and Phoebe to a stop as well. After exchanging another one of those incomprehensible looks with Phoebe, she grinned. "Are you thinking what I'm thinking?"

Phoebe returned the grin. "I am, if you're thinking that since Seth is too old for us at the moment, and he'll be off the market by the time we reach our majority, we should encourage Miss Merriweather to set her sights on him." Phoebe turned eyes that were now sparkling in a somewhat concerning fashion on Annaliese. "My friends and I will be more than happy to plan out the particulars for you, and I bet we can have the two of you married off in no time at all, and probably before Christmas, if we get right down to plotting."

Named one of the funniest voices in inspirational romance by *Booklist*, **Jen Turano** is a *USA Today* bestselling author, known for penning quirky historical romances set in the Gilded Age. Her books have earned *Publishers Weekly* and *Booklist* starred reviews, top picks from *Romantic Times*, and praise from *Library Journal*. She's been a finalist twice for the RT Reviewers' Choice Awards and had two of her books listed in the top 100 romances of the past decade from *Booklist*. She and her family live outside of Ormond Beach, Florida. Readers can find her on Facebook and Instagram, and at JenTurano.com.

Sign Up for Jen's Newsletter

Keep up to date with Jen's latest news on book releases and events by signing up for her email list at the website below.

JenTurano.com

Follow Jen on Social Media

 Jen Turano   @JenTuranoAuthor   @JenTurano

More from Jen Turano

When society's most eligible bachelors confront the most renowned matchmakers of the Gilded Age, can sparks of love outlast the danger closing in? With spunky humor and mischief, high society takes center stage in Turano's comedic series. Stakes are high to make the perfect match, but the match of the century might just prove to be their own.

THE MATCHMAKERS: *A Match in the Making,*
To Spark a Match, Meeting Her Match